21/8/2018

THE DROWNING CHILD

When Special Agent Ren Bryce is called to Tate, Oregon to investigate the disappearance of twelve-year-old Caleb Veir, she finds a town already in mourning. Two other young boys have died recently, but in very different circumstances. As Ren digs deeper, she discovers that all is not as it seems in the Veir household — and that while Tate may be a small town, it guards some very big secrets. Can Ren uncover the truth before more children are harmed?

Books by Alex Barclay
Published by Ulverscroft:

DARKHOUSE
THE CALLER
BLOOD RUNS COLD
BLOOD LOSS
HARM'S REACH
KILLING WAYS

ALEX BARCLAY

THE
DROWNING
CHILD

Complete and Unabridged

CHARNWOOD
Leicester

First published in Great Britain in 2016 by
HarperCollins*Publishers*
London

First Charnwood Edition
published 2017
by arrangement with
HarperCollins*Publishers*
London

To a Dying Girl © Sue Booth-Forbes and Diane Porter
To a Dying Girl was first published in *The Lord of Experience* by BYU Press in 1967, page 21

A catalogue record for this book is available from the British Library.

ISBN 978-1-4448-3495-6

Published by
F. A. Thorpe (Publishing)
Anstey, Leicestershire
Set by Words & Graphics Ltd.
Anstey, Leicestershire
Printed and bound in Great Britain by
T. J. International Ltd., Padstow, Cornwall

This book is printed on acid-free paper

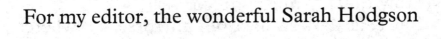

For my editor, the wonderful Sarah Hodgson

To a Dying Girl

How quickly must she go?
She calls dark swans from mirrors everywhere:
From halls and porticos, from pools of air.
How quickly must she know?
They wander through the fathoms of her eye,
Waning southerly until their cry
Is gone where she must go.
How quickly does the cloudfire streak the
   sky,
Tremble on the peaks, then cool and die?
She moves like evening into night,
Forgetful as the swans forget their flight
Or spring the fragile snow,
So quickly she must go.

Clinton F. Larson

Prologue

February 12

Jimmy Lyle was lying, bleeding, by the pond in Montgomery Park. Behind him, at the water's farthest edge, four ice-white swans moved with mechanical serenity, necks as long as their bodies, black eyes on brighter views.

Jimmy drifted in and out of consciousness, aware of rallying bystanders, footsteps, the tones of cell phone keys, raised voices, concern. He could smell his own blood. He had taken multiple blows to the face before he dropped to the ground, powerful kicks to the ribs and abdomen as he lay there. His left eyeball was swollen like a nut. His right eyelid flickered. Darkness to light, darkness to light.

When Jimmy was a boy, his favorite toy was a slide puzzle. He remembered how quickly his little thumbs pushed the tiles around to put the photo of a gray duckling back together again. Sometimes, he would close his eyes as he clicked the final piece into place, hoping that when he opened them, the duckling would have turned into a swan.

'His little girl!' someone was shouting. 'His little girl! She's gone! She was right there! Then a guy showed up . . . he just . . . he beat the shit out of him! Took his little girl!'

There was a man's voice, an authoritative one.

'Do you think you could give me a description of the attacker, ma'am?'

'Short white guy, stocky, brown hair, khakis and a dark polo shirt, white sneakers too,' said the witness. 'Early thirties is my best guess.'

'Could that have been a uniform of some kind he was wearing?' said the officer. 'Like a store uniform?'

'I . . . don't think so — it was just, you know, those boring guys, what they wear. Guys with a boring job and a nice wife back home.'

'And the little girl?' said the officer.

'She was seven years old, eight?' said the witness. 'Pink leggings, pink top with a rainbow on it and something writ across it and . . . white socks, white sneakers? She'd been crouching down, right there, feeding the swans with her daddy.'

'This man right here,' said the officer.

'Yes!' thought Jimmy Lyle. 'Yes!' Blood bubbled from his mouth. More footsteps, two men, crouched beside him.

'Yes — him!' said the witness. 'I'm sorry. I can't look at him. Is he . . . gonna make it?'

'He may be able to hear you, ma'am,' said the officer. 'Keep talking me through what you saw.'

'The rest was a blur,' said the witness, 'except that the little girl must have fallen in, her daddy tried to pull her out, but next thing that man was down on him, beating on him, taking his little girl. It was crazy.'

Jimmy Lyle felt a presence beside him.

'Can you tell me your name, sir?' He was checking his pulse. He was a paramedic. Jimmy could feel a second man kneeling to his right.

'No — I can't tell you my name,' thought Jimmy Lyle. 'I can't.'

They could search his pockets for ID, but he had none. He had no cell phone. He felt a hard pinch on his finger and recoiled from the pain. Then the paramedics' words, back and forth, interchangeable voices, descriptions, instructions. 'His GCS is nine, get the collar, put on O_2 and put it on fifteen liters . . . '

Jimmy could feel hands on his head, holding it secure, as a collar was strapped around his neck, the padding tight against his ears, the sound sucked from the world. The paramedics inserted the IV, delivered the shot of dopamine that would increase his blood pressure, hung the bag that would fill his veins with circulating fluid.

At first, it worked. Then, the numbers changed; his respiratory rate dropped from twelve breaths per minute to four, his GCS fell to six.

They were about to tube him when Jimmy Lyle coughed, and his heart surged like a lagging runner in the home straight.

★   ★   ★

As he was stretchered past the pond, Jimmy Lyle thanked God for misperception, for absent facts, for the blind faith of good hearts and decent souls. The passersby should have passed on by. That little girl wasn't 'his little girl'. The man who beat him to a pulp was the little girl's father. He had told her to turn away and cover her ears

3

as he dragged Jimmy into the bushes and beat him without letting up, without caring whether it would send him to the ER or his grave. Then he fled, covered in Jimmy's blood, his thick arms clutching his weeping, soaking-wet daughter to his chest.

★ ★ ★

Jimmy Lyle was a piece of shit, and, thanks to the kindness of strangers and the dedication of paramedics, remained a living, breathing, piece of shit.

1

March 6

Lake Verny spat and crackled with a relentless, piercing rain. Clyde Brimmer sat at a table in the window of The Crow Bar, looking beyond his reflection, beyond the candlelight that captured a face plowed for years by whiskey and the elements. In his tight right hand, he was holding a round white moonstone.

'That lake has secrets that the rain wants to tell.' Clyde spoke loud enough to be heard, but there was only one person there to hear him, and she was doing nothing more than standing behind the bar and staring ahead, her amber hair and freckles glowing in the dim light above her. She had showered today, at least. She had made it. Strike another day off the bleak remainder of the life of Shannon Fuller.

'It won't stop 'til it gets to the bottom of something,' said Clyde. 'Might be the lake bed, might be . . . '

Clyde liked to trail off; it was his lonely man's way of leaving a door open to further engagement, of luring more questions from whoever might be listening. He spoke to customers of his careful choosing, and he spoke to Shannon. He trusted her, without even realizing that in all his years of drinking, she was the only bartender who could set his pace, who

5

could keep him a civilized man until closing time. He had better nights when she was on.

He shifted the moonstone into the grip of his two smallest fingers, then hammered the rutted tabletop to mimic the rain.

'I have no doubt,' said Shannon, dealing another card from the bartender's conversational deck — I have no doubt, it sure is, they sure do, can't argue with that, who're you telling, can't beat it, you bet, sounds about right . . .

Nothing moved except her mouth.

'One for the road,' said Clyde, and Shannon Fuller moved like someone had put a coin in a slot and a mechanism was kicked off. It came to an end when her reflection joined Clyde's in the window as she set a Scotch down in front of him.

'One for the road to Tate,' she said. Tate was the town five miles away; halfway there was the brokedown house Clyde inherited from his grandmother. Some nights, Shannon gave him a ride home. Other nights, it was whoever else was high on pity.

Clyde raised his hands, gripping the air. 'It's got the wrong energy,' he said. He looked up at Shannon. 'Can you feel it?'

'I can't feel much of anything right now,' thought Shannon, but she kept that line in the buzz-kill deck — the cards no good bartender dealt; I'm lonely, I'm divorcing, I've got cancer, I've been abandoned, I'm lost, I'm fucking dying inside, I'm alone, I'm alone, I'm alone.

'*I* can feel it,' said Clyde, clearing her pain to vault into his own — in his chest, in his heart, as he watched the lake rising, watched the water

6

slap up over the banks.

Shannon Fuller knew that, in a sober state, Clyde never would have spoken about the energy of the lake that had taken away her eleven-year-old son, Aaron, only six weeks earlier. Aaron's was the last body Clyde had embalmed before he was fired for drinking on the job. Two weeks earlier, when Shannon crawled back to work to pay the bills, Clyde had stood weeping at the bar, clutching her clasped hands, swearing he was sober when he tended to her boy. And she believed him.

She gave him some work since then, odd jobs at the cabins and in the grounds. And when he wasn't doing that, he was in The Crow Bar, drinking until eleven at night, he and Shannon overlooking the killing lake, finding unspoken comfort in their somber bond, as the last two people to lay their hands on Aaron.

* * *

The door to the bar slammed back against the wall and Seth Fuller walked in, his tall, thin frame swamped in oversized rain gear. He snapped his head back to shed the hood, and pulled the door closed behind him.

'Lady and gentleman, we've got an escaped convict,' he said, in a dramatic old-style newsreel voice. He smiled, then switched back to his own — a slow, young and dumber one. 'He broke free from my alma mater yesterday afternoon. Well, during a hospital visit.' Seth glanced down at Clyde's full glass, then shook his jacket off, turning back to hang it on a wooden peg. 'So,' he said, 'BOLO for bald brick shithouse, Franklin J. Merrifield — white male, dumb as a box of frogs, forty-eight years old, meth-cooking, drug-dealing, motherfucking, teen-raping, fire-starting — '

'You knew the guy?' said Clyde.

'I knew the guy,' said Seth. 'Approach with caution.' He smiled. 'And that was tonight's public service announcement from Tate PD with a few insider extras from reformed maker of trouble, prisoner number G65746.' He walked up to the bar. 'Aunt Shannon, I am at your service.'

They shared the same glow, the same amber-colored freckles, but the rest of Seth — the shaven head, the narrow features, the flesh, the bones beneath — came together in a colder, darker way.

Seth tilted his head toward Clyde.

'Take a seat,' said Shannon. 'Let me pour you a drink. He's like a scared puppy tonight.'

★ ★ ★

Clyde's right leg was bouncing now, striking the underside of the table, rippling the whiskey in his glass. It wasn't long before it tipped over. He chased it across the table with his hand, but the rich flow of liquor through his veins and his shot reflexes meant all that happened was the moon-stone slipped from his grip, skidded over the edge, and landed in the fallen whiskey.

Shannon grabbed a cloth and rushed to Clyde.

'Do not move,' she said. She knew he had no balance, drunk or sober. She knew Clyde as well as he didn't know himself.

He stopped, then settled again in his seat, Shannon crouched down beside him, stopped when she saw the moonstone.

'Is this yours?' she said, picking it up.

He nodded. She stood up and shook the whiskey off it. A drop struck the candle's flame. It sizzled and died.

'It's a moonstone,' said Clyde. 'The traveler's stone — it protects those who cross water when the moon shines.'

His gaze moved from the wet black candle wick to what lay beyond the window.

'You can't trust water and you can't trust fire,' said Clyde. 'And out there? That lake's ablaze.'

★　★　★

Franklin J. Merrifield drifted awake from a profound, distressing sleep. What followed was the slow realization that he was not in his cell. He could smell rain, grass, trees, earth. The last time he smelled those smells was on that final shackled walk from the courthouse.

The only sound he could hear was rain hitting glass.

Glass?

He waited for his eyes to adjust, for shapes to form, for light to filter in, but the darkness was absolute. His heart started to pound wildly. His head felt strange, like it was overstuffed with packing materials; foam or twisted-up pieces of brown paper. His body felt solid, weighted down. His jaw was clamped shut. When he opened it,

9

he felt the skin on his lips tear. He could taste blood.

He had just one question:

How the fuck did I get here?

2

Special Agent Ren Bryce was sitting in Manny's Bar on 38th and Walnut in Denver.

It has been six months since my last alcoholic beverage.

She was five beers down.

Until tonight.

It was six months since a shooting at the Rocky Mountain Safe Streets Task Force, when a serial killer called Duke Rawlins had taken the lives of two of her friends and colleagues, and her boyfriend of one year, Ben Rader.

She picked up her cell phone.

Don't.

She put it down, slumped back in the bar stool, closed her eyes.

What if that had no back on it oh my God I am so fucking hammered imagine falling off a bar stool hitting your head and dying what a way to go appropriate Jesus.

She opened her eyes, and picked up her phone again. She went into Album.

Don't.

She found a photo of the boyfriend she had yet to call her former, her late . . . Ben Rader. The Late Ben Rader.

Tears filled her eyes. In the photo, Ben was cooking, smiling at her over his shoulder. He had a beaming smile, and was one of the most beautiful men she had ever known; short, tanned, dark-haired, fit.

You look so young.

A man as handsome as Ben Rader could have relied on his looks, developed nothing more than his body, but Ben developed a soul that radiated kindness.

I loved watching you cook Jesus you're dead now you're fucking dead this is so screwed up dead Jesus and you only look about eighteen you are so hot were no I can't do past tense are are are amazing arms steady grip strength of all kinds love love love gone gone gone stop stop stop.

She still had his texts; they felt like a weight in her phone that she was always aware of, but could never remove.

Can't imagine ever sending another loving text filthy text miss-you text to any other man I don't want a stranger in my bed I don't want another man in my head.

Her cell phone rang. GARY flashed on the screen.

No way.

Her boss, Supervisory Special Agent, Gary Dettling.

Yeah hey Gary I'm in Manny's yeah the bar where the serial killer who killed our friends picked up one of his victims yeah what is that telling you what is it telling me who fucking cares have you been drinking Ren yes Gary two beers and I'm about to leave . . .

She let it go to voicemail.

Gary left a message, and followed it with a text.

12

Call me — CARD

Shit.

Three months earlier, she and Gary had joined the North West Region's Child Abduction Rapid Deployment team — CARD. There were sixty members in the country, split across five regions, ready to deploy at the invitation of local law enforcement to help in the crucial early stages of a child disappearance or abduction. Though an invitation was welcome, it wasn't a requirement — when it came to a 'child of tender years', twelve years old and under, the FBI was automatically involved, whether there was an interstate element or not.

Ren called him back.

Breathe speak slowly breathe speak slowly enunciate.

'Hi, Gary — sorry I missed you.'

'Get a good night's sleep,' said Gary. 'We're — ' He paused. 'Where are you?'

Um . . . 'On my way home.'

'From a bar?'

'From a bar.'

Pause. 'We're booked on a six a.m. flight to Portland, Oregon, heading for the town of Tate. Missing twelve-year-old boy: Caleb Veir, last seen by his father at seven forty-five this morning when he left the family home to take the fifteen-minute walk to school.'

'OK.' *Say as little as possible.*

Pause. 'Ren — '

'See you at five.' Ren hung up.

Step away from the phone.

She put it on the bar, picked up her beer and

drank the last of it. She ordered another. She checked her watch.

Ugh Denver airport five a.m.

Denver airport — where memories flew at her like razors, where she had welcomed Ben, kissed him, hugged him, seen him off. Denver airport — the last place she was before she drove home to find out that he had been killed.

She looked back at his photograph as she waited for her drink.

That's it. Life over.

I should have taken more photos.

Her stomach turned.

You were an asshole to him that night anyway just delete it you were always an asshole to him he loved you and you were an asshole.

She started to cry.

Get your shit together you stupid bitch go home just go you're a mess everyone's looking at you you mess.

She stood up, pulled on her coat, paid for the drinks. She walked into the cold night, and her stomach spasmed, her throat constricted.

You fucking loser again fucking asking to enrage Gary you self-destructive I can still get five hours' sleep yeah whatever whatever I'm still here I'm still alive no one died yes they did you asshole yes they did fucking die.

She started to walk toward her Jeep.

Shiiiiiit. My CARD team Mac is at the office. Fuuuck.

★ ★ ★

14

Ren pulled up outside the Livestock Exchange Building where Safe Streets had the fourth floor. She put the Jeep into park, paused until her eyes could focus.

I can't believe I drove here of course you drove you don't give a shit a bit late to care now you loser you're going to die.

She grabbed her phone, scrolled through iTunes, picked a song from the filthy rap collection, and put in her earpods. Since the shootings, it was her routine any time she walked into Safe Streets alone: she didn't want to risk hearing the banging door she heard that evening, which she found out later had been the door to the basement where Ben's body had been thrown after Duke Rawlins shot him dead.

As she walked toward the building, a car door slammed behind her. She didn't see it, couldn't hear the footsteps behind her. She jogged up to the door, stood in front of the keypad.

Jesus could everything just be in focus.

She punched in the wrong code.

Shit.

She tried a second time, punched in the wrong code again.

Fuuuck.

Just as she was trying a third time, she saw the silhouette of a man reflected in the glass.

Oh oh oh fuck.

She pulled out her earpods with her left hand, went for her sidearm with the right.

'Ren! Don't fire — it's Cliff! It's me!'

Ren turned around, weapon raised, then quickly lowered. 'Jesus Christ, Cliff. You have

15

never looked more beautiful than you do right now.'

'Jesus Christ yourself! And you have never looked so deadly.' Cliff James was her big-bear buddy and colleague. 'Finally,' he said, 'after all these years, you've heard my girl voice . . . '

'It's over,' said Ren. She smiled and opened her arms.

Cliff came up to her, arms wide. He paused. 'Hey, pretty lady — have you been crying?'

'Possibly . . . '

He recoiled a fraction. 'Oh, oh, no. And drinking.' He glanced back at Ren's Jeep.

'I know. I know,' said Ren. 'But keep it coming with the hug.'

Cliff hugged her tight, kissed the top of her head.

Ren looked up at him. 'I need my CARD laptop. I'm flying to Portland with Gary in the morning.'

'Aw, Jesus, Ren . . . '

'I know, I know.' *I know I know I know.*

'For someone who knows a lot of things . . . ' Cliff reached around her, punched in the right code, pushed the door open. Ren stepped out from under his arm, let him put his foot inside the door. He dangled his car keys in front of her. 'Why don't you tell me where that laptop is, go wait in my car, and let me take the lady home.'

Aw, maaaan. 'I'm a loser.'

'You are, Renderland, you are. But nothing's gonna change my love for you.'

Ren grabbed his arm, squeezed. Then she watched how he took the stairs slower than he

16

used to and she felt a pain in her chest.

You instinctive knight-in-shining-armor with your own burden of grief to deal with.

Cliff's wife, Brenda, whom he adored, had passed away from cancer just two months after the shootings at Safe Streets.

Everywhere I turn . . .

Ren looked around the foyer.

Leave.

She stepped inside.

You come here every day why are you doing this now you've been drinking this will be a shitshow don't.

She walked ten paces in, stared at the basement door.

Bang . . . bang . . . bang . . . bang . . . bang.

And the sensation struck, the sensation that terrified her, like she was being drowned in a rush of cold air or water or something that she wouldn't rise above, that she couldn't breathe through, something she would succumb to. She sucked in a huge breath, and another, and another.

And then Cliff was back, and he had taken her in his big arms, and he had held her tight as she shook. She looked up at him, still holding on, her eyes wide. 'How did it all come to this?'

'I don't know, Renheart. I don't know.'

'It's like someone took a slash hook to our lives.'

3

Ren was settled into a dark corner of a dark restaurant in Denver airport by four thirty a.m. She ordered coffee and a pineapple juice. She popped two Advil.

Somebody fucking shoot me. Ugh. Do some work. My brain is fried. Do something easy.

She opened Safari.

Fuck, the light.

She dimmed the screen and googled the town of Tate.

Tate, Oregon, nestled in the Willamette Valley, fifty miles south-east of Portland, fifteen miles east of Salem, home to 3,949 residents.

The first images were of a quaint, well-kept town, built around one intersection, its most prominent building a two-story red-brick family restaurant with Bucky's written in red cursive at a jaunty angle on the front.

The public announcements of Tate PD were about fallen trees, storm damage, and buckling up to avoid getting a citation.

Caleb Veir's disappearance had hit the news and there was a photo of him alongside the article. He was a sturdy-looking boy with dark, side-parted hair, pale skin with freckles across his nose and cheeks, and a naturally down-turned mouth.

A mournful-looking kid.

Ren jumped as a figure came into her peripheral vision.

Gary. Jesus. Fuck hangover jumpiness.

'Hey.' He sat down beside her. He glanced at the watery pineapple juice pooled in the dying ice of her glass. He knew it was her hangover cure of choice.

Please just smell my beautiful wintergreen smokescreen breath.

'Caleb Veir was last seen by his father, John, at seven forty-five yesterday morning,' said Ren. 'When did you get the call from Tate PD?'

'Right before I called you last night,' said Gary. He nodded. 'Yes — it's strange. The kid didn't make it to school, but when his teacher called his mom, she couldn't get hold of her. She left a message, then left one for the father on his cell phone and at work. He's a corrections officer at Black River Correctional Institution outside Salem. An inmate escaped the previous day, so the teacher figured John Veir would be caught up with that and didn't want to bother him: she figured Caleb was at home being looked after by his mom anyway — a lot of kids had been off school with a virus.'

'Jesus Christ,' said Ren. 'Wouldn't the teacher have persevered? And why wasn't the mom answering her phone?'

'She wasn't home the previous night and no one could reach her the following day.'

'Why not?' said Ren.

'I don't have all the details,' said Gary.

'So, Caleb was alone with his father the night before he disappeared?' said Ren. 'What's the father's deal?'

'John Veir, fifty-seven years old, ex-military,

19

CO at BRCI for the past five years.'

Military man, corrections officer, son about to hit his teens . . . hmm.

There was a short silence.

'Sylvie Ross is flying in too,' said Gary. Sylvie Ross was an agent and child forensic interviewer. 'I'm still seeing her.'

Loving the defiant tone. 'That's your business,' said Ren.

'I just wanted you to know,' he said.

Why — so I'll know to exercise the muscles of my blind eye again?

'Thanks,' said Ren. *Honored to be part of your cheating ways.*

He turned to Ren. 'Paul Louderback's coming too.' There was weight to his gaze.

Tou-fucking-ché.

Paul Louderback was Ren's former PT instructor at Quantico. He was ten years her senior, married throughout their emotional affair, then briefly separated from his wife when he and Ren slept together. He was her kill-your-curiosity fuck, the eliminate-years-of-buildup fuck. After they slept together, Ren had officially gotten together with Ben, and Paul got back with his wife. Contact had dropped since then, until he called her when he heard about the shooting.

What will my heart do when I see you again, Paul Louderback? Because I've no control over that.

Your heart will betray Ben and you'll feel like shit.

The plane landed in Portland in torrential rain. Ren drove to Tate without music, listening, instead, to the sound of the rain pounding the car. It was soothing at first, but as it fell harder, faster, louder, she turned on the radio to drown it out. She focused on Gary's car, up ahead, copied every move he made.

I am on autopilot.

What the fuck was I doing, driving last night?

Jesus. Christ.

Cliff. God bless him.

I am a shitshow.

She shook her head.

Paul Louderback . . . his mouth . . . his hands . . . his . . . one night . . . sexy and just a little dirty . . . not dirty enough . . . like he was unleashed but didn't know what to do with it . . . an old-school gentleman trying to be filthy . . . he just didn't have that thing . . .

That Ben and I had. That fuck-me-always-any-way-you-want-to thing.

Ben.

Stop.

★ ★ ★

As Ren drove past the *Welcome to Tate* sign, she saw black ribbons tied around some of the trees.

Not very hopeful.

As she approached the gates to Tate PD, she felt her stomach clench: it was chaos — news vans, reporters, law enforcement, volunteers, a K-9 Unit.

Gary slowed to a crawl in front of her, and a young Tate PD officer parted the crowd and guided them both through and into two reserved parking spaces. The building was single-story, red-brick, with a parking lot on three sides and a strip of grass planted with trees along the other.

★　★　★

Inside, the lobby was small, clean, and pine-scented, with fresh plants and a wall covered with community photographs that spanned decades of sporting events, picnics, barbecues, charity drives, swim meets — beaming police officers, teachers, schoolchildren, and senior citizens.

Ren and Gary checked in at the desk and took a seat.

Within minutes, a short man with a tight, round stomach came out to meet them. He looked to be in his late fifties, with sad dark brown eyes and a puffy face, pockmarked on the left side. Ren and Gary stood up.

'Pete Ruddock,' he said. 'Thank you for coming.' As he shook Ren's hand, he gave her a smile that was all about the warmth that radiated from those sad eyes.

I like you already, Pete Ruddock. Whoa. Is that pity in your eyes? Oh, God — have you read about me? You have to know what happened at Safe Streets. How could you not know?

Because he wouldn't have been told which

CARD team members were coming to Tate. *Jesus.*

'Nice to meet you,' said Ren. 'I'm Ren Bryce.'

'Good to meet you, Ren.'

'Gary Dettling,' said Gary, shaking Ruddock's hand.

Ruddock picked up immediately on Gary's get-to-the-point ways.

'Something's a little hinky with the parents,' he said.

4

Ruddock guided Ren and Gary to his office. It was neat and tidy, with family photos lined across the lower shelf of a walnut cabinet. The biggest one, framed in gold, was a nineties-looking shot of Ruddock, with his arm around a short, smiling woman and two boys and a girl who looked to be in their early teens.

'What's your major concern?' said Gary.

'There are a few things,' said Ruddock. 'The delay in reporting Caleb missing is one.'

Ren nodded. 'Yes, we thought that — did they explain why? Caleb should have arrived home from school at around four thirty, right?'

'Yes,' said Ruddock. 'But Teddy Veir, Caleb's mom — didn't come home until six thirty yesterday evening. She'd been staying with a friend in Salem, Sunday night, and she was at a trade show there yesterday — she works part time in Gemstones, a kind of New-Agey shop here in Tate — sells crystals and incense and angel healing things. Her cell phone battery had died overnight and she had left her charger at home.'

'Surely someone at the venue could have charged her phone for her,' said Ren.

'She said she didn't think to ask,' said Ruddock. 'When she got home, she figured Caleb was at a friend's house and that he'd be back for supper by seven. She charged her

24

phone, called Caleb's, left him voicemails. His phone, we now know, was upstairs in his bedroom, powered off. Teddy also tried her husband's phone, which was diverted. She left voicemails for him, then called BRCI and they said they'd get him to call. When she checked her own messages, she heard one from Caleb's teacher, Nicole Barton, made at eight thirty a.m., wondering if Caleb was OK, that he hadn't shown up for school. At this point, about seven thirty p.m., with still no sign of Caleb, Teddy called neighbors and friends, but no one had seen him, and the kids from his class confirmed that he hadn't been to school that day. Now, Teddy was panicking. At seven forty-five, she called BRCI again and insisted she would wait on the line to speak with John. He came home right away when she told him Caleb was missing.'

'So, John Veir was working what shift?' said Ren.

'Well, here's the other strange thing,' said Ruddock. 'He was rostered in to work at seven a.m., but he didn't show up until the three p.m. shift.'

'Nobody called from work to check where he was that morning?' said Ren.

'No,' said Ruddock. 'They were taken up with the escaped inmate from the day before.'

'Wouldn't that have made them even more suspicious if Veir didn't show?' said Ren.

'I guess they trust him,' said Ruddock.

'I'm not buying that Veir screwed up his start time,' said Ren. 'An ex-military man who works a standard shift arrangement gets it wrong the same morning his son disappears?'

'The only thing is,' said Ruddock, 'Veir was filling in for someone yesterday. It was supposed to be his day off. So it wasn't part of his usual routine.'

'Still,' said Ren. 'And when the school called, he didn't pick up?'

'He said he was home, but he didn't realize the ringer was turned off.'

'That sounds like bullshit to me,' said Ren, 'because he brought his cell phone to work, and he would have seen the missed call.'

Ruddock nodded. 'Another thing that's bothering me is that we've gotten reports from some of the neighbors that they heard raised voices coming from the house quite regularly. The father and son. Apparently, mother and son were very close.'

'Did they say what the arguments were about?' said Ren.

'They didn't always hear everything, but the general sense is that it was about Caleb keeping in line, not talking back, that kind of thing,' said Ruddock. 'We also saw something at the house — scuff marks on the bottom of Caleb's door. On the inside. Like it had been kicked at. And the doorjamb looked damaged, as if someone was trying to open a locked door.'

'They lock him in?' said Ren.

Ruddock shook his head. 'Both parents said the door was never locked, and that they had never even seen a key.'

'We only have the father's word that Caleb was alive and well yesterday morning,' said Ren. 'No

26

one else can confirm that. What if something went down the night before? The father locks Caleb in, Caleb goes nuts, the father goes too far. And if that happened Sunday night, that would have given him a lot of time to figure out a plan to get rid of the body.'

'No traces of blood were found anywhere in the house or in the garage,' said Ruddock. 'Plus no one saw John Veir leave the house Sunday evening, which of course, doesn't mean a whole lot, but he hasn't come up on any of the traffic cams yet.'

'And what about yesterday?' said Ren.

'There aren't a lot on that route,' said Ruddock, 'but we have him at a 7-Eleven on 1–5 at 14.05. Bought a bottle of water, some gum.'

'Any dramatic eyeballing of the security camera?' said Ren. 'Any sense that he was trying to time-stamp his activity to prove he couldn't have been elsewhere?'

'Well, he looked up when he walked into the store,' said Ruddock. 'But he could have done that anyway.'

'Did he always stop on his way to work?' said Ren. 'Like, I hate doing that — I want to get in my car — bam — arrive in work, no stops.'

'Guess it depends on how long the journey is,' said Ruddock. 'His is an hour. But I didn't ask him. I didn't think it was significant.'

'Clearly you still don't,' said Ren, smiling.

Ruddock smiled back.

Lovely smile.

'What have you done in terms of a search?' said Gary.

'As much as we could in darkness last night,' said Ruddock. 'We have a search organized to start here at midday. We wanted to make that appeal at the press conference too, maximize volunteer numbers.'

'What about the missing inmate?' said Gary. 'Could he be connected to this?'

'Too early to say,' said Ruddock. 'His name is Franklin J. Merrifield — he's eighteen months into a thirty-five year sentence for robbery, homicide, rape, and arson. He was admitted to Salem Hospital on Sunday because of a seizure, and escaped while he was there — the guard watching him was sleeping, but may have been drugged. Whether the seizure was faked, and this was all planned ahead of time, we don't know. And seizure activity doesn't always show up in EEGs. He had an appeal rejected just last month. His buddy cut a deal with the prosecution and had his sentence reduced to seventeen years.'

'On what grounds was the appeal?' said Ren.

'Merrifield has maintained his innocence throughout,' said Ruddock. 'He admits to the robbery, but denies all other charges. He says he was going along for the ride, didn't know his buddy was carrying a firearm. His appeal was on the grounds that the jury was poorly instructed on accomplice liability.'

'When was Merrifield reported missing?' said Gary.

'Five p.m., Sunday,' said Ruddock.

'Do they believe he had help from someone in BRCI before he ever got to the hospital?' said Ren.

Ruddock nodded.

'Any incidents between him and John Veir?' said Ren.

'Nothing we know about,' said Ruddock.

'Could we take a look at the Veirs' questionnaires?' said Gary.

'Sure,' said Ruddock. 'I've got them right here.'

He handed them the forms that every parent of a missing child fills out as soon as they make the initial report. Gary and Ren scanned them.

John Veir, fifty-seven years old; born and raised in Tate, Oregon; joined the military in 1977, US Navy — OOD, married Teddy Veir in 2000; did one tour in Afghanistan; three tours in Iraq; one son — Caleb, born 2004; left the military in 2009, worked in different businesses around Tate, employed as a corrections officer in BRCI since 2010; mother deceased, father living in Madison, Wisconsin; one sister — Alice Veir, lawyer, living in Spokane, Washington.

Teddy Veir, fifty-four years old; born and raised in Tate, Oregon; married John Veir in 2000; one son — Caleb, born 2004; works part-time in Gemstones, Tate, suffers from anxiety, no family living in the US, but has a brother and sister-in-law in Australia.

'What's OOD?' said Ren.

'Double-oh Delta,' said Gary. 'He was a navy diver.'

Part of the questionnaire asked parents to name anyone they might want law enforcement to take a look at; anyone who might have given them a bad feeling or may have an issue with the family.

29

'Teddy Veir's written the names of five men she thinks we should take a look at,' said Ren. 'And John Veir has ten.' She raised her eyebrows.

'Well, some of his include former inmates at BRCI,' said Ruddock. 'We're going through the list.' He glanced at his wall clock. 'The press conference is about to start. Let's walk.'

'OK,' said Ren. 'I was wondering — I saw a couple of black ribbons on the trees on the drive in . . . '

'That's not about Caleb,' said Ruddock. 'Two young boys died here — one in January, one last month.'

'Oh my God,' said Ren. 'What happened to them?'

'Aaron Fuller — he was only eleven years old — drowned in Lake Verny. And a couple of weeks later, little Luke Monroe choked on a sandwich,' said Ruddock. 'Seven years old.'

Jesus. 'That's heartbreaking,' said Ren.

'And in such a small community,' said Ruddock. 'And now this . . . '

'Well, let's hope there's a favorable outcome to this,' said Ren.

The conference room was packed with police officers, reporters, photographers, Tate residents. Three tables were lined up at the top of the room. Mounted behind them on a whiteboard at the center was the Missing poster of Caleb Veir, blown up to four feet by three feet. There were twenty rows of chairs, divided by a central aisle. Gary and Ren stood toward the front, close to the wall, neither aware that they were in the exact same pose — arms folded, stiff, frowning.

30

Ren turned to Gary. 'What a sad little face that boy has. There's pain in those eyes.'

Ruddock walked over to them. 'We'll be starting soon.'

A man appeared suddenly in front of them, no hellos, no introductions, no eye contact with anyone. He had a buzz cut, a scowl, and flaming red razor burn on his neck.

'Just so you know,' he said to Ruddock, 'both parents have refused to take polygraphs.'

What an extraordinary voice. Like it's being scrambled.

Ruddock turned to Ren and Gary, irritated. 'This is Lieutenant Gil Wiley — FBI agents, Ren Bryce and Gary Dettling from CARD.'

Ah, the sharp upward nod, thank you, Mr Wiley.

'Nice to meet you,' said Ren, shaking his hand. Gary stayed silent but shook Wiley's hand. Wiley said nothing to either of them.

Ren looked at Ruddock. Beneath the endearing, doughy face, his jaw was tight.

5

Shannon Fuller gripped the edge of the bar like she was about to do a push-up, her head bent over the newspaper, her broad back hunched. She stared at the photo of Caleb Veir under the headline **MISSING FROM TATE**. Her chest tightened. She thought of her son, Aaron, and how he had been in the lake in the pitch-black all night. But his body had gotten lodged in a shallow spot, where the water was clear, so he was found. He wasn't **MISSING**. She was lucky.

Lucky . . . her only child, found under an icy, glassy surface, like a sleeping beauty who might wake up. But it was better than being down in the grim depths, rock bottom, decomposing, flesh falling from his bones. A shiver crawled up her spine. She reached out to grab a cloth, a pen, a beer mat, anything to take her mind along a different path — another useless pursuit. So many useless pursuits.

She'd replayed that evening on a loop ever since. Aaron had been at his middle school dance, she had been in The Crow Bar alone, feeling sorry for herself, drinking herself into oblivion, crying into beer after beer after beer. She had chased it all down with a row of shots to remind her of times when a broken heart was something other people got. She had staggered into the house behind the bar, fallen asleep on the sofa, never knew her baby hadn't made it home.

She sucked in a breath, stood up straight, shoulders back, head high. She figured all bars were a desolate place in the early morning, but when she bought The Crow, she thought that would change. It didn't. And, now, without Aaron, the desolation had seeped into every cell of her body too; she felt a part of the bar, as worn as the timber, as faded as the drapes, as stained as the surfaces.

* * *

She remembered walking into The Crow Bar seven years earlier, with four-year-old Aaron, and sixteen-year-old Seth, who she could feel was already pulling away from her, already worrying her with his behavior, and his friends, and his recklessness. Her sweet, handsome, loving, affectionate little nephew had turned into someone she couldn't understand. He had effectively been her son since he was eight years old, when her sister, Jessie, was killed in an instant by a brain aneurysm. Seth's father had OD'd when he was six months old, and the only family he had left was Shannon who had always adored him, and adored him still, even in this troubled teenage incarnation. She wanted to give Seth everything her sister had dreamed of for him.

Shannon hadn't known that Jessie had been saving for years, and along with her insurance policy, had left Shannon quite a large sum of money. Shannon had added to it, and by the time the battered and abandoned thirty-five-year-old Lake Verny resort was put up for sale, at its knock-down price, she could afford to buy it. It made sense to her: she had spent time there as a child, she worked in a bar, Aaron loved the water, and Seth used to love it. He used to be a champion little swimmer, and Shannon wanted to reintroduce him to what was once his passion. She also wanted to employ people in town, bring business to Tate, she wanted to do good in Jessica's honor. That day, she said yes to the real estate agent, yes to the Lake Verny Resort with its twenty brokedown cabins, yes to The Crow Bar, and yes to years and years of struggling to make ends meet. But she also said yes to something that brought her joy . . . until now.

★　★　★

In the six weeks since Aaron had died, along with thoughts of her beautiful boy, along with her tears and her paralyzing grief, she was struck with hot stabs of shame when she thought of how she must have looked to Pete Ruddock and Gil Wiley that morning, captured, as she was, like a shabby Polaroid with Bad Mom scrawled on the white strip underneath — hanging out of the doorway of a bar, puffy-eyed, messy-haired, liquor-soaked, unaware of her only child's whereabouts, neglectful, undeserving, trash.

Tears slid down her face. She thought of her pain, she thought of John Veir's, she thought of Teddy's. She pictured Gil Wiley and Pete

34

Ruddock walking up to the Veirs' front door, as they had walked to hers, with their white faces and their terrible news.

Then, for a guilty moment, Shannon thought of John Veir and how his hands felt on her body, how his lips felt against hers, how she loved him, how she feared she always would.

They had gone their separate ways before, found their way back to each other, until the last time — the time that sent her diving, heartfirst, into an alcohol haze. Now here they were, through tragedy, entwined again.

6

Ruddock appeared at the top of the conference room and silence fell. He paused to guide John and Teddy Veir ahead of him. John Veir pulled out the chair for his wife as he passed. He was a muscular, hard-looking man with a stern face, thick eyebrows and a solid jaw that he was clenching and unclenching. His wife was a delicate skinny-limbed woman. She had clear skin, huge brown eyes, and wavy light-brown hair. She shifted in her seat, pulling her cardigan closed over a floral blue-and-yellow shirt dress, holding her hand there in a white-knuckle grip.

You fragile thing. This environment is all wrong for you. But is this you as you always are or you as the mother of a missing child?

When the Veirs were settled beside the photo of Caleb and their three faces were lined up in a row, Ren could see that though Caleb had his mother's eyes, the steel in them came from his father. John Veir's stare was moving around the room like a drunk looking for a fight.

★ ★ ★

Ruddock tapped the microphone, once, twice, and started to speak.

'Thank you all for coming,' he said. 'We're here today to appeal for information on the whereabouts of Caleb Veir, who has been missing from his Burton Street home in Tate since seven forty-five yesterday morning. Caleb is five feet tall, weighs one hundred pounds, and is of medium build. This photo beside me was taken two weeks ago. Yesterday, Caleb was wearing the same gray Puffa jacket, blue denim jeans, a navy-blue long-sleeved sweatshirt with a red-and-gray graphic print, and white-and-red Nike sneakers. You will find photographs of all these items of clothing pinned to the noticeboard at the back of the room.'

Teddy Veir was rigid, her elbows pressed tightly to her body, her ankles crossed underneath the table.

'To my right here are Caleb's parents,' said Ruddock. 'John and Teddy Veir. Teddy would now like to say a few words.'

Teddy shifted the chair forward. 'Thank you, Chief Ruddock.' She looked up, her lost and panicked eyes blinking quickly before she focused on a point on the floor three feet ahead. 'Our son, Caleb, has been missing since yesterday morning. Caleb is only twelve years old. Caleb, we want you home with us, we want you to come home. To your mom and dad. We miss you, and we love you very much. Please . . . come home.'

She welled up so quickly, and the pain robbed her of her voice so suddenly, that everyone else on the platform was thrown; they weren't ready to break in, to rescue her.

Someone help!

John Veir kicked in, putting his arm around his wife, sliding the microphone that was in front of her toward himself, knocking over a glass of water as he did. The piercing sound of feedback erupted in the room.

'Caleb is a good boy,' said John. 'Just a . . . good kid, who is . . . good to everybody . . . and everyone . . . and helped his mom and me out, and . . . '

No one prepared you. You weren't planning on speaking.

'Please bring him home,' said John. 'Whoever has him, if someone has our son, please bring him home. We love him so much.' His voice started to crack. 'He's our son.' He broke down. He briefly raised his head to say: 'No matter what. We want him back. We love you, Caleb. I want you to know that. We love you very much.'

No matter what? He's our son, no matter what? Or no matter what, we want him back?

A sudden smell — powerful, stale and liquor-laced — struck Ren.

What the . . . whoa . . .

She turned to see a man take a few steps, then stop abruptly. He was dressed in a faded black sweatshirt with unraveling cuffs and crusted white stains. His pale jeans had two stripes of filth down the center, his sneakers were gray, the laces half undone. His eyes did a full sweep of the room before he walked any further.

Now, who might you be?

He took two steps closer.

And what bar's supplies have you recently depleted?

He walked past Ren. She put her hand to her mouth and swallowed.

Jesus. Christ. Wow.

I probably smell the exact same . . .

In a flash, Wiley was striding their way. He struck Ren hard with his shoulder as he passed.

Dickhead.

He grabbed the man by the arm, effortlessly dragging him toward the exit. The man's face was pinched in anger, his expression childish, petulant. There was tutting, eyerolling and nose-wrinkling from locals who seemed to know him.

The man opened his mouth wide, looked ready to speak, but he took in all the stares and his face fell and he didn't say a word.

You are a hurting man. You know you're a sideshow to these people.

Just as he was about to go through the door, a burst of courage delivered his voice:

'Lake Verny!' he shouted. 'You need to look in Lake Verny! Tell Ruddock. Tell Ruddock! You tell him Clyde Brimmer says that lake's a killer!'

Ren looked around at the crowd, gauging their reactions. There was no sense that the man's words held any meaning, that they were anything other than a terrible thing to shout in a room where two parents were hoping to reach out for a son they wanted to believe was alive and well — not sucked down into the depths of a lake.

7

Gary, Ren and Ruddock stood in the shelter of the back door of Tate PD after the press conference. Ruddock pulled out a pack of cigarettes.

'Do you smoke?' he said, extending the pack toward Gary, then Ren. Gary declined.

'For one night only,' said Ren. *Filthy habit.*

Ruddock lit it for her, lit his own.

'Sounds like Mom thinks Caleb ran away, and Dad thinks he's been abducted,' said Gary.

Ren turned to Ruddock. 'Could he have run away?' she said. 'What do you think?'

'Honestly, I don't know,' said Ruddock. 'All I know is something is not quite right with the Veirs.'

'It seems like they're blaming each other,' said Ren. 'They weren't even touching when they walked in. What vibe did you get from them when you first met?'

'It was tense,' said Ruddock, 'but under the circumstances, that's to be expected. Even if John Veir thinks his son was abducted, I agree — he sure is acting like he blames his wife for something.'

'Maybe for not being there yesterday morning,' said Ren. 'But, surely, that wouldn't have made a difference. It wasn't like we know that Caleb was snatched from their home while she was distracted. And John Veir had his phone on silent. Maybe that's what's bothering his wife.' She paused. 'What was John Veir's 'no matter what' about?'

Ruddock shrugged. 'Nerves? I don't know.'

They could hear footsteps coming their way. They looked around. Wiley was striding toward them from where he had dumped the man who interrupted the press conference. He rolled his eyes at Ruddock. Ruddock didn't respond.

'Who was that guy?' said Ren.

'Clyde Brimmer,' said Wiley. 'A drunk.'

Wow . . . what drunk fucked you over?

'Why was he talking about Lake Verny?' said Ren.

Wiley was shaking his head. 'His usual bullshit.'

Ruddock intervened. 'It's got to be about Aaron Fuller.'

'The boy who drowned?' said Ren.

'Yes,' said Ruddock. 'Clyde was fired for drinking on the job. He was an embalmer. The last body he worked on was Aaron's . . . '

'Ah,' said Ren. 'It's haunting him . . . '

Ruddock nodded.

'And that was the job he was caught drunk on?' said Ren.

'Well, it was the last straw,' said Ruddock. 'There were some earlier complaints. He swears he wasn't drinking when he was working on Aaron — '

'Clyde doesn't do himself any favors,' said Wiley. 'He showed up for work Monday to Friday in reasonably good shape, didn't go too wild on weeknights. But he drank heavily on the

41

weekends. Once you're propping up a bar regularly, slowly drinking your way into oblivion, well, you're telling people how to remember you. It's all about perception, really, isn't it?'

Jesus.

'I'll leave you to it,' said Wiley. He walked back toward the gates.

'What is Clyde Brimmer's story?' said Ren.

'A sorry one,' said Ruddock. 'We were in school together. A group of us hung out, usual stuff: playing football, going swimming, duck-diving in the lake. We were pretty innocent kids. But Clyde went off the rails when he was seventeen, when his little sister died. He started drinking, doing drugs. Got off drugs eventually, but kept on drinking. He'd get sober every now and then, then he'd fall off the wagon again. The longest he was sober was when he did his embalmer training. He was lucky he managed it at all. It would break your heart. Bad things just seem to happen a lot around Clyde. It's like life is always throwing things at him.'

You are so endearing. And I love pockmarked skin.

'What happened to his sister?' said Ren.

'She fell through one of the decks at Lake Verny. The timber was rotten. Clyde was custodian at the time. It was the spring of '84. He had already said there was a problem with the deck and the jetty of that cabin, but no one listened to him. He was concerned that sub-standard timber was used, and that it was unstable. He told the owners, but they were from out of town and said they'd get it fixed later: they

42

wanted to enjoy their next break without having any construction work going on. This one day, Lizzie — Clyde's sister, she was only ten years old — was hanging around with him, because their parents were gone to a wedding and he had to watch her. She brought a couple of her little friends along, they'd been playing around the cabins. Then she disappeared. She was found floating in the water . . . apparently she stepped right through the deck. It tore up her femoral artery, that was it, she bled out just like that. Clyde took it real bad. He always said if he had just fixed that deck when he wanted to, it never would have happened. He felt he didn't try hard enough to get people to listen. It's why he gets so agitated still if he feels something is unsafe, and people aren't listening. It drives him crazy. And you know something? He didn't even quit his job. He still stayed looking after the cabins for a long time after the accident, for whoever hung on to them. It was a control thing, I guess. He didn't want to put anyone else through what his family went through.'

'That is so sad,' said Ren.

Gary turned to Ruddock. 'Mind if Ren and I take a look at last night's interviews with the Veirs?'

'Sure,' said Ruddock. 'Follow me.'

★   ★   ★

Ruddock found Gary and Ren an empty room and left them to watch the videos of first John Veir, then Teddy, both carried out by Ruddock

43

and Wiley together.

Ruddock was an impressive interviewer, thoughtful, measured, bright and sharp, with the perfect demeanor to make two traumatized parents as comfortable as they could be with a series of uncomfortable questions while their only child was still missing.

Wiley didn't ask any questions, even though, at times, it looked like he was struggling to stay quiet.

I wonder were you under strict instructions from Ruddock. Or do you just not give a fuck?

There was a knock on the door and Ruddock walked in. 'Sign-in for the search is kicking off, if you'd like to come out.'

'OK,' said Gary.

'So,' said Ruddock, nodding toward the screen. 'What do you think?'

'They're both lying,' said Gary and Ren at exactly the same time.

8

Jimmy Lyle was driving, happily, freely, down the west coast. Home, in whatever altered state he had left it, was far enough behind him to bring comfort. He was taking quiet roads, darker ones, roads less traveled. He didn't want to be pulled over, he didn't want the trunk of his car to be searched.

★   ★   ★

The day he had the shit beaten out of him by the pond was coming up on Valentine's Day: after the operations, as he looked around the hospital with his unbandaged eye, he caught sight of heart-shaped balloons, bunches of flowers, cards, an air of buoyancy. Jimmy hadn't a face for Valentine's Day, hadn't a heart for love. He had seen it go wrong too soon. His wild and beautiful mother married his sensible teacher father. She walked out on them when Jimmy was eight years old, his father's heart spiked on her stiletto as she made her glamorous exit. She had loved Jimmy deeply, and suddenly she was gone, and his father looked at him across the table of their first dinner alone like he was a dog who he now needed to find a home for. He kept him, though. Jimmy made sure to be indispensable. He cooked his father breakfast the very next morning and Outside Jimmy and Inside Jimmy were born; one the white, tranquil, opaque shell, the other the dark, crimson, screaming, angry, bleeding, weeping soul it covered.

★ ★ ★

The day Jimmy had left the hospital, he went via the cancer ward. He stole some things, some 'personal effects'. He found an empty room and changed. He could barely look at himself in the mirror.

Afterward, as Jimmy stood, eyes on the floor, waiting for the elevator, he had heard a gasp beside him. It was to his right — it was always to his right. He turned to see a little girl standing there, wide-eyed.

She cried out. 'Mommy, Mommy!'

Jimmy froze. The little girl's mother scooped her up in her arms.

'What happened to that lady's face?' said the little girl, pointing to Jimmy.

'I'm so sorry,' said the woman. 'I don't know what to say. I'm trying to teach her . . . she's only three years old. She . . . '

Jimmy smiled. 'It's OK,' he said. 'She's just a little kid. They say what they think, don't they? We could all learn from that.'

The mother's shoulders relaxed. The little girl slowly turned to Jimmy, her head bowed. She looked up at him through teary eyes.

'I had an accident when I was a little girl,' he said.

The mother looked at him nervously, not sure what he was going to say next, not knowing whether or not he would say something that would scar her child.

'So,' said Jimmy, 'you need to listen to your mama when she tells you to stay away from boiling water.'

The little girl was transfixed, horrified. The mother nodded, took a few steps backward. 'Thank you,' she said. 'You have a good day.'

'You too,' said Jimmy.

★ ★ ★

Jimmy walked through those hospital doors, holding a bunch of red roses close to his face on one side, holding a still-buoyant balloon on the other.

I HEART YOU, it said.

I FUCK YOU UP, thought Jimmy. I ABANDON YOU.

He remembered picking flowers from the back garden for a woman once, and, even while he was handing them to her, thinking exactly those words. And later, doing exactly those things.

★ ★ ★

There were good people who had scars, people who had to fight every day to bring others past the outside to the beauty underneath. Jimmy Lyle's face and body, with their layer upon layer of damage, were the perfect complement to his soul.

9

Ren and Gary stood in the parking lot of Tate PD, watching the volunteers arrive. A table had been set up to sign them in, manned by two members of Team Adam. Ren watched as they went through a process they'd gone through countless times before — Team Adam was a program run by the National Center for Missing and Exploited Children. It was made up of retired law enforcement officers, who, like CARD, had specialist expertise, and mobilized as soon as they heard a report of a missing child anywhere in the US.

Ren studied the crowd. 'Sometimes I feel so guilty thinking some of the shit I think about these kind people,' she said. 'They're here sacrificing whatever it is their day would have held, while some stranger lady is thinking they're Ted Danson. I mean, Ted Bundy.' *Hello? Charles Manson, maybe?*

Gary glanced at her briefly.

'You know,' said Ren, 'it still blows my mind how often the guilty party shows up. Whatever about the ones who are so close to the victims that it would be suspicious if they *didn't* show. But I'm thinking of those peripheral nutjobs who put themselves in the frame by hanging around. The ones who might never have been on our radar otherwise — and they can't see how that's what they're doing. I mean, even if you change channels on your television in a micro-second these days, there's a crime show helping your ass out with these things.'

'We like the dumb ones,' said Gary.

Ren scanned the crowd again.

Is there a psycho among you?

Gil Wiley was moving through the line, greeting the people he knew.

'Wiley looks like he's on the campaign trail,' said Ren. 'His voice . . . it's like it's being garbled for a TV interview to protect his identity. Like we should only ever be seeing him in sil-you-ette.'

Gary held in a laugh, but still managed a low-volume sound of approval.

'It's not Denver cold,' said Ren, 'but it's still cold. That Puffa jacket might have been fine for the walk to school, but if Caleb Veir's been out overnight . . . '

Gary nodded. 'I know.'

People continued to arrive, and the crowd began to expand toward them.

Ren's heart started to pound.

Oh, no, please don't do this. Not here.

She swallowed. She swallowed again.

No, no, no. Not now. Not here.

And the sensation struck, again.

Drowning, drowning.

Keep it together, bitch.

'Gary . . . ' One word, and it came out like it had needed the Heimlich maneuver to make it.

Oh, God. My legs.

She pressed her hand against her thigh.

Like that's going to help.

'Gary,' she said. 'I'm not feeling a lot like

49

being around big groups of people.'

He turned to her. He was waiting for more.

Breathe. Breathe.

Speak.

Speak!

'Ren?' said Gary.

Crowds people I'm going to pass out don't you won't stop breathe in out in out breathe I can't you're going to pass out.

Gary took her to one side. 'Are you OK?'

'I'm . . . I'm feeling overwhelmed.'

He studied her face.

Oh, no. Not the grave concern. No fucking way.

'I just need a moment,' said Ren, 'I'm fine.'

No you're not.

'I just . . . don't feel like being in the thick of this right now,' said Ren, 'or, like, in the middle of search teams or lunches where I have to do small talk with people. I just — '

'If that's how you're feeling,' said Gary, 'I'm glad you told me. So I know to make sure you do exactly those things.'

You have got to be shitting me. I can't believe I said 'lunches'. Jesus.

'Come on, Ren — what did you think I was going to say?' He was looking straight ahead. 'Do you think I'm carrying around free passes for people? No. You're here one hundred per cent or you're not here at all. That's how this works. They were the conditions.' He paused. 'I know you're not a big fan of conditions, Ren.' He looked at her. 'I've got your back. Conditionally.'

'Great.' *Greaaaat.* 'Thank you.'

50

'The good news is,' said Gary, 'there's only one condition — that you do the best job you can. And that means being no more special than the next investigator or the next. Or the one standing beside you minus half his left triceps.'

Ooh, even you know that sounds like it's a competition.

A touch of awareness flickered in Gary's eyes.

'I, however, will give you a free pass for that,' said Ren.

She had been in the room, inches from him, watching as the bullet ripped through his arm, and the memory still drove a spike of pain through her core.

'I think you need to see Dr Lone more often,' said Gary. Dr Leonard Lone was Ren's psychiatrist. Her job was dependent on regular visits with him. 'Every two weeks is clearly not enough.'

Sweet Jesus. Gather yourself. Do not let him see you like this again. 'OK,' said Ren. *Oh. Fucking. Kay.*

Ren slapped a studied frown on her face as her heart pounded.

Fake it 'til you make it.

She drew subtle, slow, deep breaths through her nostrils as she scanned the crowd again. She saw a pretty blonde in her mid-forties, dressed in a pink zip-up fleece, lycra pants, and bright pink sneakers wrap her arms around a lanky, shaven-headed young man who looked to be in his early twenties.

Skin and bones and an air of the unwashed.

The woman squeezed him tight. It was a

51

maternal gesture, and he didn't fight it. There was profound sadness in both their faces.

Ren turned to Gary. 'Excuse me for two seconds.'

She walked toward the embracing pair, looking at a point past them, pausing as she reached them to take out her phone and pretend to text.

'This is a grieving town,' the woman was saying. 'A grieving town.'

Grieving agent finds spiritual home.

'I'm praying for him,' said the woman, squeezing his arm. 'Praying for him night and day.'

But he's only just gone missing. There's only been one night and one day.

'Thank you,' said the young man. 'I appreciate it. And I know Aunt Shannon will too.'

I'm lost . . .

'Hopefully,' said the woman, 'there'll be a more positive outcome for Caleb Veir.'

Oh. OK. She's talking about the other boy . . . the one who drowned: Aaron Fuller.

'Yes,' said the young man. 'I couldn't not come to help today.'

'Good for you,' said the woman.

She left quickly, and as Ren looked up, there was no one between her and the young man, and they locked eyes. He gave her a small nod, then turned and walked toward the line of volunteers.

★　★　★

When Ren went back over to Gary, Ruddock was standing with him, looking in her direction, but following the path of the young man.

'Who is that guy?' said Ren.

'Interesting you should ask,' said Ruddock. 'He's a former inmate of BRCI, got out last summer: Seth Fuller. He's a cousin of Aaron, the boy who drowned. He lives with his aunt out at The Crow Bar on Lake Verny. She owns it. In fact, she bought it from John Veir — he bought it when he came back from one of his tours of duty. He was going to set up a dive school there, or do boat tours, but it never really worked out for him, so he had to sell up.'

'How did he afford that?' said Ren.

Ruddock shrugged. 'I don't know.'

'What was Seth Fuller in prison for?' said Ren.

'Possession. He's a former heroin addict, cleaned up his act, apparently.'

Not that apparent . . .

'He wasn't mentioned on John Veir's question-naire as someone to consider,' said Ren.

'No,' said Ruddock. 'And Veir would have known him through selling the business to his aunt too.'

'What's your take on him?' said Ren.

Ruddock tilted his head. 'On Seth Fuller? He was a very bright, creative kid until he got involved in drugs — he was more a danger to himself than anyone else. That would have been my take on him . . . up until about five minutes ago. We've just learned a little something about Seth Fuller: apparently, he used to pay particular attention to Caleb Veir . . . '

10

The crowd of volunteers was moving back and forth, and at that moment, parted to reveal Seth Fuller again.

Ren watched him shift from one foot to the next, his eyes on the battered paperback in his right hand, one of the classics, folded back on itself.

What am I getting from you? And what are you reading?

'Who told you about this Fuller guy and Caleb Veir?' said Gary.

'The owner of the comic book store in town,' said Ruddock. 'He just called, said that on several occasions when Caleb was short a few dollars, Fuller would help him out. He also saw him buying the kid sodas and candy from the store across the street.'

'Did he say how Caleb reacted to this attention?' said Ren. 'Did it seem to make him uncomfortable?'

'He said Caleb just seemed happy to have someone pay his way,' said Ruddock.

'Well, he's twelve years old and he was getting free stuff,' said Ren.

Ruddock nodded. 'You know what it's like in a situation like this — everyone starts eyeing people suspiciously.'

'Well, we need to treat it seriously until we know otherwise,' said Gary.

Ren glanced up at him. *That was unnecessary.*
Ren looked at Ruddock.
Apologizing with my eyes.
'Have you seen enough, here?' said Ruddock.
'I wanted to let you know you're all set up inside.'

★ ★ ★

There were twelve desks in the temporary office, five already occupied by agents from the FBI Portland Division, which covered the entire state of Oregon. Another desk was taken up by the CAST agent — Cellular Analysis Survey Team. He had given Wiley printouts of the Veirs' phone dumps; John, Teddy and Caleb's cell phones, and the home phone.

Wiley was waiting for them like a student eager to please.

Mixed messages central.

'Nothing jumping out at me so far,' said Wiley. 'The last call made on Caleb's cell phone on Monday morning was to his aunt, Alice Veir — John Veir's sister. Veir himself made a call on Sunday morning to one of his colleagues, Rob Lockwood, a psychologist at BRCI.'

Wiley also had the reports from the lab on the Veirs' laptops. They read through them.

'Nothing here is setting off alarm bells,' said Ren. 'Caleb was looking up PlayStation cheats for *Grand Theft Auto 5*, emailing friends, posting on Facebook, checking out porn. Sure, he calls his father an asshole in a few of his emails, but that's what kids do. He hates school

55

— he's twelve years old, no surprise there.'

Ruddock's phone beeped. He checked a text. 'The Veirs are here. I'll go meet with them.'

Wiley followed him out.

Gary turned to Ren when they had left. 'You and me are talking to John Veir. I think you might unsettle him. I wouldn't say he likes strong women. You lead, and if his story starts smelling like bullshit, I'll go big guns, round two.'

'OK, but would you mind if Ruddock and I took Teddy Veir? She is so fragile: in the first interview, I'm not sure she responded very well to being faced down by two men. She looked a little freaked. She could be intimidated by male authority figures, especially if she's a cowed wife.'

'Or she could be used to male authority figures . . . ' said Gary.

'Trust me on this,' said Ren. 'You could intimidate a woman like her without even realizing it. I'll tread lightly, and Ruddock is a familiar face, with a gentle way about him. Between us, I think we can just . . . ' she shrugged, 'set the right tone.'

★ ★ ★

Ruddock came back and brought Gary and Ren to the interview room where John Veir was waiting, pale-faced, twitchy, tense. Ren and Gary introduced themselves.

'I'm sorry that we're meeting under these circumstances, Mr Veir,' said Ren. 'And I

56

apologize for having to ask you so many questions at such a difficult time, especially ones that you may feel you've already answered.'

John's eyes flicked toward Gary.

You're surprised the lady spoke first . . .

'Thank you,' said John, his eyes back on Ren, his pupils huge, his gaze fixed.

Jesus. Intense.

'It's OK,' said John. 'I understand. Go ahead.'

'Talk me through the twenty-four hours before Caleb went missing,' said Ren.

John nodded. 'Sunday morning, me, Teddy and Caleb went to the eleven a.m. service at Tate Baptist Church on 1st Street. We came home, ate lunch together. After lunch, Teddy was in the dining room — she was writing, Caleb was upstairs in his room, on his laptop or his phone, I guess. I was doing some work around the house, in the garage. It was a regular Sunday. Teddy left for Patti Ellis's house at around six o'clock — Patti's Teddy's friend, she's got cancer, so the friends are taking turns to look after her. Teddy does Sunday nights. And she had a trade show in Salem the following day. After she left, I cooked supper for me and Caleb. We ate together. Caleb went back up to his room. I was in the living room watching television.'

'What were you watching?' said Ren.

'Uh . . . well, I was watching a box set,' said John. 'I think *Breaking Bad*? Whichever one is in the machine.' He didn't take his eyes off her as he spoke.

Hmm.

57

'I was dozing off,' said John.

'Did you see Caleb again — did you check on him before you went to bed?' said Ren.

John frowned. 'Of course I did. He was fine.'

'How were things between you and Caleb in general?' said Ren. 'We've had reports of raised voices in the house . . . '

'Sunday night? No way,' said John.

'Not specifically Sunday night . . . ' said Ren.

'Well, not on Sunday, and not on Monday,' said John. 'Caleb and I were good.' He paused. 'Let me correct that, sorry — I did shout up at Caleb several times on Monday morning, because he was dragging his heels, and his oatmeal was going cold.'

'Did he respond to you?' said Ren. 'Did he hurry up?'

'He was already leaving his room,' said John.

'Did you drive Caleb to school often?' said Ren.

'When I was working the late shift, yes,' said John. 'Otherwise, it was his mom. Or he walked.'

'It takes what — fifteen minutes?' said Gary.

'Yes,' said John. 'A lot of the kids around here walk it. There are usually some parents too. It's . . . safe.'

'But Caleb was running late on Monday,' said Ren.

'Yes.'

'Why didn't you drive him?' said Ren. 'Your shift wasn't until later that day.'

'He wanted to walk,' said John. 'And to be honest, I wanted him to take responsibility for being late. I'm always trying to teach him that choices have consequences.'

'Did you argue at all, have a disagreement about anything that morning?' said Ren.

'No,' said John. 'I told you. Nothing like that. Hands up, I admit I'm strict on the boy, and, yes, I do raise my voice. I know that's not the done thing these days, but children need discipline. Without discipline . . . ' He trailed off as his voice cracked. There were tears in his eyes.

Whoa. Did you discipline him too much? Did it go too far?

'Look, I didn't do anything to my son,' said John. 'I know you look at parents very closely in these situations, but I swear to God, I did not harm my son. It's the last thing in the world I would do. And my wife . . . she's an angel.'

Fuck, that seemed genuine.

11

Ren looked through Caleb Veir's cell phone records.

'John,' she said, 'there was a call made from Caleb's cell phone to your sister, Alice, at seven thirty a.m. yesterday. Did you know about that?'

John shook his head. 'No, I did not.'

Those giant pupils. Sign of deception . . .

'Do you know why Caleb would have called your sister?' said Ren. 'And so early in the morning?'

'I have no idea,' said John.

'Are they close?' said Ren.

'They get along,' said John. 'They don't see each other a lot, but when they do, yeah, absolutely, they're close.'

'I have cell phone records here going back three months and this was the first time he had ever called her,' said Ren.

'From his cell phone, maybe,' said John, 'but he has spoken to her on the home phone when I've called her.'

'What would they talk about?' said Ren. 'Was your sister someone Caleb would open up to?'

'Honestly, I didn't pay attention to what they talked about,' said John. 'I was just glad they were talking.'

'Monday's call was ten minutes long,' said Ren.

'Honestly, I don't know what that would have been about.'

'The call was deleted from the call list on his phone,' said Ren. 'Why would Caleb have wanted to hide that?'

'I don't know,' said John. 'Maybe he was planning a surprise for me or his mom and didn't want us to know he'd called Alice?' He paused. 'Oh, hold on . . . I forgot about this — Alice is working on a wrongful conviction case that's getting a lot of attention. Caleb had mentioned her coming in to talk to his class on one of her visits here. Knowing Caleb, he was probably supposed to have someone organized for Monday, and he ended up calling Alice at the last minute.'

'Did Caleb have a particular interest in the law?' said Ren. 'Or was there something about this case?'

'It might just have been that Alice had been on television,' said John. 'You know kids . . . '

Ren nodded. *Hold on a second . . .* 'Haven't you talked to her yet? Told her that Caleb's missing?'

'No, no,' said John. 'I didn't want to bother her with it. She would worry. And she might drive down here for no reason. If he showed up after all that, it would be pretty embarrassing. She's very busy.'

Embarrassing? Busy? What the what now? 'Well, it's been a while at this stage,' said Ren, 'so we'd like to talk to her about this phone call from Caleb, at the very least.'

Eye-dart. 'Sure, I can call her.'

'Let me take care of that,' said Ren. 'We've got her number here.'

John waited for the next question. Ren held eye contact long enough for his jaw to twitch, long enough that he was the first to avert his eyes.

What's going on here?

'Have you taken a look around the house, noticed anything missing that belonged to Caleb?' said Ren.

He shook his head. 'No. Not that I can think of.'

'I'd like to talk to you about the escaped inmate, Franklin J. Merrifield,' said Gary.

'What?' said John. 'Why? I wasn't even there when that happened.'

'Did you know Merrifield?' said Gary.

'Yes, I knew him, but not well,' said John. 'I've never had any trouble with him — nothing.'

'When you heard Merrifield had escaped, were you surprised?' said Gary.

'Absolutely,' said John. 'It's the first time anything like that has happened since I've been working at BRCI.'

'Do you think he had help on the inside?'

'It's not about what I think,' said John. 'I don't know is the answer.'

'Tell me what you know about Seth Fuller,' said Ren.

'Seth Fuller?' said John. He shrugged. 'Why do you ask?'

'He was also an inmate at BRCI, and we've had reports he showed a particular interest in Caleb.'

'That's the first I've heard of that,' said John. 'Who said that?'

'I can't say,' said Ren, 'but we know that he

paid for some comics for Caleb if he was short of cash, bought him sodas at the store, that kind of thing.'

'Well, I know nothing about that,' said John, 'but Seth's a good kid. I'm not worried about him. I would have written his name down on that list if I was.'

'Can you be sure of that?' said Ren.

'Can anyone ever be sure of anything?' said John.

Yes, actually, but . . . 'So you didn't know anything about Seth and Caleb . . . '

'No,' said John, irritated. 'There was no 'Seth and Caleb'. So he bought him a couple of things — I'd like to think that was just a nice gesture.'

'So your dealings with Seth Fuller in BRCI . . . '

John shrugged. 'I didn't have any. I mean — no one-on-one dealings with him.'

Ren stood up. 'OK,' she said. 'That's all for now. Thank you.'

★　★　★

Ren and Gary walked down the hallway toward the office.

'Did you hear the amount of times he did the question-as-reply thing?' said Ren. And 'Honestly . . . ' '

Gary nodded.

'We need to break his ass down,' said Ren. 'And what is the deal with his sister? Why the hell wouldn't he tell her that her nephew had gone missing? Bizarre.' She paused. 'And that fucking stare . . . '

Black and eerie.

63

★   ★   ★

Ren went to her desk and typed Alice Veir's name into Google.

Alice. Alice. Who the fuck is Alice?

The client whose case had put Alice Veir in the spotlight six months earlier was a man called Anthony Boyd Lorden. He had been jailed for life for the murder of Kevin Dunne, a sixteen-year-old hitch-hiker who disappeared in 1991 and whose skeletal remains were found a year later. Alice Veir lay the blame with the detectives working the case, saying that Lorden, who was only seventeen at the time of his arrest, had been coerced into signing a confession.

This will be fun . . . talking to a woman who rails against the interrogation techniques of law enforcement.

Ren dialed Alice's number.

'Ms Veir?'

'Yes?'

'I'm Special Agent Ren Bryce — I'm calling about your nephew, Caleb. I'm sorry to have to tell you that Caleb has been missing since yesterday morning.'

'Yesterday?' said Alice. 'Why hasn't anyone called me until now?'

'Your brother, John, said he didn't want to bother you in case Caleb — '

'Hold on — why isn't John the one calling me now?'

Ren could hear the defensive tone creep into Alice Veir's voice.

'At this moment,' said Ren, 'he's speaking with

64

investigators here in Tate PD. I'd like to ask you about your phone conversation with Caleb yesterday morning at seven thirty a.m.'

'Of course,' said Alice. 'Of course. Yes. He wanted me to come talk to his class.' She paused. 'Sorry . . . I'm . . . I . . . can't wrap my brain around this. Caleb's missing?'

'We're doing everything we can to find him,' said Ren. 'Time is of the essence, as you know . . . '

'Sorry — yes,' said Alice. 'The phone call . . . '

'How did Caleb seem to you?' said Ren.

'Fine,' said Alice. 'Absolutely fine. Rushed, maybe, but he had to get to school, and he knew he should have asked me weeks earlier.'

'Did he seem upset to you in any way?' said Ren.

'Why would he be upset?' said Alice.

'I'm trying to get a sense of his state of mind,' said Ren. 'I'm sure you understand. You're the last person to have spoken to him.'

'That you know of, I presume . . . '

This woman is going to be a nightmare.

'Yes,' said Ren.

'Please don't tell me you think my brother had anything to do with this,' said Alice. 'I see where this is going. I know from Caleb that he was home alone with John that morning and you're now asking me what Caleb's state of mind was. Caleb is a happy kid, John is a wonderful father. He would do anything for his son. He loves that boy more than anything in the world.' Her voice cracked. 'He's such a good man, my brother.'

'And Teddy?' said Ren.

'Great,' said Alice. 'Teddy's wonderful.'

'And how are things between John and Teddy?' said Ren.

'Great, from what I can gather,' said Alice.

'Do you get along well with your brother?' said Ren.

'Yes, we're very close,' said Alice.

'And Teddy?' said Ren.

'Yes, we get along,' said Alice.

'What did you say to Caleb?' said Ren. 'Did you tell him that you'd come talk to his class?'

'Oh, yes — I was more than happy to. I told him I'd come down next month.'

'Were you surprised to hear from Caleb that early in the morning?' said Ren.

'Yes,' said Alice, 'of course. We've never spoken at that hour before.' She let out a breath. 'Please find him. Please, please find him. I've seen too much, I know what happens. I . . . can't bear the idea that Caleb could be . . . ' She paused. 'We all know about the first forty-eight hours, that they're the most important in a situation like this. And I think we both know that window is halfway down.'

12

As Ren ended the call to Alice Veir, she felt a presence beside her and looked up. It was Ruddock.

'Teddy Veir is waiting for us in Interview 2,' he said.

★ ★ ★

Teddy Veir was staring at the wall as if there was something more interesting to look at than flaking gray paint. Ren and Ruddock walked in and sat down.

'Teddy — this is Ren Bryce,' said Ruddock. 'She's with the FBI CARD team.'

'Hello,' said Teddy. 'Thank you . . . for being here.'

Ren nodded.

'What do you think of all this?' said Teddy.

Strange question. Or strange delivery?

'You do this all the time,' said Teddy. 'Is my son . . . do you think . . . what happens in your other cases?'

Oh, you do not want to know that we usually show up, a body is found, and we all go home.

'Mrs Veir — '

'Teddy.'

'Teddy, we're gathering all the facts here — '

'It's been over twenty-four hours . . . ' she said. 'I know you're already losing hope of finding him alive.'

'That's not true,' said Ruddock. 'And there are hundreds of people working hard on this.'

'But nothing showed up in the search,' said Teddy.

'Yet,' said Ruddock. 'We'll be searching again. Every day, if we have to. And the neighborhood canvass team is working nonstop. Please be reassured by that. And Ren and I are here now to focus on some answers we need.'

Teddy nodded. 'OK, OK. I'm sorry. I'm just . . . I'm going out of my mind.'

'I know,' said Ren. 'Let's start with Sunday evening. Why don't you talk us through that . . . '

'I left the house at six to go to my friend Patti's,' said Teddy. 'Patti Ellis. Caleb was home, John was preparing supper for both of them. I eat with Patti.'

'And how was Caleb, Sunday night?' said Ren.

'He was quiet,' said Teddy. 'But — '

Ren and Ruddock waited.

I know what you're thinking, Teddy. You're thinking if you finish that sentence, you will be incriminating your husband. But . . . what? But Caleb was always quiet around his father?

And you're thinking — what if your husband did do something, and you lied to the police? I am watching the weighing up. And you know I am.

Teddy readjusted herself in her seat. 'John's childhood, his time in the military . . . it made him the man he is today. He's a good man, a good husband, a good father. But . . . yes, Caleb was quiet around him sometimes.' There was a pleading look in her eyes. 'Caleb can be sullen,

68

and John is stubborn. The two things don't always sit well together. John is not an aggressive man. He withdraws. He gets distant. That can be really difficult, but it doesn't make him . . . ' She shrugged. 'His biggest crime, maybe, is being . . . intense.'

Intense? Yes. His biggest crime? Maybe not . . .

Ruddock spoke gently to Teddy. 'Men are not great with their feelings,' he said. 'My late wife had to work on me for a good ten years to get me to talk. Anything emotional and I'd close up like a clam.' He paused. 'Is that how John is?'

Late wife . . . noo.

Teddy nodded. 'That's exactly how he is.' There was a look of resignation in her eyes, and for a brief moment, a spark of anger at the realization.

'Did that bother you?' said Ruddock.

'I'm used to it,' said Teddy. 'I didn't mind. That's his way.'

She shrugged, but in a way that indicated she wanted the questions on her marriage to stop. Ren and Ruddock locked eyes.

Yes . . . let's not push it.

For now.

'Teddy,' said Ren. 'Did you ever get the sense that Caleb didn't like to be left alone with his father?'

'No — never,' said Teddy. 'Absolutely not.'

'Has John ever gotten physical with Caleb?' said Ren.

'No.'

'Have you ever felt that he came close to that point?' said Ren.

69

Teddy shrugged. 'What is 'close'? I can say to you that I do not think John would ever lay a finger on Caleb.'

Why am I unconvinced?

Possibly because you are.

'Was there any particular behavior in Caleb that angered John?'

'All the standard things that twelve-year-olds get in trouble with their parents for,' said Teddy. 'They're the same things that would have bothered me. Maybe John is more stern about it, but I think fathers of boys need to be.'

'Has there been any change in Caleb's behavior over the past few months?' said Ren.

Teddy gave it careful thought. 'No, not really.'

'Not really?'

'No,' said Teddy with more conviction. 'No.'

'There are scuff marks on the inside of Caleb's bedroom door,' said Ren, 'and the doorjamb looks damaged. Did you ever lock Caleb in?'

'Oh my God — no,' said Teddy. 'Absolutely not. I've never even seen a key for that door.'

'OK,' said Ren.

After a moment, she spoke again. *Deep breath.* 'Teddy, how are things in your marriage?'

She frowned. 'They're good — why?'

'These are the questions we need to ask,' said Ren. 'I'm sure you understand.'

She nodded, but it was clear that she didn't want to sign up for that line of questioning.

'Are you and John happy?' said Ren.

Teddy raised her eyebrows.

Oh, happiness is a tricky one, isn't it? Are people ever truly happy? That's depressing.

70

Ben. Everett. Robbie.
My happiness is over; I've had my life's share.
Is this how I feel now?
Jesus.
Christ.
'Yes,' said Teddy. 'I mean, life . . . is life, really, isn't it? Am I living a wild adventure every day? No.'

'I'm not thinking adventure,' said Ren. 'I'm just thinking of your relationship with your husband — are you getting along? Have there been any arguments? Are there any issues?'

Teddy gave a small shrug. 'No.'

'Have you noticed any changes in your husband's behavior or mood recently?' said Ren.

'No,' said Teddy.

Ooh: I don't believe you.

13

Teddy Veir shifted in her seat like a child at the principal's office.

'Teddy, did you monitor Caleb's online activity?' said Ren.

'Yes,' said Teddy.

'And was he aware of the dangers of being online?'

'We talked about it, yes,' said Teddy. 'Any time we brought it up, he made us feel stupid for thinking he would ever fall for any kind of weirdo who would try to meet up with him. Caleb knows that people aren't necessarily who they say they are online.'

Oh, how many times I've seen that change when the right fake messages or the right fake photographs are sent.

'Did you find something?' said Teddy.

'There were no interactions with anyone that we feel have a bearing on the case,' said Ren. 'So, to go through a few more things . . . he was also looking at pornography.'

Teddy's face fell. 'Oh, God. He's only a baby.'

'It certainly wasn't at worrying levels, and it was nothing extreme,' said Ren. *Like that will reassure you.* 'But I have to ask if he had a girlfriend or if there were girls around at the house or if you got any sense that this was more than just . . . ' *I can't say the word fantasy about a twelve-year-old boy.*

'He didn't have a girlfriend,' said Teddy. 'He was kind of awkward around girls. He just wasn't advanced in that way. Not at all.'

'OK,' said Ren. 'Have you noticed anything missing of Caleb's? Any bag or clothing or something he was particularly fond of, something he didn't usually leave behind?'

'Apart from his phone?' said Teddy. 'The only other thing — which I don't think is very meaningful, especially because I haven't seen it in a while, anyway — is a suitcase. Well, it's kind of a tin box — an old military one that John got for him — it's green and battered, with a brown leather handle. It's about twice the size of a shoebox. He used to keep it on the floor under the window, but then he moved it into the wardrobe, put it on the shelf at the top. But I can't really imagine him bringing it anywhere . . .'

Unless he was running away.

'Do you know what he kept in it?' said Ren.

'No,' said Teddy. 'His comic books, I figured. I don't know.'

'Can you remember the last time you looked in the wardrobe?' said Ren.

'No — Caleb tidied away his own clothes.'

'So that suitcase could have been gone for some time,' said Ren.

'Yes,' said Teddy.

Could he have fought with his father, packed this suitcase and left, unwittingly drawing attention to himself: some creep driving by sees a kid on his own, maybe running away, maybe crying, carrying a suitcase? Vulnerable.

73

'Does Caleb keep a diary?' said Ren.

'No,' said Teddy. 'He has no interest in anything like that. He's like his father — might read a sports story or two, but won't pick up a book, or write a word he isn't forced to.'

'If Caleb was in trouble,' said Ren, 'who do you think he might call?'

'Well — me,' said Teddy.

'And what about his Aunt Alice?' said Ren.

Teddy frowned. 'You mean, would he call her if he had a problem? Gosh, I wouldn't think so. I mean, she's family, and she's always perfectly lovely to him, remembers his birthday, all those kind of things, but . . . ' She trailed off. 'Was he in trouble? Do you know something? Why are you asking about Alice?'

'Caleb called her on Monday morning at seven thirty a.m.,' said Ren. 'She was the last call he made on the morning he disappeared.'

'We see Alice two or three times a year,' said Teddy. 'Caleb's maybe been on the phone to say hello to her once or twice, but that's about it.'

What? 'John seemed to think they spoke quite a bit.'

'Really?' said Teddy. 'Well, not when I was around. And when I checked Caleb's call list when I got home from work, I didn't see her name.'

'It had been deleted,' said Ren.

'That's very strange,' said Teddy.

'If Caleb had an argument with his father, do you think he could have called his aunt for help?' said Ren.

'Caleb always called *me* when he had a fight with John.'

74

Always. How many were there?
'Did that happen often?' said Ren.
'That sounded worse than it was,' said Teddy
at the same time.

★ ★ ★

Ren and Ruddock talked Gary and Wiley
through the discrepancies between Alice, John
and Teddy about the phone call.

'Why,' said Wiley, 'would there be a difference
in how two parents viewed their child's
relationship with his aunt? It makes no sense.'

'Nah,' said Gary. 'It makes total sense.'

Ouch.

'Have you got kids?' said Gary.

Wiley shook his head. 'No.'

Then, there you go says Gary's face.

'Alice Veir was very emotional about how
much her brother cared for Caleb,' said Ren. 'It
sounded genuine.' She paused. 'But what other
reason would there be for Caleb to call her? Or
maybe it was John who called her . . . '

'Looking to know his options because he had
killed his son,' said Gary.

'You'd want a pretty tight relationship with a
sibling — or anyone, for that matter — to be able
to call them up and say 'I killed my child, what
do I do next?'' said Ren.

Ruddock nodded.

'Especially when she's a lawyer who's all about
justice,' said Ren.

'And let's not forget,' said Gary, 'this was only
a ten-minute phone call.'

'This is a small thing,' said Ren, 'but when I told Alice Veir that Caleb was missing, she didn't say 'But I was just speaking with him yesterday morning', which is the kind of thing someone would say under the circumstances, isn't it? Reflexively? Not a big deal, but still.'

'Do you think she might have already known that he was gone?' said Ruddock.

'I wasn't getting that sense either . . . ' said Ren. 'It was hard to say.'

Everything's so fucking hard to say.

Gary's phone beeped with a text. He read it. 'OK — the other two CARD agents have just arrived at the hotel. It's been a long day. Ren and I will get checked in, have something to eat, get some rest.'

Eat. Rest. Noooo!

Gary turned to Ruddock. 'We can give the others the lowdown over dinner.'

'I appreciate it,' said Ruddock. 'Thank you for everything today.'

14

Astor's was a grim and grubby hotel on 1–5, a ten-minute drive from Tate PD. Ren and Gary checked in, and were given rooms next door to each other.

Hmm.

Sylvie Ross better be miles away.

'Ren,' said Gary, as she was about to open her door. 'Keep your phone close by. Dr Lone will be calling you in ten.'

Ren froze.

'Take his call,' said Gary. He went into his room and closed the door.

Nice, Gary. Nice.

Ren opened her door with a nudge of her shoulder and walked in. Her stomach tensed.

Indian Burial Ground.

She put her bag on the floor, undressed, and crawled on to the bed.

Fuck Gary if he thinks I'm going to take that call. Fuck him. That's the last time I'll open up to him if I'm struggling. Asshole.

Ren's cell phone rang, Lone's name flashing on the screen.

Ugh. She picked up. 'Hi.'

'Hi, Ren,' said Lone. 'Gary suggested I give you a call. I heard you had a difficult morning.'

'I did not have a difficult — *fucking* — morning. People were gathering for a search, and it was just . . . how the crowd was moving

. . . it was closing in on me and I felt a little overwhelmed. Honestly — it lasted for about two minutes. That was it. I appreciate the call, but I'm fine.'

'I haven't seen you in a couple of weeks,' said Lone. 'I'm glad we're able to speak.'

'Yes,' said Ren. 'But I'm in Oregon to concentrate on work right now. It feels selfish to be focusing on me. I have a job to do.' She sucked in a breath, and it didn't feel like enough.

'It might help to talk,' said Lone. 'It might be a good way to begin this case . . . to reduce your anxiety.'

He doesn't think I should be doing this job.

'I'm sorry,' said Ren. 'I'm hundreds of miles away and having this conversation over the phone and . . . '

'Maybe that's what it's going to take,' said Lone.

I don't think so.

'Are you still having intrusive thoughts about . . . '

I want to scream.

' . . . events at Safe Streets?' said Lone.

Yeah — thanks for clarifying.

He waited.

Please just stop. Stop. Stop.

'And are the thoughts still — '

Are you kidding me?

'I'm sorry . . . ' *What can I fucking say?*

'You need to be able to talk about this,' said Lone.

Ren let out a breath. 'OK,' she said, 'let's talk briefly about this monumental horror that I can do absolutely nothing about, because it is in the past. So I can't go back, I can't go forward — '

'All you can ever do is one day at a time.'

Sweet Jesus, why does that always sound so depressing?

'Small steps are all you can take at a time like this,' said Lone.

What is wrong with him? Why is he talking in clichés? Have I become a cliché? Traumatized law enforcement officer . . .

'I'm just not a small steps kind of girl,' said Ren. 'I feel that taking small steps would give me plenty of time to see that dark pit up ahead that is waiting to swallow me. I feel that taking small steps means prolonged dread, and this achingly slow passage of time.'

I feel. I feel. I feel. FUCK feeling.

'The future is not a dark pit — '

'Well, the present is a pretty dark pit and a year ago — when this would have been considered 'the future' . . . '

'You can't live your life expecting doom,' said Lone. 'We spoke before about catastrophic thinking.'

FUCK catastrophic thinking and magical thinking and all adjectival thinking.

'Well, if I had spent more time expecting doom,' said Ren, 'maybe I could have been prepared. I could have prevented what happened.'

'Ren, you couldn't have prevented it.'

'I'm sorry, but that's not true.'

'It is,' said Dr Lone. He waited. 'Ren, you need to start thinking about facing the reality of what happened.'

I don't like you any more. 'I need to', 'I should'. 'I'm sorry,' Ren said. 'I really can't do this. I can't. Not today.' *Probably not any day.*

'Please,' said Lone. 'Try to tell me what you are feeling.'

Feelings. Jesus. Christ.

I'm so tired.

'Do you want to know?' said Ren. 'Honestly? I believe that everything that happened that day was to punish me.'

Lone waited.

'Sometimes,' said Ren, 'I feel like there's a darkness inside me — a black part, like a piece of coal. Pitch-black. It's rough and hard, and . . . I feel that, because of that, I should be punished.'

'You think you deserved this,' said Lone.

'Yes,' said Ren. 'No. I . . . don't know.'

'Talk to me about this darkness . . . ' said Lone.

No! 'I know I won't be able to explain it,' said Ren. 'It's . . . obviously, I don't want to harm anyone; it's not the darkness of evil.' *Yes, it is.* 'It's not like I want to kill people.' *Really?*

'And you are taking your meds . . . ' said Lone.

'I really wish one conversation could go by without you asking me that,' said Ren. *Let me spell it out again: I. Am. Taking. My. Meds.* 'Yes — I am taking them.'

I am taking them, and I will continue to take them for the rest of my life, because I believe that not taking them killed my friends, and killed my boyfriend. There's the reality: my friends, my boyfriend, my loved ones, are dead because I didn't open a packet of pills and swallow them down with a glass of water like a good mental patient. Because I was too busy being mental. And wanting to feel good. I was too busy getting drunk, flirting with strangers, and deliberately ensnaring the man who went on to kill my friends, and my boyfriend, and I feel sick.

She dropped the phone, jumped up, ran for the bathroom, leaned over the toilet and threw up.

I am going to choke on this reality he wants me to face . . .

She walked back into the bedroom. She could hear Dr Lone's voice through the phone.

'Ren? Ren?'

She put the phone up to her ear. 'Sorry. I ate some crappy sandwich earlier. I need to take five minutes before I join the team for dinner. Thanks for the call.'

'Is everything OK?' said Lone.

Oh, fuck off. Everyone, just fuck the fuck off.

15

Ren showered, dressed, and stood in front of the mirror.

Ugh.

She grabbed her bag and did a quick no-makeup makeup job. She blasted her hair with the hairdryer, ran her fingers through it, left it down. It was five inches below her shoulders.

I have long hair now.

The last time I got this cut, Ben was alive.

Stop. It hurts. And it changes nothing.

Tears welled in her eyes.

Your mascara. Go.

Her cell phone rang. *Gary.*

'Hey,' said Ren.

'You ready?'

'Yes.'

'Meet you outside. Paul and Sylvie are at the bar.'

Ren went out into the hallway. Gary appeared from his room, freshly showered.

Handsome.

'Look, I know how you feel about Sylvie,' said Gary, as they walked to the elevator.

Jesus, why are we talking about her again?

'How I feel about her is irrelevant,' said Ren. *How I feel about Karen — your wife of almost twenty years — is ultimately too.* 'I do want you to be happy,' said Ren. 'Just . . . I can't see how this is doing it for you.'

'I thought I was going to die in that shooting,'

82

said Gary. 'When I was laying there and I thought it was all over, I kept thinking about Sylvie. I — '

'In what way?' said Ren.

'What? What do you mean — '

'I'm serious,' said Ren. 'Were you thinking about how much you loved her and didn't want to die because you'd never see her again? Or were you thinking, *If I'm going to die, I want the love of my life by my side*, and the face you saw was Sylvie's? Or were you running through the showreel — thinking of her ass?'

'Jesus, Ren — '

'I just feel no one else will ask you the difficult shit. Your buddies aren't going to — '

'No one else knows.'

'What?' said Ren. 'Well, that must be exhausting.' She paused. 'Does Sylvie think you're going to leave Karen for her?'

He nodded.

'And how's that working out for you?' said Ren. *What is wrong with me? I feel mean.*

Gary said nothing.

'Oh,' said Ren. 'I get it. Do *you* think you're going to leave Karen for her?'

He gave her a side glance, but didn't answer.

★   ★   ★

They arrived at the bar. Sitting on the arm of a sofa, dressed in a navy-blue suit, was Paul Louderback, his arms folded, his long legs crossed. He looked like he was cut-and-pasted from an elegant drawing room. He saw Ren, smiled warmly, stood up.

My heart . . .

He's married.

Ben is dead.

Nice.

Standing beside Paul, with her back to them, was Sylvie Ross, her thick sandy hair in a high ponytail. She was dressed in a white shirt, slim-fit gray pants, pointed black heels.

Great ass. Poor shoe choice.

Sylvie turned around, and her face lit up as she saw Gary over Ren's shoulder.

God, is that what that looks like?

I still don't know if you and Paul Louderback have slept together. Do I need to sleep with Gary to even this all out?

Everyone greeted each other, everyone was professional.

Oh, what a tangled web we weave.

★ ★ ★

Gary and Ren filled Sylvie and Paul in on the case over dinner.

'Paul — you'll be taking charge of the command center,' said Gary. 'I'm guessing the best thing for Sylvie to start with tomorrow is talking to Caleb Veir's friends.'

Paul nodded.

'Sure,' said Sylvie. 'Not a problem.'

She is freakishly intense with him.

Oh, now — I get it: yes, Gary nearly died, and Sylvie realized — uh-oh — how much she loves him.

84

It appears to be an alarming amount.

Sylvie started to pour Ren more wine. Ren held up her hand. 'I'm good, thanks.'

Gary and Paul both stared at her.

'Thanks, guys,' said Ren. 'Thanks.'

★ ★ ★

An hour later, Sylvie was the first to excuse herself. Gary left thirty minutes later.

When they were gone, Paul made a show of checking his watch. 'Half an hour . . . standard time for one lover to ask another to wait before running up to join them?' There was a sparkle in his eye.

'Behave,' said Ren.

'Come on . . . '

I'm committing to nada.

'So, are they?' said Paul.

'No, they're not,' said Ren.

'OK,' said Paul, with no conviction.

'And no one should use the word 'lover'.'

'I have definitely heard you say 'I'm a lover, not a fighter'.'

'No one other than me, then . . . '

He smiled. 'Now that I have cornered you alone,' he said, 'how are you doing? Really doing? You were very quiet over dinner.'

'I was enjoying everyone else,' said Ren. 'I'm finding it hard to raise my game.'

'You were perfectly pleasant, but . . . '

'Struggling — I know.'

'That's understandable, after what you've been through.'

Tears welled in her eyes. She blinked them away. 'I keep crying randomly.' *You don't cry. Tears well, you blink, they're gone. And you think the feelings go with them.*

'It's not random,' said Paul. 'We're talking about your boyfriend, your friends, your colleagues — '

'It's all so weird,' said Ren. 'I'm not a widow; Ben and I weren't 'long-term loves'. Just a year. But I did love him.'

You don't know what love is. You're not a victim. You don't know how to love. And he doesn't want to hear about love.

'Have you thought about grief counseling?' said Paul.

'I'd rather shoot myself in the ass.'

'Vivid,' said Paul.

Ren smiled, took a drink. 'But enough about me — how are you doing? How's Marianne?'

'Well,' he said, drawing out the word, 'the easy answer would be 'great' . . . '

Oh, no, no, no, no. Do not appear available to me.

'Shall I go on?' he said.

'Please do.' *Not.*

'It's a dramatic move, getting back with your ex-wife,' said Paul. 'It's exciting at the start, everyone is happy — the kids, our families, our friends — well, most of them — but then, the door is closed at night, everyone's going about their business, and we're just there, the two of us, and . . . ' He shrugged. 'It's like what people say about funerals: once it's over, everyone disappears and you're left on your own and

86

. . . Jesus Christ, Ren — I can't believe I just started talking about funerals. That was the most — '

Ren shook her head. 'Stop. I get it. I know what you're saying. Don't tiptoe around me or I *will* shoot myself in the ass. Just, be normal. Please don't look at me like I'm a victim. I can't deal with that. Relax in the knowledge that I know you're not an insensitive prick.'

'OK,' said Paul. 'OK. I'm sorry. Thanks.'

'No need to be,' said Ren. Tears welled in her eyes again. 'Ugh. This is getting ridiculous.'

'Stop . . . '

'I just . . . lost so many people I loved,' said Ren.

Paul reached out and squeezed her hand. She looked up at him through tears.

At least I have you.

'Well, I'm still here,' said Paul. He blushed. 'Not saying that you love me, or loved me, but, I just mean . . . what's wrong with me tonight?'

Ren laughed, and wiped her eyes.

Of course I loved you. In my own special and fearful way. But I have no idea what it is I'm feeling right now.

Safe?

'You . . . unsettle me, Ren Bryce.'

'Jesus.'

'Maybe I like being unsettled.'

Ren laughed. *I beg to differ.*

'Why are you laughing?' said Paul.

'It was just your delivery . . . '

She checked her watch. It was 11 p.m. 'OK, I'm wide awake. I'm going to take a drive.'

'What?' said Paul. 'Now?'

Ren nodded. 'Every second counts.'

And every second out there is one less second I spend alone in my bed with nothing but my own mind to fuck me.

'Do you want company?' said Paul.

Mos def not. 'No, thank you.'

★ ★ ★

Ren drove out of the parking lot and read the sign: left was Tate, right was Lake Verny.

The Crow Bar will still be open. I can ask about John Veir, I can check out Seth Fuller.

I can throw myself into the beautiful, icy, moonlit water.

16

Seth Fuller stood on the bottom step of The Crow Bar, clutching the handrail. Eyes closed, he sucked air through his nose, held it, exhaled slowly through his mouth — 7–11 breathing: he had been taught how to do this by the psychologist at BRCI. He had been embarrassed at first, sitting in front of this nerdy guy, Lockwood, in his brown round-neck sweater and red shirt, closing his eyes and counting in for seven, counting out for eleven.

'You've got this, Seth,' Lockwood used to say. 'And if you've got this, you'll see . . . you've got the rest of your life.'

Seth thought it was a pretty sweeping statement, but he liked the idea of having the rest of his life. He just wasn't sure if he really did, and that, if so, he'd ever be able to breathe properly through it.

He leaned hard on the handrail and vaulted up the steps. He walked into the bar, pulled a fifty-dollar note out of his back pocket and slapped it on to the counter in front of Shannon. He nodded toward Clyde Brimmer.

Shannon frowned. 'Where did you get that?'

Seth smiled his lazy smile. 'I choose to take no offense at the tone of your remark.'

'I'm serious.'

'Don't be,' said Seth. 'A friend of a friend of a friend.'

Shannon rolled her eyes, but there was anger in them. 'You better not be — '

'I'm not be,' said Seth. 'Don't worry.'

'Goddammit,' said Shannon. 'The town is crawling with police.'

'Well, if it helps,' said Seth, 'I won it playing pool *with* the police. Gil Wiley. You can ask him yourself.'

'Jesus, Seth — why do you have to create mysteries for no reason?' said Shannon. 'What's the point? 'Friend of a friend of a friend.' Why would you want to cause more stress for me than I'm already under?'

'I'm sorry, Aunt Shannon. I wasn't thinking . . . '

'I worry,' she said. 'So easily now. I get these spikes of anxiety in my chest and once they're dug in there, they're real hard to get rid of.' She touched a hand to his cheek, but didn't let it stay there long. 'And shouldn't Wiley be taking care of things at home instead of out playing pool with — '

'It's escaping home that Wiley's interested in,' said Seth.

'Not to mention he has an investigation to run.'

'Wiley is no investigation-runner,' said Seth. 'He'll never be anything more than a sidekick. And he knows it.'

He pushed the fifty closer to Shannon.

'And why are you paying for Clyde's drinks, anyway, big shot?' said Shannon.

'Out of pity,' said Seth. 'But Clyde doesn't mind pity. He is unconcerned with the emotion behind a gesture. A fresh drink materializes before his swimming eyes? Well, that's as pure a gesture as anything, far as he's concerned — a single, welcome moment that doesn't need to be weighed down by history or motive or rationale. A beer's a beer.'

'A beer's a beer,' said Shannon. She put a bottle of Bud down in front of him. 'How did the search go today?'

She poured a whiskey for Clyde.

'Well, no one found anything,' said Seth. 'But you get the sense they put the volunteers in places where they don't really think they're going to find anything, so they won't screw up the evidence.'

'Probably,' said Shannon.

'And I got nothing out of Wiley afterward,' said Seth. 'Even when he was wasted. I tried to pump him for information, but nothing.'

'You shouldn't be showing so much interest,' said Shannon. 'You know that doesn't look good.'

'I've got nothing to worry about,' said Seth. He paused. 'Then again, how many times did I hear that in prison?'

The door opened wide, and their heads jerked toward it.

Seth's eyes lit up. He turned back to Shannon. 'Introducing the future Mrs Seth Fuller . . . '

17

Well, isn't The Crow Bar a charming and battered little place? And why is Seth Fuller staring at me?

Seth nodded at Ren, then walked over to the pool table with a look that told her he would like to appear mysterious.

I would eat you alive.

Ren went to the bar. 'Shannon Fuller? I'm Ren Bryce, I'm with the FBI — '

Shannon nodded. 'Hi. Is there any word on Caleb?'

'No,' said Ren. 'Not yet. Would you mind if we talked here? I just have a couple of things I'd like to ask you.'

Shannon frowned. 'You work late. Sure — take a seat. Can I get you a drink?'

'A Coke would be great, thank you.'

Caffeine . . . after 11 p.m. Great.

There were four customers across three tables in the bar, and two guys playing pool, one of whom was Seth. Ren looked out the window to the lake.

Nothing like a bright moon sparkling on black water.

This is where her son drowned. How does she come here every day?

Shannon set down the Coke.

'Thank you,' said Ren. She took a long drink. 'I was very sorry to hear that you lost your son.'

Shannon nodded. 'Thanks.'

'I can't imagine the pain you're going through. To lose a child . . . '

'It's hard to know what to say, isn't it?' said Shannon. 'There's nothing worse. I'm just here to pay the bills. That's it. I feel that's all I'll be doing for the rest of my life. Showing up to pay the bills.'

'I wish I didn't have to bother you at a time like this,' said Ren, 'but — '

'It's OK,' said Shannon. 'Anything I can do . . . ' She looked down at the floor. 'I'm sorry I didn't help with the search today — '

'Please,' said Ren, 'no one would have expected you to. And there were plenty of volunteers.'

Shannon looked at her, her eyes filling with tears. 'I couldn't bear the idea that I might find his body. I couldn't bear it. I'm hoping to God he's alive, obviously — that goes without saying, I hope — but if he isn't . . . I . . . ' She shook her head.

I wonder were you the one who found your son's body.

'OK . . . shoot,' said Shannon. 'Ask me anything.' She tried to smile.

'You bought this place off John Veir,' said Ren.

Shannon nodded. 'Yes.'

'What can you tell me about John?' said Ren. 'What kind of man is he?'

Shannon briefly glanced away. 'He's a good guy. It was a quick sale, he wanted to offload the place, but he was kind enough to fix a lot of things up before I took it on. He's a trained military diver, so he did a lot of the underwater work on the jetty. Basically, anything I had an issue with, he took care of. He didn't have to do that.'

Ren nodded. 'Did you get to know his family?'

'Um . . . no, not really,' said Shannon.

Ooh . . . what was that?

'Did you ever see anything that gave you cause for concern?' said Ren.

'With John? No — not at all,' said Shannon. 'Why do you ask? You don't think he had anything to do with Caleb's disappearance . . . '

'Just information-gathering,' said Ren.

'OK,' said Shannon, 'because John Veir is a good man.'

'I just realized,' said Ren, 'your son, Aaron, and Caleb were around the same age. Did they know each other?'

'Well, they went to the same school — Aaron was a year behind Caleb, but I don't think they knew each other.'

What is this weird vibe?

'Can I ask you about your nephew, Seth?' said Ren. 'He was in BRCI. Did he and John know each other?'

'Yes.' Eye-dart.

'Was there ever any issue between them?' said Ren.

'No,' said Shannon. 'Not that I know of, anyway. Seth would have said.'

'We've been told that Seth took a particular interest in Caleb Veir,' said Ren.

'What? Caleb?'

Genuine shock.

'That sounds terrible,' said Shannon. ''Particular interest' — what do you mean by that?'

'We heard that Seth might buy him a soda, or pay for things for him at the store,' said Ren. 'Do you know anything about that?'

'No,' said Shannon. 'Why don't you ask him yourself, though? He's right over there. Don't waste your time looking at Seth for this. He's just a nice guy. When he's got money, he likes to look after people — that's all. Tonight, he's paying for Clyde Brimmer's drinks.'

Ren handed Shannon her card. 'If you think of anything, please feel free to call me.'

* * *

Ren turned her attention to Seth, walked over to him.

'Seth Fuller?' she said. 'I'm Ren Bryce, I'm with the FBI, working on the Caleb Veir disappearance. Could I talk to you for a moment, please?'

She tilted her head toward a table in the corner.

You have now recognized me from the search. And you are not a happy man.

Seth walked over to the table, sat down opposite her, and pulled his stool back a few inches.

'What can I do you for?' he said. He looked up at the clock on the wall. 'Isn't it a little late to be working?'

'Not when a child is missing,' said Ren.

He nodded. 'I suppose so.'

95

'How well did you know Caleb Veir?' said Ren.

'Not very well,' said Seth. 'Why?'

'Are you sure about that?' said Ren.

'Sure I'm sure,' said Seth. 'Why?'

'Is it true that you bought him sodas, candy sometimes, and that you paid for comic books when he didn't have enough money?'

Seth looked away. 'Yeah. So what?'

'So what? He's a missing child and we were informed that you paid him a lot of attention . . . '

'What?' said Seth. 'I was nice to the kid. That's it. I'm not into little boys. Fuck that. I'd happily beat the shit out of someone who was into little boys. I'm into grown women.'

Something flashed in his eyes.

Ugh. 'Was there something in particular about Caleb . . . ?'

'Nothing — I told you. Nothing. I was just nice to him. Big deal. Arrest me.'

'What about John Veir?' said Ren. 'Did you know John?'

His eyes flicked over to Shannon and back again.

'Seth, is there something you're not telling me?' said Ren. 'Or something you feel you can't say? I can promise you it will be treated in the strictest confidence. A little boy's life could be at stake here. I know you can understand the devastation that losing a child can cause . . . '

'There's nothing,' said Seth, 'except I think John Veir is a good man, OK? In case you're thinking he's not.'

Ren nodded. 'OK.' She handed him her

notebook. 'I'm going to need you to write down where you were on Sunday night and yesterday.'

'That's easy,' he said, twisting the notebook around to face him. 'I was here Sunday night — Aunt Shannon and Clyde Brimmer can vouch for that.'

Cute that he still calls her Aunt.

'From what time?' said Ren.

'Uh . . . ten thirty p.m.?'

'And where were you before that?'

'Uh . . . I was in town. In Tate. In Bucky's, having a burger, watching television.' He wrote all this down.

'And yesterday?'

'I was here, I slept late. Then I was helping Aunt Shannon behind the bar.'

'OK,' said Ren. She handed him a card and took the notebook back. 'If you think of anything . . . '

'Sure,' said Seth. 'I'll call.'

⋆ ⋆ ⋆

Ren walked down the steps of The Crow Bar. She started to check her cell phone. In the light of the screen, she noticed something shining on the ground. She turned on her flashlight, crouched down, and ran the beam across the ground. There were several small shards of ceramics in different colors. She moved the light up to the plant pots on the porch outside the door of the bar. They looked new. There were price tags on some of them.

Maybe one of the storms blew them over.

97

All of them?

Ren glanced at the time on her phone. It was close to midnight.

I am wide awake.

Can't bear that empty hotel room.

She went around the back of the bar, the thick mud pulling at her boots as she walked. She inhaled the fresh smell of the water, the grass, the soil. She jammed her hands into her pockets, stared out across the surface.

God, I love lakes.

She was drawn to the water's edge, mesmerized by the rippling water. She walked closer.

I want to be down there.

I want to be swallowed up.

18

Jimmy Lyle sat in the corner of the Internet café. He was logged in to the site under Rapid01. Seeing the name Lynn96 blinking, ready to chat, accelerated his heart rate every time.

> **Rapid01: Hey . . .**
> **Lynn96 Wr u bn?**
> **Rapid01: Sorry. Family stuff**
> **Lynn96: U still cmng?**
> **Rapid01: Y**
> **Lynn96: $350**
> **Rapid01: Y**
> **Lynn96: Y — ready**
> **Rapid01: Both?**
> **Lynn96: Y. Saturday 2pm?**
> **Rapid01: C u then**

The images filled his head. His entire body felt filled. His dick was hard. He was thinking only of the kids, not of Lynn96. Lynn was not to be visualized. Lynn, he figured, was a crack whore, a meth head, a junkie, someone willing to sell four hours with her two kids for $350. He wondered how she came to her price.

★ ★ ★

The rules of the café were printed on an A4 sheet stuck to the wall: RESPECT OTHER

CUSTOMERS, NO PORN. Jimmy looked around. There were only two other customers, in the furthest corners. He took off his jacket, put it across his lap. He slipped his hand underneath it, unzipped his fly. The guy from behind the counter came out with an antibacterial spray and a cloth. He eyeballed Jimmy as he sprayed down the surface three tables down.

Jimmy zipped up his jeans, put his hand back on the mouse, clicked a few times, looked interested. His mind was in Lynn's back garden. The sun was glistening on the pool. The children were standing beside it. He was kneeling by the water, smiling at them.

The guy from the Internet café had taken out a Sharpie, was writing in a notebook. Jimmy was hit with the smell of the ink. The image of his father replaced the image of the kids and he felt a surge of rage. The surface of the water in his mind was broken not by them, but by his daddy's powerful, muscular form. The pool was no longer a pretty garden pool in the Miami sun, but the middle school pool with its stench of chlorine and its freezing tiles.

Every morning at 7 a.m. his daddy did one hundred laps. Jimmy would watch him from the bench, alongside whatever boys or girls were there because they didn't do as they were told in the previous day's class.

When Jimmy's father was finished, he would rise like a god from the water, walk to where he laid his perfectly folded towel, dry himself off. Sometimes, one of the lady teachers would find a reason to come in, to ask his father a question or to talk to one of the kids, but Jimmy knew they were there to catch sight of his daddy, free now, single again, available.

Jimmy remembered the pretty little Mexican girl from his class, how she would sit on the bench in her red swimsuit, wrapped in a pretty pink towel with a giant swan printed on the back. He remembered her and how she would shiver, even when she hadn't been in the water, even when she was dry.

19

Ren arrived at Tate PD, gathered the CARD team, and Ruddock, and filled them in on the previous night at The Crow Bar. She avoided eye contact with Gary, but when she gave him a quick glance, she could see fire in his eyes.

Yes, I was up late . . . working. While you were up late . . . banging your side-piece.

Fight, fight, fight!

Ruddock was checking the door, checking the clock.

No sign of Wiley.

Ren turned to Ruddock. 'Could there be something going on between Shannon Fuller and John Veir?'

'Could be,' said Ruddock, 'but I haven't heard anything.'

Wiley walked in, gave a nod, and sat down on the edge of a desk with his arms crossed. He stank of alcohol. His eyes were almost swollen shut, his face bright red. Ruddock struggled to bury his fury.

Everyone loving their staff today.

Ren turned to Wiley. 'We're talking about Shannon Fuller possibly having an affair with John Veir — '

'Yeah, it's a possibility,' said Wiley. The words were scraping his throat as they came out. He coughed into his hand a few times. 'Pardon me. What makes you think there's an affair going on?'

This will not go down well. 'Shannon's eyes lit up when I mentioned his name.'

Wiley snorted.

Fuck you.

'Her number wasn't on his cell records,' said Wiley.

'Maybe they don't communicate that way,' said Ren. 'Maybe they've other phones. Or maybe they did have a thing, but it's over.'

'Do you think it matters to the investigation?' said Ruddock.

'Well, there are many ways it could if the wrong people found out about it,' said Ren. 'Blackmail, revenge . . . what if they were threatened, refused to cooperate, and, instead, Caleb was snatched? Let's find out first if anything was happening, go from there.'

Wiley looked skeptical, and was searching for support in Ruddock's face.

Can't you feel the heat of his anger?

⋆ ⋆ ⋆

The group broke up. Ren went to the ladies' room, then to the kitchen. She paused in the doorway. Paul Louderback was standing with his back to her, talking on his cell phone.

'I'm sorry, sweetheart,' Paul was saying into the phone, 'but I'm with Mom on this. I know.' He turned to Ren and smiled, half-rolled his eyes.

'I'll leave you — ' Ren mouthed.

Paul shook his head and pointed her toward the coffee machine.

He kept talking into the phone. 'I'm sorry, OK? I've got to go. I know. I love you. And don't forget — weekend after next . . . I miss you too. Bye. Bye.'

'How are the girls?' said Ren.

Paul shrugged. 'They're getting there — '

Wiley came into the kitchen, nodded, and went to the fridge. He pulled out a Tupperware container and popped the lid. The smell of onions filled the kitchen.

My faaavorite.

Ren made an apologetic face at Paul and left.

★ ★ ★

At her desk, Ren pulled an artists' pad from her briefcase. She opened a new page. At the center, she drew a circle and wrote Lake Verny. She drew lines coming out of it, wrote names, drew lines between them.

Hmm.

Paul walked over to her with a mug of coffee.

'Seeing that you fled,' he said, putting it down on the desk beside her.

'Yes — onions. Sorry,' said Ren. 'Thank you.'

'Oh, I know,' said Paul. He looked down at the page.

'Check this out,' said Ren. 'All roads lead to Lake Verny. There is some serious intertwining between the Veirs and the Fullers: John Veir, corrections officer in the same prison as former inmate, Seth Fuller, who is a nephew of Shannon Fuller, who he sold his bar to, and who lost her son in a drowning accident six weeks ago. Seth Fuller, who was also the man seen paying extra attention to Caleb Veir . . . ' She paused. 'Also, that sparkle in her eye still . . . '

'Go on . . . ' said Paul.

'Then you have a guy — Clyde Brimmer — who drinks there all the time and is fired right after he carries out the autopsy on Aaron Fuller.' She lowered her voice. 'And Wiley seems to have a major problem with him — he wrestled him out of here during the press conference.'

Paul's eyes widened. 'You think Wiley . . . '

Ren shrugged. 'I don't know.'

'You mentioned there was something about Seth Fuller you couldn't put your finger on,' said Paul.

Ren nodded. She turned to him. Her eyes were level with his belt. She got a flashback to the last time Paul Louderback was standing over her. She looked up. They locked eyes.

Annnd you're thinking the exact same thing.

The door opened and they both flinched as Sylvie walked in. She faltered in her stride when she saw them, but quickly recovered.

Fuuuck.

Paul Louderback took a step back.

Idiot.

'So,' said Sylvie, 'I spoke with Caleb's teacher and yes — he had an assignment to bring in an adult in his life with an interesting job to talk to the class, but his turn wasn't coming up any time soon. He had already mentioned Alice Veir, though, because his teacher had seen her on a news program about wrongful convictions a few weeks ago, and asked Caleb the next day if they were related, because of the last name, and he said he was.'

'I'm sure Alice told me she was going there next month,' said Ren. 'Maybe she and Caleb got their wires crossed.'

'I also asked the teacher what kind of boy Caleb is,' said Sylvie. 'She said it was her first year teaching him, so she couldn't speak for what he was like before that. She said he's a little difficult, but aren't all twelve-year-old boys? She gets the impression that Caleb feels misunderstood. He has a couple of close friends, but he doesn't mix well with most of the other boys in the class — apparently, he can be quite withdrawn. When I asked her if he could be drawn to older kids if he wasn't mixing well with kids his own age, she said she didn't know of any specifics, but he definitely looks up to the older kids. She also says he always seems a little angry, but that she felt his parents care very much for him. She said they come to all the parent-teacher meetings together, they seem on top of things. Caleb and his mom are very close. The teacher had heard Caleb was kind of sickly as a kid, and Teddy would drop everything to look after him.'

Munchausen's. Munchausen's.

'Sickly in what way?' said Ren.

'Chest problems,' said Sylvie. 'His mother had mentioned he had pneumonia a couple of times when he was younger, but the teacher says he hasn't been ill since she's known him. On to Caleb's two best friends: the united message I got was that Caleb hated his father. They both used that word. Apparently, John Veir was never

106

happy with anything Caleb did. Caleb thought living in the house was like being in a prison or in the army. And he hated being at home with just his dad.'

'Jesus,' said Ren. 'Any mention of whether things ever got physical?'

'One friend said that Caleb wouldn't take his hat off for a few weeks after Christmas. The other, however, said he was there when Caleb took it off and that it had been covering a bump. He asked Caleb about it — Caleb told him he fell, which, of course, means nothing.'

'And what about how Caleb got along with his mom?' said Ren.

'Well, this is where it gets interesting,' said Sylvie, 'According to both boys, he used to be very close to his mother, but there was a change in recent months. He and his mother were fighting too and they said he could be really rude to her, which they hadn't seen before. But we have to remember, he's twelve years old. That's the kind of age where there's a shift in the dynamics. He liked his Aunt Alice, but it wasn't like he talked about her that much. They all knew she'd been on a television show recently, though, and, apparently, he seemed really proud of that.'

'It's still weird that he called her that morning,' said Ren.

'What's even weirder is that I haven't had any coffee yet,' said Sylvie. 'Anyone want any?'

'We just got some — thank you, though,' said Ren.

'OK,' said Sylvie. 'I'll leave you guys to it.' She

looked from one to the other, and left.

'So,' said Paul. 'What do you want to do?'

'Well,' said Ren, 'I'd like to talk to Clyde Brimmer . . . under the radar of Gil Wiley. Fancy a drive?'

'Yes, ma'am.'

'And under the radar of Ruddock too,' said Ren. 'I know this might be a quaint town, but I'm thinking he leans a little too much toward the sunny side of life.'

'How terrible of him,' said Paul.

'Like, he was talking about bad shit happening 'around' Brimmer over the years,' said Ren, 'but not at all questioning whether Brimmer could actually have been involved in it.'

'Maybe not out loud,' said Paul. 'Or maybe Ruddock just knows the guy and trusts him.'

'Have I turned into one of those suspicious-of-everyone-and-everything people?' said Ren.

'Turned into?'

Ren laughed.

★ ★ ★

As Paul drove through the town, Ren pointed out the black ribbons on the trees.

'So sad,' she said.

'At least there are yellow ones on some of them,' said Paul.

'I didn't even notice,' said Ren. 'All I see is black.' She smiled.

Paul squeezed her hand.

Ooh.

She turned to him.

He is so handsome.

This is a disaster.

'What I didn't get to finish earlier,' said Paul, 'when we were so rudely interrupted by onion fumes — was about the girls.'

'Oh, yeah,' said Ren. 'You said you were working through it. Through what?'

'The divorce.'

'Oh.'

Uh. Oh.

Run.

Ruuuuuuuuuuuuuuuun.

Grow up.

Run.

20

Ren picked up her purse from the passenger well of the car, and started searching through it for gum.

Fuckity fuck. This is a development I could do without.

'I thought,' said Ren, pulling out a packet of gum, offering him one without looking, 'that you and Marianne were still — '

'Cinnamon?' said Paul. 'No thanks.'

Ren popped a piece of gum in her mouth. 'How can you not love that burn?'

'You left last night,' said Paul. 'We were cut short earlier . . . when I was trying to tell you.'

'I'm so sorry,' said Ren. 'How are you doing?'

He shrugged. 'It's the right thing.'

As it was the last time.

'It's a complex situation. I — '

I don't want to hear your depressing shit. I've got my own depressing shit. And people are dead in mine. 'Sorry,' said Ren, 'I just remembered I have to call someone before now.'

I can't believe I just said that. Jesus.

And now you have to make the call in front of him. Think quickly, bitch.

As she scrolled through her Contacts, they arrived at Clyde Brimmer's house.

Ren looked up at it. 'It looks like it was blown here by a tornado. I have a feeling it will be rancid.'

'I see your feeling and raise it.' He got out of the car, leaned into her. 'Let me do the recce. Sit tight.'

Ren watched as he went up to the door and knocked on it. He turned around to her with a face of faux terror. She laughed.

Clyde Brimmer appeared at the door, barefoot and bleary-eyed.

★ ★ ★

Ren's phone beeped with a text. She looked down.

Joe Lucchesi.

Something shifted in her chest.

Oh, no: do not like this man either. You can't handle damage.

You fucking are damage.

Joe was the ex-NYPD homicide detective who came to Denver to work the Duke Rawlins investigation alongside her. Ren opened his text.

Hey there . . .

Don't 'Hey there' me. It's adorable. Even without a comma. Men are crap at punctuation.

She read on.

. . . i hope life is treating you well.

Capitalize your fucking i's!

. . . X

Her heart surged.

From one fucking 'x'. How old am I?

She thought of the first time she saw Joe, when she was waiting to pick him up at Denver airport. He walked through Arrivals, handsome, muscular, holding his beautiful sleeping daughter in his arms. She felt an instant attraction that vanished because they clashed, but returned when he apologized, and remained, despite him telling her she reminded him of his late wife.

She remembered the night they had slept in the same bed, and how she had run from it the next morning, because she was with Ben.

Joe Lucchesi ... another man of mine wrapped up in guilt.

And more ...

Her stomach tightened at the thought; the other memories, the horrifying ones: she and Joe had been the only two there at the harrowing peak of the investigation, when Duke Rawlins announced that he was the father of Grace, that beautiful sleeping daughter: eight years earlier, Duke Rawlins had drugged and raped Joe's wife, and she had died in childbirth.

Stop.

She thought of replying to the text.

To say what? We've seen too much. We are forever altered.

She thought of Joe's face, his eyes, his strength.

He is so sexy. He is kind. He is a wonderful father.

She thought of his pain, his anger, his tears.

He is ... wildly damaged.

Run.

Ruuuuuuuuuuuuuuuuun.

Run.

Two for one!

She glanced up at the house. Clyde Brimmer was taking a while to process whatever Paul was saying to him.

Are you kidding me, though? Ben. Joe. Paul. Emotional.

Overload.

Paul turned back to Ren, gave her a thumbs-halfway-up before he disappeared through the front door.

The place half-stinks?

★ ★ ★

Ren went into the house.

The place half-stinks.

Paul was alone in the living room. He raised his eyebrows when she walked in. 'Well?'

'Good call,' said Ren. 'I can just about handle this.' She looked around. 'So many questionable surfaces . . .'

'Sit beside me,' said Paul, smoothing out the sofa cushion.

Clyde came back in. 'I feel like I should offer you some coffee.'

Feel away. 'There's no need,' said Ren. *We're happy with our current gut flora.* She stood up. 'Sorry, Clyde — I didn't introduce myself. I'm Ren Bryce, I'm on the CARD team with Paul.'

Clyde sat down on an armchair, nodded without looking up. 'You're a beautiful lady.'

Ren laughed. 'Thank you.' *Blind drunk already.*

'We wanted to talk to you about why you came to the press conference,' said Ren, 'and what you were saying about the lake, your concerns about Caleb.'

Clyde's eyes went wide, but his gaze stayed on the floor. He was kneading something between his thumb and forefinger. He held up an opaque white stone.

Ooh — moonstone. 'That's beautiful,' said Ren.

He held it out to her.

Cooties!

She took it in her hand. 'It's really beautiful.' *Hand sanitizer, hand sanitizer.*

He beamed. She handed it back to him. 'Thank you. Did you get that in Gemstones in town?'

Are you connected to Teddy Veir?

Clyde shook his head. 'No, no . . . ' He kept shaking his head.

'Where did you get it?' said Ren.

He shrugged. 'Been such a long time, I can't remember.'

Ren nodded. 'So,' she said. 'The lake . . . what can you tell me?'

There was a haunted look in his eye. 'Aaron was a strong swimmer.'

Aaron? She and Paul exchanged glances.

'He'd lived by that lake for seven years,' said Clyde. 'I was so shocked . . . ' He trailed off.

'That he drowned?' said Paul.

Ren could see Clyde's hand shaking. His foot started to tap the floor.

'Clyde,' said Ren. 'You can trust us. I promise. What is it?'

'The lake . . . '

Ren leaned into him. 'Are you . . . afraid of the lake?'

He thought about it, brought his gaze a little higher, his eyes pale, watery, flickering with questions.

'I'm afraid of Gil Wiley.'

The what now? 'Wiley?' said Ren.

'Wiley . . . ' said Clyde, 'is going to kill me.'

'Why do you think that?' said Ren.

'Cos I drive him crazy — that's why. That's why I'm always trying to get past him to Pete. But Wiley stands in my way the whole time.'

Always? How many times do you come forward with shit?

'He's a dismissive man,' said Clyde. 'Very dismissive.'

'What do you feel he's dismissing?' said Paul.

'What I've been trying to tell him,' said Clyde. 'About Aaron Fuller.'

He lowered his head, then brought his wide, fearful eyes for the first time to meet Ren's. 'I don't think it was an accident,' said Clyde. 'Or maybe it was. I don't know.' He shrugged. 'But something else definitely happened to Aaron. I think . . . maybe he had been hurt before he went into the water.'

21

Ren's heart was pounding. She nodded calmly.

Let's not freak him out.

Let's not hang on his every word, either.

Reliability level? Blood alcohol level?

'OK,' said Ren. 'Talk us through why you think that. We're listening.'

Clyde nodded. 'Thank you. OK, so when you get a bruise, you break capillaries and blood leaks out, but it could take ten or twelve hours for the bruise to come up. If you die, your heart stops, the blood's not pumping around any more, so the bruise might never appear. Aaron was found floating in the lake — lucky to be found, too. If he didn't go in somewhere shallow, he wouldn't have been.'

'It would have been spring before the body surfaced,' said Ren.

'Exactly.'

'At autopsy,' said Clyde, 'the ME figured he drowned — that's what the evidence pointed to. But, you know, an ME will only resect the back tissue if it's an abuse case, or he suspects abuse and therefore hidden bruising. But, otherwise, if the back looks fine, he would have no reason to do that.'

Ren nodded.

'How it works is, embalming fluid replaces blood in the vascular system,' said Clyde. 'It makes any blood that's in the tissue stand out better . . . '

It's so weird listening to words like that coming out of a man like him. He loves this. And it's been taken away from him.

'When that happened with Aaron,' said Clyde. 'I saw a large bruise at the center of his back . . .'

Ren's heart rate shot up.

'That bruise could have been because he was hurt before he died,' said Clyde. 'Or . . . because someone was holding him under the water.' He shifted forward in his seat. 'That could've been the mark of a knee in his back is what I'm trying to say.' He shrugged. 'At the very least, though, I think he suffered an injury of some kind.'

Holy shit. 'Absolutely,' said Ren.

Clyde's face was flooded with relief.

And now for the awful part. 'I have to ask,' said Ren. 'I'm aware that you lost your job that day — '

'I was stone-cold sober when I worked on Aaron,' said Clyde.

'Please look at me,' said Ren.

Clyde shook his head, his lips pursed.

Ren reached out and squeezed his forearm. 'We're not here to judge you, not in any way. We just need you to tell us the truth. I can't stress to you enough how important this is. We need the absolute truth, here, OK? Whatever that is. Because we can do something about it, once we know . . .'

Tears filled Clyde's eyes. He wiped at them with his sleeve. 'I'm a goddamn mess, I'm a mess . . .'

'No, you're not,' said Ren. 'That was a difficult job for you. Embalming a child, the child of

117

someone you knew . . . '

'Yes!' said Clyde. 'It was terrible.'

Ren waited. She could hear his breathing, growly, uneven. She looked at his fingers and noticed, for the first time, the nicotine stains. She imagined his hands before they spent most of their time gripping a bottle of liquor, younger, paler hands, years from being gnarled and ruddy, and yellowed.

All that alcohol flowing through your veins. Then embalming fluid.

I'm a terrible human being . . . who loves alcohol flowing through her veins.

'I may have had one drink . . . ' said Clyde.

Fuck. 'One?' said Ren.

He kept his eyes on his hands.

'Look at me,' said Ren. He didn't.

'It was only . . . it . . . it . . . took a lot out of me,' said Clyde. 'Brought back some bad, bad memories. This boy, only a boy, laid out, his life over, only eleven years old. Do you remember being eleven? I do. I was having the time of my life, it was all ahead of me. You never for a second think anything bad's going to happen to you, you just think that whatever dreams you have will come true. And . . . ' He shrugged. 'You never know when your life is going to be taken — gone, up in smoke. I know that, after I left the job, a seven-year-old kid was brought in — choked on a sandwich. Gone. Just like that . . . '

'Pete mentioned that to us,' said Ren. She paused. 'What bad memories did Aaron's death bring back for you?'

118

'I . . . my sister,' said Clyde. 'My sister, Lizzie, died. She was only ten years old. She fell through a rotted deck at Lake Verny. No one listened to me . . . I . . . was the custodian there. It was a summer job when I was in high school, but I took it seriously. But, I guess, no one took me seriously.'

Ren nodded. 'That must have been very hard for you. But your sister's accident wasn't your fault.'

He looked up at her. 'I should have pushed harder. I should have ignored the owners when they said not to fix the deck yet.'

She looked at his eyes, red-rimmed, sad, and prickling with fear. Her heart sank. *You poor guilt-ridden man.*

'No one listens to me,' said Clyde. 'Maybe if I didn't do this . . . ' He swept a hand across the empty beer bottles on the floor.

'Please don't beat yourself up,' said Ren. 'We're not doubting your memory. But I do have to ask you about your drinking that night.'

'I understand. I understand.'

'How much had you had to drink?'

'I did the job, sober, like I said,' said Clyde. 'I prayed over Aaron's body. Then I walked away from it. I was in a bad way. I had a bottle of vodka in my locker, I . . . I took a few swigs, maybe . . . drank half of it.'

Fuuuck. 'Half of?'

'A liter bottle.'

Fuuuck once more.

'Can you really be sure of what you saw?' said Ren.

119

'One hundred per cent,' said Clyde.

'Why didn't you say it to Pete yesterday?' said Ren.

'I said it to Gil Wiley!' said Clyde. 'When he was dragging me through the gates. And he told me to shut the hell up. I asked him to tell Pete. And he told me to shut the hell up again. I asked him could I tell Pete myself, and he said: 'If you mention one word to Pete Ruddock about this, you'll be the one with the bruises.' Then he said Pete couldn't stand the sight of me, that he was only ever nice to me because he had a reputation to protect, that Pete just pities me.'

What an asshole.

'He told me I was no different to any other alcoholic out there,' said Clyde, 'except for the fact that Pete hated me the most. Then Wiley said if I dared to interfere in a police investigation, he would have me hauled up in front of a judge and I would be incredible.'

Don't laugh.

'An incredible witness,' said Clyde. 'I mean, I wouldn't be considered credible.' He blushed.

Ugh: this is awful.

'He said that would mean even more people not taking me seriously,' said Clyde. 'Officially — in a court of law. He told me if he had to do one page of paperwork because of my bullshit, that he would throw me into Lake Verny himself.'

'Let me talk to Wiley,' said Ren.

'Don't tell him I told you!' said Clyde.

'Could anyone else in the crowd have heard him at the gates, telling you to shut the hell up?' said Ren.

'Yes,' said Clyde. He paused. 'Just . . . 'hell' wasn't the exact word.'

Ren laughed.

'You know — you're a lady,' said Clyde.

A lady who says fuck more times than you know.

'OK,' said Ren, 'Well, I can let on to Wiley that someone else overheard this — I don't have to bring you into it yet. And, Clyde — just so you know, Pete Ruddock considers you a friend. He speaks very fondly of you.'

Clyde gave a broad smile. 'Thank you,' he said. 'That's really nice to hear.'

Ren leaned toward him again. 'Have you spoken to anyone else about this, apart from Wiley?'

'No.'

'Good,' said Ren. 'We're going to need you to keep this to yourself, OK? I promise you that we are taking this seriously. We're going to go back to Tate PD right now to speak with Pete.'

Clyde nodded. His face was a mix of relief and fear.

Someone is taking you seriously.

But even you're not sure if they should.

I know the feeling.

22

Back at Tate PD, Ren met Wiley on her way to the ladies' room.

'Wiley, could I have a word, please?'

Wiley shrugged, stopped.

God, you hate me. 'I was wondering,' said Ren, 'the other day with Clyde Brimmer . . . someone said that you told him to shut the fuck up about the bruise on Aaron Fuller's back. He does seem to be a real nuisance, but I was just curious what the bruise was, and why you didn't give it any consideration.'

'Oh, I gave it consideration,' said Wiley. 'Here's what I considered: is this man ever sober? And are drunk people reliable witnesses?'

'He swears blind that he wasn't drinking while he embalmed the body.'

'Swears blind drunk.'

'Come on,' said Ren, 'give him a break.'

'Look, you're not from around here, you don't know the shit that goes on. You don't know Clyde, you don't know what a pain in the ass he is; 'nuisance' — sounds cute — is an understatement, you don't hear the paranoid, conspiracy-theory shit he comes out with. Oh, the world is going to hell in a hand basket, according to Clyde. Lake Verny is haunted, 'the lake has secrets that the rain wants to tell' — I've heard that a hundred times. The Pope has never and will never shit in the fucking woods. And on and on and on.'

'This wasn't about the lake being haunted,' said Ren. 'This was him saying that Aaron was possibly hurt before he went into the water.'

His look was a giant fuck-you. 'Sure, he might think he was hurt, but he still thinks the lake is haunted,' said Wiley. 'He probably figured it would make him sound too nuts to say it to you. It's pretty simple: Clyde Brimmer embalmed a body while he was drunk. He was already freaked out, because of the haunted lake thing. Now he's got one of its victims lying right there in front of him. Think about it: does Clyde want his worst fears confirmed? That the lake itself is actually killing people? Or would he like to find some evidence on that body that, in fact, someone — a person — is responsible?'

'But, wouldn't a 'victim of the lake itself' vindicate him?' said Ren. 'Wouldn't it go a little way to have people believe his claims that the lake is haunted?'

'Yes,' said Wiley, 'absolutely. It's just that, at that moment, it probably boiled down to what was more important — for him to be terrified for the rest of his life, or for there to be a more rational explanation for Aaron's death.'

He's not talking complete horseshit.

'Look,' said Wiley, 'he says he saw a bruise on Aaron's back. You could look at that two ways: a) sure, there could have been a bruise if Aaron slipped into the water and hit something on the way in and b) there was no bruise, because it would have been picked up at autopsy. And c) does it actually matter at this point? The kid drowned. It's tragic, sure, but why would anyone intentionally drown Aaron Fuller?'

Wow: where do I start with all that is wrong with that?

Don't start.

'OK — thanks,' said Ren. 'Just one thing, though — Clyde did admit that he drank only after he finished embalming the body. And I believe him.'

'Like I said, you're not from around here.'

Missing out daily on you serving and protecting me, dickwad.

★   ★   ★

Ren and Paul gathered the CARD team and Ruddock together and filled them in on what Clyde claimed he saw.

Gary looked at Ruddock. 'You might want to look into getting an exhumation order. I'm not saying this is connected to Caleb Veir, but something's not right here.'

Go, Gary!

Paul Louderback nodded. 'Yeah, I agree.'

Ruddock nodded.

Sylvie paused. 'I'm sorry, I don't. The guy's a drunk . . . '

'He's terrified,' said Ren. 'He's been fired. He could lose his license. And still, he came forward. Especially considering he's already in trouble, he's already marked out as someone who breached his professional code of conduct.'

Oh. Hold on . . . 'Can you give me half an hour?'

Gary looked at her patiently.

'Well, that's a resounding no,' said Ren.

'What is it?' said Gary.

'OK . . . the guy's breached his professional code of conduct by drinking. He's already in trouble . . . what else might he have done that would get him in trouble if it got out?'

'Ooh — quiz,' said Sylvie.

Ooh — miaow. 'He might have taken a photo on his cell phone after downing his vodka,' said Ren. 'I'd take a photo if I thought something looked suspicious. But as soon as I was sober, I'd know that that would be a major breach of the whole respect, care, and dignity part of my code of professional conduct. And if that got out, I'd be in serious shit for doing it. So I'd be disinclined to 'fess up . . . especially to law enforcement.'

'Did he respond well to you?' said Gary. 'If you asked him, do you think he would show you?'

'Of course he responded well to Ren,' said Paul.

Jesus, Paul. 'I think we got along,' said Ren. 'Let me talk to him.' She turned to Ruddock. 'With you?'

'Sure,' said Ruddock.

'Is there any update on Franklin J. Merrifield?' said Gary.

'There's been no sign of him,' said Ruddock. 'Investigators have gone to all his former addresses, to the homes of his family, known associates, known hangouts. They're checking out whether there's anything in his personal life he might have wanted to get out for.'

'Merrifield has maintained his innocence throughout,' said Ren. 'His appeal just got rejected. Say it's true — he is innocent. That means he got royally screwed over by his accomplice, got a longer sentence than him, and is now branded a rapist — his first time with a sex crime conviction — and he'll be in prison for the rest of his life. That's a man with nothing to lose. If something happened between Veir and Merrifield in BRCI . . . ' said Ren. She paused. 'Did anyone talk to the prison psychologists about Merrifield's state of mind? Didn't one of their names show up on John Veir's phone dump? Lockwood, was it? Maybe it's worth making a call to him. And isn't it worth talking to Seth Fuller about Merrifield, see if they crossed paths? Or if he's aware whether Merrifield and John Veir did? Veir might be too afraid to talk.'

★ ★ ★

Ren left the meeting first, and walked toward the kitchen to get coffee. She felt someone coming up beside her and turned to see Wiley.

Now he shows up . . .

'When we spoke earlier?' said Wiley. 'I think you may have forgotten to tell me about Clyde Brimmer? That you and your buddy, Paul, had already gone to talk to him? Without a word to me or Pete?'

You immediately checked up, you asshole!

'I'm sorry,' said Ren. 'You can understand

how I may have had concerns after your interaction with him yesterday.'

Wiley snorted. 'You're something else.'

Oh, fuck off, Wiley. 'I'm just doing my job,' said Ren. 'Someone comes forward, I want to hear them out — whoever they are. Why were you so adamant he would have nothing of value to say?'

'I told you already,' said Wiley. 'But going over my head like that — '

What the fuuuck? 'Over your head?'

Wiley stepped toward her.

This guy is nuts.

Ren leaned into him. 'Back the fuck up.'

Without saying another word, Wiley turned and walked away.

★ ★ ★

Ren walked in the opposite direction, and saw Ruddock standing at the end of the hallway.

Shit.

'Mind if I have a word?' said Ruddock.

'No problem,' said Ren.

'Firstly, I would like to apologize for whatever happened just there,' he said.

'Please,' said Ren, 'there's no need.'

Ruddock gave her a kind look. 'There are no excuses for Gil's behavior, but . . . he's going through a rough time at home. I'm not betraying any confidences here, it's common knowledge — his wife's got an alcohol problem, and it's been getting a lot worse lately. Now, I know Gil came in this morning smelling of alcohol himself, but that is one of only a handful of times that has happened in all the years I've known him. Usually, he doesn't drink. He can't stand it. Apparently, his wife had some kind of meltdown yesterday. It probably tipped him over the edge, with the stress of the investigation, the fact that she clearly didn't care about that. I just want you to know — he's never late and never that unprofessional.' He paused. 'I know Gil doesn't have the best manner in the world, but this is just who he's been since all this with his wife.'

'Well, thanks for letting me know,' said Ren. 'That's very sad.'

'Back there — he was probably more angry with himself than he was with you,' said Ruddock.

I don't give a fuuuck who he's angry with as long as he keeps it out of my face. But, Jesus Christ, how hard can it be, guys? Feel Angry at X = Get Angry at X. Leave Y the fuck out of it.

'Wiley completely disregarded what Clyde Brimmer had to say,' said Ren. 'Do you think there could be anything else going on there?'

'You mean — could Gil be involved in something?' said Ruddock. 'Absolutely not.'

Ren nodded. 'OK — I had to ask. You can vouch for him.'

'Of course I can,' said Ruddock.

First flash of anger . . . or as close to anger as a man like Ruddock might get.

'Are you ready to go?' said Ruddock.

'Sure,' said Ren. 'Let's do it.'

* * *

Two hours later, following a consultation with the Medical Examiner, with Shannon Fuller, and on studying a cell phone photo provided by Clyde Brimmer, a Marion County judge issued an exhumation order for the body of Aaron Fuller.

23

Shannon Fuller sat in her living room, the same three words on a loop running through her head: rest in peace. It had been short-lived for Aaron, and here she was again, in a fresh hell. She couldn't imagine who would want to hurt him. Maybe something happened at the dance — a fight, or maybe it was just an accident. Aaron was a sweet boy. She couldn't imagine anyone wanting to deliberately hurt him.

But then, she figured most mothers would think the same way. She had a sudden thought that turned her stomach — most children know their abusers. She pushed the thought away, but a whole stream of names came into her head — the names of people who knew her, who knew Aaron.

She stood up and walked down the hallway to Seth's door. She knocked.

'Enter!' he said.

She walked in, but stopped, hovering in the doorway. She looked at his sweet face. She didn't want to say anything.

'They're taking my baby out of the ground, Seth . . . ' She started to cry.

'What?' he said. 'What?' He stood up.

'There was a bruise on Aaron's back,' said Shannon. 'He may have been injured before he drowned. Or . . . maybe he was drowned . . . deliberately.'

Seth started to shake. 'What?'

Shannon nodded, sobbed harder. Seth went to her, put his arms around her. 'Oh my God,' he said. 'Who would do that?'

'I don't know,' she sobbed. 'I don't know.'

'Why do they think that?' said Seth.

'Clyde . . . Clyde saw the bruise when he was embalming him. Apparently, a bruise won't always show up right away, so that's why the Medical Examiner didn't see it. She's going to do another autopsy.'

'But why didn't Clyde say anything to us?' said Seth.

'Would you say that to a grieving family?' said Shannon. 'She pulled back from him. 'You're shaking,' she said. 'You're white as a sheet. Sit down.'

'Don't worry about me,' said Seth. 'You're the one . . . ' He trailed off, struggled to catch his breath.

Shannon gripped his arms, and guided him to the bed, sat him down. 'Are you OK?' she said.

'I . . . don't know why someone would do that to Aaron,' he said. 'He was only a boy, only a little boy.'

Seth fell sideways on the bed, clutching his chest.

'Seth!' said Shannon. 'Seth! Oh my God.'

Sweat poured down his face. Shannon ran into the living room, came back with a brown paper bag. She sat him up, held the bag to his mouth.

'Breathe, sweetheart, breathe,' said Shannon. 'Come on, deep breaths.'

Seth did as she said, and before long, his

breathing was back under control.

'Thank God,' said Shannon. 'Thank God. Was it just the shock?'

She looked into his eyes, and saw fear.

Shannon frowned. 'Is there something else, Seth?'

'No . . . '

'You're making me nervous, sweetheart,' said Shannon. 'I'm sorry.'

'No,' said Seth. 'No — I swear to God. I'm just . . . freaked out. I . . . ' He shrugged. 'I mean, I was here that night too. I was so close, and . . . I couldn't help.'

Shannon looked at him. 'Seth, I know you weren't here that night.'

Seth went very still.

'I was here alone,' said Shannon. 'I was drinking. I drank a lot, and I was worried about how drunk I was and I went to your room to let you know to watch out for me. I opened your door. Your room was empty. Your bed was cold.'

Seth still didn't move. 'I . . . '

'Where were you that night?' said Shannon.

Seth stared away from her. 'Why didn't you say anything before?'

'It didn't matter where you were,' said Shannon. 'Until now.'

24

Ruddock and Ren met in the parking lot of the ME's office in Salem on Thursday morning.

'A heads-up,' said Ruddock as they walked toward the building, 'call the ME Beckman. Her name is Lois Beckman, but she's our youngest ever ME and she looks a lot younger than her years. So she's trying to prove herself, which I think is why she prefers the last name, but also — she can come across as a little abrasive or defensive. And considering why we're here . . . '

'But she should know that she didn't do anything wildly irregular here,' said Ren. 'It's not standard practice to resect the back, unless they suspect abuse, and no one had any reason to here.'

'Knowing Beckman, she won't see it that way.'

'Well, if a drunken barfly was the one drawing attention to the flaws in my work, I might be feeling a little defensive too.'

Ruddock laughed, but there was a hint of surprise in it.

Am I actually funny or do people just laugh because they're expecting Clarice Starling? I'm intense too, people. No screaming lambs, but lots of fucking voices.

★   ★   ★

Lois Beckman came down to the lobby to greet Ren and Ruddock. She was very short and very

133

pretty, with a don't-mess-with-me walk. She had thick blonde hair to her shoulders, and warm brown eyes with long dark lashes. Her smile had a sweet earnestness.

I see why you have to work harder to get people past your youth and beauty.

'Nice to meet you,' said Ren.

'You too,' said Beckman.

Southern accent too! Could you be any cuter?

'Hi, Pete,' said Beckman. 'This is a first for me — autopsying an embalmed body.'

'Well, it's not a common thing,' said Ren. 'And the circumstances here are most unusual. I mean — this boy was found dead, floating in a lake. The logical — '

'The logical thing in my line of work, as it is in yours, is not to make assumptions,' said Beckman. 'I know that.'

I'm screwing this up already. 'I know,' said Ren, 'but . . . why would you have resected the back tissue?'

Beckman gave a concessionary nod.

Phew.

'We're just finishing getting set up,' said Beckman, 'if you'd like to take a seat. The water sample from Lake Verny was delivered earlier by your crime scene tech, and I've prepared the slides from the sphenoid sinus fluid. I've also had my assistant prepare lung tissue samples, taken at the original autopsy. This is all going to come down to diatoms. When a person goes into the water alive, obviously, they're taking in water. Whether it's fresh water or salt water, it contains diatoms — these microscopic algae. They

134

circulate around the body and settle in the organs. Diatoms vary across different bodies of water — you can tell this just by looking at a sample under a microscope: the diatoms are different shapes, colors and sizes, depending on where the water's been taken from — it's not as hardcore as a fingerprint, but you can definitely determine if the victim was drowned in the same body of water he was found in.'

'And what about the bruising?' said Ruddock.

'Well, I've seen that before in cases where a victim has been held under water, like with a knee in their back,' said Beckman. 'I'm not sure how someone could use a knee to hold someone under a lake — how exactly would that work? Though, I do know to keep an open mind on these things.' She paused. 'OK, sit tight. I'll have someone come get you when we're ready.'

★ ★ ★

Twenty minutes later, Ren and Ruddock were suited up for the autopsy. Ren went into the morgue ahead of him.

The fucking smell!!!

'Beware the embalming fluid,' said Beckman, looking up at them.

'Jesus Christ,' said Ren, stopping short. 'That is caustic.'

'It'll get better,' said Beckman. 'Thank the Lord for our ventilation system.'

Very earnest Lord-thanking. You really mean it.

Ren was about to walk on, but stayed rooted

135

to the spot as soon as her gaze went to the stainless steel table ten feet from her, where the body of Aaron Fuller was laid out, eerily preserved in some gray and ghoulish version of who he once was.

Ren's stomach flipped.

Thank God your mother doesn't have to see this.

Ruddock had walked up beside Ren and stopped at exactly the same point. She turned to him, knowing that the look in his eyes mirrored her own. They both let out a breath.

I hate these masks.

Beckman was looking at them with compassion in her eyes. She nodded at her assistant across the table. 'Let's turn him over.'

Slowly, they turned Aaron's body on to his stomach. They all gasped. There, exactly as Clyde Brimmer had described, exactly as his photo had shown, was an area of darkened skin between the shoulder blades.

Ren and Ruddock locked eyes.

'There it is,' said Beckman.

Oh, God.

Beckman drew the scalpel down the back, opening up a deep cut from the lower neck to the buttocks.

'This will reveal any occult bruising,' she said. She made three more cuts, parallel to the first.

Ren's stomach spasmed.

'You can see here that there is blood deep in the tissue, consistent with an injury, or with force having been applied between the shoulder blades. It's impossible to tell from what, but it

136

could be something like a knee, if he was being held under water.'

Holy. Fuck.

'Could the bruise just be a separate thing?' said Ren. 'Like, could it have happened hours before he died? Maybe he fell against something, it was an accident . . . the embalmer said that it takes ten to twelve hours for a bruise to appear on the skin.'

Beckman nodded. 'All I can say for definite is that it happened around the time of death, while the victim was still alive.'

They were silent as Beckman made cuts into the arms and legs. 'I'm checking here again for occult bruising.' She looked up at them when she was finished. 'I'm not seeing anything here, but I think you've got what you're looking for.'

★   ★   ★

They gathered in Beckman's office afterward. She bent down over the microscope and looked at the first slide. 'This is the sample from Aaron's sphenoid sinus,' she said, 'if you'd like to take a look.' She stepped back. 'Diatoms look like those kaleidoscope things you had as a kid.'

Last year, in your case.

Ren looked through the lens. 'They're very purty.'

'They are.'

Ruddock looked too, but it was out of politeness.

All you're thinking is that there is a child killer on the loose in your lovely little town.

'Now,' said Beckman, taking another slide, 'this is the sample from Lake Verny.' She took a look, then stepped back again. She shook her head. 'It's totally different.' She turned to Ren. 'You were right: Aaron Fuller drowned, but it wasn't an accident, and it didn't happen in Lake Verny.'

25

Jimmy Lyle was seven years old. His daddy was taking him to Rainbow Rapids, and they were going to stay in an inn nearby overnight. Jimmy had stood on the front porch in his shorts and T-shirt with his little suitcase packed, waiting for his daddy to get the house in order. He was going around each room, cleaning it, tidying it, making sure it was as neat as it could be for when they got back.

Jimmy knew his daddy had already cleaned the bathroom, so if he used the bathroom, his daddy would have to clean it all over again. Jimmy looked at his yellow plastic watch. If he went back in there, they would be late. They had to leave at exactly 9 a.m. He knew that much. Exactly that time. He shouldn't have had more juice. Daddy told him that as he was standing at the bathroom door with the mop. He gave Jimmy the last-chance warning. Jimmy told him he didn't need to go.

Jimmy listened as the vacuum cleaner moved back and forth across the hall carpet. His daddy was nearly done. Jimmy checked his watch. It was four minutes to nine. His chest filled with a surge of excitement. He forgot about everything else, he forgot to hold on tight. He ruined everything.

His daddy stripped him from the waist down right there on the porch. Jimmy remembered the smell of the rubber gloves, the feel of the breeze on his damp skin, the power in his daddy's arm as he pulled his sneakers off, struggled with the slow, wet socks. He remembered looking over his daddy's shoulder, drawn to the sound of bicycle pedals, then brakes, then feet hitting concrete. Then the kids' laughter, so much laughter.

Then the front door slamming, the click of the locks, the clatter of the mop and bucket, the stench of bleach, the ice cold of the bathtub's edge against his chest.

★ ★ ★

Jimmy's cell phone started to ring, startling him back to reality. He glanced down at it. DEAD TO ME flashed on the screen. He was proud when he came up with that name. He pictured his daddy with the phone up to his ear, with the mournful expression of an abandoned hound, his wide-set eyes heavy-lidded, the right drooping lower than the left, his thick lips. Jimmy remembered his glasses and how they would steam up, the blood rising to the surface of his skin, the sweat on his upper lip, and how he would lick it, over and over.

★ ★ ★

DEAD TO ME left him a voicemail. Jimmy listened to it right away.

'Jimmy, it's your daddy. Please . . . please call me back when you get this.' He paused. 'I . . . I . . . need your help, son. I . . . I . . . need you. I — '

Jimmy felt a surge of rage. His hand shook. He

140

ended the call. There was a choking knot of emotions inside him, ever since his mama left him with a broken daddy who would fall away from him, leaving him alone, then return, searching for common ground, reaching out to drag Jimmy on to it, when it was only the size of a pin-prick. And they would teeter there, clinging to each other for a balance that they could never achieve. Then, as their failure was once again revealed, Jimmy would watch as his father would reach for something else . . . for someone else.

Jimmy sucked in a breath.

Breathe, breathe, breathe.

And the words, the words, always the same words:

Daddy loves you, Jimmy. Daddy —

Sometimes, his daddy was naked, on his knees beside him. He remembered the cold edge of the tub as it pressed against his chest. He remembered his daddy's pale skin, the darkness of his armpits, the darkness between his legs. He remembered his words, the smell of him, his fingertips buried into his neck, his words.

You are nothing and I will return you to nothing. You are everything and I will restore you to everything. You are nothing and I will return you to nothing. You are everything and I will restore you. You are my everything. And I will restore you.

Jimmy listened to the voicemail again, listened to it all the way through this time. It ended with 'You know Daddy loves you, don't you? Daddy loves you, Jimmy.'

Jimmy deleted the message. He remembered a different version of that proclamation, a different ending.

Daddy loves you, Jimmy.
Daddy loves you to death.

And back again.

26

Ren and Ruddock arrived at The Crow Bar. The door was open, but there was no one inside.

They're dead.

Jesus.

Ruddock called into the house. 'Hello? Shannon?'

There was no answer. Ruddock went in behind the bar. Ren followed him into the living room.

Cozy, homey, traditional. Not what I expected. Poor Shannon, a single mom working so hard to give her boy a home, then losing him so young.

Shannon appeared from the darkness of a short hallway, carrying a stack of towels. She stopped, stared at Ren and Ruddock.

She doesn't want to know.

But, still, she came toward them.

'Why don't we take a seat,' said Ruddock.

Shannon had tears in her eyes before they even sat down. She fell apart when they told her what the autopsy had revealed.

You cannot fall apart with her.

'We're so sorry,' said Ren.

'I . . . can't believe it,' said Shannon. 'I just . . . I can't. Who would want to kill my baby?'

This is gut-wrenching.

'A lot of things are going to happen that we need to prepare you for,' said Ren. 'Your home, the bar, the entire property will be searched

143

— the grounds and the cabins. We'll be accessing your phone records, Aaron's, and Seth's. We'll be accessing your financial records.'

'When will people start coming here?' said Shannon.

'The crime scene techs? Within the hour,' said Ren. 'And it's likely that once the media get a hold of this — '

'Well, they won't be hearing a word from me,' said Shannon. 'Or Seth.'

'We also need you to fill out this question-naire,' said Ruddock. 'It's standard practice. And we'll need Aaron's father to do the same . . . '

'Aaron's father left when Aaron was six months old,' said Shannon. 'He died three years later in a car accident.'

Poor kid.

'Can we take you and Seth anywhere?' said Ren. 'To family? A friend's house?'

'No,' said Shannon. 'We'll figure something out. Thank you, though. I appreciate it.'

★ ★ ★

Ren and Ruddock went back to Tate PD and filled the others in on the autopsy results. Ren drove to the Veirs.

'What is it?' said Teddy, when she opened the door.

'I wanted to let you know before you might hear it from another source,' said Ren, 'that Aaron Fuller's death is no longer being treated as an accident.'

'Oh my God,' said Teddy.

144

She brought Ren into the house, guided her into the living room. John came in, and sat beside Teddy, holding her hand. Ren talked them through the autopsy results. When she finished, John Veir stood up, ran for the bathroom. After a moment, they could hear him throw up.

'I should go to him . . . ' said Teddy, sliding forward on the sofa.

Ren put a gentle hand on her forearm. 'Please . . . he'll be back.' *I can't have you discussing this with each other.*

'What does this mean for Caleb?' said Teddy. 'Have you lost hope for him? Do you think this is what happened to him? Aaron was found very quickly . . . is that a good or a bad sign for Caleb?'

'Let's wait until John comes back,' said Ren.

They sat in silence. Ren looked around the room. It was exceptionally tidy, with few decorative touches, except for a narrow wall of family photographs to the left of the archway into the dining area. There was one of John Veir in his army uniform, his face set, his eyes dark and blank.

'When was that photo taken?' said Ren.

'Gosh,' said Teddy, turning to follow her gaze. 'He must have been thirty years old in that.'

'He looks so young,' said Ren.

Teddy nodded. 'He always did.'

Where all three Veirs were in photos together, Teddy was smiling, and her husband and son looked, at best, tolerant; at worst, tense.

I'd hate to be with a man like that. And have a son who looks miserable even on vacation. You

145

have zero clue what was going on that day. And maybe they just don't like getting their photo taken.

John came back, white-faced, with beads of sweat along his hairline. He sat down beside Teddy, and took her hand again.

'Sorry,' he said. He wiped his forearm across his brow.

'You've had a shock,' said Ren. 'But this news about Aaron doesn't mean that something bad has happened to Caleb. No one wants to alarm you, but it would be foolish for us not to at least consider a connection, based on their age profile and geographic proximity. And I want to reassure you that looking into what happened to Aaron won't impact on our efforts to find Caleb.'

'Oh, come on,' said John. 'It'll take a chunk out of your resources, for sure. How couldn't it?'

'We'll be bringing more officers in,' said Ren. 'And more agents from the FBI offices in Salem and Portland.'

'Is there anything we can do?' said John. 'I can't just sit here and do nothing. There's a maniac out there who's drowned a boy, who might have our son, and we're just sitting around?'

'There's nothing you can do except be here and support each other,' said Ren. 'But you will have to come in later to talk to Gil Wiley and Pete Ruddock.'

'There was something I discovered this morning,' said Teddy. 'It's probably no big deal, but I noticed that John's sleeping bag is missing from the attic.'

146

John's head spun toward her. 'What?'

'Yes,' said Teddy. 'I was going through the things Caleb kept up there, in case there was anything that might help us find him, and I realized it was gone. When was the last time we used them?'

John shrugged. 'I can't remember. The summer before last?'

Teddy nodded. 'You're right.'

'Do you have a photo of it?' said Ren.

'I can get you one,' said Teddy. 'I know that it's got a pretty distinctive black ink stain on it from a Sharpie.'

'When was the last time either of you were up in the attic?' said Ren.

Eye-dart from John Veir.

'Several months,' said Teddy.

'Caleb was talking about getting an action figure from up there on Sunday night,' said John, 'but I don't know if he did in the end.'

How convenient . . .

Teddy sat forward, her eyes bright. 'Could this mean that Caleb did run away? The suitcase, the sleeping bag . . . '

Caleb, dead, rolled into a sleeping bag, sealed inside a sheet of plastic, his father closing the trunk of his car.

'Not necessarily,' said Ren.

Suddenly, a car screeched up outside the house. Everyone stood up. A car door slammed, and there was the sound of footsteps rushing up the path. The doorbell rang, then a fist pounded on the door.

'Get out here! Get out here!'

147

It was a woman's voice.

John went to the window. Ren walked toward the front door.

'Stay where you are, Teddy,' said John.

'Who is it?' she said.

John went into the hall, and started to open the door, trying to push his way through the gap, to get out on to the porch.

'Don't you dare! Let me in, John!' *That's Shannon Fuller.*

John gave in, and Shannon appeared in the hallway, just as Teddy came out from the living room.

'It was you, you fucking psycho!' said Shannon.

'What are you talking about?' said John.

'Shannon,' said Ren. 'Please calm down — '

'No!' said Shannon. 'No.'

'John, step back, please,' said Ren. 'Shannon, I'm going to come over to you and — '

Shannon Fuller was pale-faced. Her eyes locked on to Ren's. 'There's something I should have told you right after I heard that Caleb was missing, but I didn't want to sound like some psycho too — '

Her gaze turned to Teddy.

'What is it?' said Ren.

'Tell her!' said Shannon to Teddy. 'Tell her!'

'Tell her what?' said Teddy.

'Tell her!' said Shannon.

'What . . . what are you talking about?' said Teddy. 'I don't know what you're talking about.'

'I was just told my son was drowned!' said Shannon. 'Did you hear that? Someone deliberately drowned my son — '

'We don't know that for sure,' said Ren.

Shannon talked over her. 'Someone held him under water until he couldn't breathe any more. Someone killed my beautiful boy! Tell her, Teddy. So help me God — '

Teddy's eyes were filled with tears, but she looked utterly bewildered. 'I have no idea — '

'I'll tell her, then,' said Shannon. 'I'll tell her — '

'Stop!' said John. 'Shannon, stop. Don't — ' He stepped toward her.

'No!' said Shannon. 'No way!' She turned to Ren, her eyes alight, but she was speaking to Teddy. 'Tell her! Tell this woman! Tell her!'

'John,' said Teddy, pleading. 'What is she talking about?' She was shaking. 'I don't know what you're — '

'Don't!' roared John at Shannon. 'Don't say a word. Don't do this.'

The pain in his eyes.

Shannon saw it too, and it drained the fight from her. 'I'm sorry,' she said. 'I'm sorry. I'm . . . angry. I'm confused. I . . . someone drowned Aaron. Someone drowned my little boy. Why would someone do that?'

And why would you come here directing your anger at Teddy Veir? And what does John Veir know about it?

Ren looked at John Veir over Shannon's shoulder, and nodded him toward his confused wife. 'Can you please take Teddy into the living room? Thank you.'

★ ★ ★

149

Ren took Shannon to one side. 'What is going on?'

Shannon lowered her voice, out of earshot of Teddy. 'When Caleb was a baby, Teddy tried to drown him.'

Oh.

Dear.

God.

27

Ren led Shannon into the kitchen.

'Talk to me,' said Ren.

'When Caleb was a newborn,' said Shannon, 'I came across Teddy early one morning, kneeling down by Coolwater Creek, lowering Caleb into the water. I ran, got there just as his face was going under. It was horrific. I jumped in the water, and pulled him out of Teddy's grip. Teddy was just sobbing, rambling on about no more pain. She was hysterical. She lashed out at me, scratched my face, tried to take Caleb out of my arms. She kept telling me that Caleb would only ever be safe if he was in heaven.'

Jesus. 'What happened next?' said Ren.

'Well, I managed to talk Teddy into coming with me back to the car,' said Shannon. 'I was going to drive them both to the police station, or the hospital, but Teddy begged me not to. She said her husband was in Iraq and that the baby would be taken away from her. So I brought them both back home. I told Teddy I wouldn't call the police on three conditions: one — that she called a family member to come stay with her; two — that they brought the baby to the doctor immediately; and three — that she got psychiatric help.'

'So, what family member came?' said Ren.

'It was a friend, in fact,' said Shannon. 'Patti Ellis.' She shook her head. 'I'm so sorry. I'm sorry for coming in here like that today. Teddy obviously has no memory of any of this. She must have blocked the whole thing out. I'm a mess. I'm sorry. Who would want to hurt Aaron?'

'We're going to do our very best to find that out,' said Ren. 'But first, I have to ask you, why did you think Teddy might? I know what you've just told me, but why would you think Teddy would have reason to harm *your* son.'

Shannon flushed. 'I — '

'Are you and John having an affair?' said Ren.

Shannon sat down on one of the kitchen chairs. Tears welled in her eyes. 'Yes . . . we were.'

'Let's talk about this in my car,' said Ren. 'If you could wait outside, I just want to have a word with John.'

Shannon left. Ren called John into the hallway. 'What did you say to Teddy?'

'I told her it was about . . . ' He shrugged.

'The affair,' said Ren. 'She knows?'

He nodded.

'But she has no memory of what happened with Caleb when he was a baby,' said Ren.

'No,' said John. 'I wanted to protect her.'

'I understand,' said Ren. 'For right now, I need to go speak with Shannon. But I will need you and Teddy to come into Tate PD this afternoon.'

★ ★ ★

Shannon Fuller was standing beside Ren's car, her arms crossed, her head bowed. Ren walked over, unlocked the car, and they both got in.

152

'So . . . ' said Ren. 'You and John . . . '

'Yes . . . ' said Shannon.

'Is it ongoing?'

'No . . . not really. It's — '

'Complicated . . . ' Ren smiled.

Shannon's shoulders relaxed.

'Tell me . . . ' said Ren.

'Well, we met when I bought the resort,' said Shannon. 'We'd see each other every now and then. Everything I said to you about him is true — how kind he was, what a good guy. At that point, though, that's all I thought. Then one day last summer, I ran into him in the store at Lister Creek — he was on his way home from work, I was on my way in to visit Seth. We got to talking . . . '

There is still such a sparkle in your eye for that man.

'There was just . . . a connection,' said Shannon. 'Plus, he knew I was worried about Seth, and he sort of implied he'd look out for him, which I thought was really kind. Maybe that's what it was . . . his compassion. I guess we don't expect it in men who look so . . . tough.' She sucked in a breath. 'I know I should have stayed away from him.'

'Life isn't that simple, though, is it?' said Ren.

'No,' said Shannon. 'No.'

'How did it progress from the meeting in the store into an affair?' said Ren.

'Well, we already had each other's cell phone numbers,' said Shannon, 'but that evening after we met at Lister Creek — he texted me, checking if I got home OK after my visit. A couple of days later — '

'When was this exactly?' said Ren.

'The end of July last year,' said Shannon. 'So a couple of days later, I asked him to come fix something at the bar . . . and it went from there . . . until Teddy found out in October. She was trying to hook up her phone to the Bluetooth printer at home and his second phone — he'd forgotten to power it off — showed up as an open device or whatever that's called. She searched all over for it, and she found it in his sports bag. It was all there.' She blushed again.

'So, the 'not really' part,' said Ren. 'I'm guessing it hasn't really ended . . . '

'We tried,' said Shannon. 'But it was just too hard. It started up again in December, ended in early January . . . and . . . when Aaron died, John was here to support me — emotionally. As a friend.'

'Did Teddy know in December that it had started up again?' said Ren.

'Yes,' said Shannon.

'And nobody thought to mention this to us . . . ' said Ren.

'I didn't think it was my place,' said Shannon. 'Not when they're going through this. I don't want to add any more pain. And I didn't see how it mattered. It's over now.'

'Did Seth know about it?' said Ren.

'Seth? No — he might have had his suspicions, but no. Why?'

'What about Aaron or Caleb?' said Ren. 'Could they have known?'

Her eyes widened. She took her time to

answer. 'That never entered my head. No . . . ?'

'Your plant pots out front . . . ' said Ren.

Shannon had a resigned look on her face.

'Someone trashed them?' said Ren.

'Yes.'

'Teddy?' said Ren.

Shannon nodded. 'She showed up New Year's Day, totally lost it.'

'Was Aaron there?' said Ren. 'Did he see it?'

'Yes,' said Shannon. 'But he didn't know what it was about. I told him it was to do with the bar and money I still owed the Veirs. It was the first thing that came into my head.'

'Did Teddy know that John was back offering you emotional support when Aaron died?'

'Yes,' said Shannon. 'He decided to just come clean — he told Teddy I needed him, and that it wouldn't feel right for him not to be there for me.'

'How did she take that?' said Ren.

'He didn't say,' said Shannon. 'And I didn't ask.'

'When you came here today,' said Ren, 'did you really think that Teddy Veir could have done something to harm Aaron?'

'I know you're expecting me to say 'no',' said Shannon, 'and that saying 'no' is the right thing to say, but yes . . . yes, I did. And I'm not sure I feel any differently now.' She paused. 'You'll look into it, won't you?'

'Yes,' said Ren. 'Of course.'

Shannon stared out the window. 'Do you think it's karma?'

The what now?

'Bad things happening to both our sons . . . ' said Shannon, turning to her. 'John and me. I mean . . . is God punishing us?'

'No,' said Ren. 'No, no, no.' *Why would you even think that?* 'I don't know why this had to happen,' said Ren, 'but it is not karma.'

'But, wouldn't you think it was karma if you did something shitty and someone you loved died?'

'No,' said Ren. 'Now, if you'll excuse me . . . I need to get back to the Veirs. Thank you for your time.' She got out of the car. Shannon got out, and started to walk after her.

'I'm sorry,' said Shannon. 'Did I say something to upset you?'

Ren kept walking.

Blink.
Blink.
Blink.

28

Back at Tate PD, Ren filled the team in on the Veirs and Shannon Fuller.

'I've asked both the Veirs to come in later,' said Ren. 'After I spoke with Shannon, I went back in to ask them for a photo with the sleeping bag in it. Teddy was in pretty bad shape. We need to know more about her mental health from her doctors. The episode with Caleb as a baby, particularly as he was only a week old, would suggest post-partum psychosis to me. Does that make someone susceptible to future psychotic episodes? I don't know.'

'I can try speaking with her doctor,' said Ruddock.

'Is she taking any meds?' said Ren.

'Xanax for anxiety,' said Ruddock.

'I was thinking,' said Ren, 'if there was an affair between John Veir and Shannon Fuller, that brings up the possibility of blackmail. Not everyone would know that his wife already knows about it. If someone thought they could blackmail John Veir . . . ' She paused. 'What about Merrifield? Could he have wanted John Veir's help to escape? And something went wrong . . . '

'How would Merrifield know that John Veir was having an affair?' said Wiley.

Ren thought about it. 'Seth Fuller? He's a common denominator.'

'And there's Seth's 'interest' in Caleb,' said Ruddock. 'Plus, if Seth has Caleb's trust, too, that could make it easy for him to lure Caleb somewhere.'

'What is the word on Merrifield?' said Ren.

'No leads,' said Ruddock. 'It's like he vanished into thin air.'

'Another thing occurred to me after talking to Shannon Fuller,' said Ren. 'She mentioned running into John Veir at Lister Creek rest area. I'm wondering if it's somewhere he stops regularly. Did anyone call in video from the store there for Monday?

'I can do that,' said Wiley.

Why do I not trust anything you do?

'He may not have gone inside the store,' said Ren. 'I think he went into the gas station for our benefit, hoping we would assume he wouldn't make a second stop on the way to work.'

'We'll put a piece in the *Marion County Gazette* and the *Salem Journal* about items we want the public to look out for,' said Ruddock. 'We'll include photos of the sleeping bag, the clothes Caleb was wearing, the suitcase, his school knapsack . . . '

'We also got a photo of John and Teddy Veir standing in their driveway — maybe their cars will jog someone's memory,' said Wiley.

Ren nodded. 'We also need to see if we can establish a connection between Aaron and Caleb — maybe there's something we've missed.'

'Plus,' said Paul, 'if this bruise was caused by him falling or someone striking him, most of his final hours were spent at the middle school

158

dance — we need to check if anything happened there.'

'I can go back and talk to Caleb's teacher,' said Sylvie. 'Make it clear to teachers and parents that if they have information, it's crucial they speak up, that they won't get in trouble.'

A young officer stuck his head in the door. 'The Veirs are here, Chief.'

Ren turned to Ruddock. 'Can you and I take John?'

Ruddock nodded.

Gary said, 'Wiley — how about you and I speak with the mom?'

* * *

John Veir looked like he had been crying.

I don't know what to feel about you. I have no idea who you are.

'John,' said Ren, 'can you talk us through what happened with Teddy and Caleb?'

'I was in Iraq when Caleb was born,' said John. 'Teddy got post-partum psychosis when Caleb was only a week old. I got a call from her friend, Patti, saying that Teddy had to be hospitalized. Patti said she would take care of Caleb, that she'd move into our house, so he was in familiar surroundings and he would be comfortable. Patti's a really kind lady.' He paused. 'She didn't tell me at the time what had happened at the creek. She didn't want to distress me while I was so far away, but she did tell me as soon as I got back. I went and spoke with Teddy's doctors. We figured it was best not

159

to tell her what happened.'

'So Teddy was hospitalized . . . ' said Ren.

'Yes, and put on medication,' said John. 'She was in and out of psychiatric care for several years after that. And I was redeployed at different points during that time. But what happened that day was a one-off event, the doctors explained everything — that's not who Teddy was.'

'I understand,' said Ren.

'I can't believe that Shannon connected that with what happened to Aaron — I thought she'd have more compassion.'

'Well, it's safe to say that Shannon isn't exactly thinking straight herself at the moment,' said Ren. 'Her entire world has been turned upside down. She's suffered a tragedy — she probably thought it couldn't get any worse than losing her only child, and then she finds out yes, yes it could.'

John nodded. 'I guess so.'

Ren looked at her notes from Sylvie Ross's interviews. 'John, we heard that there's been some tension between Teddy and Caleb recently. Neither you nor Teddy mentioned that to us when we spoke with you before. Were you unaware of that?'

John shrugged. 'No — not really. It just seemed like a hurtful thing to say in the middle of all this, when she is so devastated. To be honest, I didn't think it was relevant. I know Teddy wouldn't hurt a fly. And none of this has anything to do with me and Shannon. Besides, I don't believe Caleb would have run away from home. I know that for absolute sure.' He started to cry.

This is a shitshow.

29

Everyone reconvened at the command center to swap notes on their interviews with the Veirs.

'Teddy Veir admitted to the meltdown at The Crow Bar,' said Gary. 'She backed up what Shannon already told you, Ren. I also asked her whether she'd told anyone else about the affair, and she said no.'

'Sounds to me like the anger was specific to the circumstances,' said Ruddock.

Ren shrugged. 'Unless she's one of those people who's prone to explosive rage.'

'Do you think she might have done something to Caleb?' said Ruddock.

'It's a possibility,' said Ren. 'She clearly has a temper, but ... exceptional circumstances. Though maybe she did lose it with Caleb, and that's why the Veirs seem like they're lying? Maybe John is protecting her.' She shrugged.

Sylvie came into the office.

'OK — I just spoke with Caleb's teacher again,' she said. 'Caleb told one of his friends back in December that he was getting a PlayStation for Christmas — apparently he found it in the garage. Only — here's the weird part — he was never given it. So someone bought it for him, then changed their mind. Or someone bought a PlayStation that wasn't intended for Caleb and stored it in the Veirs' garage ... '

'Imagine his little face on Christmas morning,' said Ren. 'Who would do that to a child?'

Sylvie looked at her patiently. 'John or Teddy Veir, obviously.'

Ren stood up. 'Are they still here?' She didn't wait for an answer. She ran out to reception. John and Teddy were just about to leave. They turned when they heard their names.

'One of Caleb's friends said that Caleb found a PlayStation in the garage before Christmas,' said Ren. 'Do you know anything about that?'

Bing: John Veir does.

'No,' said John. 'Really?'

'I don't know anything about that,' said Teddy. 'John is the one who takes care of those kind of gifts. But we hadn't planned on getting Caleb one.' She turned to John. 'You didn't change your mind about that, did you?'

'No,' said John. 'I did tell Caleb if he behaved better — consistently — that I would buy him one. He had gotten a little disrespectful, he was creating tension in the house. He's our son, we love him, but I couldn't tolerate that kind of behavior.'

'Tolerate is a strong word,' said Ren. 'How bad had it gotten?'

'Maybe I expect too much,' said John. 'Maybe I should 'tolerate' more.'

Teddy raised her eyebrows.

'I have high expectations of Caleb,' said John.

'We both do,' said Teddy.

'If he didn't live up to them,' said John, 'there had to be consequences. So he knew it wasn't a promise or, at least, that it was conditional: if

163

these conditions are met, you will get a gift or permission to go somewhere or whatever it was he wanted at that time.' He paused. 'So the only thing I can think of is that either his friend was lying when he said that, or that Caleb was lying to his friend.'

'Did Caleb have a habit of lying?' said Ren.

'No,' said Teddy.

'No,' said John a few beats later.

'So, Teddy,' said Ren, 'you definitely know nothing about this . . . '

'No, nothing,' said Teddy.

'I'm asking because we were also told that there was a change in your relationship with Caleb after Christmas,' said Ren. 'That maybe things had gotten a little more . . . ' *God, I hate doing this. This poor woman.* ' . . . difficult?'

Tears welled in Teddy's eyes. 'Yes,' she said. 'And I don't know why.'

'OK,' said Ren. She turned to John. 'Can I just ask — did you expressly say to Caleb that he was creating tension in the house?'

'No,' said John. 'Of course not.'

'It's just a concern,' said Ren. 'If he thought that he was causing a problem at home, he might have decided to run away, thinking it would either solve the problem, or teach you a lesson, depending on how he took it.'

'Well, I probably made that sound worse than it was when I said it just there,' said John.

I can only imagine what it may have sounded like to a twelve-year-old boy.

★ ★ ★

164

As Ren walked back to her desk, her phone beeped with a text. She looked down.

Joe Lucchesi. Shit.

Are you in Denver next week?

Why would I be in Denver next week?

Do not encourage this. You would be a disaster together.

Seriously: how sane can a man be whose wife and son were almost killed by a serial killer and whose daughter was fathered by him? And whose wife died in childbirth because of what that same killer did to her first time around.

Maybe saner than a grief-stricken bipolar FBI agent.

Oh. God.

Joe and I are made for each other.

Run.

Ruuuuuuuuuuuuuuuun.

30

The parking lot of The Crow Bar was filled with police cars, SUVs, Crime Scene Investigations trucks. Ren and Ruddock stood by the hood of his car with a map of the property opened out on it. It marked out twenty-seven structures: The Crow Bar and adjoining house, twenty cabins, a reception area, a storage room, a laundry room, and a shower block.

Ruddock pointed to Cabin 5. 'Aaron's body was found in the water here.'

Ren nodded. 'By whom?'

'A woman out walking her dog. She called it in to us.'

'And have we got keys to all these cabins?' said Ren.

'I'm not sure,' said Ruddock. Shannon Fuller walked over to them. 'Hey there,' she said. 'We're missing a key to Cabin 8. Clyde reckons it's gone from the big ring he keeps all his keys on.'

'Since when?' said Ren.

'He doesn't know,' said Shannon, 'but he's only had that for the past six weeks.'

'Unless he never had that key in the first place,' said Ren.

Shannon nodded. 'It's a possibility.'

'And where were those keys before he was given them?' said Ren.

'I keep them in the house,' said Shannon.

'And when's the last time you remember

seeing that key?' said Ren.

'I couldn't tell you,' said Shannon. 'It's more Seth who's been dealing with the cabins.'

'Who else might have keys to the cabins?' said Ren, as they walked down.

'Apart from the remaining individual owners?' said Shannon. 'Just me. I don't know if John Veir kept copies, but I doubt it — he wasn't too concerned with the cabins even when he owned the place. Maybe some of the tradesmen who have worked here over the years still have keys, but I doubt it. And I guess, if any of the former owners rented out their properties privately, they would have had copies too — they could be anywhere.'

'Yeah, that's not really narrowing it down for us,' said Ren.

★ ★ ★

Ren and Ruddock took the map with them and followed the path past the shabby Reception hut with a pale rectangular space above the door where the sign used to be.

'It's hard to believe that this was the place to be,' said Ruddock. 'Well, up until about '85. Then, as it always goes, somewhere fancier was built nearby and that was that — Lake Verny was pretty much wiped off the map for most people, and all the kids around wanted to go to Rainbow Rapids.'

'And did Rainbow Rapids survive?' said Ren.

Ruddock nodded. 'Yes, it's still going strong. But the owners know to keep reinventing it.'

They walked on.

'How's your hotel working out for you?' said Ruddock.

'It's . . . OK,' said Ren. 'The food isn't exactly dazzling.'

'Well, you're not going to find sushi there, that's for sure,' said Ruddock.

Sushi! 'A roast chicken with crispy skin would do it for me right now,' said Ren.

'Despite appearances,' said Ruddock.

What the heck?

'That was a compliment,' said Ruddock.

Ren laughed. 'I'm a girl of simple tastes, really.'

They arrived at Cabin 5, the cabin closest to where Aaron's body was found. Clyde Brimmer was standing at the top of the path beside a Crime Scene Investigations van.

'Nice work, Clyde,' said Ruddock. 'Thank you for persisting with what you believed in. It's very sad news, but the kind we need to know.'

What a sweet man.

Clyde nodded sadly.

★ ★ ★

Ruddock and Ren walked down to the water's edge.

'The body was found here,' said Ruddock, pointing. He turned and waved the crime scene techs over. Three divers had arrived, and descended along with them.

'Do your best,' said Ruddock, 'but we know there's a slim chance of any evidence being found at this stage.'

Ren turned to him when the others started to work. 'So,' she said, 'was he drowned close by? Or driven here in a vehicle to be disposed of? Shannon was out for the count that night, she wouldn't have heard anyone drive in. Seth didn't report hearing anything.' She looked around. 'There's no access point here, is there?'

'No,' said Ruddock. 'All vehicles have to come through the front.'

'Where could Aaron have been drowned near here?' said Ren.

Ruddock shrugged. 'In one of the cabins . . . in a bathtub? A sink? You could drown someone in a bucket of water, if you really wanted to.'

'Is there water running to all the cabins?' said Ren.

She turned to ask Clyde. He was gone.

'Oh,' said Ren. 'Clyde has vanished.'

'It's probably all too much for him,' said Ruddock.

'Jumping-into-the-lake too much, or just having-a-quiet-cry too much?'

Ruddock smiled. 'I wouldn't say we have to worry.'

Not as simple for me.

'I'm going to go see if I can find him,' said Ren. She walked up the path and passed a crime scene tech coming down.

'Did you see a guy leaving here?' said Ren. 'Late forties, but looks a little older, short, slightly bedraggled-looking.'

'Nope.'

'Clyde?' Ren called. 'Clyde?'

She walked back to the cabin. There was no sign of him. She walked up to the edge of the lake, looked up and down.

He's fine. Relax.

* * *

Ren went back to Ruddock and they went together to Cabin 5, where two crime scene techs were at work. The place looked like it hadn't been opened in decades.

'I don't think it happened here,' said Ren. She went over to the faucet and turned it on. Water sputtered out of it.

Where the heck did Clyde go?

He's going to kill himself.

Stop.

Ruddock turned to her. 'You're worrying about Clyde, aren't you?'

She laughed. 'I am.'

'Why don't you call The Crow? All he might have needed was a stiff drink.'

Ren called the bar. Shannon picked up.

'Shannon, it's Ren Bryce. Firstly — is there water running to all the cabins?'

'Yes,' said Shannon.

'And is Clyde with you?'

'No,' said Shannon.

'Can you take a look out the window and see if you can see him on his way?'

'Sure,' said Shannon. Ren could hear her move out from behind the bar, she heard her footsteps on the timber floor. 'No,' said

Shannon. 'I can't. Is everything OK?'

'I wanted to talk to him, but he's disappeared.'

'Where are you?' said Shannon.

Shit. Not far from where Aaron was found.

'Try Cabin 8,' said Shannon, sidestepping the answer that had just dawned on her.

The cabin with the missing key.

'Why eight?' said Ren.

'Because Clyde's in beating-himself-up mode — he feels responsible for Aaron, no matter how many times I tell him he's not. Cabin 8 is where Clyde's sister fell through the deck all those years back. The kids all think it's haunted. Clyde sometimes goes there to feel bad about himself.'

Bad things happen around Clyde Brimmer.

Stop.

31

Clyde was sitting on a rock beside Cabin 8. Ren walked down to him.

'Hey,' said Ren, gently. 'How are you doing?'

He shrugged. 'I've been better.' He was holding a tattered photograph in his hand.

His sister. 'Who's that in the photograph?'

'My sister, Lizzie,' he said.

'How old was she?' said Ren.

'Ten,' said Clyde. 'This was taken the year she died.' He handed her the photo. Lizzie was a skinny, tanned little girl, dressed in a navy-and-white striped swimsuit, her wavy, sandy blonde hair falling around her shoulders, one hand trying to push it back off her face.

'She's adorable,' said Ren. She paused. 'I'm so sorry.'

Clyde nodded. 'Thank you.' He looked at her. 'I wish I could go back in time . . . '

'It wasn't your fault,' said Ren.

'That's what everyone keeps telling me,' said Clyde. 'But if I had just insisted on fixing that deck . . . '

'You're being too hard on yourself,' said Ren. 'You did what you were told to do by the owners. And you were only seventeen years old. Do the same owners still own this cabin?' said Ren.

'No. It was part of the sale when John Veir bought the site.'

Ren nodded. He looked up at her, expectant.

Why am I here? Well, I thought you might be dead. That's why. Jesus.

'OK,' said Ren. 'Is there anything you can think of, Clyde, anything you saw, anyone you saw here the night Aaron drowned — someone who looked out of place or was acting suspiciously?'

'No,' said Clyde, 'not that I can think of. I would have said. I told you about Aaron's back.'

'You did,' said Ren. She looked around. 'When was the last time you were here?'

'Christmas Eve.'

Jesus Christ. He comes here at Christmas.

Ren looked at the cabin. It was in a worse state than all the others, the timber battered, the paint flaking, roof tiles missing, a section of the roof caved in. The windows she could see were boarded up.

'I feel so bad about Aaron,' said Clyde. 'If I'd been here . . . '

'Don't,' said Ren. 'You weren't responsible for what happened to Aaron.'

He looked down at the photo of Lizzie.

'And what happened to your sister was a tragic accident,' said Ren.

She squeezed his shoulder, and walked away. As she made her way up the slope, a chill swept over her.

Bad things happen around Clyde Brimmer.

She turned back to look at him. His shoulders were shaking. He looked so small, hunched and weeping, against the vast expanse of the lake, next to the tumbledown cabin that haunted him still.

That's why you sit in the window of The Crow Bar; you find comfort in being vigilant, you think you need to make amends.

'Clyde?' she said.

He turned around and looked up at her with his soft blue, watery eyes.

Bad things happen around Clyde Brimmer.
No.
No: this is just a damaged, heartbroken man.

'Look after yourself,' she said.

* * *

When Ren got to The Crow Bar, Shannon was putting plates of sandwiches on the tables. She looked up. 'Just if any of your guys are hungry,' she said. 'They've a lot of ground to cover.'

'That's very kind of you,' said Ren.

'Did you find Clyde?'

'I did, thank you,' said Ren. 'That poor man.'

'I know,' said Shannon. 'I'm not sure he's ever going to be right.'

Ren heard a shout from inside the house. It was Seth.

'Fuck this shit!' he said. 'No!'

Ren was startled.

'PlayStation,' said Shannon. Her expression was a tolerant one.

PlayStation . . .

'Mind if I go in?' said Ren.

'Sure — go ahead,' said Shannon. 'It's down that hallway, where I was when you came in with Pete.'

Ren knocked on Seth's door. There was no answer. She walked in. Seth was sitting on a black beanbag on the floor, his back up against the bed, with headphones on, playing *Grand Theft Auto*.

His fingers were furiously, effortlessly, working the controls.

I have Nintendo muscle memory.

Caleb . . . Grand Theft Auto . . . PlayStation cheats . . . did Seth Fuller lure kids in here with this?

PlayStations are everywhere.

This one looks new. But there's a dent at the corner.

'No!' said Seth to the screen. 'Motherfucker! Fuck you! Fuck, fuck, fuck!'

He caught Ren out of the corner of his eye and jumped. He pulled off his headphones. 'You scared the crap out of me!' he said, struggling to sit upright in a black beanbag. On screen, his car crashed. 'Damn!' he said. Then he paused. 'Sorry. Is everything OK? Why are you here? Where's Aunt Shannon? Is she all right?'

'She's out in the bar — she's fine,' said Ren.

She looked at the PlayStation. 'How long have you had that?'

'I feel bad, but since Aaron died. It was Aaron's.'

'And when did he get it?'

'For Christmas. From Aunt Shannon.'

'What happened to the corner?'

Seth leaned in. 'What?'

175

'Do you see that dent in it?' said Ren.

'No,' said Seth. He walked over to it, crouched down, got to within three inches of it. 'Oh, yeah, now I see it.' He ran his thumb down it. 'No idea. Never noticed it before.'

You're a checked-out kind of guy.

'Did Caleb Veir ever play this?'

Seth shook his head. 'No.'

'Did Caleb ever mention getting a PlayStation to you?' said Ren.

'No,' said Seth. 'Why are you asking about PlayStations?'

'Just wondering,' said Ren. 'Can you call up the player list?'

'Sure,' said Seth. He did as she asked, and pointed to the names. 'That's me, and that's Aaron.'

'OK,' said Ren. 'Thanks.'

Shannon appeared in the hallway.

'Everything OK?' she said. Her eyes were filled with fear.

You have so much invested in this kid, you don't want him to be in any more trouble.

'Yes,' said Ren. She turned back to Seth. 'I hate to break your heart, here, Seth, but I'm going to need to take that PlayStation away.'

'What?' said Seth. 'Why?'

'We'd just like to take a look at it,' said Ren.

'Come over here, take a look at it right now,' said Seth.

'If they want to take it,' said Shannon. 'Let them take it.' She turned to Ren. 'The trauma.'

'Seth, I wanted to confirm something with you,' said Ren. 'You were here on the night

Aaron died, is that right?'

'Yes,' said Seth.

'Yes,' said Shannon at the same time.

Ren turned to Shannon. 'I read in your questionnaire that you were drinking that night . . . '

Shannon nodded. 'Yes.'

She knows where I'm going with this.

'But I checked on Seth before I went to bed,' said Shannon. 'And I could hear him snoring when I got up in the middle of the night to use the bathroom.'

'OK,' said Ren. 'Seth, do you know anything about a key that's missing from Clyde's keychain? It's the key to Cabin 8.'

Seth looked at Shannon, then back at Ren. 'No,' said Seth. 'But get him to check again — Clyde's got a million keys on there.'

Shannon nodded. 'I think he collects them as he goes, never gets rid of them, even ones he knows he'll never need again.'

Seth splayed his fingers, wiggled them. 'He's probably on an eternal search for the one that will unlock the mystery of Clyde Brimmer.' He smiled.

I like you, Seth Fuller.

I hope you're not a killer.

32

Jimmy Lyle walked the aisles of the strip-mall toy store, and it was his measured walk, the one he practiced in his mirror sometimes, so he could look less noticeable, so he would look calmer than he felt. He took a box down from the shelf, and looked at the picture. The girl in it looked so happy, in the sunshine, her black hair falling around her shoulders. He was hard right away. He looked around, saw a restroom in the corner, and moved quickly toward it. He pushed the door in, kicked off his heels, pulled off the tan pantyhose he was wearing, pushed his dress up around his waist, and took his dick out.

He closed his eyes, wallowed in visions of the girls he was going to see, their hair dark and floating, their skin white, their eyes, wide, alarmed, panicked. Wide. Alarmed. Panicked. Wide. Alarmed. Panicked.

Jimmy didn't last long. He collapsed against the wall, exploding, sucking in huge breaths, rolling toward the mirror to smile at his bright red face and bulging, streaming eyes. He could smell himself, all his smells, he could feel his heart pounding. He didn't wash his hands.

★ ★ ★

The sales assistant behind the counter tilted the box toward her to get a better look at it. Jimmy already had the cash in his hand. He wanted her to hurry the fuck up.

'A white inflatable swan,' she said. She beamed as she swiped the scanner across the barcode. 'These are all the rage.' She smiled brightly at him.

He knew his scars made people conscious of being extra kind to him. So many of these brief exchanges in his life were filled with effort on the part of other people. Sometimes he could see the little sparks of something else in their eyes.

Jimmy smiled back. 'It's for my daughter.'

'I'm sure she'll love it,' said the sales assistant.

Spark, spark, spark.

Jimmy knew it was fear. Sometimes he wanted Inside Jimmy to come out, he wanted to open his mouth wide and let his screams out like a searing blast that would melt away flesh, right down to the bone.

★　★　★

As he left the store, Jimmy Lyle's cell phone started to ring. He took it out, looked at the screen.

It was DEAD TO ME again.

This time, he picked up.

'Jimmy? It's Daddy.'

Jimmy said nothing.

'Did you get my message? I left you a message.'

Jimmy didn't reply.

'I had a visitor . . . and . . . it's not good. That little Mexican girl . . . '

179

Still, Jimmy didn't reply.

'She's goddamn loco,' said his daddy. 'Loco.' He chuckled.

There it was again — the reaching out, searching for commonality. Jimmy could feel the blood pounding at his temple.

'I'm sorry, son,' said his daddy. 'I'm sorry for everything.'

A surge of anger shook Jimmy. Inside Jimmy was pushing against his ribcage. He could picture small fissures breaking out across his bones. He was trembling. Inside Jimmy flared up again, vibrated, hurt.

'No, you're not,' said Jimmy. At first, his voice barely made it, and it felt as if the strength inside him was going only to fuel the pounding in his head.

'What was that, son?'

'No, you're not!' roared Jimmy, Inside Jimmy, out. 'You're not sorry! You're *afraid* is what you are. You're a scared old man. You're weak and you're terrified and alone. Don't dress that up like sorry and try to sell it to me. I'm not buying.'

'Please, Son. I need you to — '

'Don't need me, Daddy! Don't need me! It won't end well.'

'Please . . . '

'We had a deal,' said Jimmy, 'and I'm done.'

His daddy's voice dropped to a snarl. 'No, you're not.'

The line hummed. Jimmy's heart hummed along with it. Tears welled in his eyes. He wiped them away. His lips trembled.

'OK, Daddy,' said Jimmy. Inside Jimmy, in again. 'What do you need?' He swiped at his tears. He mouthed the word 'no' over and over, so he could try it the next time. *Out loud*, so he could be strong. He mouthed again. 'No, Daddy, no. No — this time. This time? No.'

'What do you need me to do?' said Jimmy. 'Tell me, Daddy.'

Jimmy heard sounds; breathing, shuffling.

'Daddy? Are you still there?' said Jimmy.

'I am, Son. I need you to . . . maybe bring me a few of my things. Something to watch.'

With a lightning-fast reflex, Jimmy's thumb shot out and ended the call.

★   ★   ★

Jimmy got to the car, carrying the bag from the store, his heart pounding. He popped the trunk. It was an automatic gesture. It was foolish. He quickly slammed it shut, looked around, as if anyone would be able to see what was inside.

His eye was drawn to the line of dumpsters along the wall. He looked for cameras. There were none. He checked his watch: it was two hours to darkness. He had some ideas how he could spend the time.

33

Ren got back to the hotel at nine that night. She parked outside, closed her eyes and listened to the rain pounding on the roof, pouring down the windshield. She reached into the back seat and pulled her raincoat toward her. She struggled into it, and pulled the oversized hood up. She took a deep breath, opened the car door, and ran.

★   ★   ★

The Do Not Disturb sign was still hanging on the door knob of her hotel room where she had left it that morning. She went inside, straight into the bathroom to hang up her coat. She glanced around. Her heart plunged.

Someone's been in here. It smells different. It smells like man. And it hasn't been serviced.

She looked at the space around the sink.

I did not leave my soap bag there.

She felt a spike of anxiety.

Paranoia.

No.

Someone was in here.

She went into the bedroom. In the shadows, she could see her suitcase, some notes, her file folders. She had left more notes out on the bed because she was running late. She had left the Do Not Disturb sign on the door.

Like that's a security measure.

Anyone could have been able to look at those notes.

Shit. Shit. Shit.

She sat down on the bed and called Reception. She hung up before they answered.

Paranoia.

She was about to call Gary.

No way: he will kill you. She had done it before, and he went ballistic, bawled at her in front of everyone about running a command center out of her hotel room.

She called Reception again. 'Hi there, it's Ren Bryce in 310. Was anyone in my room today while I was out?'

'Yes, ma'am,' said the receptionist.

Noooooo! How unbefuckinglievably unprofessional.

You're the one who left your notes out.

It's a small-town hotel . . . what did you expect? More! Always!

'We've been having problems with some of the showers on your floor,' said the receptionist. 'I know yours has been working OK, but we had our plumber check them all. We just need to make sure everything is OK.'

Oh, thank God. 'Would you mind letting me know the next time someone needs to access my room?' said Ren. *Because I can't fucking stand my privacy being invaded.* 'And if you can't reach me in my room, can you please call my cell phone before allowing anyone to come in?'

Or maybe I could tidy my stuff away . . .

'Yes, ma'am,' said the receptionist. 'I apologize

183

for any inconvenience.'

Inconvenience . . . a great sweeping fuck of a word.

'Could I get the name of the plumber?' said Ren. *Just in case . . .*

Pause. 'Sure . . . it's J. J.'s Plumbing Services — J. J. Nash.'

'Thank you,' said Ren. She googled J. J. Nash on her phone. His company was five years old, based in Tate. His testimonials all ended with four and five stars. The photo was of a smiling but slightly sad-eyed man in his mid-twenties.

Move along, nothing to see here.

★ ★ ★

Ren still hadn't turned on the lights in the bedroom. She stood up, made her way over to the window. The rain was relentless. She stood in the darkness, separated from the night by the icy glass. She started to unbutton her shirt.

Ben ripping my shirt off . . . losing my buttons.

Ben.

Ben.

Ben.

Tonight, it is just you.

I want you. I want your arms, your beautiful face. I want every part of you.

And I can't have it. I can't have it ever again.

She took off her shirt, threw it on the back of the chair. She unhooked her bra, threw it on top. She went to her bag and took out a faded black Dropkick Murphys T-shirt with a skull and crossbones on the front. She held it up to her face, breathed in.

Loser.

Don't.

She put it on, looked at her reflection in the glass. She finished undressing, then pulled on a pair of loose black shorts that were shorter than the T-shirt. She tied her hair in a ponytail, grabbed her laptop, went over to the bed, lay down and curled toward the window to lose herself in the drenched and clouded world outside.

Her phone beeped with a text.

Go away.

She reached out, took the phone from the nightstand and pulled it toward her. She held it above her face, squinted at the screen. The text was from Paul Louderback.

Are you OK? Missed you at dinner.

She replied.

Just shy. ;-)

He replied:

One of my favorite things about you.

Then:

Want company?

Ren punched in:

Are you fucking high?

She deleted it. And replied:

Working . . .

He typed back.

Sure you're OK?

Sure you're not just looking to get laid?

She sent:

Yes, honestly. Sleep well. And thanks. XX

I should just send him a text:
I am wearing my dead boyfriend's T-shirt.
She touched her hand to her heart.
Ben Rader, I miss you so much.
Work. Forget.
She sat up, propped against the pillows and opened a photo of Caleb Veir.

Where are you? Did your daddy kill you? Did your mommy?

Did you run from a home you didn't love? Why did you fall out with your mother? Did she do something to you? Did your daddy come home after work, bitching about the inmates at BRCI, calling them psychos, or did he make sure they were humanized? You knew Seth Fuller had been at BRCI . . . did you allow him to befriend you to provoke your father? Did it provoke your father?

Were you a trusting kind of kid? Would an adult buying you comics and candy just seem like kindness to you, seem unthreatening? Or what if a man like Franklin J. Merrifield approached you? Would you have been afraid of him? Could he have mentioned your father to earn your trust? What made you afraid? Who made you afraid?

Ren opened a new document and started typing.
John Veir lost his temper and killed Caleb accidentally . . .

John Veir killed Aaron and Caleb because he is a pedophile and was abusing them.

Teddy Veir lost her temper and killed Caleb accidentally . . .

186

Teddy Veir killed both boys to get back at John and Shannon for having an affair.

Teddy Veir killed her son to get the same attention her husband gave his mistress when her son died.

Franklin J. Merrifield killed Caleb Veir.

Franklin J. Merrifield abducted Caleb Veir, but has not killed him.

Another former inmate from BRCI abducted/killed Caleb to get back at John Veir for something.

Seth Fuller killed Aaron Fuller and/or Caleb Veir because he is a pedophile.

Aaron's death and Caleb's disappearance are not connected.

Caleb Veir ran away to see if his parents really cared about him, to give them a fright.

Caleb Veir ran away to bring his parents closer together, because he knew his father had been having an affair.

Caleb Veir ran away because he was disgusted about his father's affair and thought his mother was weak.

Caleb Veir is still alive, being held by person(s) unknown.

Ren's eyes started to close.

It's all too depressing.

Make it go away.

34

Ren woke up with a start at midnight. Her laptop had slid on to the bed beside her. She sat up, pulled it on to her lap and re-read her list. She added Alice Veir's name at the bottom with a string of question marks. She re-read everything again. She stopped at Merrifield.

Hold on . . . Merrifield . . . claims he was wrongfully convicted. Alice Veir . . . is on a wrongful conviction case. Caleb's last phone call was to . . . Alice Veir. Alice Veir has no children. Caleb is the only child in her life. Could he have been seen as a weak spot? Could Merrifield have wanted Alice Veir's help on his case? Would he have gone to any lengths to get it?

★ ★ ★

Ren went to YouTube and searched for the TV show that Alice Veir had appeared on. She pressed Play.

'Ahead of next month's International Innocence Program Conference in Portland, Oregon, tonight our panel consists of four lawyers working in the field of wrongful conviction. It's a hot topic right now, following the recent success of Netflix documentary, *Making a Murderer*, which seems to have gotten the entire world talking . . . '

The presenter introduced the guests. Alice Veir

was striking in her sternness, stiff posture, and conservative dress. Her deep brown hair was wavy, cut in a short, unflattering style. She had the same broad lower jaw as her brother, the same dark, steely eyes.

You are the kind of lawyer who is hired to be unleashed.

The presenter turned to Alice: 'Let me start with you, Alice Veir. You are the odd one out here tonight, in that you are not affiliated with the Innocence Project, and this is, in fact, your first wrongful conviction case. Why don't you talk to us about your client, Anthony Boyd Lorden? He was jailed for life back in 1995 for the murder of sixteen-year-old high school student, Kevin Dunne, who he had picked up hitch-hiking . . . '

'If I may,' said Alice, 'I'd like to begin by saying that Anthony Boyd Lorden is an innocent man, who has spent twenty-one years in prison for a crime he did not commit. There was not one piece of evidence that linked my client to the body of Kevin Dunne.'

'But what you haven't mentioned is that your client confessed,' said the presenter.

Alice nodded. 'Yes,' she said, 'and I know this is one of the toughest things for people to wrap their brain around — why someone would confess to a crime they didn't commit. Let me try to explain: there's a type of false confession called coercion-compliant. It's when people confess because they are so broken down, so desperate, so exhausted, so *lied* to, that they will say anything to get out of an interview room. Sometimes, it can be as simple as that. Many suspects — or witnesses — believe that because they didn't commit the crime, there will be no evidence to back up their confession, therefore they couldn't possibly be convicted. But, of course, sadly, as everyone on this panel knows, that's not how it works.'

The other panelists nodded.

'It's my view,' said Alice, 'that the investigation into Kevin Dunne's death was fast-tracked for political reasons. It was not carried out in the interest of justice. The lack of evidence is staggering.' She raised a finger for each item on her list. 'No DNA — not a hair, a fingerprint, a droplet of sweat, blood spatter — nothing. There was no *motive*. There was no *weapon*. Let me make this very clear: I'm not denying that my client stopped on the side of the road and picked up Kevin Dunne, who was hitch-hiking on a dark, rainy night. Anthony admitted that from day one. What I am saying, though, is that when Anthony let Kevin Dunne out by the side of the road, Kevin Dunne was very much alive and well. That he was not seen by passing motorists can be explained by the fact that it was raining, it was a rural road, therefore, extremely dark, and he was dressed in dark clothing: he would have been almost invisible.'

'What do you believe happened to Kevin Dunne?' said the presenter.

'I believe he was beaten to death, consistent with the autopsy findings,' said Alice, 'but I know that my client had nothing to do with it.'

'Your client was the last person to see the victim alive,' said the presenter.

190

'With all due respect,' said Alice, 'the last person to see Kevin Dunne alive was his killer.'

Ooh. Nice one.

Ren expected that was Alice Veir's parting shot — she had delivered the facts of the case, she had delivered a memorable closing line. But the presenter wasn't ready to let her go just yet.

'Now,' said the presenter, glancing down at her notes, 'there was also an eyewitness who placed Anthony Boyd Lorden close to the location where Kevin Dunne's body was eventually found one year after he disappeared.'

'Eyewitness testimony is notoriously flawed,' said Alice, 'and that's been proven time and time again. There are a huge number of parameters that impact on its reliability: the lighting, the distance from the eyewitness to the suspect, how the selection of suspects is shown to the eyewitness, what is said to the eyewitness. To give you one example: if I'm a police officer and I show you six faces on a sheet of paper and I ask you 'which one of these men did you see on XYZ road?', you will deduce that the suspect is among those men, right? However, if you are asked, 'Is the man you saw that night one of the men on this page?', then, that's a whole different matter. You cannot underestimate the factors that can lead to misidentification. As human beings we want to please, we want to help, we want to give the right answer. While I do believe that the eyewitness was acting in good faith, this was a case of mistaken identity, affected by various other factors. And one year on — how could this eyewitness have been sure?'

'Why did you take on this case, Ms Veir?' said the presenter. 'After all this time?'

'It was in 1991 that Anthony Boyd Lorden stopped to pick up Kevin Dunne,' said Alice. 'At that time, I was a young law student at the University of Washington. I was studying the law so I could help people, so I could make a difference. And that's exactly what I'm going to do here: make a difference in Anthony Boyd Lorden's life.' She paused. 'Or what remains of it, after this travesty of a conviction.'

I wouldn't want to be on the other side of a courtroom to you, Alice Veir.

Alice was resisting the presenter's attempts to move on to the next panelist. As she was thanking her, Alice interrupted.

'For any of your viewers who are interested,' said Alice, 'I'd like to direct you to Anthony's interrogation video, which has been posted on the website justiceforanthony.com. Remember, this boy was seventeen years old, and this was a seven-hour interrogation without a break. The video has been edited — in a fair and unbiased manner — down to three hours just in the hopes that people might watch it. If you do, what you will witness is the brutal, relentless, and devastating abuse of a young man. Those two detectives knew exactly what they were doing: they knew the power of their words, they chose the volume at which they delivered them. They knew the power of their physicality, their facial expressions. They knew the effect of their threats, the delivery and withdrawal of praise . . . ' She paused. 'Anthony Boyd Lorden was one of the unlucky ones — someone who put himself in the frame, who volunteered to become a part of our justice system, a system that has drastically failed him, that has robbed him of the best years of his life. Anthony came forward to give information he thought would aid in a homicide investigation. He drove twenty miles to do that, because he remembered that boy who died, he had met him, he had kindly offered him a ride on a dark, wet night. And he let him out on the side of the road where he had asked to be let out. Anthony reluctantly watched Kevin Dunne walk away into the darkness: he had urged him to wait until they reached the next town where there would be more light. And one year later, when Anthony learned that the boy had been found dead, he was devastated. He went straight to the investigating officers to offer help again. And one year after that, he was rewarded by being robbed of the next twenty-one years of his life. Where is the justice in that? I believe in justice. And I will do everything in my power to make sure that not another moment of Anthony Boyd Lorden's life is taken away from him.'

The presenter turned to the next woman. 'I'm now going to go to our next panelist, Emma Ridley, who is a lawyer with the Innocence Project Northwest.' She paused, then clearly went off-script. 'Maybe you ladies need to come together on this one . . . this falls into your region, Emma, am I right?'

Eye-dart from the Innocence Project lawyer. 'Well, yes, that would be great,' she said. 'We would very much welcome that opportunity.'

Tense smile from Alice Veir, and the light of a small flame in her eyes.

What the heck was that about?

* * *

Ren went to justiceforanthony.com. The interrogation video was front and center of the home page. Ren checked the time. It was twelve forty-five.

I have three hours to spare. I've probably got twice that if I incorporate the time I usually spend staring at the ceiling.

She hit Play. Anthony Boyd Lorden appeared on screen. He had tight-cut brown hair, good skin, broad shoulders. He looked fit and healthy, young, eager, and trusting.

There is something about you . . .

He was sitting in a chair that had been backed right up against the wall of a cramped interview room. Two huge detectives sat opposite him, dwarfing him, their backs to the camera.

* * *

Ren had tears in her eyes before the first hour was up.

You fucking assholes.

This is what Alice Veir fights against. This is the good fight.

Ren watched the video again on fast forward, and it was like a flicker book showing the deflation of a soul.

Outside, in the quiet night, the sound of sirens erupted.

Ren's cell phone beeped with a text. She looked down at her screen. The text was from Gary.

Fire at the Veirs' . . .

35

Two fire trucks, an ambulance and two squad cars were parked outside the Veirs' house. Ren parked across the street. A weak strand of smoke drifted up from behind the house.

There were neighbors standing out front, others watching from their windows. Ren walked up to the open ambulance doors. An EMT was finishing his checks on John Veir, who was sitting in the back, dressed in pajama bottoms and a T-shirt, his bare feet on the metal step. There was a blanket around his shoulders. He jumped up when he saw Ren, stormed over to her. He raised his hand and stabbed a finger at her, sending a waft of kerosene her way.

'This is your fucking fault!' he said. 'All your fault. This was Merrifield! You're all wasting your time on me when it's clearly fucking Merrifield — '

Whoa, whoa, whoa. What the fuck? 'OK,' said Ren, 'first of all — stop pointing at me.'

'How else can you explain this?' said John, gesturing toward the house. 'The guy's a fucking arsonist!'

Ren held her two palms up to him. 'John, we asked you about Merrifield, day one, and you told us there were no issues between you, that you didn't really know him. Is there anything you'd like to say now?'

'How has Merrifield not been found?' said

John. 'And we have to pay the price — '

This is all very strange. 'Why don't you sit back down, and tell me why you would think that Merrifield would abduct your son, then come back and carry out an arson attack on your house? Or do you think he's responsible only for the arson attack?'

He looked at her, dead-eyed. 'Both, obviously.'

'Yet — you were the one to shut that avenue down immediately.'

John sat back down on the step of the ambulance. Ren nodded to the EMT to give them space.

'Maybe I'm just clutching at straws . . . '

Ren looked around. 'Where's your wife?'

'Luckily, she's at Patti's — she swapped nights with one of her friends.'

'OK, talk me through what happened tonight,' said Ren.

'Someone spray-painted the wall and lit the garbage on fire.'

'Let's start at the beginning,' said Ren.

'Uh . . . OK,' said John. 'I was taking a shower. When I came into the bedroom, I saw smoke at the window. I threw on some clothes, ran down and out into the back garden, saw the flames. I called 9-1-1. Then I thought of the garden hose. I went around the side of the house, got that going. I was putting it out by the time the fire trucks arrived.'

Hmm.

'What did they spray paint?' said Ren.

'Pedophile killer,' said John. 'F-I-L-E, though. And K-I-L-L-R, no 'e'. Whoever did it emptied out the recycling container, lit that on fire. Looks like they took a drum of kerosene out of the garage.'

'The garage was open?' said Ren.

John nodded. 'I leave it open . . . in case . . . ' he shrugged. 'In case Caleb comes back.'

'You don't think he would ring the doorbell?' said Ren. *I'm sorry, but seriously.*

'None of this makes sense,' said John. 'Anything's a possibility, as far as I'm concerned.'

Yes. Such as you are the person responsible for this circus.

* * *

Ren walked over to the officer guarding the driveway, flashed her creds, and went around the back of the house. Smoke was rising from a damp pile of garbage. There was a heavy smell of burnt plastic and kerosene.

Ruddock was standing with his hands on his hips in the middle of the garden. A hose was discarded on the grass. The patio was drenched. Ren followed his gaze to the back wall of the garage where PEDOFILE KILLR was spray-painted shakily.

'Needs a plus sign . . . or ampersand,' said Ren. 'Unless they're saying he killed a pedophile, whereupon I don't see a problem. I might look through my cabinet of pedofiles . . . '

Ruddock smiled.

'Any sign of the paint can?' said Ren.

Ruddock shook his head. 'No.'

198

'Veir did this, right?' said Ren.

Ruddock gave her a measured look.

'Where's Wiley?' said Ren.

'I don't know,' said Ruddock. 'He got the same message as everyone else.'

Ren walked down to the back of the garden, and turned to face the house. She took a step back. She tripped, landed on her butt.

'Shit.'

Ruddock rushed over to her, helped her up.

'Thank you,' said Ren. *Wet ass. Great.*

They both looked down to see what she had tripped over, ran the beams of their flashlights over the grass. It was a small piece of a flagstone.

'There's another one,' said Ren. 'It looks like part of a path . . . to nowhere.'

'Maybe there was another structure down here at some stage,' said Ruddock.

They walked back toward the house, and met Gary, Sylvie and Paul coming toward them.

Ren filled them in.

'Did you talk to Veir on the way in?' she said.

'Not yet,' said Gary.

'Isn't it a little convenient?' said Ren. 'An arson attack while an arsonist is on the loose? And who spray paints a message on the *back* wall of a house? Isn't the point to expose someone to their whole community as a KILLR? With no 'e' . . . '

'Someone might have wanted the message to go only to John Veir and were covering their own ass by choosing the back of the house — quick escape over the back fence,' said Gary.

'We all know that bad spelling bullshit is done

199

by people trying to seem dumb,' said Ren. 'Is anyone buying the fact that this anonymous arsonist arrived with no kerosene, fingers crossed the garage door would be open, would contain fuel, etc., etc.?'

Yeah, didn't think so.

'I think Veir did it,' said Ren. 'And when Teddy wasn't home? There could be a pattern there: Teddy's gone, John Veir does bad things . . . ' She paused. 'Can I just say that I don't think there's a lot more for me to do here? I have a pounding headache.' *She lied.* 'So I'd like to absent myself from thinking about this big wet fiery distraction any further. Night, everyone.'

She walked away.

Fuck this bullshit.

She went around the front of the house, and had no choice but to walk past John Veir.

The smile is for the EMTs. The burrowing eye-fuck is for you.

What are you hiding?

Oh. Just one more thing . . .

She jogged over to him. 'John — was there ever a building behind your house?'

Eye-dart. 'Yes.' He paused. 'We bought the house off a family — they had built a separate dwelling for the grandmother.'

'What happened to it?' said Ren.

'We knocked it down to have more room for Caleb to play.'

Why the eye-dart?

36

The first person Ren walked into the next morning was Paul Louderback.

'How's your head?' he said.

'What?'

'Your headache . . . last night.'

Shit. 'Oh,' said Ren. 'Yes. It's fine.'

'You look tired.'

She stared at him. 'You know that's right up there with asking a woman when she's due . . . '

'Ooh . . . cranky.'

'Cranky — wow. You're on fire this morning.'

He raised his eyebrows. 'Have I done something?'

Yes. 'No, I'm sorry. I'm . . . just . . . ' *fucking bereft . . .* 'it's the case.'

Paul nodded. 'That's understandable.'

Really — you're buying that? I'm . . . fucking sad . . . I'm heartbroken. I don't want to sleep with you. I want to cry. And, yes, in your arms would be a great place to do that, but I don't trust your hands not to go anywhere else. I will lie there and cry, but part of me will be expecting to ward off an advance and where's the comfort in that?

'I'm sorry for being short,' she said. 'It wasn't a great night, even before I got to that shitshow at the Veirs.'

'So he got you at a bad time,' said Paul.

'What? John Veir?' said Ren. 'Do you believe

him? That it was Merrifield?'

Paul shook his head. 'No, but . . . '

Oh, I get it. 'But I shouldn't have let it get to me.'

'No, you shouldn't have.'

'Sorry.'

'No need.' He paused. 'I hope you know you can pick up the phone to me any time.' He looked at her with great kindness. 'And it doesn't have to be about the case.'

Oh, God, I'm such an asshole. 'I do know that,' said Ren. 'Thanks.'

'So . . . before the shitshow?' said Paul.

'Memories,' said Ren. 'Sadness.'

'I'm sorry,' said Paul.

'Also, though, I looked into Alice Veir's wrongful conviction case.' She filled him in.

'Do you think it's relevant to this?' said Paul.

'I don't know,' said Ren. 'If we're taking Caleb's disappearance in isolation, maybe. Could Alice Veir be a target through her work? What if Caleb was calling her because someone had approached him about her? Mentioned her name? Or he was concerned someone was following him? I don't think Alice Veir would tell us if she'd been threatened in any way. If Caleb's been abducted, his safe return could be dependent on her doing something.'

'It's worth looking into,' said Paul. 'Do you think her wrongful conviction guy is innocent? Could the real killer be getting nervous?'

Ren nodded. 'I do think he's innocent. There was one thing that was slightly odd, though: the show was a panel format and there were three

202

Innocence Project lawyers on it with her, one of whom was from Innocence Project Northwest — which covers the area where the Kevin Dunne murder happened — but there was definitely some tension between this lawyer and Alice Veir when the presenter suggested they collaborate.'

'So, let me get this straight — Alice Veir — a strong, smart woman — is a lone wolf,' said Paul. He gave Ren a meaningful look.

Ren laughed. 'Screw you, man.'

★ ★ ★

Ren went to her desk and looked up the Innocence Project Northwest. She found Emma Ridley's contact details and called her direct line.

'Emma, my name is Ren Bryce, I'm with the FBI — I'm in Tate, working on the Caleb Veir disappearance — '

'Yes,' said Emma. 'I'm familiar with that. How can I help?'

'It's actually about his aunt, Alice Veir,' said Ren. *How do I put this?* 'We're looking at every possible angle here, and whether this could be connected to anything that Alice Veir was working on. I watched the show you and Alice appeared on together, and I was wondering if you were aware of any particular reason that Alice had not come to you with the Anthony Boyd Lorden case?'

Emma let out a breath. 'Well, she didn't need to come to us — I went to her.'

'Oh,' said Ren.

'Yes,' said Emma. 'Before Alice Veir ever got

203

involved, we reached out to Lorden's original lawyers, and asked them if he would agree to us taking a look at his file, and he did. I studied Kevin Dunne's autopsy report very carefully. I consulted with a forensic anthropologist, who offered an alternative as to what happened to Kevin Dunne — that it was not, in fact, a homicide.'

Holy shit. 'Really?'

'Yes,' said Emma. 'Dunne had signs of two separate head traumas, but according to the anthropologist, they could also have been caused by him being struck from behind by the side-view mirror of a high vehicle, like an SUV or a pickup: this would have accounted for the skull fracture at the back of his head where he was hit by the mirror, and the skull fracture at the front of his head from when he hit the ground. Dunne was dressed in dark clothing, it was late at night: yes, it would have been a freak accident, but it's a very strong possibility. Because Lorden confessed, the autopsy photos weren't analyzed in any great detail, and even if they were, I think the idea that it was an assault was so ingrained in people's minds that there would have been a reluctance for opinion to shift. We see that a lot: we see, for example, victims' families still insisting that whoever was convicted for their loved one's murder was guilty, even after DNA evidence has exonerated them.'

'It's too much for people to bear that they may have contributed to someone's life being destroyed,' said Ren.

'Exactly,' said Emma.

'Did you talk to Alice Veir about your theory?' said Ren.

'Well, yes,' said Emma. 'What happened was that by the time I had received the report back from the forensic anthropologist, Alice Veir had approached Lorden and taken on his case.'

'So, he didn't reach out to her?'

'No — she approached him,' said Emma.

'And how did she react to your findings?' said Ren.

'She shut me down completely,' said Emma. 'I thought I'd made this amazing breakthrough, I was so excited, but she ruled it out completely, she said absolutely not, that she still believed that Dunne was the victim of an assault, just that it wasn't at the hands of her client.'

'Did she look at your evidence?' said Ren.

'I sent it to her,' said Emma, 'but I didn't hear anything back. I tried her a few times, but I had no luck. And then we were doing that show together. Awkward . . . '

'Do you think it might have been an ego thing?' said Ren. 'That she's not the type to want help?'

'I don't know,' said Emma, 'but she's an intimidating lady, so I didn't want to push it. I don't get it, though — it's excellent for her client. If Alice is only focusing on the confession being false; well, juries have a real hard time understanding why a person would make a false confession. When I started out doing this, it was the one thing that my family and friends found really hard to understand about my world

205

— why someone would confess to a crime they didn't commit. Now, though, my mom is online finding cases she wants me to take a look at, looking out for confessions, checking out who might have been coerced.'

'Good for her,' said Ren. 'Emma — would you mind emailing me that evidence?'

'Sure,' said Emma. 'No problem. It'll have to be Monday, because I'm in court all day and then out of town for the weekend.'

'That's no problem,' said Ren. 'And if you could keep this confidential . . . '

'Of course,' said Emma. 'I really feel for Lorden. I'm not sure that Alice Veir is going about this the right way. We have a lot of resources here, and we're happy to help. She doesn't seem interested.'

37

Ren went back into the CARD team and Ruddock and told them about her conversation with Emma Ridley.

'Well,' said Paul, 'see what the evidence says. Maybe their expert is mistaken or it's a flimsy argument.'

Ren nodded. 'Yeah — I can't see Alice Veir taking too well to someone who's not doing a flawless job — that could have been what the tension was all about: Emma Ridley thinking she's nailed something, Alice Veir begs to differ.'

Paul nodded.

'How are you getting on with the middle school dance night follow up?' said Ren.

'Nothing so far,' said Paul.

'Nothing from me, yet,' said Sylvie.

'We'll have footage from the traffic cams, and any CCTV or private cameras in the area called in,' said Ruddock.

One of the young Tate PD officers stuck his head in the door. He was holding a remote control.

'You might want to come out and see this,' he said.

The news was on and the anchor, a handsome guy in his mid twenties, was very excited about his next story, flagged by the photo of Caleb Veir in the top right-hand corner of the screen.

'In a dramatic twist in the investigation into

the disappearance of Tate boy, Caleb Veir,' he said, 'the Veir family home came under attack late last night. Speaking outside his home, John Veir, father of the missing boy, had this to say:

'This is devastating for my wife and me, as you can imagine. Our son is missing, we're suffering through that, and then this happens. The only thing that I'm grateful for is that my wife wasn't here at the time, and that no one was injured, or that the house didn't go up.'

'Mr Veir,' said the reporter, 'you've said yourself that there's been speculation on the Internet that you were somehow involved in the disappearance of your son. Would you like to take this opportunity to address those rumors?'

John nodded. 'Yes. I'd like to make it clear to anyone who's watching that I had nothing to do with the disappearance of my son, I love my son very much, and I just want him home. Those kind of rumors can cause real damage to people, and they can distract from an investigation. My wife and I want all law enforcement's resources to be focused on finding our son, not on looking at me as a suspect. Thank you.'

It returned to the studio. 'Sources close to the investigation are saying today that there could be a link between last night's attack and missing Black River Correctional Institute inmate, Franklin J. Merrifield, who escaped from BRCI just twenty-four hours before Caleb Veir was last seen. John Veir, as we know, is a corrections officer at that prison. Merrifield was eighteen months into a thirty-five-year sentence for robbery, homicide, rape, and . . . ?' He paused.

'Arson.' A photo of Merrifield appeared in the top right hand corner of the screen. 'Merrifield was last seen wearing his orange BRCI prison jumpsuit, but may now be dressed in civilian clothing. He has a history of violence, and should be considered extremely dangerous. If you do see him, do not approach him, but contact Salem PD on their tips line: 555-45-95-25.'

'Mute that,' said Ruddock to the officer.

'Who leaked the Merrifield connection?' said Ren.

'Me,' said Ruddock. He smiled. 'I'm thinking if Merrifield finds out that his name is being connected to a murdered boy, a missing one, and an arson attack, he might be very willing to come forward to clear his name. I don't think it matters that he was in prison when Aaron died. That could have been organized through an associate . . . '

Go, Ruddock.

'I need to talk to Alice Veir about Merrifield,' said Ren.

She went to her desk and called her.

'Alice? It's Ren Bryce here. Are you familiar with the missing inmate from BRCI — Franklin J. Merrifield?'

Pause. 'Yes,' said Alice. 'I believe he attacked John's house last night.'

'Do you?' said Ren.

'Well, it certainly makes sense to me,' said Alice.

Even without any evidence? You've changed your fucking tune. 'There's no evidence pointing to him,' said Ren. 'But, of course, we have to explore it as a possibility, which is why I'm calling you. Has he ever reached out to you about his case?'

Pause. 'Why would he do that?'

'Well, Merrifield claims he's innocent, he's just lost an appeal, and you're a lawyer working on a high-profile wrongful conviction case. He knows your brother from BRCI — '

'No, Merrifield has not approached me.'

Definitive, yet unconvincing.

Ren paused. 'How is the Anthony Boyd Lorden case going?'

Silence.

'I watched the news program you appeared on,' said Ren.

'It's progressing,' said Alice.

Ren waited.

'The whole thing was a travesty,' said Alice.

'What do you think happened that night?' said Ren.

'I believe that Kevin Dunne suffered a serious assault, but that it was not carried out by my client.'

'But you're not offering an alternative killer?' said Ren.

'That's not my job,' said Alice. 'There is no physical evidence linking my client to the assault, and his confession is not worth the paper it's written on. Did you know there have been three hundred and twenty-nine exonerations based on DNA testing since 1992, and one thousand six hundred and eight exonerations identified by the National Registry of Exonerations since 1989 when DNA was first used in US courts? Did you know that of that number, thirteen per cent of those adults had falsely confessed, but that that percentage rose to forty-two per cent in the case of juveniles? Forty-two per cent!'

Jesus. Blind me with stats. 'Have you spoken about it with Emma Ridley from the Innocence Project Northwest?' said Ren.

Silence. 'Yes,' said Alice. 'I'm sorry, but what is your interest in this case?' Her tone had sharpened. 'With all due respect . . . shouldn't your focus be on Caleb?'

'It is,' said Ren. *Of fucking course it is, you snippy bitch.* 'I'm just curious what you thought of the theory proposed by Emma Ridley. That Kevin Dunne may have been clipped by the side-view mirror of a passing vehicle? Have you read her report?'

'I scanned it,' said Alice. 'It's not the focus of my defense.'

Your hackles are skyward.

'Did you show it to a Medical Examiner to maybe try to get a second opinion?' said Ren.

'I'm sorry,' said Alice. 'I'm under a lot of stress . . . '

You've noticed I've noticed.

'I'm worried about Caleb, about my brother, about Teddy,' said Alice. 'And this case is all-consuming. The trial is coming up. I'm raising awareness about false confessions too, so I've a lot of speaking engagements. I'm trying to do the best I can for my client. He was *seventeen years old*, zero evidence showed he did anything, but here we are: twenty-four years later. The prosecution constructs a wonderful, convincing narrative, and bam, Anthony is jailed. It's terrifying, is it not? He's forty-one years old — just four years younger than me. I've had my life — what has he had?'

'You're discounting Emma Ridley's alternative scenario,' said Ren, 'So your case is based on . . .'

'A golden triangle of police coercion, flawed eyewitness testimony, and incompetent legal representation.'

★ ★ ★

Ren got off the call, sat back, and thought of Anthony Boyd Lorden, his eager face.

Imagine being so utterly broken, so distraught, so traumatized, so terrified, that one word transforms your entire future: yes. In one horrifying swipe, your twenties are taken away, your thirties, your milestones, decades of significance, where love happens, where life happens, where relationships are formed, relationships with good people, not charged, violent, petty, feuds behind prison walls.

That one word: yes. Yes, I did it. Yes, I took a weapon no one ever found, and I bashed in the skull of a boy who I gave a ride too. A stranger with whom I spent just twenty minutes of my seventeen years, talking about football, talking about summer jobs, talking about school, talking about cars. YES. I am a monster. A monster who stopped to pick up a guy dressed in black who was walking in the dark. I am a monster. Right? I am a monster. Am I not? I did this. Didn't I?

* * *

She thought of John Veir.

Am I damning him?

What if it was Merrifield? What if John and Alice are being forced to lie?

Jesus Christ. Imagine being part of the team who wrongfully convicted someone.

I don't think I'd ever get over it.

* * *

She went back through her notes and found one person she thought might shed light on Merrifield and Veir: Rob Lockwood, Veir's friend, and Merrifield's psychologist.

38

Shannon Fuller was lying on her living room sofa in the dark, staring at the television. It wasn't on. Her son had been murdered, her property had been trampled on, her house and bar had been torn apart, she had spent hours putting it back together again, then she had shut out the world, crying on and off all night. She had heard the vans arrive again this morning, heard the search teams talking, shouting, laughing, told Seth to take care of everything.

She got up slowly, sat on the edge of the sofa, bent down and picked up the pile of damp tissues from the floor. She put them in the garbage in the kitchen and wandered out into the bar.

Seth was leaning on the counter, playing with a piece of card. He jumped when Shannon came out.

'You scared the crap out of me,' he said.

'It's very easy to scare the crap out of you these days,' said Shannon. 'What time is it?'

'Lunchtime,' said Seth.

'You didn't fix any food for them.'

He shook his head. 'No. I'm sorry. I didn't want to disturb you.'

'That's OK,' she said. 'I'm glad you didn't.'

She looked around the bar. 'I guess everyone will steer clear of us now,' said Shannon. 'We're bad luck, we're too sad, or we're crawling with police.'

'John Veir was on the news this morning,' said Seth. 'Someone torched his house.'

'What?'

'Well, not torched — lit his garbage can on fire.'

'Are they OK?' said Shannon.

Seth nodded. 'They're linking it to that missing inmate . . .'

'Really?'

Seth nodded.

Shannon walked around the front of the bar, pulled up a stool in front of him. 'Could you get me a Coke, please?'

Seth was about to turn around when Shannon placed her hand on top of his, pressed down on it hard, so he couldn't move it.

'I'm drawing a line right here, right now,' said Shannon. 'I agreed to trust you that wherever you were the night Aaron died is your private matter. I watched you lie so easily to that FBI agent. And I lied for you. You're jumpy as hell. I'm not sure why, but you're going to have to be honest with me about everything from now on. So let's start with what's in your hand.'

She grabbed his wrist, turned his hand over and he opened his palm. There was a business card in it. She looked up at him. 'Special Agent Ren Bryce? OK . . . what's going on here? The truth: now.'

Seth let out a breath. 'Nothing.'

'Nothing is never nothing with you, Seth Fuller. You're thinking of contacting an FBI agent? Talk to me.'

He weighed it up, his shoulders sunk, he

opened his mouth to speak.

Shannon smiled. 'You've been doing that since you were four years old: slumping your shoulders, dragging yourself into a conversation you really don't want to be a part of.'

He smiled, but there was sadness in it. 'You got me.' He paused. 'Let me pour your Coke.'

He handed it to her, took his time getting eye contact. 'You have to promise me you won't judge.'

'Have I ever judged you?' said Shannon.

'No,' said Seth. 'No. I'm sorry, but . . . there's something that's been on my mind about John Veir . . . '

'John?' said Shannon. 'What about him?'

'Did he ever tell you about Franklin J. Merrifield . . . and me?'

'You?' said Shannon.

Seth took a deep breath. 'Merrifield was dealing in BRCI — '

Shannon put her hands over her face. 'No, Seth. Please don't tell me — '

'You promised not to judge.'

He took her hands gently away from her face, squeezed them.

'I'm sorry,' said Shannon. 'Go ahead, sweetheart . . . but, you're breaking my heart, here.'

'So Merrifield was dealing heroin and TNT — '

'Heroin!' said Shannon. 'You — '

'No!' said Seth. 'I didn't do heroin, I swear to God.'

'TNT, then?' said Shannon. 'I don't even know what that is.'

'Fentanyl . . . patches.' He lowered his eyes.

Shannon's eyes were lit with anger. 'Jesus Christ, Seth. Fentanyl? And you were taking it?'

Seth nodded.

'What?' said Shannon. 'Chewing patches? I saw a news program about that. It's an overdose waiting to happen. It's, like, fifty times stronger than heroin.'

Seth looked away. 'About a hundred, actually. And I only did it once.'

'Jesus Christ — once is all it takes! What were you thinking? That patch is for putting on your skin! To *slowly* release it — if you've got cancer or you've had an operation or . . . it's not for you! And after getting off heroin, you don't have a clue what your tolerance is like. Why would you gamble with your life that way?'

'I know, I know,' said Seth. 'I haven't touched it since that last time with Merrifield. I swear to God.'

'When was that? What happened?'

'Like, eight months ago,' said Seth. 'That's what I'm trying to tell you about. This one night, I got a patch from Merrifield. You know how Fent makes you; sleepy, slows your breathing and shit. I started nodding out, but it was weird, I was kind of aware that this wasn't good. And I remember Merrifield, he was still in the cell with me, I remember thinking, 'He's going to let me die right here, he doesn't give a shit if I die right here.''

Shannon was shaking her head, struggling to hold back tears.

'Then John Veir showed up,' said Seth.

39

Ren called Rob Lockwood, the BRCI psychologist, and agreed to meet him in a coffee shop in Salem, instead of going through the visitors' procedure at the prison. She ordered coffee for both of them, and they sat in a quiet corner.

'So, how long have you been treating Franklin J. Merrifield?' said Ren.

'For the past year or so,' said Lockwood.

'Were you surprised he escaped?' said Ren.

'Yes, actually,' said Lockwood. 'I mean, I knew he was unhappy with the outcome of his appeal, and he was angry and very bitter at his buddy, his accomplice, but Merrifield's not very bright. I don't think he would have the smarts to pull something like that off.'

'That's slightly different from having the desire to escape, though,' said Ren. 'If he got help on the inside and bought his way into someone else's plans, or made himself indispensable for other reasons, then anything could have happened.'

'Merrifield is a loner,' said Lockwood. 'I just can't see how that would work.'

'Were you aware of any contact between him and John Veir, outside of routine interaction?' said Ren.

'No.'

'Do you think Merrifield could have had anything to do with Caleb's disappearance?' said Ren.

'I don't know,' said Lockwood. He shrugged. 'I wish I could give you a better answer than that.'

'What was his reaction to losing his appeal?' said Ren. 'Just anger, or was there more to it? Did he have any plans to do anything further about it?'

Lockwood nodded. 'He mentioned reaching out to a lawyer who specialized in wrongful conviction lawsuits.'

Holy. Shit. 'Did he mention a name?'

Lockwood shook his head. 'No.'

'You know John Veir's sister has quite a high-profile wrongful conviction case,' said Ren.

'Really?' said Lockwood. 'John didn't mention that.'

'Did Merrifield?'

'Not to me.'

'Was Merrifield the type to want revenge?' said Ren.

'Yes,' said Lockwood. 'Absolutely. He held grudges. That was the kind of guy he was. Small slights, big ones — it didn't matter.'

'I know John Veir is a friend of yours,' said Ren. 'I'd like to ask you about him.'

'Sure,' said Lockwood. 'Go ahead.'

'Do you think it's likely that he could have carried out the arson attack on his own house?' said Ren.

Lockwood's eyes went wide. 'John? No way. No . . . what makes you think that?'

'Do you think Merrifield could have done it, whether he took Caleb or not?'

'Well, it wasn't exactly a wise move,

considering the law enforcement and media attention around the house,' said Lockwood, 'so, yes — like I said, Merrifield wasn't the smartest of men . . . '

'John's very intense,' said Ren. 'I get the sense that he's suppressing a lot of anger. Am I right?'

Lockwood tilted his head. 'John suffers from PTS, so that explains the intensity. But he's not an angry man, not in my opinion, whether I'm speaking as a friend, colleague or psychologist. He's very compassionate, in fact. He saw some terrible things when he was overseas.'

Ren nodded. 'Do you know much about his relationship with Caleb?'

'They have their ups and downs,' said Lockwood, 'but he adores that boy.'

'Has there been any change in John's behavior recently?' said Ren.

'No.'

'Have you met Caleb?' said Ren.

'No,' said Lockwood, 'but John talks about him a lot.'

'In what sense?'

'Mainly positive,' said Lockwood, 'but he mentions the bad behavior too.'

'Has he looked for your advice?' said Ren.

There was a flicker of a frown on Lockwood's face. 'Not in the professional sense — but more like a 'what can you do?' attitude. Caleb was like a teenager a little before his time. I told John to give him some responsibility, have him do volunteer work, do some odd jobs for a neighbor. It would teach him to work hard, it would give him goals, a sense of achievement. So, that's what he did, and it seemed to help.'

'Good idea,' said Ren. 'I hadn't heard about Caleb doing that.'

Could he have crossed paths with a killer that way?

'Why did you call John last Sunday?' said Ren.

'Just to chat,' said Lockwood. ' "How's your weekend going . . . ?" '

'Did John mention Caleb?' said Ren.

'Just that he was there with him, that's all.'

Ren nodded. 'OK.'

★ ★ ★

Back at Tate PD, Ren filled Ruddock in on her conversation with Lockwood. 'Did you know Caleb did odd jobs for someone?'

'Yes,' said Ruddock. 'It's somewhere on one of the Veirs' questionnaires.'

'How did I miss that?' said Ren.

'It was a recent addition,' said Ruddock. 'Neither of them had put it on the original . . . it came up in a later interview. Caleb had stopped working there a month before he disappeared, so the Veirs just didn't think of it.'

'OK,' said Ren. 'Let me go take a look.'

★ ★ ★

Ren went back to her desk and looked through the Veirs' questionnaires. The woman Caleb worked for was called Rose Dennehy. She was eighty-three years old, a widow with three grown-up daughters, two of whom lived out of

221

state, one of whom lived in Salem. Ren called Paul in the command center.

'Did you send anyone to talk to a Rose Dennehy?' said Ren. 'Caleb did odd jobs for her.'

'No,' said Paul. 'She wasn't a priority.'

'Mind if I go talk to her?' said Ren.

'Not at all,' said Paul. 'Go ahead.'

40

Rose Dennehy brought Ren into her kitchen, and immediately put the kettle on, without even asking if she wanted a drink. She was a little slow on her feet, but moving around steadily, eager to make Ren feel at home. She set coffee and cake down on the table.

You sweet woman. 'Thank you,' said Ren, taking a drink. 'So, we're trying to figure out who may have crossed paths with Caleb, either once-off or regularly, while he was here. Can you help me with that?'

Rose nodded. 'Caleb comes here every second Saturday to shovel snow, bring logs in from the woodshed, clean the gutters or help me out with whatever small jobs I need. His father drops him off at eleven a.m., and he usually finishes up around two.'

'And the last time he was here was a month ago,' said Ren. 'February eleventh?'

'Yes.' She paused. 'The poor dear. I hope he's OK.'

'I know,' said Ren.

'About who he would have met,' said Rose, ' . . . my neighbors, if they were around. And every Saturday, my daughter, Eileen — she lives in Salem — she stops by around eleven thirty to take me shopping, and drops me home by one. So Caleb would know Eileen a little.'

'So when Caleb's here — you're out for part

of that time,' said Ren.

'Yes — I'm always here when he arrives to let him know what needs to be done, but I don't like having to listen to whatever banging is going on, so that's why I leave while I can.'

'You trust Caleb to be here on his own,' said Ren.

'Oh, yes. He's a hard worker, a serious kid. He doesn't fool around if there's work to be done.'

'Is there a reason he hasn't come back to you since?' said Ren. 'Or did you not need him?'

'No — he was supposed to be here two weeks ago, but he never showed up. I called his house, and his father apologized and said that Caleb would no longer be working, that he was going to have to devote more time at weekends to his homework.'

No one mentioned this.

'How did Caleb seem to you that last day?' said Ren. 'Could something have happened that bothered him, that maybe meant he didn't want to come back here?'

Rose was taken aback. 'Lord, I hope not,' she said. She paused. 'Now that I think about it, he did seem a little off that day. He was very eager to get paid and leave. In fact, I owed him one hundred dollars — it had added up. I kept forgetting to go to the machine.'

'And the neighbors you mentioned — did they talk to Caleb, did they know him?'

'In passing,' said Rose. 'I wouldn't say he's the chattiest of kids.'

'Did Caleb have access to your house while you were out?' said Ren.

224

'Yes,' said Rose, 'for washing up, using the bathroom, getting a drink — whatever he needed.'

'Do you think he would have ever let a stranger in?' said Ren.

'No,' said Rose. 'He's pretty street smart.' She looked at Ren with great compassion. 'It must be very hard for you to deal with things like this every day.'

'Finding the bad guys makes it all worthwhile,' said Ren.

'I'm sure it does.'

Ren glanced over at a photo of Rose and her family.

'What a beautiful family,' said Ren. 'And what a handsome man your husband was. You look so happy.'

Rose beamed. 'We were. He passed eleven years ago, and I miss him every day.' She glanced down at Ren's ring finger.

Uh-oh. Don't ask.

'Have you someone special in your life?' said Rose.

'I . . . did,' said Ren. 'I did. I miss him too.' *I will die alone. And be eaten by neighborhood cats. Not even my own cats.* She stood up. 'Thank you so much for your hospitality, Rose, and for answering my questions.'

'I hope I was of some help,' said Rose.

'You absolutely were,' said Ren.

'I can't believe any man would let a nice girl like you go.'

Oh, Jesus. 'You're very kind,' said Ren. *But I killed him is actually what happened. I'm not a nice girl at all.*

225

'You'll find your Mr Right,' said Rose. 'And you'll know it in your heart.'

Then I'll doubt it, then I'll fuck it up.

'Is there anything else you can think of?' said Ren. 'About that Saturday?'

Rose looked toward the counter. 'Sorry, I was looking to see where my cell phone is, but I lost it a while back — Eileen's trying to organize a replacement for me. You could talk to her as well, actually, if you wanted, because, like I said, she was here that day too, but I'm not sure you'll be able to get a hold of her — she told me she's headed off on one of her 'switched-off' long weekends. If you can't, I can let her know when she gets back.'

41

Ren saw a calendar stuck to the side of the refrigerator with a magnet. It had notes scattered throughout the month. 'Could you maybe go back to February on that?' said Ren.

'Good idea,' said Rose. She went to the calendar and flipped it back a month. 'Yes!' she said, stabbing a finger into one of the boxes. 'Plumber! He came that day. It was an out-of-hours call. He was in and out, quickly. He didn't have the part he needed, said he had to order one in.' She paused. 'I haven't been able to get him back here since.'

'What?' said Ren. 'In a month?'

'I know,' said Rose. 'And I've called him several times, but no luck.'

'Could I get his name from you, please?' said Ren.

'Yes,' said Rose. 'It's JJ's Plumbing Services.'

Ren's heart rate shot up.

The plumber from the hotel . . . the one who was in my room . . .

'J. J. Nash is his name,' said Rose. 'His mother is a sister of Pete Ruddock's late wife. So, I guess that makes him the police chief's nephew.'

Uh.

Oh.

41

Ren sat in her car outside Rose Dennehy's house, her mind on J. J. Nash in her hotel room, going through her things, reading her notes, taking photos with his cell phone . . . showing them to his uncle.

Stop.

It could all be completely legitimate.

There's no way it is.

Yes, there is.

We've been here before.

Paranoia. Paranoia.

Why doesn't it ever go away? I'm taking drugs!

Mood stabilizers, not paranoia eliminators.

Imagine trying to do this job on antipsychotics. Snoozing in the corner.

She ran a background check on Nash, then called Gary.

'Well, here's a delicate one,' she said. 'Rose Dennehy — the woman who Caleb Veir used to do odd jobs for? There was a plumber in her house the last time Caleb was there. It's Ruddock's nephew, a guy called J. J. Nash.' She paused. 'And I happen to know that he was in my hotel room one of the days I was at work. The hotel said there had been a problem with the showers.'

'Does he have a record?' said Gary.

'No,' said Ren. 'I ran him, and he's negative in NCIC. He's twenty-six years old, lives on the outskirts of Tate, has his own plumbing business: JJ's Plumbing Services. It's just him — no staff.'

'Does Ruddock know about this yet?' said Gary.

'No,' said Ren. 'I'm hoping to slam that ball into your court, if you don't mind. I'm getting along just fine with Ruddock.'

'You don't want to be the bad guy,' said Gary.

'No, I do not.'

'Let's go talk to him together when you get back,' said Gary. 'You're the one who met the woman.'

'I'm not going to bring up Nash's visit to my hotel room,' said Ren. 'That could come across a little paranoid.'

'Ruddock was the one who invited us to consult on this, so he can't have suspected his nephew . . . unless he found something out afterward.'

'Or,' said Ren, 'he knew all along it was his nephew, but didn't want to be the one to have to take him in.'

*   *   *

Back in Tate PD, Ruddock was surprised to hear that J. J. had met Caleb at Rose Dennehy's.

'He never mentioned it,' said Ruddock. 'And, with my job, I would have expected that — you know, he'd say 'I met that missing kid', or whatever. It makes sense you'd like to bring him in. But he's a good guy, J. J. — I can vouch for him one hundred per cent. I'm sure all his clients would say the same thing. He's very well-liked.'

'Are you and J. J. close?' said Ren.

'Yes,' said Ruddock.

'Have you discussed the investigation with him?' said Gary.

'In passing, yes,' said Ruddock. 'But I didn't tell him anything that wasn't already in the media. And there's also the fact that J. J. goes in and out of a lot of houses, I'm sure he loses track of who he saw where or when.'

Hmm.

'What kind of hours does he work?' said Gary.

'Usually eight to five,' said Ruddock, 'but he'd work late if he had to, and he does call-outs, obviously. He's a hard worker.' He paused. 'Do you want me to tell him to stop by this evening?'

'No,' said Gary. 'We'd appreciate it if you didn't talk to him about this for now.'

'Sure,' said Ruddock. 'I understand.'

'Do you have a cell phone number for him?' said Gary.

'Yes,' said Ruddock. He got his phone and called out the number.

'Thanks,' said Gary.

'Do you have a list of sex offenders living in the area of Rose Dennehy's house?' said Ren.

'Yes,' said Ruddock.

'Did we get their alibis checked for last Monday?' said Ren.

'Yes,' said Ruddock. 'We cast the net wide. They all checked out.'

'Have there been any reports of suspicious activity on that street or nearby?' said Ren. 'Has any kid reported being followed or cars slowing down . . .'

Ruddock shook his head. 'No. The only thing that happened near there was that little boy I mentioned who choked.'

'What was his name?' said Ren. 'Monroe?'

'Luke Monroe.'

'When did that happen?' said Ren.

'Last month,' said Ruddock. He turned to his computer, typed in Luke Monroe's name and called up his memorial page. 'February eleventh.'

What the what now?

'That's the same day Caleb was last at Mrs Dennehy's,' said Ren. 'So the same day John Veir was in the area, dropping his son off.' *And the same day your nephew was.*

It was clear from Ruddock's face that he knew exactly what she was thinking.

★ ★ ★

There was a truck in front of J. J. Nash's house with JJ's Plumbing Services written on the side. The shades on the house were down.

'Despite the truck,' said Ren, 'I'm getting the sense no one's home.'

They rang the doorbell, knocked on the door, called out his name, but there was no answer.

They walked around to the back of the house. They could see a cell phone on the kitchen table. The screen was black.

Ren could feel her heartbeat quicken.

'Did Ruddock tip him off?' said Ren. *I hate when I think these things.* 'Could Nash have known I was speaking with Rose Dennehy?'

'Leaves his cell phone behind,' said Gary.

231

'Doesn't want to be tracked.'

'Or,' said Ren, 'he's a tradesman who doesn't want to be bothered outside office hours. Or maybe he knows the police are on to him. Or the FBI, at least.'

Stop.

They came back around to the front of the house. A skinny guy in his sixties, with long dark hair streaked with gray, came out of the next-door house, smoking a cigarette. He was dressed in a sleeveless checked shirt and khaki board shorts. His only concession to the weather was a pair of black fake Uggs.

'Are you looking for J. J.?' he said.

'Yes,' said Ren.

'I think he might have gone away on vacation,' said the man. 'He kind of rushed out about a half-hour ago, packed up his Harley, and was gone.'

Fuuuuuck.

42

Ren and Gary flashed their creds at the neighbor. He looked a little stunned.

'We're with the FBI,' said Ren. 'Anyone call at his house before J. J. left?'

'Nope.'

'Does he have a lot of visitors?' said Ren.

'Nope. But' — he raised the fingers holding his cigarette — 'I do believe he has a lady in his life.'

'Do you know her?' said Gary.

'I get the impression she's from out of town — she's only ever around on weekends, drives a red car — I'm not good on makes and models — arrives Friday night, leaves Saturday mornings, comes back Saturday afternoons, stays the night again, then leaves Sunday evening.'

Jesus, you don't miss a trick.

'Could you describe her for us?' said Ren.

'She's an attractive woman — older than him by maybe twenty years, I'd say. Nothing wrong with an experienced lady. She has that blonde hair, nicely styled, dresses real well, nice jewelry — the real deal, good shoes, nice nails . . . '

I'm just going to keep nodding here, you nosy, but helpful, weirdo.

'Did you catch her name?' said Ren.

' 'Babe',' he said, smiling.

'So he never introduced you,' said Ren. *Even*

though you were right up there in manicure-judging distance.

'No. To be honest, it felt like he was going out of his way to avoid introducing her to me.' He took a step back. 'I mean, do I look like the kind of guy's gonna steal your chick? Not a lady like her, anyway. Nothing to worry about with me. They're not lining up at my door.' There was a wistful look in his eye.

★ ★ ★

Back at the station, Gary and Ren went into Ruddock's office.

'We have a problem,' said Gary.

Ruddock looked up, wide-eyed. 'What?'

'J. J.'s gone,' said Gary. He let it hang there.

'He packed a bag, hopped on his Harley and left a short while ago,' said Ren.

'What?' said Ruddock.

Genuine shock.

'Did you speak with him?' said Gary.

'No,' said Ruddock. 'Of course not.'

'Was he planning a vacation?' said Ren. 'A weekend away?'

'Not that I know of,' said Ruddock. 'But it's not like he keeps me posted on all his movements. Most of the time, I only know he's been away after he gets back.'

'Looks like his cell phone is on the kitchen table,' said Ren.

'Do you have keys to his house?' said Gary.

'Yes,' said Ruddock. 'Would you like me to take you over there? Or are we being a little dramatic? Maybe, I'll call my sister-in-law — his mother — first.'

'Do you know about the woman J. J.'s seeing?' said Ren.

'No,' said Ruddock. 'What woman?'

'His neighbor said she's blonde, quite a bit older than him, she's only ever there on weekends.'

'First I heard of her,' said Ruddock. 'But it could explain if she's only free on weekends why he might not be around. They could have gone away.'

'True,' said Ren. 'And the nosy neighbor said no one had called to the house.'

Ruddock called J. J.'s mother. It was clear they had a warm relationship. He put down the phone. 'She doesn't know where he is, she doesn't know anything about a girl-friend, but she says absolutely go over and take a look around.' He shrugged. 'She knows there's nothing to this.' He paused. 'But, obviously, I understand why you have to look at him.'

He was in my hotel room!!!

★ ★ ★

Gary stayed at the station. Ren returned to J. J.'s house with Ruddock. The first thing she went for when he let her in was the cell phone. She turned it on. There was no password set up. She scrolled through the text messages. They were all straightforward: work, family, and friends. There were none that looked like they were sent to a romantic partner. Email hadn't been set up on the phone. There was nothing immediately off about the last-dialed calls.

'Oh, hold on,' said Ren. 'He called Rose Dennehy after I'd been there.'

'I know you're doing what you have to do,' said Ruddock, raising his hands, 'but you're barking up the wrong tree. I'd just hate for you to waste your time on this.'

'Why don't you ask your sister-in-law to call around J. J.'s friends,' said Ren, 'and if nothing comes back, we can put a BOLO out for him tonight.'

Ruddock looked resigned. 'OK,' he said. 'I'll do that.'

★ ★ ★

On the drive back to Tate PD, Ren turned to Ruddock when a silence opened up.

'I'd like to go take a look at Luke Monroe's autopsy file.'

Ruddock's eyes went wide. 'But, why? He choked on a sandwich. It was an accident.'

'I know,' said Ren. *But . . .*

★ ★ ★

Beckman was in the middle of an autopsy when Ren and Ruddock arrived unannounced. She stepped outside to meet them, pulling down her mask.

'You're lucky you caught me,' she said. 'I'm only here late because there was a suicide out your way. A guy hanged himself at the Harvest

236

Road Retirement Home — he'd only been there two weeks. Lesson: do not farm your seniors out to Harvest Road.' She paused. 'What can I do for you?'

'Did you do an autopsy on a seven-year-old boy from Tate — Luke Monroe?' said Ren. 'He choked on a sandwich.'

Beckman gave her a you've-got-to-be-kidding-me look. 'Yes.' Pause. Deadpan: 'He choked on a sandwich.'

I like your style.

'Would you mind if we took a look at the file?' said Ren.

There was fire in Beckman's eyes this time. 'May I ask why?'

Ren nodded. 'Tate's a very small town: in just under three months, two children have died, and one is currently missing — that's not very common in my experience.'

'Luke Monroe was an accidental death,' said Beckman.

And the response that hovered, unspoken, between them all was: *So was Aaron Fuller's.*

★   ★   ★

Ruddock and Ren followed Beckman to her office. She set them up at a desk, left them the file and went back into the morgue.

'Tense,' said Ren.

'Yes,' said Ruddock. 'Are you OK to start without me? I have a call to make. I'll be right back.'

'OK,' said Ren.

She started with the first responder's report:

'Boy, seven years old, found unresponsive in garden of family home, holding a peanut-butter sandwich with one bite taken, piece of sandwich found lodged in boy's throat.'

She pulled out the autopsy photos.

I can't deal.

She slipped them back into the folder. There was another photo in the file — of Luke Monroe, alive, grinning, gripping the handlebars of his red bicycle. He had wild blond curly hair, huge, eager blue eyes, long lashes.

How do your parents function? How do they get up in the morning? What levels of strength does that take? What could possibly get them through this?

Ren took a deep breath. Tears welled in her eyes. She put her elbows on the desk, pressed her palms against her forehead. Her nose started to run. She reached into the drawer.

Not your drawer. Not your desk.

She grabbed her handbag.

No tissues.

She held her head back until the tears were gone, sucked air through her nostrils until her nose stopped running.

Gross.

She picked up her cell phone. She was about to text her brother, Matt.

I can't text him. He is a father. He doesn't do what I do.

She texted her best friend, Janine.

Little angel autopsy photos. Literally feel a crack opening in my heart. Not literal. But still. Unbearable. XX

She took another breath, looked back at the autopsy photos. There was one of Luke, face down on the morgue table.

What is it? What is wrong with this picture?

She felt a spike in her chest, a shift, a realization.

What happened to your purty curls, Luke Monroe? Your hair is very flat at the back of your head.

Her heart rate shot up.

Oh, God: your hair was wet. Your hair was wet, then it dried as you lay on it.

Not exactly stark evidence. It could have been from the paramedics working on you.

She looked through the photos of the Monroes' garden. There was no pond, no water feature, no vessel nearby that would hold water.

That doesn't mean there wasn't one there beforehand.

Her phone beeped with a text from Janine.

Hang in there, lovely lady. That angel is blessed your wise eyes are on him. X

Aw, maaan.

Ren replied:

Teary eyes. Thank you, maaan. Hope all is dazzling where you are. XX

Ren went back through the file.

This is too weird. John Veir nearby . . .

There was no sign of Ruddock. Ren called his cell phone. He was walking in the door as it rang.

'Sorry,' he said. 'That took a little longer than I expected.'

'No problem,' said Ren, turning to him.

His face fell when he saw her expression.

'I might be jumping to conclusions,' said Ren. 'But . . . I'd like Beckman to take a look at his lung tissue. She didn't take a sphenoid sinus sample, understandably — drowning was not part of the picture.'

'No,' said Ruddock.

After a short silence, he added, 'Please God, no.'

43

Jimmy Lyle had missed seven calls from the same number. His phone was on the passenger seat beside him, ringing now for the eighth time.

'No!' he shouted, gripping the steering wheel. 'No, thank you!'

It stopped, then rang again.

'Fuck you all! Fuck you all, people!'

He reached out, and picked up. 'Yes?'

'Is this Mr Jimmy Lyle?'

'Yes, ma'am.'

'This is Nadine Jacobs from the retirement home. Have you got someone there with you, Mr Lyle?'

'It's Jimmy. And yes. I've got my friend here beside me.' He rolled his eyes.

'I'm afraid I'm calling you with bad news . . . '

Jimmy's heart started to pound.

'It's your father,' said Nadine. 'I'm sorry to have to tell you that your father passed away, Jimmy. He took his own life early today.'

'Well, thank you for letting me know.'

Silence.

'Are you all right, Jimmy?' said Nadine.

'I'm all right.' He paused. 'How did he do it?'

'Well, I'm not sure you — '

'You can tell me.'

'He . . . well, he hanged himself. We're so terribly sorry. I know he wasn't with us long, but he seemed like he was settling in, he showed no signs of depression, he wasn't taking any meds.'

'He 'passed away' by hanging himself,' said Jimmy. He laughed. 'Sounds so gentle *'passing away'*. None of that writhing about, eyes bulging, face bright red, being starved of oxygen, scratching at your neck, trying to pull the noose off at the last minute . . . ' He paused. 'Though I doubt Daddy was having second thoughts.'

A silence stretched between them. 'You've had a shock,' said Nadine.

'I'm not so sure that I have,' said Jimmy.

'Oh,' said Nadine. 'Well, you could have let us know if you thought — '

'I'm not holding you or anyone else there responsible for this,' said Jimmy. 'I didn't really know. I'm just saying . . . ' He paused. 'I've had a shock.' He rolled his eyes again.

'Could anything have triggered this?' said Nadine. 'Did anything happen that might have upset him?'

'Not that I'm aware of.'

'We have very strict rules in place here,' said Nadine. 'I don't know how your father could have — '

'Nadine, Daddy had a way of getting to do whatever it was he wanted to do.'

'He didn't leave a note,' said Nadine.

'That wouldn't have been his style,' said Jimmy.

'I didn't think he was lonely here,' said Nadine. 'I mean, like I said, he seemed to be getting along with people.'

'He had a way of seeming like that,' said Jimmy. He paused. 'But I don't think loneliness is the number one cause of suicide, Nadine.'

A silence stretched between them.

'Well, his personal effects are here for you to collect,' said Nadine. 'And again, we're terribly sorry for your loss. His body is currently at the Medical Examiner's office, and will be removed to Longacres Funeral Home, as per your father's wishes — he left quite detailed instructions with us when he moved in. They're in his file. You might want to call Longacres to confirm the arrangements . . . '

'Thank you for the call, Nadine. I'm on vacation right now, but I guess I'll be turning this ship around.'

He ended the call, and roared into the windshield. 'Fuck you, Daddy! Fuck you! Fuck you!' He hammered his hands on the steering wheel. 'I hate you, I hate you, I hate you. I hate you, I hate you.'

44

Ren and Ruddock stopped off at the Veirs' house on their way back to Tate PD. Only John was home.

'We just wanted to talk to you about the last day you dropped Caleb off at Rose Dennehy's house — February eleventh?' said Ren.

'Sure,' said John.

'Did anything happen to Caleb that day?' said Ren. 'Anything that made him afraid to go back? We believe you told Rose that Caleb needed to concentrate more on his schoolwork, but Sylvie Ross spoke with Caleb's teacher again, and she said nothing had changed in his grades during that period, and no extra assignments had been given.'

'It was a white lie,' said John. 'Caleb just didn't want to do the job any more.'

'But wasn't the whole point of him having a job to teach him work ethic?' said Ren. 'Responsibility? Wouldn't letting him quit, and covering for him by lying about it, kind of defeat the purpose?'

'Maybe,' said John. He shrugged.

'Talk to us about that Saturday,' said Ruddock.

'There's not a lot to say,' said John. 'I dropped Caleb off at Rose's. I came back three hours later and picked him up. During that time, I was home with Teddy. I can get her to call you when

244

she comes back. I don't know what else to say to you.'

★ ★ ★

That night, Ren arrived back alone at the hotel, and was walking past the bar when she saw Paul Louderback sitting on a high stool with a vodka tonic.

I need a drink.

She went over to him.

'Well, hello, there,' said Paul.

'Hello, yourself.'

'I heard we may have another victim,' said Paul.

'Hopefully not,' said Ren. 'I mean, it's not like I've got hardcore anything. Apart from the twisting in my gut.'

'How was the ME about it?'

'Not a happy bunny,' said Ren. 'But, I'm not exactly hoping I'm right, here. We'll know by tomorrow night. Lung slides take a while. Poor Ruddock. He knows the family, told me all about them, they're in his church, he says they're the nicest people you could meet. Cut to: nice, earnest, blond Christian dad's a child killer.'

'I don't know whether to be more depressed at that being a possibility or at the fact that inside that beautiful head is the beautiful brain that can come up with that shit so quickly.'

Ren laughed. *Jesus.* 'What a suckfest of a fucking day.'

'Would a glass of wine make it better?' said Paul.

'No,' said Ren, 'but a bottle might.' She paused. 'You look a little sorrowful. Is everything OK?'

'It is now.'

Hmm.

'OK — let me go take a shower,' said Ren. 'I'll be back. Five minutes.'

He raised an eyebrow.

'OK — ten.'

She left, hurried to the elevator.

What are you doing, exactly? Wine. Just wine. Mmm-hmm . . .

★ ★ ★

As Ren was going into her room, a text came in from Gary. She opened it.

You need to be back in Denver: Tues a.m. Inspectors re Safe Streets shooting.

Her stomach plunged. She had been interviewed twice already about the Duke Rawlins shooting.

This is why Joe Lucchesi was asking about Denver.

Inspectors . . . Fuck. Fuck. Fuuuuuck.

Let's relive the worst moments of my entire life over and over forever and ever! Amen!

So, I guess I will be going to Denver after all.

★ ★ ★

Ren came back down to the bar fifteen minutes later, dressed in black trousers, a black turtleneck, her lightning strike cuff, her black patent high heels. Her hair was wet, combed back off her face. She had minimal makeup on. She slapped her phone on to the bar, and slid up on to a stool beside Paul.

'Wow,' he said. 'You look beautiful.'

Aw, man. Nooo. I'm dressed like a fucking nun.

A non-fucking nun.

Maybe nuns don't wear patent heels. But still . . .

'Sorry,' said Paul. 'I probably shouldn't have said that.'

Ren laughed. 'No — thank you.'

'You're negating the effects of possibly the least sexiest bar in the universe.'

We're not supposed to be anything to do with anything sexy.

He raised a bottle of red wine. 'I took the liberty . . . '

'I love your liberties,' said Ren. 'I've missed them. And I welcome them.'

He poured. They clinked glasses.

'There's nothing a bottle of wine won't fix,' said Paul.

Your voice is saying 'a bottle of wine' and your eyes are saying 'acts of a sexual nature'.

Will levels: weak.

Paul topped up her glass. Very generously.

He wants to get me drunk. And I shall oblige. Jesus.

'You know, I'm fascinated by couples in crisis . . . ' said Ren.

'Who are we talking about?' said Paul.

'Sorry — I was just thinking about the Veirs.

And all the couples I meet in this job. Just — how trauma impacts on them. Who's caring for whom? Are they both? Is one reaching out, is the other withdrawing? Do they care? Are they suspicious of each other? And who *loves*? Truly loves. It's rare. And that depresses the shit out of me.'

He was staring at her.

What are you thinking?

'You know, though, the boring couples can be more rock-solid than the ones who swing from chandeliers,' said Ren. 'I will never reject a chandelier, but I like the idea of having someone with big strong arms standing underneath it to catch me.'

I just can't for the life of me imagine anyone other than Ben.

'But for now . . . ' said Ren. *Stop.*

'For now . . . ?'

Ugh. I'm just going to stand back and watch the chandelier sparkle. That's the best I can do. There's a little light in that.

Paul reached out, took her hand, squeezed it.

'I'm fine,' said Ren. She tilted her head back, blinked, and the tears were gone.

She breathed out. They drank. They drank more.

Before long, Paul called the barman over. 'Same again.'

He was still holding Ren's hand.

Yup.

Same again.

45

Ren woke up alone. The space beside her in the bed was empty.

Oh my God.

She sat up.

No one has ever done this to me before.

She looked around.

What an asshole.

He took advantage of me. And he sneaks out of his own fucking room! What an absolute fucking asshole. He's supposed to be my friend. I am such a fucking sucker.

The bathroom door opened.

'Hey,' said Paul. He smiled wide. 'I hope I didn't wake you. I was trying to be quiet.'

'Well, you succeeded . . . ' said Ren.

He took a few steps toward her. 'Did you think I had abandoned you?'

'No,' said Ren.

'Good.'

Uh-oh. What's that look? Please don't be nice to me. Or like me in any way. Oh, no. Don't sit on the edge of my bed like I'm ill. Do I look ill? Am I ill?

Paul paused, and walked back around the bed as if he had read her mind.

'You're feeling guilt-ridden,' he said. He lay on the bed beside her, pulled her into his arms.

'Yes.' *This is too intimate. That word I hate. That feeling I hate.*

'Well, I'm sorry if I've put you in that position,' said Paul. He kissed her head.

Are you? 'Thanks.' *That was a crap, sterile kiss.* 'I'm sorry for getting emotional the first night.' *And not sorry for not being emotional on any level last night.* 'I do want you to know you can rely on me. Professionally. I know I wouldn't be on the team without you and Gary batting for me. I really appreciate it.'

'We wouldn't have given you our backing if we thought you weren't capable.'

'So, it wasn't a pity move?' said Ren.

'I don't do pity.'

'Thanks,' said Ren. 'I love this job.' *I love being able to escape. Even though I keep showing up wherever I go.* She squeezed his arm, rolled to her side of the bed, got up and went into the bathroom. She stood in front of the mirror.

Here we go again.

No pride to be found in that reflection. Don't waste your time.

⋆ ⋆ ⋆

Ren went back to her room, took a shower, got dressed, and rode the elevator down to the lobby.

I walked by here holding Paul Louderback's hand, oh, about, four hours ago.

I've come so fucking far!

She went straight for the coffee machine in the restaurant and poured a large one into a take-away cup. She grabbed a napkin and wrapped two raisin Danishes in it. She became aware of a

250

presence beside her. An arm reached across her to take a cup.

'Late night?' said Sylvie.

Ren went very still.

Sylvie smiled. 'Your secret's safe with me.'

Oh.

Dear.

God.

★ ★ ★

Ren arrived in Tate PD, walked through the room with her head down and sat at her desk.

Everyone needs to stay away from me today for their own safety.

She had been there only an hour when Paul Louderback came over to her desk. She looked up at him.

Seriously?!

'Are you OK?' he said. 'About last night.'

'Jesus — straight to missiles. Yes — I'm just tired.'

He smiled.

'Do not smile at me like that,' said Ren. But she smiled back. 'Any word on J. J. Nash?'

Paul shook his head. 'No.'

'Has Ruddock said anything?'

'Nothing.'

'It's so strange.'

'Do you trust him?' said Paul.

I'm afraid to trust anyone. 'Ruddock?' said Ren. 'I do.' She paused. 'Do you?'

'Don't look so nervous,' said Paul. 'Yes, I do.'

Ren tilted her head. *Go on, now go.*

'OK, OK,' said Paul. 'I just wanted to make

251

sure you were all right.'

'You have a nice day, sir,' said Ren.

He laughed as he walked away. 'Cold,' he said. 'Cold.'

* * *

Ren checked her email. There was one from Ruddock with the video from the Lister Creek store on the Monday Caleb disappeared. She downloaded the file and pressed Play. The camera captured the side of the cars as they drove into the parking lot at the side of the store, and whatever cars parked out front. Ren watched as a car drove in, parked, then another car, another car, then John Veir's.

You lying son-of-a-bitch.

A bus drove in after John Veir, but stalled before making the turn into the parking lot for buses, blocking Veir's car from view. Three more cars arrived. One car left. Another car left. Another car arrived. Another car left. John Veir left. He was there for a total of fourteen minutes.

Ren wrote down the license plate numbers of all the cars that arrived or left within an hour of his arrival.

'Fuck you, John Veir. Fuck you.'

* * *

She went to see Paul in the command center. He raised an eyebrow.

'Can't keep away from me,' he said.

'Yeah, yeah,' said Ren.

She handed him the sheet of paper. 'John Veir's been lie-telling,' said Ren. 'I just watched the video footage from the store at Lister Creek: he did make a second stop last Monday. I took down the license plate numbers of all the cars that were there around the same time — to do with what you will.'

'I'll give it to Wiley,' said Paul.

'I haven't seen him this morning,' said Ren. 'Let me go check with Ruddock.'

★　★　★

Ren bumped into Ruddock in the hallway outside his office.

'Hey,' said Ren. 'How are you doing?'

'I've been better.'

'We don't know for sure yet about Luke,' said Ren. 'But . . . one thing I do know is that John Veir lied about Monday. He made a stop off at Lister Creek rest area.'

Ruddock shook his head.

'Paul wants Wiley to follow up on the other cars that were there,' said Ren.

'Wiley's not in yet,' said Ruddock. 'It's Isabella again, his wife. She had a very public meltdown on Thursday afternoon — sitting on the curb in Harvest Road, bawling her eyes out, drunk as a skunk.' He paused. 'I told Gil to take as much time as he needs. It seems she's just not ready to get help . . . '

'Jesus — that's really bad,' said Ren.

Ruddock nodded. 'An intervention is the next step.'

Intervention.

Ren's heart flipped.

Intervention . . .

The word went through her like a knife. The evening of the shootings at Safe Streets, her loved ones and friends had been gathered by Gary to sit her down and tell her they knew she had stopped taking her meds, that she would have to go back on them or risk her life, her career, her relationships. They were all in the Safe Streets building that evening because she had gone off the rails. She knew the word 'intervention' would forever haunt her.

Ruddock was staring at her. *Fuck.* 'Yes,' she managed to say. 'That sounds about right.' *I need to get out of here.*

She could feel him watching her as she left.

46

There was a subdued atmosphere in the command center all day. Under the buzz of activity, was the pulsing fear that Beckman could call to tell them that another child had been murdered, that they would now have to look at the possibility that Caleb Veir could have, or was set to, succumb to the same fate.

* * *

Later in the afternoon, Paul came over to Ren's desk. 'In the absence of Wiley, I got one of the other Tate guys to trace the vehicles that were spotted at the Lister Creek rest area — no one with a record, no name that's come up before in the investigation.'

'Have they called them all to see if they saw anything?' said Ren.

'They're still going through the list,' said Paul. 'On the rental cars, I got the details from Avis: one car was a family from Vermont on vacation, another was a student couple on vacation, the third was a lawyer — '

'Lawyer?' said Ren, sitting up. 'Alice Veir?'

'No such luck,' said Paul. 'Lawyer's name is Paula Leon, forty-nine years old, visiting from Maine. I couldn't reach her, so I left her a message.'

'OK,' said Ren.

Investigators who were supposed to go home that day, stayed late, pizza was ordered, conversations moved to brighter places, until silence brought everyone back again to what could lie ahead.

At nine p.m. Ren's phone rang. She looked down. Beckman. She walked out of the command center into the quiet of the Tate PD foyer. Beckman hung up before Ren answered.

Shit.

Ren tried her again. The line was busy. She texted her.

Am here. Call when you can.

Ren stayed in the foyer, her gaze moving to the photographs.

I can't believe I only arrived here four days ago.

Ruddock and Wiley featured in some of the photos, as did some of the investigators from the command center, most of them looking a little thinner in the face, thicker in the hair. Then there was a group of kids standing by a pool, all wearing medals around their necks. She wouldn't have stopped except she saw something familiar in a little boy with auburn hair to his shoulders, standing proud, his chest out.

Bless your heart, Seth Fuller. And you used to have hair! And smile . . .

Her phone rang again. She picked up right away.

'Beckman . . . '

'Hi, Ren. Sorry about that. I've called to

confirm your worst fears.'

Fuck. Fuck. Fuck.

'The choking was staged,' said Beckman. 'Luke Monroe was drowned. I looked at the lung-tissue samples. It's clear there are diatoms, so I can tell you for sure that the drowning happened in fresh or salt water, not, for example, in the bathtub, kitchen sink, etc. I'm sorry I missed this.'

'Don't be,' said Ren. 'This was not an easy call. I get how it works. I did a seminar on water deaths. People make a whole lot of assumptions about fluid in the lungs meaning that someone drowned, but we both know there are lots of reasons why someone could have fluid in the lungs. Luke Monroe was found in his garden. There was no water — '

'Thank you,' said Beckman.

I'll shut up now. 'I'll share this with the team. We'll gather water samples from around the area and send them your way.'

★ ★ ★

Ren went to Ruddock's office first to tell him the news. He sat at his desk, white-faced, his gaze traveling far beyond the walls of his office.

'I can't help thinking,' he said, 'that this is my town . . . ' He paused. 'And I have failed my town.'

Ren was sitting on the edge of his desk. She looked down at him.

Oh my God . . . he's going to cry.

No fucking way. No, no, no. 'That's not how

this works,' said Ren. She reached out, squeezed his forearm. 'Absolutely not. This is the last thing anyone would have expected somewhere like here.'

'You did,' said Ruddock. There was a gentle respect in his tone. 'You were here a couple of days and you knew something wasn't right.'

'I'm an outsider,' said Ren, 'from . . . a darker world, unfortunately.' *And with a darker shitshow of a mind. I would hate for you to have this mind, you sweet, adorable man.*

'I don't know how you do this all the time,' said Ruddock.

'Neither do I,' said Ren. 'I guess it's all about getting a missing person safely home and saving the next person from an encounter with a psycho.'

He nodded.

'If you don't mind,' said Ren. 'I think we should call in an expert on this. There's a woman called Deb McLean — she specializes in aquatic deaths and homicidal drownings — I went to one of her seminars. She's outstanding.'

'You do that,' said Ruddock. 'Get her here as soon as you can.' He paused, looked up at Ren, studied her face. 'Ren, I was wondering, would you like to join me for dinner tomorrow night?'

Oh. Um . . .

'Just — you did mention you'd like roast chicken,' said Ruddock, 'and as luck would have it, the butcher in town sent me a nice big organic one . . . to thank me for getting him off a nasty murder charge.'

Ren laughed.

'The chicken part is true, though,' said Ruddock. 'And what I did was catch the brat who threw a rock through his store window.'

'Did you ever think your butcher was offloading a chicken because it was showered with glass?' said Ren.

'That's exactly what I said to him, but he assured me this chicken was alive and clucking on a farm when the attack happened.'

Ren smiled. 'Well, if the chicken has a solid alibi, count me in.'

'This won't be a long dinner, don't worry — I know we've got a lot to get through,' said Ruddock. 'I just don't know if I could stand cooking a whole roast chicken for one.'

Aw, maan.

'Well, I would be very grateful to bypass the hotel restaurant,' said Ren. 'And I can't face pizza again. Thank you.'

She could see Ruddock drift back into the brutal reality he had just been trying to escape. A profound sadness swept across his face.

'I went in to talk to Luke Monroe's class about my job,' he said. 'It was a few months back. He was sitting right at the front, and he hung on my every word. He asked the most questions, he told me he wanted to be a doctor or a police officer or a firefighter when he grew up. All jobs to help other people. He stood out — he was one of those kids people are drawn to, they have something special, you think 'they're going to be a star', 'the world will know this child.'' He paused. 'And the world will never get to know Luke Monroe. For most people, he'll just be a face from a news report about a killer. Just like Aaron Fuller's.' He looked up at Ren. 'I don't want Caleb Veir's to be alongside them.'

47

Shannon Fuller walked through the living room and down the hallway to Seth's bedroom. She knocked.

'Enter!' he said.

She opened the door. He was sitting on his bed, watching a video on his laptop.

'Did you hear who died?' said Shannon.

'No,' said Seth. 'Who?'

'Roger Lyle.' She waited for a reaction. 'You remember Mr Lyle? The swim coach.'

Seth nodded. 'Of course I remember him. What happened?'

'Well,' said Shannon, 'apparently, he killed himself. He was out in the retirement home and he went into his closet, hanged himself.'

'Well, they won't be putting that in the brochure,' said Seth. ' 'Lots of hanging space', 'sturdy closet rails to take the weight of your abandoned loved one'.'

Shannon's eyes widened. 'Seth, that's not very nice — Mr Lyle was always very good to you.'

Seth nodded. 'He was.'

'You won so many medals.'

'I did,' said Seth. 'What a champ.'

'Where *are* your medals?' said Shannon.

'I have no idea,' said Seth. 'They weren't anywhere when we were moving here.'

'Really?' said Shannon. 'That's a shame. They would have looked great on the wall.'

Seth looked at her with a patient expression. 'You'd want to be pretty desperate to rely on glory dating back over ten years. Child swimming champ . . . '

Shannon smiled. 'I have no doubt you will go on to great glory in the future, so I guess you won't need your medals to fall back on.'

'Jeez. I hope not.'

'The memorial service is on Thursday,' said Shannon, 'they're waiting for some family members to arrive from overseas. Do you want to come with me, pay your respects?'

Seth nodded. 'Sure.'

'Poor Jimmy — ' said Shannon.

'Yeah,' said Seth. 'Poor weird Jimmy.' He paused. 'Well, at least a space has opened up in the retirement home. Pay it forward.'

Shannon was frowning. 'I think you got out of the wrong side of the bed this morning.'

'The cold side,' said Seth. He stood up, stretched his arms. 'I'm going to go take a walk.'

He grabbed a hoodie and pulled it on.

'Walk?' said Shannon. 'At midnight? Where?'

'Just into the woods,' said Seth. 'I thought maybe I could check the cabins, see what kind of mess the cops made of them. I feel people are stepping all over our lives.'

'Aw, Seth, sweetheart,' said Shannon. 'We're going to be OK.' She hugged him tight.

'I know,' he said. 'I know.'

★ ★ ★

Seth kept the beam on the flashlight low as he walked the path down to the cabins. The air was freezing, he had forgotten his jacket, his eyes were streaming. His hands were stuffed into his pockets for warmth. There was a bunch of keys in the right one, two single keys in the left.

As he walked, his shoulders were tight, he was hunching, holding his breath again.

'Breathe,' he said to himself. 'Breathe.'

He tried to relax his body. He was tired of having to keep reminding himself to. It didn't come naturally. He couldn't remember a time when it had. But he guessed it was before his eighth birthday. He remembered his eighth birthday. It was the last one he spent with his mama — she was dead before the year was out. It was the best birthday he ever had.

His eyes were streaming now, not from the cold, but from the tears. He was aware of every sound in the woods, the leaves as the breeze blew through them, whatever critters were scurrying about, the lapping of the water. The crunch of his boots on the path felt loud and almost unbearable. But he loved all these sounds, because they weren't prison sounds. They weren't the sounds of caged men, desperate to avoid silence. Twenty-four seven the noise went on and sometimes he thought his head would blow.

★ ★ ★

He stopped at the farthest cabin. Instead of going left down to it, toward the water, he went right, up a slope with no path, no trail, no evidence that there was anything up there. There

263

was certainly nothing that made it on to any map, nothing that would have appeared on an aerial view of the property.

It was a small hut, no bigger than eight by ten. The roof was covered over by earth, ivy grew around it, and it was sheltered by trees. It had thin windows with wooden shutters, and strong locks. Clyde Brimmer had built it back in the late eighties, and spent a little time every spring maintaining it as best he could.

Seth had just taken the key from his pocket when he heard footsteps coming toward him. He froze. He turned around. A woman was standing in the shadows, close enough that he could smell the liquor on her breath. She was swaying back and forth.

A cloud shifted in the sky, and she was illuminated by the moon. Seth squinted into the hazy light.

'Isabella?' he said.

'I can't stand this any more,' she replied.

48

Deb McLean was leaning against the table at the top of the Tate PD conference room, her legs crossed at the ankles, her arms folded. Ren was studying her from the front row. Her blonde hair had been cut stylishly short since Ren last saw her. She was dressed in a smart black suit, white shirt, and heels that were hidden under bootleg pants that hit the ground.

Deb had her cell phone in her hand and was typing. Every now and then, she looked up from her screen to watch the investigators filing into the room. Ren's phone beeped with a text. From Deb.

OK — have spotted three potential future husbands.;-)

Ren looked up. Deb smiled and winked at her then put her cell phone down on the table.

'Hello, Tate,' she said, when Ruddock gave her the nod. 'Happy Sunday. My name is Deb McLean, I'm a court-certified expert in aquatic deaths and homicidal drownings. I also train divers, water rescue and recovery teams, and I carry out ongoing research in the field.'

She stood up.

She has to be four ten, max. I know she has sneaked at least three-inch heels under there. She's never going to be ready to ditch the bootlegs.

'I'm happy to help you in any way I can on

your investigation,' said Deb. 'I read through the details of the case on the flight here. So we know: the death of Aaron Fuller was no tragic accident, the death of Luke Monroe was no tragic accident. Lake Verny is innocent, the peanut butter sandwich is innocent. Ladies and gentlemen, the only tragic accident here was the birth of their killer.' She paused. 'It may or may not be one and the same person, but, nevertheless, there are people out there who get their kicks from drowning or near-drowning their victims. There is no evidence of a sexual nature to the crimes you are dealing with, but, very often that evidence will no longer be present on the body. I'll explain more about the sexual element later.' She looked around the room. 'I'm here today to talk to you about ASSes.' She smiled. 'That would be Aquatic Sexual Sadists. My term.

'An ASS tortures his victims for his own sexual gratification, using water as his weapon,' said Deb. 'I'm saying 'his' because it's easier, and because it's more likely it's going to be a man. OK — an Aquatic Sexual Sadist doesn't *just* want to torture and cause pain. He wants to bring you, his victim, to the brink of death and show you that he — and only he — can give you your life back. Your torturer is also your savior. This is the most powerful feeling an ASS can have.'

There were some chuckles around the room.

'He wants to be god,' said Deb. 'He wants to be *your* god.'

Clever lady, bringing us directly into the story.

266

You. You. You. You. You.

'If you think of a domestic violence situation,' said Deb, 'where your partner strangles you until you pass out, then releases the neck pressure to allow blood flow to return to your brain. Well, he or she uses this behavior — and the ongoing, oppressive threat of this behavior — to have control over you in all areas of your life. ASSes, however, *only* need the near-death-to-life experience. That is their thrill.' She paused. 'Some ASSes concurrently commit rape as they're drowning their victims, though we've established that this is not the case here. What *we're* dealing with is a killer who wants to drown his/her victim entirely, who no longer wants to be a savior, or who maybe never did; someone who simply wants to end lives. This category of killer falls under the subcategory of lust killer. These type of Aquatic Sexual Sadists may torture their victims with repeated near-drowning sessions prior to killing them.'

I wonder what it feels like to almost drown.

'There is no greater urge than the urge to breathe,' said Deb, 'so when you are preventing someone from doing so, it's torture in the most horrific form. Unlike other tortures where the victim can pass out — like, as I mentioned, in strangulation — with drowning, you don't pass out, plus you suffer the excruciating pain of inhaling water.'

I no longer wonder what it feels like to almost drown.

'Drowning is a silent death,' said Deb. 'There is none of the flailing and shouting and

267

arm-waving you see in movies. Drowning does not happen the way you might think it does.'

'Sorry, Deb,' said Ren, 'back to what you said a minute ago: are you saying there could be victims out there who were near-drowned by this guy, but are still alive, that he let them go?'

'It's a possibility, yes,' said Deb. 'But, if that is the case, we don't know yet when near-drowning became 'not enough' for the killer. We don't know when drowning to death became his thing.' She paused. 'So you'll want to know, what kind of person your killer is. ASSes are smart: what they do to their victims happens silently, and, usually, leaves no marks. If I electrocute you, if I beat you, if I stab you, there will be clear evidence of this on your body. If your head is being held under water and, like I said, breathing is your greatest urge, that is what your body will put all its strength into: you will not be able to reach back and prize someone's fingers off you, you will not be able to claw at them. You'll be too busy fighting for your life. There are parents who use near-drowning to torture their children *because* it leaves no marks. In a domestic setting, the perpetrator is 'lucky' to have a private area in which to do it: a bathroom. They're locked in, they have control, privacy is automatically given by others. But even outside of that, not a lot is required to carry out this punishment — I could drown you in a bucket of water if I wanted to. I could drown you in a busy lake on a summer's day and no one might notice.'

It's really not safe to go back in the water.

'Any fetishistic behavior, like aquatic sadism,

268

develops when something causes you a pleasant sensation, when something arouses you. It might be an image, an object, an event, an item of clothing. It stays with you and you are compelled to return to it — you recreate the circumstances of whatever that was in order to feel that sensation again. So your killer is likely to have been near-drowned himself, or has certainly connected drowning or water with feelings of arousal. Maybe he or she witnessed a drowning — '

'If this is sexual, why have none of the victims been raped?' said Wiley.

'Because, for this killer,' said Deb, 'the power and the rush comes from the drowning.'

'So it's not a sexually motivated crime,' said Wiley.

Not as simple as that, Wiley.

'It's possible that there is a masturbatory element,' said Deb, 'though, obviously, like I said, there will no longer be evidence of that on the bodies of Aaron Fuller and Luke Monroe.

' "Tragic accident",' said Deb, and she had the full attention of the room again. 'We hear those words paired together a lot, we read about them in news reports. They're powerful words, with an unspoken story behind them. We immediately think of innocent, weeping relatives. But what saddens me the most about the words 'tragic accident' is that they're often the first words that people will attribute to a drowning death. We're programmed to think that way, to be afraid of water, to be afraid of what water can do to us. But we're not made aware of how someone could *use* water to do something to us.'

Good point.

'You have patrol officers going to a six-year-old child lying dead in a field,' said Deb. 'En route, they're thinking 'why is the child in the field and why is it dead?' They arrive, they secure the scene, there's no question about it. Take that child out of the field, put it into a pond, without realizing it, the officers are thinking 'tragic accident' before they even get to the scene: child in a bathtub, teen at a pool party, woman in a hot tub . . . ' She looked around the room. 'So, while I have you all here, hanging on my every word, I will shamelessly use this opportunity to implore you all not to jump to 'accident'. Instead, I ask you to wait, to observe, to process, to look around you, to look all over the home, or all around the pool, or around whatever body of water holds the body of your victim. It is a crime scene like any other. It should be preserved. And, like any other crime scene, you can't be told by the witness or witnesses what went down and take that at face value: 'I turned my back for thirty seconds', 'I didn't know he was in the bathroom', 'he must have filled the tub himself', 'he had been depressed for weeks', 'she had always threatened to do something like this' . . . '

I love listening to you, Deb McLean.

'I'm sure you're all aware now about how the diatoms in the water showed that Aaron Fuller was not killed in Lake Verny,' said Deb. 'Once you have a five-hundred-milliliter sample of water from other possible sources, you can test it against the water from his sphenoid sinus to see if there's a match. There is also a way of linking the UNSUB to the body of water: diatoms have a shell called a frustule. It's made of silica, is really durable, and withstands all kinds of conditions. These little shells can hang around a long time. I worked a case where a guy was caught because he had drowned a victim in a lake, put her body in the trunk of his car, and driven two hundred miles away to dump it in woodland. We found silica shells in the trunk of his car that matched the ones found in the water from the victim's sphenoid sinus. So you might find them in the UNSUB's vehicle, on his clothing, his sneakers, etc.' She paused. 'And hopefully, you will stop him before he takes another life.'

Caleb Veir, please be alive.

49

Ren sat in the kitchen having coffee with Deb when she was finished.

'I was thinking, after what you said, that we should take a look at any previous drownings in the area,' said Ren, 'or any unusual water-based incidents, if the UNSUB has a history.'

'Definitely,' said Deb.

'And in terms of previous victims of near-drownings, apart from hospital admissions . . . '

'See, that's the problem,' said Deb. 'What I said before — it's a sinister crime. It leaves very little trace. And, you know what, it's the type of thing that people don't seem to take seriously. Child victims have tried to report these things before and people just don't believe them. I think if a child said he was being molested, he would be believed quicker.'

'I guess it seems so unreal,' said Ren. 'Or just, I don't know — someone could construe it as 'of course your mother/ father/brother, etc. wouldn't do that to you'. Like, what a screwed-up thing to do. As if all the other shit that people do to each other isn't.'

'I know,' said Deb.

'Are ASSes drawn to water in general?' said Ren. 'Like, John Veir is an ex-military diver, Seth Fuller was a child swimming champ.'

'Not really, no,' said Deb. 'That in itself

wouldn't ring my alarm bells. But if the victims are children, well, we all know UNSUBS will put themselves where they'll be around them.'

'Are there any other signs that someone is or was a victim of near-drowning?' said Ren.

Deb let out a breath. 'Depending on how long-term the abuse is, maybe lung issues, recurring pneumonia . . . '

'OK,' said Ren.

Deb checked the time on her phone. 'OK — I better go or I'll miss my flight.' She took a printout from her bag and handed it to Ren. 'My parting gift to you is this — a list of aqua erotic and drowning fetish sites.'

Ren scanned the list. 'You do know I'll be exploring these on my own in my hotel room tonight . . . '

'Would you rather watch them with that adorable police chief? Or his angry lieutenant?'

'You spotted that too,' said Ren.

'Issues . . . ' said Deb. 'Now, when you are checking those out, you might want to have another screen open beside it with cartoons on.' She paused. 'Not *The Little Mermaid*, though.'

'Or *Finding Nemo* . . . '

★ ★ ★

Gary walked in after Deb had left.

'Your friend is good,' said Gary.

'Really good,' said Ren. She slid the printout over to him. 'Fancy a late-night aqua erotic porn screening? My treat.'

That evening, Ren sat at Ruddock's dining room table after a dinner of roast chicken that was mercifully perfectly cooked. He lived in one of the homiest homes she had ever been in. Ruddock was easy company, a man who lit up when he talked about his late wife. He told Ren she'd been heavily involved in life at Tate PD — organizing the community photo displays in the foyer, tending to the plants. She would bring in cakes and cookies during the day, and casseroles when the team was working late. It was clear Ruddock missed her terribly.

He didn't ask Ren about her own relationship situation, but she knew at this stage he was bound to have googled her and found out what happened in Safe Streets.

Were you sent to me, Ruddock, you gentle soul? My inadvertent healer.

She could hear him in the kitchen, putting the dinner plates in the dishwasher.

'Are you sure I can't help?' she called in.

Please say yes.

'Positive,' said Ruddock. 'You relax out there.'

'OK!' *Yay.*

She heard the oven door open, and she could smell cinnamon.

Life brings wonderful surprises.

People die.

Surprise!

Good people.

Surprise!

Ruddock's wife. Robbie. Everett. Ben.

Surprise!

Aaron Fuller. Luke Monroe. Caleb Veir?

No.

She could feel her chest tighten.

No, not here. This is a nice fucking night. Give me a break.

Ruddock walked in. She took a deep breath, then looked up with a smile. Ruddock had his hands in his wife's floral oven gloves, and he was carrying a steaming apple and cinnamon pie.

Jesus Christ, he is so fucking adorable.

She burst into tears.

Without saying a word, Ruddock set the dish down on a trivet at the other side of the table, slipped his hands out of the oven gloves. He sat down beside Ren, reached out and squeezed her hand, held it there, didn't let go.

I am a fucking lunatic.

'I know you lost your friends,' said Ruddock. 'And your boyfriend.'

Ren nodded. She grabbed a napkin and pressed it into the corner of her eyes.

'Yes,' she said.

'I'm so sorry,' said Ruddock.

'Me too,' said Ren. 'For you. Your wife . . . '

He managed a nod too.

'You must think I'm nuts.'

'Well, if you are, I'm nuts right along with you.'

'It's so sad,' said Ren. 'No one tells you . . . all the weird stuff. Not the normal stuff — the texts, the emails you keep, the songs that remind you of them.' She sucked in a breath. 'Weird stuff. Like . . . not buying the shower gels you used to use. Mugs I can't drink from, but I can't bear to throw away. TV shows I can't watch any more — I'd feel like I'm cheating. Meals I can't eat. And if I do cook something we used to have, I just end up crying through the whole thing and I can't even eat it. And I still have his toothbrush, his razor, his deodorant.' *Which I still take the lid off and smell. Which I would use if it wouldn't make me feel like I was losing my mind.* 'I still wear his T-shirts.' *And his shorts. Jesus. Christ. When will it go afuckingway?*

Poor Ruddock.

'I wish you weren't going through all this,' said Ruddock. 'It's not easy.'

'Everyone is grieving,' said Ren. 'Everywhere I look. You're such a lovely man. I'm so sorry you lost your wife. Life is so unfair.'

'It will get easier,' said Ruddock. 'You won't believe me now, but you'll be saying the same thing to someone else down the line. That's just how it goes. I'm the person to tell you. You'll pass it on to someone else.'

'Thank you.' *I should be more embarrassed than I am. But you're just so fucking nice.*

She gave herself one minute of crying, then excused herself to go to the bathroom. She stared in the mirror.

I have those lost eyes. Oh, God. I do. They're only for other people.

My mascara rocks.

She wiped the tiniest of smudges from the outer corners of her eyes. Her hair was damp at the temples. She pulled it off her face into a high ponytail, then pulled out the elastic and let it fall down. She washed her hands, dried them, and went back out. As she was walking down the hallway, she could hear the click of the front door closing. She stopped.

She heard voices. Ruddock's . . . and another man's.

Oh, God. What's going on? Why do I always go to the dark side?

'I didn't want to mess it up!' the other man was saying. 'I'm lying to everyone, I'm lying to you, I'm lying to her — '

Ren felt her sadness cut away by a stab of anger.

I can't trust anyone. Even Ruddock. My instincts about him. My instincts are gone. I never know who to trust. I shouldn't be doing this.

She reached for her sidearm. She felt steady, preternaturally calm. She raised it, walked forward quietly, listened. Their voices had dropped, were hushed, urgent.

Fuck.

She looked into the living room, her weapon raised. There was a tall, dark-haired man standing with his back to her, dressed in a black biker jacket, black jeans and boots.

Fuck. That's J. J. Nash. The plumber. The nephew.

Her heart started to pound.

I've been set up.

50

Ren walked into the living room.

'J. J. Nash?'

J. J. raised his hands in the air immediately. Ren could see Ruddock standing behind him in the same pose, an I'm-as-surprised-as-you-are look on his face, a pleading in his eyes.

You did this on purpose. You suckered me into a low-key, out-of-school-hours first encounter with your fugitive suspect nephew.

'Ren,' said Ruddock, firmly, 'you can lower the weapon. J. J. will explain everything. I had no idea he was going to show up.'

'He didn't,' said J. J. 'I was away. I just wanted to stop by and let him know I was thinking of him.'

Thinking of him? What?

'I just didn't like the idea of him being here alone tonight,' said J. J.

What? I'm totally lost.

Ruddock picked up on it. 'It's my wife's anniversary tonight.'

Oh, Jesus. He didn't want to be alone tonight — he wanted to be with someone who would understand. Grieving woman, grieving town. Poor, adorable Ruddock. What a great fucking support I turned out to be.

'I'm so sorry,' said Ren. 'I had no idea . . . '

Ruddock batted away the apology, but she could see his compassion for her. She realized she was still pointing the gun at a terrified J. J. He couldn't take his eyes off it. He looked like he had never seen one before.

Ren lowered the weapon, put it back in its holster.

I thought that went well.

Ruddock stepped forward. 'J. J. — this is Special Agent Ren Bryce with the FBI.'

'Oh,' said J. J. 'I thought . . . you know.' He gestured to the table, shrugged. 'It looked like a date, which I thought was weird anyway.'

I'm blushing. I never blush.

'And then she's got a gun,' said J. J. 'And . . . I can't wrap my brain around it. I thought you were being tricked by one of those women who prey on lonely men, those Black Widow ladies — '

By the time J. J. had finished, Ruddock was laughing hard. 'Ever since J. J. could talk, he didn't know when to stop,' said Ruddock. 'No filter.'

Keep a straight face. This man could still be a child killer.

'J. J. — you know we've been looking for you, right?' said Ren.

'Yes, yes,' he said. 'I'm sorry, OK? I'm here now. I came back. I just . . . didn't want to do that until I could. Until I had an alibi for those days. I knew I didn't look good, OK?'

'Sit down,' said Ren. 'Talk to us. Who are all these people you're lying to? And why?'

Ruddock cleared space at the dining table.

J. J. shrugged. 'My alibi . . . for the dates in question . . . I read about them in the paper

. . . was, well, it was Mrs Dennehy's daughter.'

Ren exchanged glances with Ruddock.

I know what you're thinking: a daughter of Mrs Dennehy's is bound to be at least fifteen years older than him? And: Go, Mrs Dennehy's daughter? So, she was the older blonde woman with the great nails.

'Keep talking . . .' said Ren.

'I've been seeing Mrs Dennehy's daughter,' said J. J. 'She's back in town — she's over there now with her mother, breaking it to her that she's in love with a plumber 'twenty years her junior' is how she describes it. I didn't want to talk to you until she talked to her mother first.'

'OK — can we stop calling her Mrs Dennehy's daughter?' said Ren. 'It sounds like a bad Irish movie. Does she have a name?'

'Eileen.'

Ruddock laughed. 'Because that'll knock the Irish out of the whole thing.'

'Look,' said J. J., 'she's divorced with a mean ex-husband. It's a . . . sensitive situation. Hence, we disappeared for a while.' He spoke like 'hence' was a new word in his vocabulary.

Perhaps discovered in the script of Mrs Dennehy's Daughter.

J. J. turned to Ruddock. 'I'm so sorry if I made things awkward for you on a professional level.'

Ruddock nodded. 'It's OK.'

J. J. talked them through his nascent love affair with Eileen Dennehy, whom he met when he was fixing a radiator in her mother's bedroom in December.

J.J. the twenty-six-year-old biker plumber,

with Eileen, the close-to-fifty divorcée, on the back of his Harley with the wind in her hair. It explains why her mother was saying she was having a 'switched-off' long weekend.

'We'll talk to Eileen tomorrow,' said Ren. 'Now that we've cleared up your whereabouts on the other dates, on February eleventh a young boy died — Luke Monroe — right around the block from the Dennehy house. So, I'd like you to talk me through the last Saturday that you were there . . . ' She paused. 'That Rose knows about . . . '

J. J. laughed. 'Ha — good point. Not that we'll be talking to her about any of that. She doesn't need to know, right?'

'No,' said Ren. 'No, she doesn't.'

'We didn't get it together in her mother's house, so you know,' said J. J.

Thanks for that.

'I called to the house,' said J. J. 'Mrs Dennehy was there, she brought me in, and I went to check out the downstairs bathroom. There was a problem with the toilet, but I didn't have the right part, so I told her I'd go order it as soon as I could, and be back to her.' He paused. 'It was a busy time. Then I was kind of afraid to show my face again.'

Ren nodded. 'Did you see Caleb that Saturday?'

'Yes — he was in the garden.'

'Do you know Caleb?' said Ren.

'Not really,' said J. J. 'But I said 'hi'. He didn't answer. He might have had headphones on. I don't know.'

281

'Where did you park your truck that day?' said Ren.

'I parked on another street, cut through a laneway down the side of one of my other client's gardens into Mrs Dennehy's.'

Ren got her phone and went to Google Maps. She showed him the Monroes' street. She went wider.

'Where were you parked?'

'Here,' he said, pointing to a house two blocks away.

'Would you have had to drive past the Monroes' house to get where you were going when you were finished at Mrs Dennehy's?' said Ren.

'No,' said J. J. 'I would have gone out the way I came in — through the neighbor's garden, got in my van and went in the opposite direction.'

Shit.

'Did you see anything suspicious that day?' said Ren.

'Nothing,' said J. J. 'Nothing I can think of.'

'Could you email me details of all your clients when you get home tonight?' said Ren.

'Sure,' said J. J. 'No problem.'

'And we're going to need you to come down to the station in the morning, to make a formal statement,' said Ren.

J. J. nodded. 'Sure.'

'In the meantime, don't go anywhere,' said Ren. She smiled. 'And keep your cell phone with you.'

'Yes, ma'am.'

★ ★ ★

When Ren got back to the hotel, she spent two hours going through Deb McLean's list of websites. She texted her when she was done.

Jesus Christ, Deb. I've been 'surfing' your aqua erotic sites of shame. I'd say 'I need a shower', but no: I never want to go near water again. I haven't even made coffee.

Deb phoned her. 'It's pretty grim, isn't it?'

'Yes!' said Ren. 'Why do men want to hurt women so much? Why do they get off on women who look like they're dying? These women look so fucking terrified. There are women chained to the bottom of pools. And these fat fucks in scuba masks offering . . . I can't even go there. And if all that wasn't bad enough, the aqua-erotic stuff ended up being my gateway drug.' She let out a breath. 'God, I love breathing. There's some fucked-up shit out there. I mean, it's not like I don't know that already, but when you are actively looking for it, and you open the portal . . . I mean — there are photos of women in all kinds of torture gear and then — and this is the true horror — a separate selection of women in torture gear *while wearing socks*. Socks . . . I swear to God, please strap me up in leather and chains, but if you use the opportunity to put socks on me, you'll see how quickly I can get out of a ball gag.'

'I know, right?' said Deb.

'There are so many forums — posts by people talking about all kinds of reasons they do what they do. Lots about how they nearly drowned as kids, and the sexual high that gave them, and how they've tried to reproduce that feeling or

283

those circumstances ever since. *I* nearly drowned as a kid and it was about as sexual as thinking you're going to fucking die at any moment. And it's what you said — they associate whatever was going on, or whatever was happening around them, with that sexual experience. Some of these people are really anguished, though — it's like 'take the pain of this obsession away'. They want to be normal . . . '

'Most of them think they are,' said Deb.

'I kept getting this horrible feeling — '

'Sinking sensation?'

'Stop! I kept thinking I was going to see a photo or a video of someone I know.'

'That's why I avoid amateur porn sites . . . hello, neighbor! Hello, kind man from the dry cleaner's!'

Ren laughed.

'OK — step away from the ASSes,' said Deb. 'You get it. There's no need to water-torture yourself . . . '

'I know too much,' said Ren. 'You know, like, next time I'm in a hotel pool . . . '

'You know as well as I do,' said Deb, 'that people go where their needs are likely to be met. You won't find a pedophile hanging around a retirement home. Terrible example — I'm ignoring the ones who might be residents or employees — but you know what I mean.'

'I'll do one more tour of duty,' said Ren. 'But, Deb . . . it is not purty.'

'Try seeing them after the fun and games. Losing an eye would be the best-case scenario.'

51

Ren woke up at six a.m. the next morning, on her back, sweating, her hands in fists, her jaw clenched.

One week . . . nothing.

Fuck this shit.

She got up.

I need to get rid of this energy or I will beat someone.

She packed her overnight bag for Denver, then changed into shorts, a tank, and sneakers, put her hair up in a pony-tail and went to the third-floor gym.

This is not a gym; it's a supply room.

An empty one, at least.

She got on the only treadmill there and started jogging. She speeded it up after five minutes.

Run, bitch, run.

Fuck John Veir, the fucking liar.

Why were you at Lister Creek? What have you done?

She pictured grabbing him by the throat, slamming him up against a wall, and asking him.

Stop.

What is wrong with me?

Where are you, Caleb Veir?

She pushed the speed button three times and ran faster. She upped the speed again. She took deep, rhythmic breaths, could feel it beginning to calm her. She started to go back over everything, all the conversations, the files she had read, who she had believed, who she didn't, why she didn't. She got flashes of all the images that came with the case over the previous week.

What the fuck is going on?

★ ★ ★

When she got into Tate PD, she checked her email — there was one from Emma Ridley from the Innocence Project with the Anthony Boyd Lorden file. Ren read through the original autopsy report, then the second report, including the forensic anthropologist's views on it being a possible accident.

I'm buying this. I wonder why Alice Veir isn't.

There was also a police sketch in the file: the flawed eyewitness testimony that Alice Veir had mentioned, but that wasn't featured in the television show. The face looked familiar: a little like Lorden, but not a lot. Not enough that it should have been taken as seriously as it was. The eyewitness claimed he saw a man pulled in at the side of the road not too far from where the remains were ultimately found . . . at the time Lorden claimed he was at home with his parents.

Hold on . . . the TV show. The lawyers. They were all introduced as going to be speaking at 'next month's International Innocence Program Conference in Portland'. That means it was on this month.

Ren grabbed her laptop and googled it.

Holy shit: day three of the conference was last Monday, the day Caleb went missing.

286

Ren clicked on the conference program. One speaker's name popped out at her: Alice Veir. And a second: Paula Leon, a lawyer from Maine.

Ren called the team over. 'I've found a link between Alice Veir and Paula Leon, the lawyer whose rental car was seen at Lister Creek rest area at the same time as John Veir's.' She pointed to the screen.

'This video is of Leon — she spoke at two p.m., exactly when her car was at Lister Creek rest area. So, someone else was driving her car. And the chances of that being anyone other than Alice Veir are pretty slim.'

Everybody was silent, processing what she was saying.

'Alice Veir borrowed Leon's car to go meet her brother,' said Ren. 'John Veir *was* the one who called Alice that morning, told her he'd killed Caleb, asked her to drive down and meet him there, so she could take the body, get rid of it.'

Gary looked at Ren.

Unreadable.

'Why else would he be meeting her that afternoon, around that time, and lie about it?' said Ren.

'Do you really think she's going to go along with that?' said Gary. 'A woman like her? A high-profile lawyer with a strong sense of justice?'

'Yes!' said Ren. 'If she had no choice.'

'Of course she'd have a choice,' said Gary. 'Seriously — would your brother cover up for you like that?'

They locked eyes when they realized what he'd said.

Yes, my brother has covered for me. He's covered for all of us.

But not quite like this. Not fucking quite.

Gary turned to Paul Louderback. 'If your sister called you, and said she'd killed your nephew, would you cover for her?'

'Depends on which nephew,' said Paul.

Everyone laughed.

I'm right. I know I am.

'We need to bring John Veir in,' said Ren.

'We need to wait until we have more on Lister Creek,' said Gary. 'It may not have been Alice Veir driving, there could be another reason why John Veir stopped there. This could be nothing to do with Caleb.'

Don't be so fucking measured.

'He could have been getting rid of something in the garbage,' said Ruddock. 'We'll check which landfill site their garbage collection goes to, organize a search.'

'He could have gone to the men's room, left something behind there for Alice to pick up,' said Gary.

'And we need to wait to get a hold of Paula Leon,' said Paul. 'I think your theory is right about the car, Ren, but if we can hear it directly from Leon . . .'

Fuck you all: I want to hear it from John Veir right now.

★   ★   ★

The group broke up and went their separate ways. Ren checked the time.

My flight!

She grabbed her purse and went into Ruddock's office.

'I wanted to apologize for getting emotional last night,' she said.

Ruddock batted her away. 'I won't hear a word of it.'

'You're very kind,' said Ren. 'And then I pull a gun on your nephew . . . '

'Well, I think he's proven he likes a little excitement from the ladies.'

Ren laughed.

'I called Eileen Dennehy,' said Ruddock, 'which was probably terrifying for her — this is her first encounter with the family and she's at the receiving end of an interrogation . . . '

'Interrogation . . . ' Ren laughed.

'She had nothing new to add,' said Ruddock, 'except she did ask me to check lost property for her mother's cell phone, which I did, but no one had handed it in.'

'I'm off to Denver,' she said. 'I'll be back late tomorrow night, so I'll see you first thing Wednesday.'

Ruddock nodded. 'Safe trip.'

She turned to walk away.

'Do you still have that thing,' said Ruddock, 'when you get on the plane, or the plane's about to land?'

She looked back at him.

'That feeling of 'there's no one to care if I've got here on time, or if I've landed safely'? No one to text.'

'I do,' said Ren. 'I do.'

'Well, lots of people care,' said Ruddock. 'Remember that.'

What a gorgeous soul. 'Thank you.'

'Safe trip.'

★ ★ ★

When Ren landed, as soon as she turned on her cell phone, it beeped with a text.

R u in Denver yet?

Her heart flipped.

Joe Lucchesi.

Screw you, heart, you independently operating asshole.

★ ★ ★

Ren decided to stay at a hotel in Denver instead of staying in her apartment. She didn't want the coldness, the bareness, the memories.

She knew where Joe Lucchesi would be staying — where he always stayed when he came to visit his son: The Maker Hotel, sleek, stylish, sexy. Ren booked an olde-worlde, cozy, chintzy hotel.

Safe. Unsexy.

★ ★ ★

She checked in, sat on the bed, looked out at the lights of the city. She took out her phone, opened Joe's text, and stared at it for a while.

This will be a shitshow. We are both fucked-up, damaged beyond repair. If you meet,

290

you will feel worse.

If that's at all possible, you will feel worse.

She texted one of two letters of the alphabet that had caused her so much trouble in the past:

y.

Followed by a double-dose of the other:

XX

52

Joe Lucchesi was sitting at a table in a corner of the bar that they had gotten drunk in together the last time — the bar whose serene gentleman's-club atmosphere they had happily ruined. The place hadn't changed, the barman was the same, the customers just as conservative. And then — Joe. She had a chance to look at him, because he was lost in thought. He had gotten bigger, broader, more muscular. He was wearing a black long-sleeved T-shirt and it was bursting at the arms. He stood out. In a room filled with suits, he looked like a bodyguard, and he had the don't-fuck-with-me frown to go with it. And then he turned to her.

He smiled and it was a warm, genuine, light-filled smile.

My heart.

I witnessed one of the most devastating moments of your life. I am the only other person alive to know your secret, your daughter's secret. Will I ever see your face and not quickly replace it with the expression I saw that night?

She returned the smile, knew it was a reflection of his.

It is good to see you. I don't even know how it could be, but it is.

She walked over to him, and he was standing, and he hugged her in those arms.

You smell so good. You are freshly showered,

freshly shaved, and . . . fucking sexy.

'So,' said Joe, gesturing for her to sit in the booth opposite.

She sat. 'So . . . '

'Seems like a long time ago we were here.'

'It was,' said Ren. 'And it hasn't changed.' *Unlike us.*

They looked at each other, and it was as if they were having the same thought.

'How are you?' said Ren. 'How are Shaun and Grace?' *Let's be normal.*

'They're great,' said Joe. 'Shaun is still looking for a job, Grace is doing real well at school. You know she asked about you when I said I was coming to Denver. You have a fan there.'

'And so does she,' said Ren.

'So . . . ' said Joe. 'How have you been?'

Ren shrugged. 'I'm OK . . . '

'Really?'

'No,' said Ren. 'Not really. I don't know . . . ' It hung in the silence.

Joe waited.

'I feel like I'm defined now by everything that happened,' said Ren. 'Do you? I feel like I have a flashing neon sign 'victim' over my head. And I'm not a victim kind of girl. I'm tired of talking about it.'

Joe nodded. 'It's probably healthy to, though.'

'Yeah — how healthy are you?' said Ren. 'On a scale of sashimi to Heart Attack Burger.'

He laughed, clinked his glass against hers.

★ ★ ★

Four hours later, Joe was opening the door of his hotel room. Ren was standing behind him.

The last time I went back to his room, we talked around things, we had many drinks, we slept side by side, but we didn't —

She was barely inside the door, still in the short hallway, when Joe turned to her, looked for something in her eyes, looked for permission.

Granted.

He reached out, slid his right hand up her neck, pulled her toward him and kissed her hard as he did.

Fuck. Me. I want this man.

She pushed him back against the wall, kissed him harder, slid her hand under his T-shirt.

But I may not mean it.

With his left hand, Joe grabbed her jacket, yanking it down one arm. Ren helped him pull off the rest. He struggled with the buttons of her shirt, but kept going, kissing her hard as he did.

You are rough. Beautifully rough.

When her top was off, he slowed down, held her by the waist, ran his finger down the two studs at the center of her black bra, then looked into her eyes as his hands moved up her back, unhooked the bra, sliding it off her. He stared at her breasts.

'You have incredible — ' said Joe.

'Thanks.' *Jesus.*

He lowered his head to her nipples, raised his hands gently up to them, worked them perfectly.

Ren pulled at his T-shirt, dragged it over his head, threw it on the floor. She slid her hands down from his chest, grabbed on to his belt buckle, pulled at it, but didn't open it. She moved her finger along just under the waistband of his jeans.

Not yet.

'Fuck, I want you,' he said. He kissed her deeper, ran his hand down to her ass, squeezing hard. 'I want you so fucking bad,' he said. 'I've wanted you since — '

Ren's words were muffled against his mouth, his tongue.

This guy is so fucking sexy, I can't stand it.

Ren went for his buckle again, opened it with one move, popped the top button of his jeans. The zip slid down by itself.

Rock. Hard.

She slid her hand down.

Oh.

She looked down.

Oh.

Fuck.

Fuck me.

He took her into the bedroom, and threw her on to the bed. He took off her shoes, her skirt, her stockings, everything. He knelt down in front of her, grabbed her hips and yanked her toward him. She tightened her legs around him, closed her eyes.

Fuck.

When she opened her eyes, he was looking up at her.

Gets me every time.

She grabbed his head, guided him up toward her. He slid his hand between her legs, kissed her gently at first, then firmer, deeper.

He is amazing.

I won't last.

Stop.

'Stop,' said Ren. 'Fuck me. Just . . . slam me up against that wall and fuck me. Hard.'

Hurt me.

Joe stopped, looked like he was going to take his jeans off.

Ren shook her head. 'Don't.' In three strides she was at the wall, her hands on his back, pulling him with her, kissing him deeply. He kissed her again, let her drag his jeans and shorts down around his ankles. She kissed him harder. He grabbed her ass and pulled her up, so she could wrap her legs around his waist. He slammed her against the wall. Over and over.

Holy.

Fuck.

⋆   ⋆   ⋆

In the moments afterward, Ren lay in bed, curled away from him, staring at the wall. She could see the red light of the alarm clock out of the corner of her eye.

That was fucking amazing.

Tears streamed down her face.

Shit. Shit. Shit.

Behind her, she heard a sharp intake of breath.

He's . . . he's crying too.

What a shitshow.

She reached her arm back, touched him, and he rolled toward her, pulling her into his arms, his chest pressed to her back.

They eventually slept, tightly wrapped together, bound less by sex and more by shared horrors.

53

Seth Fuller stood in the doorway of The Crow Bar, waiting for his opportunity. He found it when Shannon bent down over Clyde Brimmer's table to serve him a beer.

'Aunt Shannon?' said Seth. 'I'm going into town — do you need anything?'

His heart was pounding. His T-shirt was shaking. He held his hand to his stomach to steady it.

Shannon was too far away to notice. She glanced at the clock. It was ten p.m. 'What are you going into town for?' she said.

'I'm going to go to Bucky's, maybe play a game of pool, see who's there . . . '

'Why can't you play here?' said Shannon.

'With whom?' he said.

'I like that you say 'whom',' said Shannon, 'but I'd like it more if you didn't go anywhere this late.'

'Sometimes I think you forget I'm twenty-three years old.'

'You're right,' said Shannon. 'You're my sister's baby, and now you're mine. You haven't aged a day . . . ' She smiled.

'Go on — be back by midnight, OK? Can you promise me that much?'

'I most certainly can.'

'Hey,' she said, 'before you go.' She walked over to him, gave him a hug. She patted his back.

'You're on fire,' she said.

He nodded. 'It's hot in here.'

She was about to pull her hand away when she felt something against his lower back. She patted it harder. Before he had a chance, she had turned him around and lifted up his T-shirt.

'What the hell?' said Shannon. She grabbed him by his skinny arm, and shoved him behind the bar. 'You better start talking, mister. What the hell are you doing with a gun? Are you out of your mind?'

His cheeks were flaming red. Tears sprung into his eyes. 'For protection,' he said.

'That's the most ridiculous thing I've ever heard,' she said. 'Who do you need protection from? Give me that right now.'

He pulled it out of his waistband and slapped it on to her open palm. She grabbed it and slid it to the back of a shelf.

'Tell me,' she said. 'Who do you think is after you?'

'No one!' said Seth. 'No one. But I just — '

'Just what?' said Shannon. 'Want to feel tough? And you know that would just be taken off of you and used against you. You don't know how to fire a gun. I've never had guns in the house. I don't even have one in the bar, and there's a damn good reason for that: nothing good comes from guns, Seth. You see it every day on the news.'

'I do know how to fire it,' said Seth. 'I've been practicing in the woods.'

'Well, shooting at some tin cans is not the same as shooting a human being,' said Shannon.

'You're twenty-three years old — do I really need to explain that to you? Do you have a death wish, Seth? A prison-sentence wish? Do you miss being in prison? What is wrong with you? Are you taking drugs again?'

'No!' he said. 'No way! You know that. Never again.'

'I believe you,' said Shannon. 'But tell me what's going on — talk to me. Why is your internal switch set to self-destruct?'

He wiped away his tears. 'It's not,' he said.

'It is!' said Shannon. 'Misbehaving at school, damaging people's property . . . you were so young, Seth, so reckless, and I gave you a break, because you lost your mama. You were acting out. But it didn't get much better. And then drugs. Again, I figured, you'd had a hard time, you were a teenager by that stage, your daddy was gone at a time you really needed him . . . then prison . . . and now this! What is wrong, Seth? Something has to be.'

'Nothing's wrong!' he shouted. 'Nothing's wrong. Just leave me alone. You're suffocating me. I know you've lost everyone else, so I don't know why you're trying to push me away too.'

'What? I'm not trying to push you away!' said Shannon. 'I love the bones of you, Seth Fuller — '

'Stop!' he said. 'Just stop.'

'Stop loving you?' she said. She tried to smile. 'That's never going to happen.'

'You don't know me,' he shouted. 'You don't really know me. I think you just love who I was when Mama was alive. Who I used to be.'

He brushed past her, strode for the door, and pushed through into the night.

* * *

Seth parked his truck a five-minute walk from Bucky's, but he had no intention of going there. He looked around at the mix of houses along a street that was mainly residential, but had some doctors' offices, lawyers' offices, and other small businesses based out of them.

He got out of the truck and walked the length of the block, his breath white in the cold air. He stopped at the corner, at Longacres Funeral Home. He remembered standing there when he was eight years old, holding his Aunt Shannon's hand, looking around at the other kids his age, and thinking that this was it — he had no parents, now. At just that moment, Shannon had squeezed his hand three times — I. Love. You. He had looked up at her, and she had looked down at him, and there was so much love in that small gesture, so much love in her eyes for him, in her smile, that he believed that everything was going to be all right. He was wrong.

Then they were back again for Aaron's funeral.

Seth's heart was racing, and he was amazed that it worked at all despite the slash of pain that felt like a hot blade, slicing down through it, carving out a trench that felt like it was widening with every breath.

How is my heart still pumping? How are my lungs functioning?

What am I doing here? What am I doing?

He turned back, walked toward his truck, hands in his pockets, head down. He heard heavy footsteps coming toward him. He looked up and saw Gil Wiley.

'Hey, Wiley'

But Wiley, face was red and twisted, and he was closing the gap between them in huge strides. Before Seth had a chance to pull his hands from his pockets, a powerful right hook had sent him to the ground, with nothing to break his fall. As his head struck the concrete, through the ringing in his ears, he could hear Wiley shouting: 'Are you fucking my wife, you piece of shit? Are you fucking my wife?'

54

Ren sat across the table from Joe. She was dressed in a white hotel robe, he was in his boxers. They had ordered room service. She looked at him when he wasn't looking, buttering toast, pouring coffee for both of them.

Couple-y.

He looked up at her and smiled.

No one is going to get my heart again. Or whatever amount of it is left. One used heart, broken in places, black in others.

The heart that was moved when he looked at you . . .

Shut it.

'I've always felt weird eating breakfast with no underwear on,' said Ren. 'Is that normal?' She paused. 'Or with someone topless.'

Joe got up, grabbed his T-shirt from the floor, put it on, sat back down, and smiled. 'I don't want to turn you off your pancakes.'

'It would take more than that. I didn't mean for you to actually go put your T-shirt on.'

'And I hope you didn't mean yourself to go put underwear on.'

She laughed. *Oh, God. I hate doing it again in the morning after breakfast when it's a one-night stand.*

One-night stand?

Stop.

He poured her more coffee, gave her another

303

big smile, stayed looking at her a little longer.

No, no, no. No.

She focused on eating her pancakes.

Why is it that I feel like Paul Louderback took advantage of me and Joe Lucchesi didn't?

Because I wanted Joe more. Because of the chemistry. Because . . .

No one took advantage of you.

'What's going through that pretty head?' said Joe.

'A tiny tumbleweed.' *That's what Everett and I used to say.*

'Hmm,' said Joe. 'Is it last night? Are you having regrets?'

She shook her head. 'No. Not at all. It's just — ' She looked away.

Do not tell him.

'Come on,' said Joe. 'You know you can say anything to me . . . I hope.'

She looked at him.

You are a sweet, sweet, tough guy sexy fucking fuck. 'I think that . . . I think I'm to blame for all the . . . everything. I think I should have ID'd — and located — Duke Rawlins sooner. I think I shouldn't have gone to the Ostler Building alone, that I should have been at the meeting I was ordered to be at — on time. I think that . . . ' *I didn't love Ben enough for the universe to have allowed him to live.* 'I think that I didn't do my job as an agent, a friend, a girlfriend. I think that I should have followed my gut that there was something wrong with Janine when I arrived at Safe Streets. I think — '

Everyone I touch turns to dead.

304

Don't let me touch you.

'Whoa,' said Joe, 'There are too many things to respond to there. You're to blame for 'all the everything'? No. You need to remember that Duke Rawlins was a psychopath. In my opinion, he would never go out on anything other than . . . how he went out. He is the only person to blame. You have to know that. And to take your last point — you should have sensed there was something wrong with Janine? And done what — left the building? Called for backup? She wouldn't have allowed you to — you would have jeopardized everyone if you did. She would definitely have been killed, and Gary would have too. I believe that you saved *me* with your actions, that's for sure. You saved me twice over: by having Rawlins break through that guardrail, and by stopping me from strangling him to finish him off. I could be dead or locked up, if not for you.'

I never thought of that. Is it even true, though?

'You couldn't have known Rawlins' plans,' said Joe. 'He was insane.'

'Parts of him were predictable.'

'Not enough parts.'

She checked the time on her phone. 'You better hurry. You have to be at Safe Streets in forty-five minutes.'

'I know,' said Joe. He moved his chair back. 'What do you think I could use some of that time for?'

'No, no, no — I haven't finished my pancakes.'

He stood up, took her hand, pulled her up, opened her robe, slid it off. 'From behind, real

305

quick,' he said. 'You can be back to your pancakes while they're still hot.'

'You're a considerate man,' said Ren. *Serious brownie points for thinking of the pancakes.*

He looked like he was about to speak, but he was too focused on keeping his promise. She watched him in the mirror.

Fuck me, you are sexy.

★ ★ ★

She lay in his arms afterward, turned away.

Always, turned away.

What are we doing?

And are we doing the same thing?

Joe took her gently by the shoulder and pulled her back to face him.

She looked into his eyes: brown, beautiful, troubled eyes.

Something shifted in her chest.

The twist of a thick wooden stake,

This is how vampires feel when it's all over.

She looked away.

It's all over.

She got up, put on her robe and went back to the table to pour more coffee. She could sense Joe watching her. She turned around.

He is unreadable.

'That was amazing,' he said.

'It was.' *It really fucking was.*

She thought of never seeing him again. Her heart did not like it.

'You really need to leave,' said Ren. 'You'll be late.'

'All right, all right,' said Joe. 'I get the message.' He rolled to the edge of the bed and sat up.

He has no clue how gorgeous he is.

'What do you mean, you get the message?' said Ren. 'The message was pretty straightforward: you will be late. Not a huge amount of interpretation required.'

He made a face. He looked a little wounded.

'I have tone-of-voice issues,' said Ren. 'Sorry.'

'It's not that,' said Joe. 'It's just I'm not sure the 'you'll be late' was the main message in that sentence.'

Fuck. 'Technically, there were two sentences.' She smiled.

Joe went toward the bathroom, but paused in the doorway. He looked at her.

Do not ask me to come in the shower with you.

He didn't say anything. He just looked sad.

* ★ ★

Ren climbed back into bed, stared at the ceiling.

I hate this.

She listened to him in the shower, pictured him in there, imagined him coming out afterwards, clean and cool, and fucking her again. He reappeared ten minutes later, with a towel around his waist, and his head down. He glanced up briefly and gave her a smile that flickered with something else.

What was that?

He got dressed and packed without saying anything.

I have no idea what's going on here.

*Oh my God . . . I can't read emotional cues.
Oh my God: I'm on the spectrum.*

When Joe was finished, he came over and sat on the bed beside her. He brushed her hair off her face, held his hand there.

'Hey,' he said. 'What's up? What just happened?'

'Nothing.'

'Are you sure?'

She nodded. He waited.

'OK,' he said. 'Well, can I kiss you goodbye?'

Ren laughed. 'Of course you can.' She sat up. He kissed her.

He is incredible.

Don't cry.

'So,' he said, 'can I see you later — after your interview?'

'I'd love to, but I can't.'

I just remembered I have to call someone after then . . .

'OK . . . ' said Joe. 'Well, maybe . . . ' he studied her face ' . . . another time?'

She nodded. 'Yes. Good luck later.'

'You too.'

She watched him walk to the door. He looked back. 'Bye.'

'Bye. Thanks.'

She rolled over in the bed, and buried her head into the pillow.

Ugh. Bye.

It was only sex.

Spectacular sex.

More than sex.

Stop.

She came again, thinking about what he'd done that morning, how amazing it was, and what he'd done the previous night, and how amazing that was, and what she wanted him to do the next time and how amazing that would be.

Next time?!

You're nuts.

She took a shower, then went for her purse, pulled open the inside zip.

Noo! No backup underwear!

Going commando to face two inspectors. Professional.

Just not that kind of professional.

★　★　★

She went out on to the street and called Janine. She got her voicemail.

'Janine, I'm just going to lay it all out there,' said Ren. 'I slept with Joe Lucchesi, very drunk, and very sober, and it was incredible, and I feel like the biggest piece of shit in humanity. Call me.'

A text came back within five minutes:

Meet me in Crema?

Ren replied:

Bring underwear . . .

55

Janine was smiling at her as soon as she walked in. Ren ordered coffee and sat down opposite her.

'Seriously, though,' said Ren, 'is there a decent wait time? Is there some kind of etiquette? I wait — oh, six months — and sleep with two men in one week — '

'Whoa, whoa — two?'

'Sorry, yes, I slept with Paul Louderback on Friday night.'

'I thought you had a threesome!'

'Well, when you put it like that, I guess it could have been worse. Or better. Is this normal? Are mine the actions of someone grief-stricken? Or a whore?'

'Isn't Paul married — not that I'm judging.'

'No, he left her again,' said Ren. 'And he'll go back to her again. He's a boy in a man's body. He needs a wife to mother him. But he doesn't find the mothering part sexy, so he roams free every now and then and gets the sex part. But — and here's the crux of it — he needs the mothering part more than the sex part, which is why he goes back. He will never admit that to himself because it's not cool. So I think this will be the loop for the remainder of his life. I will sidestep him next time, though. It's kind of depressing.' She let out a breath.

'You know you're not at the mercy of these

men's choices,' said Janine. 'You get to make your own choices too.'

'True,' said Ren. She paused. 'But I do need Joe Lucchesi to seriously decide to get the fuck out of my life. I can't handle it.'

Janine shook her head, groaned. 'I don't know if you want to hear this, but it's pretty clear that you have — already — really fallen for that man.'

'Oh my God. No, I haven't.'

'You are useless.'

'I know that, but, separate to that, I have not fallen for Joe Lucchesi.'

'Useless.'

'Ugh,' said Ren. 'I don't know what's going on. I guess I'm finding it hard to process who I should be after all this.' She laughed. ''I don't know who I am any more . . .''

''It's not you, it's me,'' said Janine. 'Just be what makes you happy.'

'Happy at the time, or happy afterward?' said Ren. 'I think that's my issue. Happy at the time gets me in a lot of trouble — '

'Largely with yourself, though,' said Janine. 'What standards are you holding yourself up to?'

''Ladies',' said Ren. 'Like you.'

'You know that you don't actually know my sexual history,' said Janine.

'Oh, thank God: you're a closet whore.'

Janine smiled.

'Oh my God — you are!' said Ren.

'Are you waiting for more information?' said Janine.

'Now I feel like a weirdo.'

'Does any of it matter in the end?' said Janine.

'Is sex something to feel guilty about?'

Ren paused. 'I'm Catholic, remember. But good point. I guess I've spent so long thinking . . . '

'Overthinking,' said Janine. 'You overthink everything. It must be exhausting. You're not hurting anyone. And if you're hurting yourself, well, then don't do it.'

'It's not that simple, though, is it?' said Ren.

'Stop. Be kind to yourself.'

I don't deserve kindness.

Joe is kind.

Fuck him.

'OK, so here's my issue,' said Ren. 'Can you have a guy who makes you want to be slammed up against a wall every time you see him, and still he could be faithful to you?'

'So, you're thinking about a relationship,' said Janine. She smiled.

'Jesus. Paging Dr Lone, paging Dr Lone. No, I'm not thinking about a relationship . . . I don't know what I'm thinking.' She paused. 'I guess I like . . . different types, and I'm afraid of the Joe Lucchesi types. Why would he want to be with me?'

'Good point, because you're a loser.'

'But, also, can anyone really, truly commit to one type?'

'Basically, this is about the fact you slept with two entirely different types of men in one week?'

'Four days if we are to fully nail down the sluttiness. But yes. I guess so.'

'But, you don't have a type,' said Janine. 'You're personality driven. Yes, you happened to

312

have been with some gorgeous guys, but that was incidental.'

'Yes!' said Ren. 'You're right. I really don't care what guys look like . . . within reason. Make me fucking laugh . . . and you're fucked.'

'Hey, I make you laugh,' said Janine.

'Be afraid.'

'OK — here's my advice,' said Janine. 'Stop worrying. Enjoy! Stop torturing yourself. And I don't see no ring on that finger.'

Ren looked down at her hand. 'It's very bare.' She looked up at Janine. 'It suits me bare.'

'Well, lucky you haven't put the panties on yet,' said Janine. 'Because they would be totally on fire right now. And they cost me thirty dollars.'

'Thirty dollars — did you get me a multi-pack? Thanks for your optimism. Or your belief in my continued whoredom.'

'No, I did not get you a multi-pack,' said Janine. 'I got you one pair. Of very nice ones. I know who I'm dealing with.'

Ren's phone beeped with a text from Joe Lucchesi.

See you before you go? x

Oh, God: the kiss.

Her heart sank. But she was smiling. She looked up. Janine was smiling back.

'Love . . . ' said Janine, 'is a wonderful thing.'

'Is a fucking nightmare,' said Ren at the same time.

★ ★ ★

313

Half an hour later, Ren arrived at Safe Streets. She went to the ladies' room and put on the very pretty pink underwear.

She texted Janine.

Excellent taste, ma'am. Thank you. And it's not love . . . XX

Janine replied.

They're flame-retardant

Ren wondered if Janine had the same, sudden realization, and whether it turned her stomach too. Because they both knew that, within minutes, Ren would be sitting down in front of two senior FBI investigators and telling lies, lies, lies.

56

Ren walked into the bullpen and shook off her jacket. Cliff James came over to her without saying a word and put his big-bear arms around her.

'You and me against the world, sweetheart,' he said, kissing her head.

'God bless you.' She pulled away gently and sat down at the edge of his desk. 'What would I do without you, Clifford James?'

'Ren, what you do without me is your business . . . '

She laughed. 'If you only knew.'

'I don't want to. I mean it. How's Oregon?'

Ren nodded. 'Looks like we could be dealing with an Aquatic Sexual Sadist, drowning children for kicks.'

Cliff shook his head. 'How long can I keep doing this job, I ask myself.' He tilted his head toward the conference room. 'Are you nervous?'

'You bet.'

'No reason to be,' said Cliff. They locked eyes. 'You just tell your story.' There was weight in his words.

★   ★   ★

There were two people waiting for Ren in the conference room — a dark, bulky man with a big gut, an unreadable face, blank eyes. His gray suit was a little too tight. The female agent with him had blonde hair swept tightly back, a stern, masculine face, but compassionate eyes. They stood up when Ren walked in. The man reached out first.

'Agent Bryce, I'm Inspector Neubig, this is Inspector Brinks.'

Whoa, whoa, whoa. They're not the names Gary said would be here.

Ren clenched, unclenched her fists under the table when she sat down.

What is going on here? This doesn't feel routine.

'Thank you for meeting with us today, Agent Bryce,' said Neubig. 'I believe you're working on the missing boy case Oregon. How is that going for you?'

'Good, thank you,' said Ren.

'Well, we don't want to hold you up,' said Neubig. 'We'll get straight to the point. We'd just like to talk to you about why a meeting was convened by Gary Dettling in his office at Safe Streets on the evening of the shooting?'

Oh.

Fuck.

Ren's heart started to pound.

Stop. Stop. Stop.

'Gary wanted to go through elements of the investigation with the core team.'

'That would be . . . ' Neubig looked at his notes, 'Janine Hooks, Robbie Truax, Everett King — '

'No,' said Ren. 'Not Everett King. He just happened to be there.'

316

'But,' said Neubig, 'was he not involved in tracking down' — he looked at his notes — 'the suspect who was shot when you and Robbie Truax came under fire at his property? Would you not say that Agent King was a key player in the investigative team?'

'Of course,' said Ren, 'but he was a newer member of Safe Streets, and perhaps Gary was — out of familiarity — choosing to — '

'But,' said Neubig, 'was Agent Hooks not hired at the same time as Agent King?'

Fuuuck. 'That's correct,' said Ren. 'I'm sorry. It's really not my place to offer up suggestions as to why Gary chose the team he chose to be there that evening.' She paused. 'Actually, I think Everett may have had a personal engagement that night.' *Phew.*

'Moving on to your — we'll call him your boyfriend — Ben Rader,' said Neubig. 'Can you tell me again why he had flown in to Safe Streets?'

We'll call him your boyfriend? Nice. 'Well, he'd flown to Denver,' said Ren.

They fucking know. How could they possibly know? 'As I found out afterwards,' said Ren, 'Gary was considering Ben for an undercover assignment.' *Not, in fact, asking him to be part of an intervention for his crazy fucking girlfriend.* 'Ben wanted to surprise me, so he asked Gary not to mention it to me.'

'And your brother, Matthew Bryce,' said Neubig. 'He flew in to Denver that day, and had had prior phone conversations with Agent Rader.'

She nodded. 'They got along very well,' said Ren. 'Ben called Matthew to see if he would come — '

'We have it that it was Matthew who called Ben,' said Neubig.

Jesus Christ. I'm going to fuck this up so bad.

'I didn't mean that literally,' said Ren. 'I meant they were talking on the phone and when Matt heard that Ben was flying in, he decided to do the same thing. I hadn't seen Matt in five months, he had to use up some annual leave in work . . . it all worked out . . . ' She paused. ' . . . would have worked out . . . very well.'

The blood is draining from my body.

She remembered the night of the shooting, when Matt was waiting at her apartment, waiting to tell her that Ben had been shot dead, then Gary arriving out of the blue, well after midnight, and the confusion, the shock, and the snapping out of it. The abrupt change, the setting aside of the horror and grief to focus. To focus on concocting a story over coffee that no one wanted to drink, but everyone had to drink, to keep them awake, which they didn't want to be, because they wanted to sleep through their nightmare.

I want to sleep through this nightmare.

Agent Brinks poured a glass of water, and passed it over to Ren.

'Thank you,' said Ren, turning to her, sensing she was rooting for her. *People are so kind.*

'Would we be correct in saying,' said Neubig, 'that the people who were gathered in Safe Streets that evening were your closest friends?'

318

Don't cry. Ren nodded. *That's the best I can do. I can nod.*

That night, sitting in my apartment, Gary turning to Matt. 'Matt, you're the writer: I'll give you the facts. We need a strong, convincing narrative that will dead-end a potential line of questioning for ever. Something that will hide the fact that Ren was off her meds, that I organized an intervention, that that's why you and Ben were in Denver, that Rawlins was likely aware of Ren's condition despite the fact that she told him otherwise.'

Looking at Matt, my heart breaking all over again. Matt was a journalist: an honest, thorough, fact-checking, morally upstanding, award-winning investigative journalist. Telling the truth was his vocation. But how quickly he stood up, and how Gary had looked at him like he thought he was leaving. But, how, instead, without a word spoken, Matt had walked over to the printer, slid out some pages and started to write notes.

They were up all night, they learned their lines.

Remember your fucking lines.

'They were also my colleagues,' said Ren.

'You were late for the meeting,' said Neubig.

'Yes,' said Ren.

'Why was that?'

'I was with Detective Joe Lucchesi investigating a building that I believed Duke Rawlins was holed up in.'

'And Rawlins was not there,' said Neubig.

'No,' said Ren. 'But he had been. I told

Detective Lucchesi that I would go to Safe Streets and bring the team back to the Ostler Building.'

'You said in your original statement that you believed Duke Rawlins was watching Safe Streets from that building,' said Neubig.

'Yes,' said Ren.

'Yet you didn't think that the purpose of that was, perhaps, to gain access to that building at some particular point?'

'It wasn't as simple as that,' said Ren. 'I believed that he was in pursuit of Detective Lucchesi . . . and possibly Gary Dettling. Yes. But I couldn't have predicted what Duke Rawlins was going to do. It was unlike anything he had ever done before. I had studied him, Detective Lucchesi had, the profilers at Quantico had, even Detective Lucchesi's son had studied him for his Master's degree in Forensic Psychology. No one predicted this.'

'OK, thank you, Agent Bryce. That's all for now.'

For now? Jesus. No more. No more. No more.

57

Jimmy Lyle walked through the airport terminal, angry and red-faced, dressed in a black jacket, blue jeans and black boots. He was coiled like a spring waiting for a reason to launch; his broad shoulders hunched, his arms rigid, ending in tight fists. But he'd kept his eyes down, because he couldn't launch, he couldn't draw attention to himself.

He'd do one night in the house, that was it, then get to the retirement home, pack up his daddy's things, show his face at Longacres, stand there mourning his fucking eyes out for a couple hours and get the fuck back to his vacation, his car, the plans he'd been forced to rearrange.

★   ★   ★

After fifteen minutes driving Jimmy's rental car was suddenly illuminated by flashing blue lights. His breath caught. He felt like his head was going to explode. His leg spasmed and, for a brief moment, his foot struck the accelerator and the car jerked. He looked in the rear-view mirror and saw the police car, its presence like a looming tank that would roll over the rest of his life.

Jimmy got his breathing under control, because his mind had quickly taken him to an image of an officer asking him to pop the trunk of his car. Jimmy knew how to tame the wild breaths because it was what he had learned to do. Just as he was regaining the rhythm — and visualizing an alternative scenario, picturing charming the officer, instead of sitting in the driver's seat, pale and sweaty and suspicious — the police car drove on.

Jimmy's relief came out as something between a growl and a cry.

You're in a rental car. You're in a rental car. Idiot. You emptied the trunk. Idiot.

You are nothing. You are nothing. You are nothing.

58

Ren arrived back at Tate PD on Wednesday morning. Ruddock was in his office. He had ordered proper coffee and blueberry muffins from a café in town.

'God bless you,' said Ren.

'Welcome back,' said Ruddock. He pointed to the table. 'Good timing . . . '

'Thank you, kindly,' said Ren, grabbing a muffin. 'Yes — it is. I can sense four things from a thousand yards: coffee, pancakes, blueberry-flavored foodstuff, and Cinnabons.' *Plus wine, beer, champagne, and carnal opportunities.*

There were three long black boxes on his desk, the kind that held photos.

His wife's . . .

Ruddock saw her noticing. 'I'm channeling my wife. The local newspaper is running a memorial for an old teacher from town who died.' He paused. 'Took his own life, in fact.'

'Was that the guy in the retirement home?' said Ren. 'Beckman mentioned it.'

Ruddock nodded. 'He was the swim coach for years at the school.' He paused. 'You just never know what's going on in people's heads, do you?'

You sure don't. 'You sure don't,' said Ren. 'Any updates on the case?' She looked at him properly.

Jesus — he looks shattered.

'I'm sorry to say, there was an incident

323

Monday night,' said Ruddock. 'With Gil . . . and Seth Fuller.'

What?

'Gil assaulted him,' said Ruddock. 'He messed him up pretty badly, but we got him to the hospital, he's been patched up, he's OK . . . some damage to his back, but mainly cuts and bruises, a black eye. He's had a few stitches, he's in pain, but he'll live to fight another day.'

'What happened?' said Ren.

'According to Gil, it was over a pool debt. Seth owed him fifty dollars.'

Buuuullshit did this happen over $50. She scanned Ruddock's face. *You don't believe that either, surely . . .*

She nodded politely.

'Our saving grace,' said Ruddock, 'is that Seth's keeping it quiet, and he's not pressing charges. At the hospital, he told doctors he didn't know who the assailant was. And it wasn't his plan to tell his aunt either.'

You are so fucking lucky. But why would Seth cover for Wiley? Is he afraid of him, like Clyde is?

'And where's Wiley now?' said Ren.

'Well, he's taken a short leave of absence,' said Ruddock. 'But, he's extremely contrite, nothing like this has ever happened before. He's under . . . personal stresses. I don't want his standing in the community to be impacted on, either — it's a very visible post — so once he's cooled off, I will have him back on different duties. You won't have to deal with him any further on the investigation.'

Damn fucking right we won't.

'Well,' said Ren, 'I'm sorry to hear all that. You look like you've had a long night.'

Ruddock nodded. 'Yes. Yes, I have.'

I want to hug you.

★ ★ ★

Gary was waiting for her outside the CARD team's office.

'How did Denver go?'

'They're circling around me,' said Ren.

He held up a hand to stop her walking on through the door.

'This meeting was about me, Gary. This was person — '

'What? No, it wasn't,' said Gary. 'It was standard going-back-over-the-facts — '

'It wasn't,' said Ren. 'They know something, I'm telling you. Why else would they have told you two inspectors were going to be there who weren't.'

'What? Who was there?'

'Neubig and Brinks. Do you know them?'

'No, I do not.'

'Well, that's reassuring,' said Ren. 'They switched them at the last minute to fuck with us.'

'Ren, that sounds a little paranoid.'

'It's not paranoia,' said Ren. 'They're questioning me, wondering if I should be working at all. They're — '

'You've been cleared to work,' said Gary. 'You've passed your psych eval — '

'But — '

'Ren!' said Gary. 'Pause for one second. Do you think there is any evidence anywhere that that meeting was an intervention? Think about it: none of this was in writing. The only people who knew were me, Ben and Matt. It was only spoken about on my landline. And you know that neither Ben nor Matt would have betrayed either mine or your confidence. Janine didn't know, but would have been no less trustworthy if she did. Everett didn't know. Joe Lucchesi didn't know. OK? So relax.'

'Why are they asking those questions, then?' said Ren.

'Standard procedure,' said Gary. 'It was a major incident.' He looked at her. 'It's over. You're back here. You still have your job.'

'For now,' said Ren. 'They want me to come in again.'

'They know nothing. Relax.'

Why do people ever tell people to relax? Who reacts well to 'relax'? Who actually relaxes?

'Yikes about Wiley,' said Ren.

Gary nodded.

'It was only a matter of time,' said Ren. 'I thought if he was going to assault anyone, it would be me.'

* * *

When they went into the office, Paul Louderback waved them over. His laptop was open on a screen-grab from a traffic cam. Ruddock walked in to join them.

'So,' said Paul. 'It turns out Seth Fuller was

not at The Crow Bar the night Aaron drowned. Not for the entire night, anyway. He was parked for a lot of it on Richmond Road — a residential street. He doesn't get out of his truck. It looks like he was the only one in it.'

'Any recent burglaries in the area?' said Ren to Ruddock. 'Could he have been up to no good? Why else wouldn't he have told us?'

'No burglaries reported,' said Ruddock.

'He could have been waiting for a woman,' said Ren. 'One who didn't show. A married woman? Stalking someone? How long was he there?'

'Three hours,' said Paul.

Ren opened up a street view of the area on her laptop.

'Can we get a list of the addresses on this street?' she said. 'Who owns them, who's living there?'

She zoomed out. 'Hold on — this is the Middle School right here? And there was a dance on there that night? He was parked here for three hours during that time?'

'Yes,' said Ruddock.

Everyone looked at each other.

No, Seth. No. You need to be innocent for me to have faith in humanity . . . and trust in my gut.

'And now for my next trick,' said Paul. He handed Ren a printout. 'Nice call on the Play-Station.'

She read the results. 'So, Caleb Veir *has* played it,' she said. 'I fucking give up.' She read the results again. 'Hold on — he was the first person to play it?'

327

Paul nodded.

'That's very weird,' said Ren. 'No kid is going to let another kid play it before they do.'

'No,' said Paul.

'I think I may need to pay another visit to The Crow Bar,' said Ren.

59

Ren winced when she saw Seth Fuller. 'Ouch . . . '

He looked up from the sofa where he was watching television.

'I'm just here to clear a few things up,' said Ren.

Seth paused, then turned off the television. He struggled to sit up straighter.

'Seth, we know that Caleb Veir was the first person to use your PlayStation. That's what the lab came back with when they analyzed the hard drive. Did he play that with you?'

'No!' said Seth. 'No way. And remember — it was Aaron's PlayStation. As far as I know, he wasn't even friends with Caleb.'

There was a noise behind them, and they both turned around. Shannon was standing in the doorway, looking at Ren.

'I can explain about the PlayStation,' she said. 'If you'd like to talk privately?'

'Sure,' said Ren. She followed her into the kitchen.

'Seth doesn't know anything about this,' said Shannon. 'It was John who bought the PlayStation — for Caleb. He paid cash, so it wouldn't have shown on his credit-card receipt. John and I bumped into each other at Target in the middle of December — we were both looking for it for our boys, but there was only one left and John got to it first. He was planning to give it to Caleb for Christmas, but because of Caleb not behaving the way he said he would, John changed his mind and gave it to me for Aaron. He didn't know that Caleb had already found it in the garage, and had already sneaked it out to play with it. He dropped it, which is why it has a dent in the corner.'

Ren stared at her. 'How do you know that Caleb had found it?'

'It's not a pleasant story. Caleb cycled out here one day. He had climbed a tree, and was just sitting there — '

'What do you mean 'just sitting there'?'

Shannon flushed. 'I didn't say anything to John, but that tree overlooks my bedroom window. Whether that was a coincidence or not, I don't know.'

'Do you think he might have suspected the affair?' said Ren.

She shrugged. 'I don't think so, because he fell from the tree — I think it was the shock of seeing John arrive, pull up outside the house, and . . . well, I came out to greet John. It was a fairly passionate encounter. Caleb fell, banged his head. We rushed over to him, brought him inside, lay him down on the sofa, made sure he was OK. While he was there, he saw the PlayStation — he recognized the dent, so he knew it was the one he had found in the garage. He went nuts. We had to calm him down. He wanted to take it home — he said he'd tell Teddy about us. We . . . asked him not to. John promised to buy him one with his next pay check, and Caleb promised not to tell Teddy.'

Poor Caleb. So that was how he got the bump on his head. 'Thanks for letting me know,' said Ren. 'But why didn't you say it before?'

'More lies for Teddy Veir to hear,' said Shannon. 'Not a lot for any of us to be proud of.'

'I'm going to go back in to Seth,' said Ren. 'And I'd like to talk to him in private.'

Shannon nodded. 'I'm sorry for intruding earlier. I heard 'PlayStation' and I just figured something was up.'

★ ★ ★

Ren went into Seth's room, and sat on the windowsill.

'Everything OK?' he said.

'Yes,' said Ren. *Here goes.* She took out the traffic-cam photo.

'Why was your truck pictured on Richmond Road on the night Aaron died?' she said. 'We got this from a private camera. You told me you were here all night.'

Seth stared at the image for a while, twisting his mouth left and right. 'I needed a drive. I wanted to clear my head.'

'Why did your head need to be cleared?'

'I get anxious sometimes,' said Seth. 'Driving helps.'

'And does parking?'

He side-eyed her. 'I just stopped there — there was no particular reason. It was just where I felt like stopping.'

'Were you going to see anyone on that street?'

331

He frowned. 'No, ma'am.'

'You know the grounds of the middle school back on to that street,' said Ren.

'Uh . . . yes.'

'And that there was a dance on there that night?'

'Yeah, obviously,' said Seth. 'I dropped Aaron off at it.' He paused. 'Look, I went for a drive — that's all that was, OK? I promise.'

'I promise.' There's something so young about you.

She took a breath. 'You know I'm separate from Tate PD,' she said. 'So anything you tell me about anyone who works there won't go back to them, right?'

'Really?' said Seth.

'Really.' She paused. 'What happened Monday night with Wiley?'

He shrugged. 'It's no big deal . . . '

'It looks like a big deal from here,' said Ren. She walked over to him and bent down. 'And an even bigger deal close-up.' She smiled.

'That was about fifty bucks I owed him from a pool game,' said Seth.

Ren returned to her seat on the windowsill. 'Seth, I'm not sure what I've said or done to give you the impression that I'm stupid . . . but whatever it was, I apologize for misleading you. And I'm sure Pete Ruddock feels the same way about why Wiley thought that story would float.'

Seth stared at her. 'What do you mean?'

'Come on . . . ' said Ren. 'No police officer — *lieutenant* — is going to beat the shit out of someone in the street over a fifty-dollar bet. This was a lot more personal than that.'

'I'm telling you — it was about the fifty dollars. I owed it to him for months.'

'You can change the timeframe all you like,' said Ren, 'but I'm still not buying it.' She paused. 'What were you doing in town last night?'

'I was going to Bucky's to play pool. I was actually going to see if Wiley was there.'

'OK . . . but you were found collapsed a block from the other side of Main Street, beside your truck, which was parked outside the church car park.'

'I couldn't get a spot by Bucky's.'

'I'm trying to be a grown-up here and not roll my eyes,' said Ren, 'but do you know how easy it is for me to check if there were parking spaces close to Bucky's that night? Very.'

Seth's shoulders slumped.

'What's going on?' said Ren. 'Are you protecting Wiley? Because Wiley doesn't need protecting. And *shouldn't* be protected — he's an officer of the law. Or are you protecting yourself?'

'Look,' said Seth. 'There's something I was going to tell you about John Veir, but I was afraid to say anything . . . and then, it didn't seem to matter any more.'

'What do you mean, it didn't seem to matter?'

'I want immunity.'

I want to laugh. 'Immunity?'

'From prosecution.'

'For what?' said Ren.

He shrugged. 'Just . . . in case there might be

something unlawful I've done in this story.'

Ren smiled.

'What?' said Seth.

'Honey, you've got ten seconds.'

His eyes widened. 'OK, OK: Merrifield was dealing in BRCI, he hooked me up with a patch — fentanyl — and I OD'd, by accident. John Veir walked in, saved my life. Merrifield was still in my cell, happy to watch me die. When he was leaving, he said to John: 'If you breathe a word of this to anyone, I will watch you burn.'

Jesus Christ.

And I meant ten seconds to begin your story. Not to tell it in. But, hey — works for me.

'Why did you think it didn't matter?' said Ren.

'Because Merrifield was linked to John Veir anyway. I saw the news report the day after the fire. Merrifield was linked to it.'

But there's the small matter of who was supplying Merrifield and what they may have thought of John Veir stumbling on to their little enterprise.

Jesus. Christ.

60

Ren went back to Tate PD and told everyone about Seth Fuller and the fentanyl story.

'I believe Seth,' said Ren. 'But what I don't get is why John Veir didn't say it to us the night of the fire — it would have bolstered his case.' She turned to Ruddock. 'Have you heard anything about dealing in BRCI? I mean, they must be doing a thorough investigation, considering Merrifield is out there.'

'No,' said Ruddock. 'But I can make inquiries.'

'He's been gone ten days,' said Ren. 'There's no way he hasn't had help somewhere along the way. Someone is harboring him.'

They all nodded.

I think I'm stating the obvious . . .

'Let's call John Veir in again,' said Gary. 'To rattle him. We won't mention the video from Lister Creek until we have more, and until we can get Alice Veir in here too, face to face.'

★ ★ ★

Half an hour later, John Veir was sitting in the interview room, his fingers linked, his head bowed. Ren and Ruddock walked in. He looked up at them, tolerance and challenge flickering in his eyes.

'OK,' said Ruddock, sitting down, 'looks like there are a couple of things here that you neglected to mention to us, John.' His manner was warm, non-threatening. He made John go through everything about the day Caleb went missing, about the night Aaron Fuller died, about the day he dropped Caleb off at Rose Dennehy's. He repeated the facts as he had first given them, then collapsed back in his seat.

'Is that OK?' he said, raising his hands up. 'Everyone happy with that? Can I go?'

'Can you go?' said Ren. *Not before I punch you in the face.* 'I'm sorry, but we're here to try to find your son, and we're doing everything we can. Is this tedious for you? Does it sound like a terrible thing? I can't understand this. It's like you're angry with us, when we're here to help you — '

'You're accusing me!' he said, rising from his seat.

'Sit down, Mr Veir,' said Ren.

'Don't patronize me — '

'We're not accusing you of anything,' said Ren. *Yet.*

Deep breaths. 'Why don't we all just take a moment?' said Ruddock.

There was a knock on the door. Gary stuck his head in. 'Chief — I'm sorry to interrupt. If I could have a word with you, please?'

Ruddock stood up. 'Excuse me.' He nodded to John and Ren, and left the room.

Oh, John, you have no idea what's about to go down here.

Ren sat in silence, watching John Veir staring at his fingernails. Instead of Ruddock, Gary walked back in, stood beside Ren, right in front of John Veir, then slammed his good fist down hard on the table.

336

John jumped.

Ding, ding. Round One.

'You need to start telling us the truth,' said Gary, his voice booming. 'We know you know the truth, and you need to start talking or things are going to get a whole lot worse for you.'

Jesus Christ, Gary is scary.

I may want to fuck him.

Eye on the prize.

'I told you,' said John. 'I've gone through — over and over — what happened that Monday morning. Nothing has changed since the statement I made. It's all there.' He had lowered his voice, taken the edge off the tone.

'Well, I need you to go through it again,' said Gary. He sat down.

'I know you're looking for inconsistencies,' said John, 'but there are none. I've told this a million times now.'

'And we're ready to hear it again,' said Gary.

John Veir looked like he was about to blow. But he went through the details again, and they were the same. Gary cut in at the point where John Veir ran up the stairs to get Caleb to hurry up.

'You walked in on your son in his bedroom,' said Gary. 'You had called up to him several times, he had ignored you, you were late for work, he didn't care, he was disrespecting you, something he was increasingly doing, something you had called him out on many times. And it infuriated you. You grabbed him — '

'I did not lay a finger on him,' said John.

Steely. Calm.

'You didn't mean to hurt him,' said Gary. 'You

337

shook him, he lost his balance, he fell . . . '

'No, sir.'

'He struck his head against the wardrobe, or against the bed, he fell back on the floor — '

'No, sir. That is not what happened.'

'You knew it was too late,' said Gary. 'You'd gone too far. You panicked. You knew you couldn't tell your wife what you'd done. You took your son's cell phone and you called your sister. You asked for her help. You asked her to talk you through what you should do — '

'There's no way my sister would — '

'Then you went up into the attic, you took down your sleeping bag, you placed your son's body inside, carried him down the stairs, into the garage . . . '

Tears welled in John Veir's eyes.

Tears of . . . what? Guilt?

'No!' said John. He wiped away the tears. 'That is not what happened. My son walked out of our house on his own two feet. He — '

'You opened the trunk of your car and placed your son's body inside,' said Gary. 'You closed the trunk. You were now late for work. Your only option was to show up at three p.m. and say that you got the shift time wrong. You could have called in sick, but that would have set off alarm bells.'

John shook his head. They all sat in silence. Moments passed.

'And that's it,' said John. 'You don't know any more. Where did I put the body? Where is that sleeping bag now?'

In the landfill site?

'In fact, where is there any evidence for what you're saying?' said John. 'You talk about my sister? Well, you better watch out for her. You better watch out. That's all I'm going to say.'

'You tell me where the body is,' said Gary. 'And where that sleeping bag is.'

'I don't know anything about the sleeping bag,' said John. 'I have no idea why that's not there.'

And the body?!

'And I hope to God there's no body,' said John, his eyes boring through Ren as if he had read her mind. 'You think I want to think about that? Are you that fucking cruel?'

Gary recalibrated. 'I can see that you're a good person, John. You're an honorable man, you fought for your country, your boss respects you a lot. Apparently, you're a disciplined and fair corrections officer. You like to be in control. I understand that. But I also understand what happens when things get out of control, when the pressure gets too much, or just when someone doesn't have respect for the things you value. Caleb was twelve years old — it's a difficult age.'

'I agree with you,' said John. 'But that doesn't mean I did anything to my son.'

61

'John, we need your help on this,' said Ren. 'We need you to give us everything you got. You see all the people we have here coming together to help find your son. We care deeply about this. We need the truth. I believe you can tell us the truth.'

'I am telling you the truth,' said John.

'I'm afraid I don't believe that you are,' said Ren.

He looked at her, his eyes suddenly black with anger. 'I did *not* harm my son. If you hooked me up to a polygraph — '

Hello? 'You declined a polygraph,' said Ren.

He held eye contact with her. 'I know. What I'm saying is, I'm telling the truth. And separate to that, I don't trust polygraphs.'

'That doesn't make a whole lot of sense,' said Ren. 'You either believe that the polygraph would prove you're truthful, or, as per your original reason for refusing, you believe that it wouldn't.'

'I'm exhausted,' said John. 'I'm just . . . so exhausted. I am so goddamned stressed that I don't know how my body's going to react: my heartbeat, my sweat glands, whatever the hell else you measure. You know who my sister is. There is no way she would ever recommend anyone taking a polygraph, guilty or innocent. I know how these things work.'

'Taking a polygraph means that, if you pass,'

said Gary, 'we can eliminate you, and focus on — '

'You won't eliminate me,' said John. 'Do you think I'm an idiot? Not after the way you're talking. At the very most, you might set me aside, until you can come up with a new fairy tale about how I hurt my own son.'

'Of course we'll eliminate you if new evidence arises pointing to someone else,' said Gary.

John threw up his hands. 'See what I mean? Now you're thinking, 'Oh, hold on — why would he think we won't eliminate him if he's innocent? He must know that no evidence will point to someone else!''

'We've been in this job a long time,' said Gary. 'You can't be part of the CARD team without having logged the hours on child abduction cases. We don't walk in, pick one of the parents, and go from there. We look at the evidence. And some of this evidence, I won't lie to you, is not looking good for you right now, John.'

John looked away, sullen and dark-eyed. 'What evidence? I had nothing to do with this. I'll keep answering your questions, if you think that will help, but I'd rather you were spending your time focusing on finding my son.'

★ ★ ★

Ren and Gary left John and went back into the office. Paul Louderback was putting down the phone.

'OK,' he said, 'I finally got a hold of Paula Leon. She apologized for not getting back in touch. She was in lock-down, preparing a case. Ren, you were right — she loaned her rental car to Alice Veir, who told her her own car wouldn't start and that she had to run an errand. Alice brought it back with a full tank, so Leon couldn't tell how far she'd traveled.'

'And why would she give a shit, either way?' said Ren.

Paul nodded. 'She said Alice Veir was definitely back in the hotel by six p.m., and that she left right away. Her own car seemed to have come back to life. Alice Veir missed the dinner that night. She went straight home to Spokane.'

'Jesus Christ,' said Ren. 'Was she transporting a body in that? We need to get on to AVIS — get that rental car in.'

'I'm on it,' said Paul.

Sylvie looked up from her desk. 'Sorry,' she said, 'but I'm just not buying the idea that in a matter of ten minutes on a Monday morning, Alice Veir gets involved in such a heinous crime.'

'I know,' said Ren. 'The only rationale is that she owes her brother big time. The question is: what for? I mean, could she have taken away the body of his son and dumped it? And where? And how would she even manage that — she doesn't seem like a very strong woman.'

'She went home,' said Paul, 'she could have dumped him somewhere that was familiar to her.'

'We can call in video from the conference hotel,' said Ren, 'but I doubt she would be stupid enough to have done this where she could be seen.'

'I don't need to stress how carefully we need to tread here with Alice Veir,' said Gary. 'That woman is ready to pounce on anything she can use to justify her war against law enforcement. We can call in Paula Leon's rental car, send it to the lab, no problem. Getting a search warrant for Alice Veir's property is not going to happen. She is going to resist every move we make. We need more evidence.'

Ruddock walked into the office, just as Ren's cell phone rang. 'Oh, shit: that's Alice Veir,' she said. 'What are the chances?'

'Pretty high, after what Gary just did to her brother,' said Paul.

Ren picked up.

'Agent Bryce?' said Alice. 'I just got off the phone with my brother. It is scandalous what you're doing to him. His son is missing, he's heartbroken, and he has to be subjected to what you've just subjected him to? It's despicable. He's under incredible strain right now, as you can imagine. This does not give you and your colleagues an excuse to take him into a room and attack him the way you did. He's made himself available to you at all times, he hasn't called in a lawyer because he feels he has nothing to hide, and he trusts in the system, which, to be honest, amazes me.

'What this entire investigation should be about is finding out facts that will help us find Caleb.'

'That's exactly what we're trying to do,' said Ren. 'Is there anything else you can think of that might help us in that regard?' *Like your visit to Lister Creek, you lying-ass bitch!*

343

Ren allowed a silence to open up. Alice Veir didn't close it.

What the fuck are you two hiding?

Ren looked up at Gary and Paul, and mouthed. 'Can I call her in?'

They nodded.

'Alice — where are you right now?' said Ren.

'In Spokane — why?'

'We'd like you to come in to Tate PD, please.'

'What?' said Alice. 'Why?'

'For a chat,' said Ren.

Pause. 'A chat?' said Alice. 'About what? I'm very busy. It's going to be hard for me to travel. I can tell you anything you want to know right now.'

'There are a couple of things we'd like you to take a look at,' said Ren. 'It won't take too long. I know you're very eager to do anything you can to help us find Caleb, and, clearly, to help your brother too.' She smiled sweetly at Gary and Paul. Paul smiled back.

Ren ended the call. 'She can't not come in, because if she's hiding anything, the last thing she's going to want to do is come across as uncooperative.'

* * *

Ruddock's cell phone rang. He picked up, listened.

'It's CVIP,' said Ruddock to the others.

Child Victim Identification Program? What?

'Let me put you on speaker,' said Ruddock, punching the button, holding the phone out to

344

the others. 'I'm with SSA Gary Dettling, SA Paul Louderback, and SA Ren Bryce.'

'Hello, everyone — Bob Freeborn here, CVIP. I'm calling to let you know we got a hit on that sleeping bag image that you guys released to the media from the Caleb Veir disappearance.'

What the fuck? 'What kind of hit?' said Ren.

'There's a distinctive black ink stain on it. We've picked it up across a series of over a thousand images and videos of abused children.'

62

Ren's heart started to pound.

'It was an unusual find,' said Bob. 'Boxes of photos and videos in a dumpster beside a strip mall toy store called the Toy Box in Redding, California on Friday. That's just off I-5, which is obviously a route out of Salem. We're still scanning them. By my estimates, so far, though, they look like they're from the seventies/eighties/nineties.'

'So, before Caleb Veir was born,' said Gary.

'Yes — so far,' said Bob. 'The kids look to be anywhere between four and eleven — boys and girls.'

'What kind of abuse are you seeing?' said Gary.

'It's almost exclusively near-drowning,' said Bob.

Ren's stomach lurched. 'And is there sexual abuse?'

'In some cases, yes,' said Bob. 'I'm aware of your drowning deaths in Tate. Is that the route you're going down?'

'Yes.' *The log flume to hell.*

'It looks like the same abuser throughout,' said Bob. 'You're likely looking at someone who's minimum mid-sixties now.'

'Definitely?' said Ren. 'Could it be John Veir, the father? Have you seen a photo of him? He's fifty-seven.'

'Can I say definitely sixties?' said Bob. 'Well, no — but thereabouts. I can say, though, that it's definitely *not* John Veir. I saw him on the news. This man has darker skin and very dark hair, lots of it. We can really only see an arm, a knee, and . . .'

We all know where the camera is aimed in those videos.

'I'm presuming the sleeping bag wasn't with the porn,' said Ren.

'No.'

'How often is the garbage collected at the store?' said Ren.

'Those boxes could have been dumped there any time from the Thursday before,' said Bob.

'No CCTV, I presume . . .'

'No,' said Bob. 'We'll keep inputting the images, and I'll send everything on as I get it.'

'We can't presume whoever dumped them shopped at the store,' said Ren, 'but what pedophile could resist a toy store?'

That was grim.

'Yup,' said Bob, 'they go where their needs are met. And I've got one hundred and fifty-five million unique images to prove it.'

Jesus. Christ.

'And these guys are getting more and more tech-savvy,' said Bob. 'They're editing out anything identifiable that might be in the background, anything that we can pick up on our system.'

Imagine sitting at your desk, using editing software for that. It's beyond depressing.

'Well, thanks for the call,' said Ruddock.

'What the fuck?' said Ren. She put a call into the Toy Box to email her their video files for the previous week, and a list of all the purchases made.

'And we can at least get a list of men in that age group from around Tate,' said Ruddock. 'Not that the abuser necessarily has to be from the town, but it's a start.'

'Really looking forward to Bob's email,' said Ren. *Ugh.*

Like a juggernaut, the images and videos from the fetish sites moved in.

Ugh.

Jesus.

Ren's heart rate accelerated.

'*People go where their needs are likely to be met.*'

'*You won't find a pedophile hanging around a retirement home.*'

Oh my God . . . the suicide at the retirement home. Wasn't that guy a swim coach? He taught kids for years. He killed himself last Friday. That was the day it got out that Aaron Fuller had been drowned.

She looked reflexively at Ruddock. *This will crush him.*

'Ruddock, maybe you could check with the Veirs about that sleeping bag — find out where it came from and how long they had it,' said Ren. 'If there are images from the seventies, and it's an older man . . . who could that be? A sibling? Uncle? Family friend?'

Ruddock nodded. 'OK — I'll do that.'

She waited for him to leave, then opened up a

legacy. com page for Roger Lyle. 'Pillar of the community alert,' she said, pointing to the screen.

Gary and Paul looked at her.

'Did you know that a local swim coach committed suicide last Friday at the retirement home?' said Ren.

'A couple of the guys in the command center were talking about it,' said Paul.

'Did they say anything else about him?' said Ren. 'Any weird vibe?'

'No,' said Paul. 'Nothing.'

'Ren — want to swing by, check it out?' said Gary.

'Sure,' said Ren. She googled it, then typed the owner's name into her phone.

★ ★ ★

Ren took the ten-minute drive to the Harvest Road Retirement Home, and went up to the front desk.

'Hello,' she said. 'I'm looking for Nadine Jacobs.' She showed her creds.

'Just one moment,' said the receptionist.

Nadine Jacobs came down to Ren, with the look of someone who had not been sleeping well. Her eyes were puffy, her hair in need of a brush.

Suicide is not exactly great for business.

'Hello, Ms Jacobs — I'm Ren Bryce, I'm with the FBI — could we talk somewhere privately? It's about Roger Lyle.'

Nadine frowned, but nodded. 'Sure, absolutely — come with me.'

349

They walked a hallway that was painted a dismal shade of gray and hung with wall art that was angular and aggressive. The lighting was cold and bright and the heating was high.

What sensory fuckery is this?

No wonder Roger Lyle didn't want to hang around.

Oh . . .

I could do this all day.

'Here we are,' said Nadine, pushing her office door open, letting Ren walk in ahead of her. 'Take a seat.'

'Can you tell me a little about Mr Lyle?' said Ren, settling in a chair.

'About what happened on Friday?' said Nadine.

'Well . . . if you want to start with that. Or you could just talk to me about him as a person.'

'OK,' said Nadine. 'Well, he was the swim coach here in Tate for many years. He taught most of the kids coming up, did extra classes, took them on trips . . . '

Ding. Ding. Ding. 'Was he a popular man?' said Ren.

Nadine gave a one-shoulder shrug. 'Depends on who you ask,' she said. 'He got results. The kids did well, but they didn't like his discipline. Obviously, a lot of the parents did — the stricter ones. The more laid-back ones thought he needed to lighten up — not that they would say that to his face.'

'Are you from here?' said Ren. 'Did he teach you?'

'Oh, no,' said Nadine. 'I'm terrified of the water.'

Me too now.

'Have you cleaned out Roger's room yet?' said Ren.

'No,' said Nadine. 'We were going to wait until his son came by to pick up his personal effects. He asked that the room be left as is. And, he's paid up until the end of the month, anyway.'

'Did he have a wife?' said Ren. 'Are there any other family members?'

'There's just Jimmy,' said Nadine. 'He's on his way here for the memorial. Roger's wife — Jimmy's mother — left him years ago. From what I can gather, it broke Roger's heart. He threw himself into his work. It became all about the kids after that.'

I bet it did.

This could all be a coincidence. 'Could I take a look at his room, please?' said Ren.

'Sure,' said Nadine. As they walked the next hallway, this one a dirty shade of blue, Nadine turned to Ren. 'May I ask, Agent, what your interest in Roger Lyle is?'

Yes, you may. And I may feel free to lie in response. Can't think of anything. 'I'm afraid I'm not in a position to discuss that.'

They arrived at Roger's room. Nadine unlocked the door and pushed it open. It looked like a hurricane had swept through it. It was small, with a single bed, a closet, a chair and a table. There was a newspaper on the table, folded back to a completed crossword. Ren unfolded it to the front page. It was Tuesday's edition of the *Marion County Gazette*, leading with Caleb's disappearance.

351

She turned to Nadine. 'Could I trouble you for a glass of water, please?'

'No problem,' said Nadine. 'There's a cooler at the end of the hallway. I'll just be a minute.'

Ren bent down as soon as Nadine left, put on her gloves, and grabbed the wastebasket, tilting it toward her to get a look inside. There was a balled-up piece of paper. Ren opened it, flattened it out, read what was on it.

What.

The.

Fuck?

There were two dates handwritten on it: the date Aaron Fuller died, and the date that Caleb Veir disappeared.

63

Ren stood up, flipped the newspaper on to the crossword again, and compared the handwriting in the two.

Not his writing on the note.

There was a faint smell of citrus from the paper.

Perfumey. Female.

Ren took a paper evidence bag from her purse, put the page inside, and put it back in her purse. She opened the drawers, all of them half-filled with neat piles of clothes. She looked through them, found nothing. There was a stack of crime novels beside his bed. There was a suitcase underneath the bed. She slid it out and opened it. It was empty.

Nadine came back in as Ren was standing up, and handed her a cup of water.

'Thank you,' said Ren. She drank it and put the empty cup on the table.

'Do the residents get out much?' said Ren.

'There are various outings organized every week,' said Nadine, 'residents can decide whether they want to go. If you mean Roger specifically — he hadn't been on any of them.'

'Has he had any visitors recently?' said Ren.

'Not since the Sunday before last — his son Jimmy came in that morning — he was heading off on vacation.'

'Is your visitor log computerized?' said Ren.

'Yes,' said Nadine.

'Can you forward me details of visitors from last week?'

'Sure, no problem.'

Ren handed her her card. 'Thank you.' She paused. 'Where did Roger Lyle live?'

'Well, the house is for sale now,' said Nadine. 'But it's on Richmond Road, just by the middle school.'

Holy. Fuck.

* * *

Ren drove to Richmond Road, and parked opposite the one house that had a FOR SALE sign in the front garden. She opened up her laptop and called up the CCTV photo of Seth Fuller on the same street. He was pretty much parked in the same spot.

What is going on?

* * *

Ren arrived back in Tate PD and filled everyone in on Roger Lyle, and Seth Fuller. Ren turned to Ruddock. 'What do you know about him?'

Please do not tell me he's your best friend.

'He's very well-known in the community,' said Ruddock. 'He always kept very much to himself. He was strict with all the kids, strict with his son. He was a private man.'

'Could you see him doing anything like this?' said Ren. 'He wasn't in Harvest Road when Aaron and Luke were killed. Going in there could have been some very convenient timing.

354

Have there ever been any rumors about him?'

'No,' said Ruddock.

'CVIP's estimate is that the man in the photos would be minimum mid-sixties now,' said Ren. 'He fits the bill in that sense.' She put on gloves and pulled the piece of paper from the evidence bag. 'This was the note from his wastebasket.' She held it in front of Ruddock. He stared at it.

Ooh . . . what do you know? 'Do you recognize the writing?' said Ren.

Ruddock looked up at her. 'No.'

There is a battle behind those eyes.

'It smelled a little citrusy earlier,' said Ren. 'It's worn off now. It might be a woman.'

Ruddock nodded. 'Could be. Let's see what the lab comes back with, in terms of prints.'

'What did the Veirs say about the sleeping bag?' said Ren.

'Both thought that the other brought it from before they were married,' said Ruddock. 'After that, their best guess was that the previous owners left it behind. But we contacted them, and it wasn't theirs. The Veirs were horrified the sleeping bag had appeared in images of abuse.'

Ren turned to Paul Louderback. 'Can we send some guys to Richmond Road to check out Roger Lyle's house?'

'Sure,' said Paul, 'but that was already done as part of the neighborhood canvas last week.'

'Can we get into the house?' said Ren. 'Get the keys from the real estate agent? Unless Lyle's son lets us in when he arrives. Pretty shitty, though, when he's coming back for his father's memorial.'

'If the house is up for sale, it's likely we're not going to find much in it,' said Gary.

'Let's find out if they've got anything in storage,' said Ren. 'We need to know.'

★ ★ ★

By the time Ren checked her inbox, there was one from Bob Freeborn in CVIP, forwarded by Ruddock. It had the first of the indecent images and videos. Ren started to look through them.

Grim. Grim. Grim. Grim. Grim.

64

Jimmy Lyle pulled up in his rental car and parked on Pleasant Lane. He couldn't park in the driveway on Richmond Road, he couldn't alert the neighbors that he was back. He couldn't stand to hear the doorbell ring, to see the porch fill up with casseroles, to feel his ears fill up with condolences, his eyes flooded with pitying looks, or tears, his body squeezed by warm, fat ladies who left their scent behind on his neck, and their unreliable fucking memories caught in his throat.

He unlocked the gate, and started walking up the path through the back garden, his hands in his pockets, his head bowed. He stopped and looked up at the small bathroom window. He imagined being a boy, floating up to it, like the window scene in that old movie, *Salem's Lot:* one boy on the inside, one on the outside. Inside Jimmy, Outside Jimmy. But in the movie, the horror, the ghastly boy, the smoke — everything was on the outside. Not in the Lyle house.

Jimmy remembered that bathroom blurred with steam, the bath, this time, one time only, filled with boiling water. It was night time. His father was drunk. He didn't notice. He didn't notice until he heard Jimmy's piercing screams, saw his red, falling-away flesh. He didn't know that Inside Jimmy wanted someone to know, but that when they arrived at the hospital, Outside Jimmy won. Daddy won.

Jimmy walked on. He was used to steeling himself when he knew he was about to face a reflective surface — this time, the windows at the back of the house, the glass kitchen door. He looked up when he got there and his reflection was clearer, starker than he expected. It took him a moment to realize why. The glass was black. Maybe the real estate agent had drawn the curtains. But he hadn't heard from her all week. There had been no viewings. He walked closer. The curtains were moving. He walked closer again.

The curtains were flies. Lots and lots of flies.

65

Seth Fuller stood by the pool table in The Crow Bar with his jacket on, waiting for Shannon to come out from behind the bar. It was midnight and there were only three customers left.

'I'm going for a walk,' said Seth.

Shannon paused. 'OK . . . ' She hugged him. He winced.

'I forgot about your back — sorry,' she said. 'And I'm sorry — I know I hug you too much.'

He smiled. 'That's OK. I don't mind.'

'Should you really be walking that much, though?' said Shannon. She touched his cheek lightly. 'Your poor face. It's so strange to see you with a black eye.' She studied him. 'Are you sure you're all right?'

'Please stop worrying about me all the time,' said Seth. 'You're freaking me out.'

★ ★ ★

Seth walked through the woods by Lake Verny, down into Clyde's workshop. He unlocked the door. He lit some candles on the worktop. He grabbed an empty crate from under the counter, flipped it over and sat down, elbows on his knees.

He reached into his back pocket and slid out a slim white packet. He read the yellow print: FENTANYL 100mcg TRANSDERMAL SYSTEM. The warning — white on a triangle of red in the bottom right-hand corner — read: ATTENTION: ONLY FOR USE BY PATIENT FOR WHOM PRESCRIBED.

Seth wasn't sure if that was good English. Should it not have an 'it is' in there? 'For whom it is prescribed'?

He turned the packet over and over in his hands. He thought of the night he overdosed, how that prick Merrifield would have been happy to watch him die.

It probably just looked like falling asleep, when, inside, your body was firing all kinds of pain around you, while you stayed. He liked being numb.

And now he was in pain, all over. And he was in pain from the hug Aunt Shannon had given him. He thought of her, and it was just too overwhelming. When they lived in Tate, it was a little easier. But then she bought a bar on a lake. Then he was hanging over water. At first, he looked at it like a therapist would. Water hung over you — now you're hanging over water. You have the power now.

Tears slid down Seth's face. He didn't have any power. He was powerless. He would never have power.

But he thought he would. He had made up his mind months ago that, one day, he would go back to face Roger Lyle — but only after he had made something of himself, when he was better, when he was running cruises on the lake or hiring out speedboats, when he was making money for himself, for Aunt Shannon, when he'd managed to abandon his fear of water, reclaim his love for it. He would wait a few years until he was married, maybe, when he had a beautiful wife who would help him heal from all the fucked-up shit that he had seen, all the fucked-up shit that had been done to him, all the fucked-up shit that had led him to drugs, to numbing, to prison, to almost dying, to wanting to die, over and over.

And then Roger Lyle fucking killed himself. They'd laid him out in Longacres Funeral Home so people could pay their respects. The thought of mourners filing past that casket, paying tribute, had filled Seth with rage. He began to fantasize about walking in there, standing over that casket and firing a bullet into Roger Lyle's brain so everyone could see just how damaged his head was.

On Monday night he'd made up his mind to do it for real. He got hold of a gun and Clyde's key to the funeral home and was all set to go. Even after Aunt Shannon took the gun from him, he'd been determined to go through with it, figuring he'd find some other way to mess with Lyle's head — smash it with a crucifix or one of those cheap fucking swimming trophies lined up around the coffin.

He'd made it all the way to the gates. And then an image had come into his mind of that beautiful girlfriend, whoever she would be, as he held her hands at that part of the relationship, the honesty part, the part where you laid it all out: your past, your fears, your regrets, the secrets you could only ever entrust to someone extraordinary, to someone you loved deeply. He knew he would love deeply. He knew he could.

Then his heart had started to pound like a warning, his stomach had tightened, tears had spilled down his cheeks as he imagined looking a girl in the eye and telling her that he desecrated the corpse of an old man. The tears didn't stop when he imagined looking her in the eye and *not* telling her.

He couldn't do it, so he'd walked away, walked into Gil Wiley's fists. As if he'd fuck Isabella. She was beautiful, but she was married, and she was as damaged as he was. They knew what had happened to each other. They had been Roger Lyle's favorites. They had never spoken about it until last Saturday when she showed up at Lake Verny. She had told him about going to see Roger Lyle, confronting him, trying to find out whether he was responsible for the drownings she had just heard about. And Roger Lyle had been hideous to her. He had been nasty, and dirty, and racist, and abusive. She had stayed strong in front of him, but had collapsed halfway down the road. Roger Lyle was undistilled evil. Isabella Wiley was brave.

★ ★ ★

Seth tore the packet open, slid out the patch. He thought of Aunt Shannon again. Her sister was dead, Aaron was dead . . . all she had was him. He felt bad for her that an ex-junkie jailbird screwed-up piece of crap was all she had left in this sorry-ass world. He thought of her walking in on him, slumped on the floor, his sleepy, druggie eyes, knowing how weak he really was, after all the time she believed in him.

She's not going to walk in on me.

I'll be back in a while.

He thought of her finding him dead.

Like I'm going to freakin' die. It's just one patch.

One grain . . .

No way I'm going to freakin' die. Like I'd let Roger Lyle win. Fuck, no. No way.

★ ★ ★

Seth peeled the clear cover off the patch. He sucked in air, first through his nostrils, then his mouth, his chest swelling, more air, more, more. He stared at the patch again.

I just need to dissolve for a little while. I just need my chest to rest.

He placed the patch on his tongue. He closed his eyes. He breathed like Lockwood taught him.

He thought of some lady lying all skinny in her bed, one patch down. Cancer-stricken. Stricken.

What am I stricken with? The shittiness of people's screwed-up fantasies, of early deaths, of just life, of injustice, of children in pain with no voices and no breath.

Warm and liquid.

His eyes started to close, his heart slowed.

I don't want to die. I've got this.

You've got this, Seth.

I've got the rest of my life.

I'm tired.

I'm so fucking tired.

66

Ren woke up with a start, her chest heaving, slick with sweat.

Fuck. Fuck. Fuck.

She grabbed her cell phone and checked the time. *Eight thirty.*

Fuck. Fuck. Fuck.

What happened?

Nightmares. Neubig. Brinks. Courtroom. Matt. Gary. Witness box. Faces. Gunfire. Prison. Jesus. Christ. I hate this shit.

She turned to the empty side of the bed. *I don't want to be alone. I'm tired of being alone. I want someone to tell me it will all work out.*

★ ★ ★

Ren arrived at Tate PD at nine, hurrying across the parking lot, struggling with her purse, and her briefcase. The command center had been overtaken by a sense of urgency — voices were raised, detectives were mobilizing.

Sensory overload. Sensory overload.

Her phone beeped with a text, just as she met Paul Louderback rushing toward her, pulling on his jacket.

'That's from me,' he said.

Her phone beeped three more times.

'What's going down?' said Ren.

'A report just came in,' said Paul, 'a body

— badly decomposed, as yet unidentified — has been found in Roger Lyle's house on Richmond Road.'

'Oh, no,' said Ren. 'Oh, fucking, no.'

★ ★ ★

Ren and Paul drove together to the scene.

'I thought you said that area was searched during the week,' said Ren.

'Because I was told it was,' said Paul. 'Wiley again — abandoning his duties. He crossed this off his list.'

'His wife,' said Ren. 'She had a meltdown on Thursday. He had to go tend to her. He probably figured leaving an empty house off his list wasn't the end of the world. Fuck, though.'

★ ★ ★

Ruddock was gray-faced, coming down the path as they arrived.

'Got an ID?' said Ren.

'One Franklin J. Merrifield,' said Ruddock.

'What?' said Ren.

'Looks like an OD: drug paraphernalia around the body.'

'This is where he's been hiding out?' said Ren.

'He was chained to a radiator,' said Ruddock. 'This is where he was being held captive.'

'Yet supplied with drugs,' said Ren. 'So, this has to be connected with his supplier in BRCI. He probably helped him get away, but may have wanted him out of commission and deliberately

365

facilitated the OD. How did they access the property?'

'No signs of forced entry,' said Ruddock.

'Who has keys?' said Ren.

'The son — Jimmy Lyle,' said Ruddock. 'There are footprints in the back yard and one of the neighbors saw him getting out of a car yesterday on Pleasant Lane — that's the road at the back of here. He may have come back, found the body and then taken off.'

'He would only have done that if he had something to hide,' said Ren. 'I'd be getting everyone the fuck inside my house if I came home and thought there was a dead body in there.'

'We've put a BOLO out on him,' said Ruddock.

'Could Jimmy Lyle have helped Merrifield escape?' said Ren. 'Could he have left him here?'

'No,' said Ruddock. 'He was going on vacation, and he needs to sell that house.'

Ren nodded.

'We spoke with the boss of the real estate agency,' said Ruddock. 'The woman handling the property has been away on business for the past week. There were no viewings lined up.'

'Find out her address,' said Paul, 'find out who she lives with, who she works with, who might have access to her keys.'

'The call between John Veir and Rob Lockwood on the Sunday Merrifield escaped,' said Ren. 'What if that was about this? Could . . . Lockwood have been the supplier? Could this have all been about to hit the fan? Could Merrifield have been about to blow Lockwood's cover, and Lockwood needed to get him the fuck out of there?'

'But how does John Veir fit in?' said Paul.

'Well, John Veir didn't reveal the whole fentanyl story to us,' said Ren, 'which would totally have bolstered his claim that Merrifield had taken Caleb.'

Her phone beeped with a second email from Bob Freeborn at CVIP.

'We'll leave this with you, Ruddock,' said Paul.

She waited until she was back at her desk to open Bob's email:

We cross-matched one of the structures in the sleeping-bag photos to later photos . . . these ones were taken between six and eight years ago.

Ren started to look through them. She stopped at one that had a yellow inflatable kiddie's pool and stepping stones trailing back through the garden.

Where did I see those stones in the grass? That shape?

She closed her eyes.

The stones in the grass.

Darkness. Moonlight. Grass. Wet. I . . . fell.

Ruddock appeared in the doorway.

'It's not just Jimmy Lyle who's gone AWOL,' he said. 'Teddy Veir just called to say that John Veir has been missing since last night. And he left his cell phone at home.'

'I might know why,' said Ren. 'I just got more photos from CVIP and, if I'm right, they were taken in the Veirs' back garden.'

* ★ ★

There were two cars in the Veirs' driveway when Ren arrived: one was Teddy's. Ren rang the doorbell. She could see Teddy through the glass, at the bottom of the stairs. She opened up right away.

'Can I come in?' said Ren.

'Of course,' said Teddy, panic flashing in her eyes. 'What is it?'

'Have you had any word from John?' said Ren.

'No,' said Teddy.

'Who's here with you?' said Ren.

'My friend, Patti.'

Patti Ellis, who you were looking after the night before Caleb disappeared.

You look better than I thought you would.

'Can we all take a seat?' said Ren. 'This is a very difficult subject, but considering everything, I have no choice but to tell you about this. We received photos from CVIP — that's the Child Victim Identification Program. Your sleeping bag, Teddy, came up as a match with one that was seen in the background of photos of child abuse, dating from the seventies to the nineties.'

'OK,' said Teddy, 'but we wouldn't have used it during that time. It was years later. Like we said, we never really knew where it came from.'

'Some of the photos from the garden are more recent,' said Ren. 'I'm going to show you parts of some of the photos — obviously, I won't be showing you anything distressing, but I think you might recognize the background.'

She showed them to Teddy. 'Yes,' said Teddy, horrified. 'That's our garden.'

368

Patti Ellis burst into tears. Her body folded in on itself, her head bowed against her knees. Ren and Teddy turned to her.

'Oh my God,' said Patti. 'Oh my God.'

'What?' said Teddy. 'What is it?'

Patti gestured toward the photographs. 'I remember that time . . . you were in the hospital, John was in Iraq.' She looked up at Ren, her eyes filled with pain. She pointed to an arm in one of the photos, where there was a triangle of dark freckles. 'I know who that is.'

★ ★ ★

Ren's heart rate shot up.

'It's Jimmy Lyle,' said Patti.

'Jimmy Lyle?' said Ren. 'Roger Lyle's son?'

Patti wept. 'I'm so sorry, Teddy, I'm so sorry. This is my fault — I brought Jimmy into Caleb's life. I was seeing him back then. He was married, but we had this thing, on and off for years. I didn't say anything, because I was ashamed, and he didn't want his wife to find out, and . . . '

Teddy was momentarily speechless. Then, 'Did you know about this, though?' pointing towards the photos, her voice edging immediately into hysteria. 'That Jimmy was into this?'

'No!' said Patti. 'Of course I didn't! I trusted him completely!'

'Did you leave Caleb alone with him?' said Teddy.

'Yes,' said Patti. 'But not for a second did I think — '

'How could you not have known?' said Teddy. 'How?'

Ren cut in. 'A lot of people don't know these things,' she said. 'People are very good at hiding those parts of themselves.'

Teddy turned to Patti. 'You were supposed to be looking after my son!'

'I was!' said Patti.

Teddy looked at Ren. 'Do you have photos of Caleb? 'Have you seen any? Is it definite?'

'No,' said Ren. 'I haven't, however, received all the photos, yet.'

Teddy turned to Patti. 'Does John know about this?'

'No!' said Patti. 'Wouldn't he have told you?'

'No,' said Teddy. 'He likes to protect me from things.' She glanced at Ren, and got a compassionate look in return.

Shit . . . if John Veir knows about this, and knows that Jimmy Lyle is back in town . . . maybe John has gone to find him. Or maybe if John found out Jimmy left town last week, he might have thought he took Caleb with him. He didn't tell us, because he wanted the chance to confront him.

67

The full investigation team were gathered in the command center when Ren arrived back at Tate PD. Ruddock was at the top of the room.

Whoa: this looks serious.

'OK,' said Ruddock. 'We have an update on Merrifield. The real estate agent shares a house with a divorced woman called Serena Jones, whose boyfriend is a courier for a pharmaceutical company that delivers to Salem Hospital. Jones's maiden name is . . . Lockwood.'

He waited for everyone to process the information.

Oh my God. 'Lockwood was the supplier in BRCI,' said Ren.

'According to Salem PD, Jones and her boyfriend have admitted to getting Merrifield out of the hospital that day in his delivery van,' said Ruddock. 'He deliberately held back some of his Friday delivery so he had a reason to be there on a Sunday.' He paused. 'Then Jones used her roommate's key to gain access to the Lyle house.'

'And was there a plan?' said Ren. 'Why were they doing this?'

'Because Lockwood told them Merrifield threatened to blow his cover,' said Ruddock. 'They're keeping quiet on the rest of it. They admit to supplying Merrifield with the heroin, but they're not going to admit the OD was deliberate.'

'So Merrifield thought they were going to

release him into the wild?' said Ren.

'Apparently, so,' said Ruddock.

'Have they taken Rob Lockwood in?' said Ren.

'He's waiting for his lawyer,' said Ruddock.

Paul Louderback turned to Ren. 'Do you want to fill everyone in on the Veirs?'

'Sure,' said Ren.

★　★　★

After the meeting, Ruddock called Ren into his office, closed the door behind them.

You look haunted in the eye.

'What is it?' said Ren.

'There's something I want to show you,' said Ruddock. He handed her a Christmas card.

She read it. 'It's from Wiley. And his wife.' Then she looked up at him. *The handwriting — it's the same as the note in Roger Lyle's room.* 'Written by his wife?' said Ren.

'Isabella, yes,' said Ruddock. 'It looked familiar when I saw it, but I didn't want to say anything . . .'

Because you know I have my doubts about Wiley.

'I wanted to make sure I was right,' said Ruddock. 'It took me a while to find the card. I haven't said a word to Gil,' said Ruddock.

Isabella Wiley's drink problem, Isabella found wandering drunkenly on Harvest Road the previous Thursday.

'She must have gone to confront Lyle,' said Ren. 'Hearing about Aaron pushed her over the edge.'

'Knowing that it was the night of the middle school dance and Lyle's house was so close to the school . . .'

'Lyle probably said something vile to her, as these assholes do,' said Ren, 'and whatever it was left her in a weeping mess on the side of the road for her husband to pick up. She obviously can't bear to tell him.'

'You know, I still have my wife's photos,' said Ruddock. 'I went through the boxes.' He handed Ren a photo. It was a beautiful, beaming little Latina girl in a swimsuit. A towel was thrown on the bench behind her. Ren could make out the image of a swan.

'Oh, God,' said Ren. 'She's in one of the CVIP videos.' She shook her head. 'Poor Isabella.' She paused. 'And poor Wiley.'

* * *

Ren went back to her desk and continued going through the images. She stopped when she saw something familiar in a little boy of about ten years old with auburn hair to his shoulders, standing proud, his chest out, a swimming medal on a ribbon around his neck.

The next images were him again, but they were all wrong.

Oh, God. Oh, God.

Not you too.

Fuck.

Ren called Ruddock. 'I'm going to go out to The Crow Bar,' said Ren, 'I need to talk to Seth Fuller. It looks like he was one of Roger Lyle's victims, too.'

'I just got a call about Seth Fuller,' said Ruddock. 'I'm afraid it's not good.'

68

Ren parked the car in the parking lot, but sat holding the steering wheel, her head bowed. She thought of Seth Fuller as a little boy, his long hair being grabbed by Roger Lyle, so he could torture him, so he could be his killer or his savior, so he could twist him all up inside and damage him and make him reach out to dissolve the pain. She thought of him watching the world going on around him, seeing dumber kids get better grades than him, feeling a terrible emptiness inside where he had been robbed of his innocent soul. She thought of him tearing open a fentanyl patch and how tragic it was that to take that was worth more to him than his life.

Just do this.

★   ★   ★

Seth Fuller looked up at Ren from his hospital bed, panic in his eyes, his face ghostly, his skinny body hooked up to monitors, tiny little lines making sure everyone knew that his heart still beat, that his blood still flowed, that he was alive, that he had a chance, that he had a future.

She blinked back tears. 'Hey,' she said. 'I'm so glad you made it.' She sat down on the chair beside his bed, touched his arm.

He struggled to speak. 'Are you here to arrest me?'

374

Ren smiled. 'I am definitely not here to arrest you.'

'Phew,' said Seth.

'I am so sorry, Seth,' said Ren. 'I know about Roger Lyle. I know what he did to you . . . and a lot of others.'

Tears slid down Seth's face. He turned away.

'I can't imagine what you went through,' said Ren.

'I told one of my friends once,' said Seth. 'We were ten. He just laughed. He thought it was a joke. I don't think people believe that anyone would do this. I don't think people understand. My hair . . . I hated how he grabbed my hair. When I shaved my head, I was twelve years old, and I got sent home from school, because it was against the rules. But Lyle called me in for extra classes and Aunt Shannon thought that made me was special. That cliché. And I couldn't bear to tell her the truth. Her sister was dead, she was looking after me, she was so proud of how well she was looking after me. And that son-of-a-bitch just clamped his hand around my skull and pressed his fingertips right in, and it didn't matter . . . '

'These kind of abusers are very clever,' said Ren, 'and there are almost no signs.' She paused. 'Who gave you the patch, Seth?'

'I got it from a guy in Salem.'

Ren looked at him. 'That's a lie.'

He looked away.

'I want to help you,' said Ren. 'And whoever gave you that patch did not. You owe them nothing, Seth. You owe it to your Aunt Shannon to tell me the truth. From what I heard, you wouldn't be here without two people: Clyde Brimmer and your Aunt Shannon. The most obsessive safety freak in town found you. Did you know Clyde carries around all kinds of emergency supplies — epi pen, Narcan — Narcan is what saved you. Do you have any idea how lucky you are?' She paused. 'So you certainly owe it to him and to Shannon to tell me who gave you that patch, because whoever it was doesn't give a shit about you, Seth. Shannon does. You owe her.'

A tear slid down his face. He looked at her. 'That's the problem . . . '

The problem? Why would it be a problem for Shannon? Ren waited for him to expand on that. He didn't.

Oh, Jesus Christ. I know who it was.

'John Veir . . . ' said Ren. 'Was it John?'

Seth looked away. 'John Veir saved my life.'

And once more in Seth Fuller's damaged story, savior and killer are intertwined.

'I know,' said Ren. 'So, why would he give you a fentanyl patch now?'

'He'd heard about Wiley beating the crap out of me,' said Seth. 'He knew I was in pain, and that my doctors would have a hard time prescribing meds, because of my addiction issues. And Aunt Shannon would have been all over it.'

There is something so strange about this.

'He just wanted to help,' said Seth. 'I feel bad.'

'Please don't,' said Ren. *Jesus Christ. Please fucking don't.*

Why the fuck is John Veir messing about in

Seth Fuller's pain, while his son is missing and his whole life has been turned upside down?

'How did it happen?' said Ren. 'Why did he give this to you? Did you reach out to him?'

'No,' said Seth. 'He just showed up. He thought he was doing the right thing by me.'

But he couldn't possibly have!

'Will he be prosecuted?' said Seth.

'Yes,' said Ren. *Oh, yes.* 'Do you know where he got the patch?'

Seth shook his head. 'I don't know — someone who's sick. Not a dealer. Some lady who's got cancer. That's all I know.'

Patti Ellis. Jesus Christ. Is anything sacred? 'Do you still have the package it came in?'

He shook his head. 'No. I don't know where it is.'

Ren stood up. 'We're going to get you some help, Seth. You won't have to deal with this alone. Not the abuse, not the addiction . . . I want to make sure you get all the help you need. You deserve a wonderful life. Do not let the actions of one sick bastard take another day away from you.'

I want to save you. I want to save you. I want to save you.

But why, the fuck, would John Veir want to risk your life?

★ ★ ★

Ren's cell phone rang. Gary. She picked up.

'Ren? We've had a sighting.'

'Of Jimmy Lyle?'

'No — Caleb Veir.'

377

69

Ren pulled into the side of the road.

'Pardon me?'

'Yes,' said Gary. 'A young woman said she saw Caleb at French Prairie rest area — it's about a forty-five-minute drive from here.'

'And what makes this so credible?' said Sylvie.

'She's an artist, she draws portraits,' said Gary. 'As she said to Salem PD: 'Faces are my thing.' She'd have that kind of attention to detail . . . '

'Jesus Christ,' said Ren. 'What the fuck is going on? Did this woman say anything about Caleb's demeanor?'

'She said that he seemed agitated,' said Gary. 'Wilsonville PD are on their way there now.'

'What do you want me to do?' said Ren.

'Tell Teddy Veir,' said Gary.

'Any sign of John?' said Ren.

'No,' said Gary. 'but we located Jimmy Lyle's rental tucked into the back of the church car park, close to the funeral home. So he has access to another vehicle — '

'Or he has someone else to help him out . . . '

★ ★ ★

Ren pulled up outside the Veirs' house. Teddy's car was there, but instead of Patti Ellis's, there was another car. When Teddy brought Ren in, she saw Alice Veir sitting on the sofa.

378

What the heck?

'Alice . . . when did you get here?'

'About two hours ago,' said Alice.

Weirdness. 'Did you stop anywhere along the way?'

She nodded, but it was as if to buy time. 'Yes — French Prairie Rest Area.'

Ren's heart started to pound.

They locked eyes.

'At what time?' said Ren.

'About four p.m.,' said Alice. 'I stopped for gas, picked up some water.'

Assured. But lying.

'Why do you ask?' said Alice.

'Just wondering,' said Ren. *Wondering why I'm getting the sense you know exactly why I'm asking.* 'Did you see anything out of the ordinary while you were there?'

'No,' said Alice.

'No?' said Ren.

'Did you see John there?' said Teddy. 'Is that what this is?'

'No,' said Ren.

What do I do here? Leave them? Alice Veir is picking up on something. I'm picking up on something.

'Ladies, can I ask you both to stay here for the time being? I'm going to have a family liaison officer come sit with you.'

They nodded.

Ren looked across their tense faces, behind them, to the walls, to the family photos.

How moments are captured, years pass, and lives are turned upside down.

379

Ren went into the hallway again and called Gary.

'Something's up with Alice Veir,' she said. 'She was also at French Prairie — two hours ago. She's here with Teddy. Can you send a family liaison officer, please? I don't want to leave them alone.'

'No problem,' said Gary. 'Also, the results came in on the Lister Creek landfill search . . . two things were found: the first was Caleb Veir's suitcase. The second was Rose Dennehy's cell phone.'

'Rose Dennehy's cell phone?' said Ren. 'What the fuck?'

'It wasn't in the suitcase,' said Gary, 'but it looks like it was part of the same garbage collection.'

'What's that all about?' said Ren. 'Caleb stole Rose Dennehy's cell phone? John Veir did?'

'We'll know more when we get into the phone.'

★ ★ ★

Ren drove in the direction of Tate PD, her thoughts back on Alice Veir.

Yet again, she's in the right place at the right time. Or the wrong place.

Is the sighting of Caleb fake? Did Alice pay that woman to come forward? What is going on? She is obsessed with the unreliability of eyewitness testimony. Does she know we know about Lister Creek? Could Paula Leon have called her?

Ren's cell phone rang. She picked up. 'Beckman.'

'Hi, Ren — just to let you know, based on the

380

samples your guys sent in, we got a match for the water in Luke Monroe's sphenoid sinus: he was drowned in Rose Dennehy's koi pond.'

Holy shit.

Ren's first thought was John Veir.

The next was J. J. Nash.

★ ★ ★

Ren called the CAST agent.

'Ren Bryce here — did you lift any prints from the cell phone?'

'Yes, ma'am,' he said. She could hear the smile in his voice. 'John Veir's.'

Ren frowned. 'John Veir? And what did you get from the phone dump?'

'I got video of Luke Monroe . . . '

Oh, no. 'Being . . . drowned?'

'I'm afraid so.'

'Jesus Christ.' *John Veir* . . . A shiver ran up her spine. 'OK, thanks,' she said. Her mind went into overdrive.

★ ★ ★

There was one other person she knew was in the area that day, one person who hadn't been questioned, who hadn't been ruled out.

Her final thought, the most horrifying one, was: Caleb Veir.

The sighting's not fake. It's real: Caleb Veir is alive. Caleb Veir killed Luke Monroe.

Jesus.

Christ.

70

Shannon Fuller was white-faced, sitting on the floor of her living room, her back against the sofa. In one shaking hand, she gripped the phone. In the other, she clutched a square of white paper.

She called John Veir. He picked up right away. 'Hey . . . '

'Please,' said Shannon. 'Please . . . please come over. To the bar. I need you.' Her voice cracked. 'I . . . it's Seth . . . it's Seth.'

★ ★ ★

Fifteen minutes later, John Veir walked into The Crow Bar. Shannon was slumped in Clyde's chair, her head on the table, her body wracked with sobs. John rushed toward her. Shannon stood up, turned to face him. For a moment, he faltered.

'You fucking asshole!' she screamed. 'You fucking asshole!'

She walked over to meet him, shoved him hard in the chest. He staggered back.

'What the . . . what are you doing?' said John, regaining his balance.

'Don't!' she said. She lunged for him, lightning fast, shoved him harder and he was on the floor.

John stared up at her, wide-eyed. 'What are you talking about?'

'Don't you fucking dare,' she said. 'Don't you

dare!' She held out the small white wrapper she had in her hand. 'He OD'd! He OD'd on fentanyl and you gave it to him. Have you lost your mind?'

John struggled to his feet. 'I did not — '

'Liar!' screamed Shannon. 'You liar! He told me about Merrifield, he told me about you. And he said he was done with it all, done with drugs. And you fucking give him fentanyl. Are you out of your — '

'I don't know what you're talking — '

'Oh my God!' said Shannon. 'Don't make this worse. But you need to tell me why. You need to tell me why, because I've been wracking my brains here, trying to work out why the man who's supposed to love me, or have loved me — or may never have loved me, let's face it — would give this fucked-up drug to the only family I've got left in the world. And I have no clue why you would do that, John. No fucking clue. I'm losing my mind here, trying to figure it all out.' She paused. 'The only conclusion I can come to is that you wanted Seth dead — but why? Why? You looked out for Seth in prison. You like Seth — '

'I do like him!' said John. 'I did not want him dead! I was trying to help him with his pain. After the assault — '

'But you know the risks,' said Shannon. 'I'm just not processing this. You hate drugs! You hate even having to take your prescription drugs. You watched him almost die in his cell, you saved his life. What changed? Why did you want to kill my baby? Why?'

'I . . . didn't think he would die,' said John. 'I didn't want him to die — '

'You're lying!' said Shannon. 'You're still fucking lying.' She walked up to him and slapped him hard across the face. 'Tell. Me. The. Truth.'

John Veir was pale. 'I . . . I'm sorry.'

'Sorry?' screamed Shannon. 'Sorry? What have I ever done to you? You loved me! I loved you! Why did you do this? Tell me!'

'I . . . I . . . can't,' said John.

Shannon reached into the back of her waistband and pulled out Seth's gun. 'Yes, John. Yes, you can.'

The door opened and they both spun around.

71

Ren's heart was pounding.

The anger at Aaron Fuller for having his PlayStation, the anger at his father for giving it away, the anger at his mother — why? — the drowning in the koi pond, quitting the job at Rose Dennehy's . . . *I know what you fucking did, John Veir. You found Rose Dennehy's phone wherever Caleb had hidden it. You knew it wasn't his, so you went through it to see who it belonged to — and you found the video he'd made.*

Ren's stomach turned at the thought that Caleb Veir recorded what he did to little Luke Monroe.

Selfies, videos — that's what kids do.

Oh, God. He's just a kid.

A damaged one. An abused one.

You saw Luke Monroe, his little neck gripped, his head pushed into the pond.

And that was the moment your world fell apart. You knew what your son had done, who your son was. Your twelve-year-old son was a killer.

You were horrified. But you love your son. You knew what Jimmy Lyle did to him. You always knew he was damaged. You just didn't know how badly. But you love your son. You felt responsible, because you went off to war and you left him behind, and you left your wife behind, and they fell apart. You love your son. More than he will ever understand. Because that's not something he can understand. Even though you thought, you hoped, he could.

Did you confront him? Did you look into those angry black eyes and ask him why he did it? Was that when you locked him in his bedroom? He'd have been crazed at this point — he hated you. He knew you knew his secret. He just didn't know what you were going to do about it. He thought maybe you were going to call the police, that he'd end up in prison. He figured you wanted to get rid of him anyway, that you never liked him. There was no way he could make it out his bedroom window on the second floor, it was too high. So he kicked at the door, he kicked and he kicked and he kicked.

You couldn't let him go to prison, could you? So you ran through your options and you chose to save him. You would have him disappear, let everyone think he was another tragic young victim — that way no one would ever suspect him of being a killer. Meanwhile you would get him somewhere he could have the help he needed, and eventually you would bring him home, cured. You believed that that was possible.

You just didn't realize what a mess you would make.

So you called your sister and asked her to help you save him. She was only three and a half hours away. You were lucky.

Why, though, why did she help you? Isn't she honorable? Doesn't she believe in justice? She is so desperately earnest to save Anthony Boyd

Lorden, to right that wrong, why would she jeopardize everything she'd fought for to save a child killer, even if he was a child himself, even if he was her own nephew? How did you talk her into getting involved?

Weren't you lucky Alice agreed — and that she was only three and a half hours away.

And weren't you lucky that Merrifield escaped the day before? He was the perfect person to pin this on. There was a history there, with you, with Seth. So easy to blame him for Caleb's disappearance.

Weren't you lucky?

Lots of luck.

Ren's heart started to pound.

Oh my God: this was planned, it had to have been. You didn't just find the phone and confront him and then everything magically fell into place. You knew weeks ago that on Monday, March 6, Alice would be in Portland on a speaking engagement. She would be close by. And Teddy wouldn't be home. And you planned everything around that.

But what about Merrifield? You knew he was dealing. You knew that Lockwood was bringing drugs into BRCI via his sister, Serena. So you worked that into your plan: you approached Lockwood and blackmailed him into helping Merrifield escape. After all, who would suspect the good, kindly, nerdy therapist?

For some unknown reason, Alice agrees to help. She knows not to drive her own car — she borrows Paula Leon's. She drives that car into Lister Creek Rest Area where you transfer Caleb from the trunk of your car into hers . . . But how did you persuade him to go along with all this?

How come he didn't fight you off? Fight her off? Or was he willing to leave Tate behind him? Had you told him enough stories about prison and inmates to terrify him? Did he trust you, was he willing to go along with your plan, spend the next few years in some facility where they could cure people like him?

No. You drugged him. That's what you did. Your wife's Xanax. Caleb had no clue what was going on. You gave him a spiked drink, and he was knocked out for the entire ride.

★   ★   ★

And Alice Veir, I know what you did. You drove back to your hotel and . . . what? How did you move Caleb? He woke up. He woke up, and you told him what was happening. And maybe he resisted, maybe not, but you parked beside your rental that evening, transferred him into the trunk, returned the keys to the innocent Paula Leon. Then you drove the four-hour journey home.

You arrived at your house in darkness. You have no close neighbors, anyway. You could enter unseen. Days pass — Caleb resents you, you resent him. Or maybe you loved spending time together. I'm guessing the former.

Then you get a phone call from your brother, he's freaking out, the police are getting closer, they're asking too many questions, he's running out of stories, his lies are catching up. Then John

Veir's final panic, the desperation to find another suspect: this time someone who wouldn't talk, his last-ditch attempt to frame someone was Seth Fuller: he nearly killed Seth Fuller to cover up Caleb's crimes.

It doesn't work. John calls you, and you get in the car with Caleb and you drive again. You have rehearsed the story he will tell, pieced together all the evidence you have been fed by your brother, used your brilliant lawyer's brain to create a convincing story that the police will believe, that will hold up to scrutiny, that will hold up in court, if it comes to that. Only problem is . . . Caleb runs. You stop at French Prairie Rest Area and he thinks: screw this. He doesn't want to go back to his father, back to the scene of his crimes, back to a home where he will be scrutinized, watched, encaged, worse than ever before.

You trusted him too much. Caleb runs, and his story is rough, and unpolished. His narrative has holes. Now, you and your brother are hoping he won't be found.

But he is seen by the wrong woman at the wrong time — a woman whose life isn't led like yours — on fast-forward, but a woman who is watchful, who knows faces, who studies them, their angles, their features. She knows she has seen that missing boy, Caleb Veir. She may say she is a little less convinced than she really is, just so she doesn't sound too crazy, but she knows, she knows it's him.

There is nothing else you can do — you have to continue your drive to your brother's house.

Anything else would raise suspicion.

Oh, fuck: Seth Fuller doesn't know where the packet is. It had to have been close to him when he was found. That means Clyde Brimmer or Shannon has it. If Shannon Fuller knows you nearly killed Seth, she will kill you, John. If you don't kill her first.

72

Shannon Fuller stood with her back against the bar counter, her thoughts on a horrifying loop, her heart shattered. Not one person she loved, all of whom she had loved so fiercely, had been honest with her: not Aaron, not Seth, not John. Everyone had lied to her. What a fool she was. How humiliating it all was. She thought her heart had been as broken as a heart could be, but it just kept on coming. She couldn't believe that there could be a lower place to which she could be plunged. The place where she now was. She was standing upright, but she felt there was another version of her, some shadow version that was collapsed on the floor at her feet. She would never recover. The hits had come one after the other. But she knew, at least, that Seth, she could forgive. Seth had more demons than she had ever known, but she knew she was right to have always trusted in his beautiful soul. And she would do everything she could to repair that, even if it took the rest of her life.

The phone rang, and it startled her from her thoughts. She let it ring. It stopped, then it rang again. When it rang a third time, she picked up.

'Shannon, it's Ren Bryce.'

'Hi,' said Shannon.

'Have you seen John Veir in the past twenty-four hours?'

Shannon's eyes flicked over to where John sat,

ashen-faced by the wall, as she pointed Seth's gun at his heart.

'No,' said Shannon.

'OK,' said Ren. 'I don't want to alarm you, but please, if he shows up, don't let him in. I need you to lock up the bar, the house. Do not let anyone in. I'm on my way over.'

'What?' said Shannon. 'Why?' She stayed calm, but her heart had started to beat wildly.

'I'll speak with you when I get there,' said Ren. 'I'll be ten minutes.'

'Please,' said Shannon. 'Tell me. Why? What do you mean?'

'I can't,' said Ren. 'I'll speak with you when I get there.'

'OK,' said Shannon. She put the phone down.

'Who was that?' said John.

'None of your business,' she said.

She was staring, now, at two people who thought nothing of taking lives, or of telling the most horrific of lies, of being colder than any two people she had ever been faced with.

And she was pointing a gun at them. And she wanted them to be gone.

73

Caleb Veir's steady gaze moved between Shannon Fuller, and his dad. Shannon, Aunt Alice, his mom, his dad . . . there were a whole load of messed-up adults in his life.

Shannon had asked him five times what had he done, what had he done to her baby. He hadn't answered her.

$\star$ $\star$ $\star$

He thought back to that day, sitting in a tree at the edge of the Fullers' front yard where he could see into Shannon's bedroom. He knew that asshole Aaron was at practice for another hour, he knew that. He figured if Shannon was going to take her clothes off and he was going to see those giant titties the boys all talked about, now would be a good time — when she was alone.

Then he heard it — the familiar sound of the engine of his father's car, as it drove into the front yard. He watched as he parked, a little haphazard, never like he would at home, as if he was desperate, heading to an emergency, parking outside a hospital where someone was dying or heading to a fire because someone had to be rescued. He thought he was caught — he thought someone had told his father that he was there, in a tree, looking to see some loser's mom's titties. But that wasn't what happened.

His father was there for Shannon Fuller, who was now rushing into the yard like a puppy dog. Caleb watched them come together like they'd been thrown in an explosion, and his father was walking her backward into the house as the rain fell, and neither of them cared, like they were in a fucking movie. His dad was old, and this made him sick to his stomach. He watched as they made it only as far as the shelter of the porch before his father had hiked up Shannon's skirt and was kissing her so hard, he . . .

★　★　★

Caleb shuddered. He remembered the week before the school dance, telling Aaron what he saw, using it like a weapon. He told him his mom was a whore. He called her Shannon Fulfiller. And Aaron answered in the strangest way. He could still remember what he said, how easy it was for him to say it, how open he was, how he hadn't even sneered.

'At least my mom loves me,' Aaron had said.

'You fucking pussy,' Caleb said. He had mimicked him. ''At least my mom loves me.' Pussy.'

'Your mom fucking hates you,' said Aaron. 'She never wanted you. She tried to fucking drown you when you were a baby, you fucking loser. She couldn't even stand you for that long, probably got sick of you soon as she saw your ugly fucking face.'

'You're full of shit,' said Caleb.

394

'It's the truth!' said Aaron. 'Only reason you're still alive is because my mom came along and saw what was happening. She took you off of your mom at Clearwater Creek. She was holding your stupid head under the water. I can't believe my mom saved your loser fucking life.'

Caleb felt cold, shivery, like the world around him was warm and colorful, and he was black and white, and he was ice. Nothing that came to mind he could say to Aaron: *But my mom loves me! My mom is the only one who loves me! We're a team! We . . . we love each other! She's . . . always there for me. You're a liar, Aaron Fuller! Aaron Full of Lies! You're a fucking liar!*

But something had told Caleb that this was the truth. He sensed it in his pounding chest, his sick stomach, his burning flesh, his flaring pupils.

My mother tried to kill me. Why? Why would she do that?

He couldn't bear to ask her. He couldn't bear it. But he would. He would come back to her, and it would be different now. She would have missed him. She would be so glad he was back. All he needed to do was get his fucking father to stay the fuck out of everything. And Alice.

★   ★   ★

The night of the middle school dance, Caleb had watched Aaron Fuller staring at Molly Gardner. The prettiest girl in the class, Molly had a dark streak; she was fun, but she liked creepy stuff. Aaron had been telling the story of Lizzie, the girl who haunted Cabin 8 at Lake Verny, how he

395

had seen her, how she had a huge slice out of her leg, how she would scream and nothing would come out.

Caleb took Molly Gardner's cell phone when she was on the dance floor. He opened SnapChat and typed three things: an emoji ghost beside a house, a clock that read midnight, and a kiss. He sent it to Aaron Fuller. Then he deleted it.

★ ★ ★

And, of course, Aaron had shown up. And Caleb was waiting. And there was a barrel of rainwater. And drowning is silent. And easy. So easy with just a knee pressed into his back.

★ ★ ★

Suddenly, he felt the urge to answer Shannon Fuller, to tell her all that. So he told her everything.

74

Ren ran into The Crow Bar, her sidearm raised. Shannon Fuller was standing with her back to her, in the middle of the floor, her arm outstretched, holding a handgun, swaying back and forth.

Oh my God. What have you done?

Caleb Veir was lying at Shannon's feet, in a growing pool of blood from a gunshot wound to the chest.

Oh, Jesus Christ.

Shannon turned to Ren, wild-eyed, pointed the gun her way. 'Don't go near him. Stay the fuck away from him.'

Caleb was still breathing, making terrible gurgling sounds.

'Give me the gun, Shannon.'

Shannon didn't move.

'Give me the gun,' said Ren. 'Don't make this any worse.'

Shannon handed it to her, fear flickering in her eyes.

'Stay back,' said Ren. 'Please let me help him.'

She checked Caleb's pulse.

Thank God, thank God, thank God.

'No!' said Shannon. 'No!' Her arm shot out, and she grabbed a fistful of Ren's hair, started to drag her backward.

Owww! Fuuuck!

Ren reached up, grabbed Shannon's wrist, dug

her thumb into the right pressure point, got her to release her grip. She kicked out, striking Shannon's knee, bringing her to the ground with a scream.

'Sorry,' said Ren, 'but you have to stay back. You don't want him to die, Shannon. You do not want this.' She returned to Caleb's side, started to do chest compressions.

'Is John here?' said Ren.

'Yes,' said Shannon. 'I locked him in the cold room. I can't stand the sight of him. I wanted him to see Caleb die, I did, I really did. What is wrong with me? I loved that man so much . . . I loved him.' She was sobbing uncontrollably, pointing at Caleb. 'He killed Aaron,' she was saying. 'And he killed Luke Monroe, told him to come look at the fishes in the pond, then held his little head under. He just told us all this terrible stuff.'

Oh, God.

'He's a psychopath!' said Shannon. 'He doesn't deserve to be saved! He's a monster, he's a monster.'

Ren turned to her. 'Listen to me, Shannon. Listen. You need him to live. *You* do. OK? You need him to make it.'

'I don't want him to!' screamed Shannon. 'I want him to die.'

'You do not want to go to prison for the rest of your life,' said Ren. 'That's what will happen if he dies. You need to be there for Seth. He needs you.'

'I don't care if I go to prison!' said Shannon. 'Don't you get it? And who gives a crap about me?'

398

'Seth does,' said Ren. 'You're more than his aunt — you're a mother to him. And you know it. I care about you. I want you to make it, Shannon. You have to make it. You deserve to. You're a good person.'

Ren looked down at Caleb, at his pale face, his grim, downturned mouth.

Her heart plunged.

Duke Rawlins: the destruction he wrought. He took my friends, he took my boyfriend.

He was a monster. And he started out as a boy monster.

What if he hadn't made it? How many horrible deaths would have been avoided? How many lives would have been saved?

My arms . . . won't move.

She thought of Luke Monroe and his curly blond hair, how his curiosity was leveraged, how he was lured to look at fishes in a pond.

The innocence.

My arms . . . what is going on?

She glanced up at Shannon. They locked eyes.

No one would know. If I just stopped trying to save this boy right now, no one would know.

Ren looked down at Caleb. His eyes began to flicker. She looked back up at Shannon.

Shannon wouldn't tell. She'd back me up. I'd back her up.

Desperate, animal choking sounds were coming from Caleb's throat. Ren looked down at him.

He's a monster.

He is twelve years old.

He's a psychopath.

Ren's arms were stiff, unmoving.

He is so fucking damaged.

But someone damaged him.

Her arms started to work, she started to push down, her movements rhythmic.

Irreparably, though.

Irreparably damaged him.

Ren stopped again. Duke Rawlins' face bloomed in her mind, how he lay dying in the foyer of Safe Streets, how she dragged Joe Lucchesi off him.

Her arms wouldn't move.

Move!

A banging sound came from behind the bar, from inside the house.

Bang. Bang. Bang. Bang. Bang.

Her heart plunged.

Duke Rawlins killed Ben.

Move!

Duke Rawlins was a psychopath.

Move your fucking arms!

Who will Caleb Veir go on to kill?

Ren looked down at him.

Who will you kill next?

Bang. Bang. Bang. Bang. Bang.

'What is that fucking noise?' roared Ren. 'Shut it up! Shut it the fuck up!' *I'm going to lose my fucking mind.*

★ ★ ★

The door to the bar burst open and suddenly the room filled: Gary, Paul, Sylvie, Ruddock, Wiley. Ren looked up, her arms working furiously.

God bless you all. God bless teamwork.

She fell away from Caleb, and Paul took over.

Ren was covered in blood. She looked down at her hands, red and trembling. She looked up at Shannon Fuller, and watched her collapse to her knees. Ren crawled over to her and took her in her arms.

'You made it, Shannon, OK? You made it, and Seth made it.'

And Caleb did.

Shannon was sobbing hysterically.

'You will get through this,' said Ren. 'I promise you.'

I can promise that . . . can't I?

75

Ren walked through Tate PD, and said goodbye to the team. Paul, Gary, and Sylvie had already gone to the airport. Ren left Ruddock until the end. She knocked on his door.

'Come in,' he said.

'Hey,' said Ren. 'I've saved the best 'till last.'

He stood up.

'Stay where you are,' said Ren.

He didn't.

I love your face. 'Thank you for being so kind, Ruddock. And it was a real pleasure working with you.'

'Thank you. You too, Ren. You take care of yourself.'

They hugged.

'Any word on Jimmy Lyle?' said Ren.

'He's still out there,' said Ruddock.

'I don't like the ones who get away,' said Ren. 'Speaking of which . . . '

'Keep in touch,' said Ruddock.

'I will.' *I definitely will.* 'Come to Denver some time,' said Ren. 'Please.'

'I might just do that.'

★　★　★

Ren drove through Tate, but instead of heading for Salem, she took a detour. She pulled into Clyde Brimmer's drive. She went up to the house and rang the doorbell. He came to the door, opened up, and once again, the smell of liquor surrounded him.

'Clyde, there's something I'd like to talk to you about,' said Ren.

He looked at her, eager, but fearful. 'What is it?'

'Can I come in?' said Ren.

'Sure,' he said. 'Please excuse the mess.'

'Don't worry,' said Ren.

He sat on the sofa, and she sat next to him.

'It's about your sister, Lizzie,' said Ren.

'OK,' he said.

'It might not be very easy to hear,' said Ren, 'but I think it might help you.'

'OK. I trust you.'

Aw, maan. 'Lizzie didn't fall through that deck,' said Ren.

'What?' said Clyde.

'This is the difficult part,' said Ren. 'Have you heard about Roger Lyle?'

Clyde nodded.

'I'm sorry to have to tell you that Lizzie was one of Roger Lyle's victims. I've seen evidence of this. She wasn't sexually abused, but she had been near-drowned by him on several occasions. He made it look like she fell through the deck that day, but I looked at all the evidence, the photos of the deck. There was an ax used on part of that. It wasn't weak enough, and I've seen the photo of Lizzie — she wasn't a heavy girl.'

Clyde was open-mouthed, silent. Tears poured down his face. Ren put her hands on his. 'I'm so sorry,' she said. 'I know this is hard for you to hear, but I hope it brings you some peace. You weren't responsible for what happened to Lizzie. Roger Lyle was a very evil, and very clever man.' She paused. 'If you want further confirmation, Clyde, there is the option of — '

'No,' he said. 'No — I don't want her taken from the ground. I want peace for her too. I know you wouldn't have come here to me today if you weren't sure. Like I said, I trust you.'

'Thank you,' said Ren. 'And thank you for everything you did for us.' She paused. 'Can I give you a ride anywhere, before I go?'

'I'd like to visit the cemetery, please.'

'Sure,' said Ren. 'That's not a problem.' *I'd have taken you to the moon if you asked.*

⋆ ⋆ ⋆

At Portland airport, Ren stood with Paul at his boarding gate — he would be flying back to DC with Sylvie.

'See you,' said Ren.

'See you?' said Paul. 'Have I done something?'

'No — not at all,' said Ren.

'"See you"? Who is this lady before me and what has she done with Ren Bryce?'

'I'm sorry. And who you callin' a lady?'

He tilted his head, narrowed his eyes. 'Can I come see you? Or . . . you could come to DC?'

For what? 'Hmm . . . '

He looked hurt. 'Not quite the reaction I was hoping for . . . '

'I'm sorry,' said Ren. *Don't you know that your 'Can I come see you?' is really 'Can you fix*

404

me?' And that the answer is 'No, I can't.'

'This is about Marianne . . . ' said Paul.

Ren laughed. *He is clueless.* 'No — it's not.' *It's about you.* 'I'm sorry. I just . . . can't be close to anyone right now, I don't think. Honestly, I'm feeling like . . . ' *you took advantage of me.*

'Like what?' said Paul.

She looked away.

He laughed. 'I love that you started the sentence with 'honestly', and then didn't finish it.'

Ren smiled, turning back to him. 'Says it all. Yes, I do not want to be honest about my feelings. Which really means: I don't want to be dishonest about them. So I'm going to go for the trailing off thing, followed by silence.'

He hugged her.

Ren stepped back, looked up at him. 'Look after yourself,' she said. 'Talk soon.' She started to walk away. 'Unless the plane goes down . . . ' She paused. 'Merciful release.'

'Ren?' said Paul.

She stopped and looked around. 'Yes?'

'You do know that the world's a better place with you in it, right?'

Ren laughed. 'The bottom line is this — whatever your triumphs or tragedies, if a movie were made of your life story, someone would be eating popcorn as you die.'

'So, who would play you?' said Paul.

'Nick Nolte.'

She walked away to the sound of his laughter. *I love making him laugh. I love his laugh. Stop being mean to him.*

As she went toward the bar, she passed Sylvie and Gary saying a passionate farewell in a dark corner by the coffee shop.

He looks like an amazing kisser.

Jesus.

Christ.

★　★　★

Ren went to the bar and sat down, ordered a vodka cranberry.

She checked her messages. The tally of ignored texts from Joe Lucchesi had reached six.

I'm a terrible human being.

She started to text back.

And say what? You are so fucking hot: goodbye. Thanks for the amazing sex: goodbye. I remind you of your dead wife: goodbye.

Something in her heart was overriding the thoughts, over-riding the words.

Go away, heart. You've been nothing but trouble.

She smiled to herself. The bartender caught her eye. He smiled back.

'I'm a million miles away,' said Ren.

'Well, wherever you are, it looks like a great place.'

'It's a fucking hellhole.'

'So you're the type who smiles on the road to hell . . . '

'I sing and dance too,' said Ren. *And fuck.*

She finished her drink, checked the time.

Gary walked in. 'I knew I'd find her here,' he

said to the bartender.

'Because I texted him where I was,' said Ren.

'On the road to hell,' said the bartender, handing a beer to another customer.

Ren laughed. Gary sat down beside her. 'Did you make a new friend?'

'Every stop I take,' said Ren. She checked the time on her phone. 'I'm going to run to the ladies. Or maybe walk casually.'

'Vodka cranberry?' said Gary.

'Yes, please.'

★   ★   ★

As Ren reached the door to the ladies' room, Sylvie was coming out. Her eyes were red.

'Oh,' they both said at the same time.

'You're still here,' said Ren. 'Are you OK?'

Sylvie nodded. 'Yes.' She tilted her head back. 'Well . . . ' She tried to smile.

'I'm sorry,' said Ren. 'Is it . . . '

Sylvie let out a breath. 'It is.'

Fuck. You are hurting. And I am judging.

Sylvie tried to smile. 'Mistresses don't have horns, you know.'

Their boyfriends, however . . .

'I know you look at me and you don't like me,' said Sylvie.

I'm not sure that's what it is, actually . . .

'I'm your worst nightmare,' said Sylvie. 'You think women like me let other women down. And here's the thing: I agree. Or, at least, I used to.'

'I don't think — '

407

'You've never had an affair with a married man,' said Sylvie, 'am I right?'

Ren nodded.

'Because you've never met one who blew your mind,' said Sylvie. 'It could be as simple as that. I'm bright, I'm strong, my self-esteem is not exactly in the toilet. I'm a psychologist, for Christ's sake. Sometimes, I have no idea who this person is when I look in the mirror . . . except someone who is in love with Gary Dettling. I honestly don't know how this happened. Have you ever fallen for someone who just takes your breath away, it makes no sense, there's no logic, it goes beyond your beliefs, your expectations, your principles?'

I'm not sure. Jesus. I've been that in love . . . haven't I? Maybe not. I don't know.

Sylvie was still talking. 'Your head is the same logical place it always has been and your heart is like something from the greatest romantic movie of all time — the type of movie you never got, where you're watching and you're like 'There's no way anyone would do that or say that or feel that strongly or . . . ' And that logical mind of yours becomes this battleground, because, when I'm not with him, I think: what the hell am I doing? And when I'm with him, or talking to him, or hearing from him, the whole world is right.'

It can't be!

'Is it worth it?' said Ren. 'Really?'

'Yes,' said Sylvie. 'Can you believe that? I don't even think I can . . . '

Ren smiled. 'I'm sorry, Sylvie — I haven't

408

been very kind to you. It's — '

'I understand, OK? I do.'

'But, maybe you're right — maybe I've never had that kind of loss-of-logic love before. Well, not with someone unattainable.' *But, then, I've never had logic to begin with. And, shit — that was terrible: unattainable? Maybe Gary is attainable. What do I know?*

'Just — I think you deserve more,' said Ren. 'Every woman does.' *His wife does too.*

'I never thought getting this little from a man could feel like so much,' said Sylvie.

Oh dear God . . . you said that out loud. To me. And I hope you say it out loud to yourself later and hear how depressing it is.

I'm such a judgey asshole.

Ren hovered in front of Sylvie, then reached out, touched her forearm. 'I'm sorry for being . . . not exactly friendly. Please . . . just look after yourself.' *Because whatever happens, I think Gary will be just fine.*

'Thanks,' said Sylvie. 'You too.' She paused. 'I'm so sorry about everything that happened to you, Ren. I . . . can't imagine. I think you're very strong.'

'God,' said Ren, 'I'm so not. But, thank you.'

They hugged.

Well, well, well . . .

76

Jimmy Lyle had left Tate behind, left DEAD TO
ME in his wake. He felt free, untethered. He was
who he was meant to be. He had a stolen laptop,
a burner phone, he had a new wig, he wore
clothes that were two sizes too big, clothes,
again, that were for women.

He sat back on the motel bed with his laptop.
He checked his messages. The only name he
wanted to see now was the newest one:
BoyUndr15. He had screen-grabbed some of
their earliest exchanges. Every time he read
them, he got hard.

The first one had blown his mind.

    Rapid01:   hw undr15 r u??
    BoyUndr15: :-) im xctly 15 . . .
    Rapid01:   ok good . . . y'undr'??
    BoyUndr15: undr
                 . . .
                 . . .
                 . . . watr

Jimmy's heart pounded now, as it had pounded
then.

    Rapid01:   y undr watr?
    BoyUndr15: cuz . . .
    Rapid01:   cuz . . . ??

BoyUndr15: its where i wnt 2 go
Rapid01:   y??
BoyUndr15: its where i wnt 2 go . . . in the end

Instantly hard. It was the same now. He started pulling at his dick. He remembered how desperately he needed to know what the boy meant, was it what he hoped.

Rapid01:   the end of??

The wait had almost killed him. He felt a head rush, like white noise. He had been rooted to the spot, his eyes transfixed by the screen. Then the words appeared.

BoyUndr15: cuz . . . life sux

BoyUndr15 had signed off, then, and Jimmy had nearly passed out. He imagined the pain of never hearing from him again. But BoyUndr15 came back, and was back almost every day since.

The last message Jimmy had sent BoyUndr15 was two hours before he checked into the motel. He described exactly what he wanted to do to him. He ended it with:

i wnt to take the pain away
let me take ur pain away

His screen lit up with a reply.

BoyUndr15: OK

Jimmy's heart was bursting.

One hour later, BoyUndr15 sent another message.

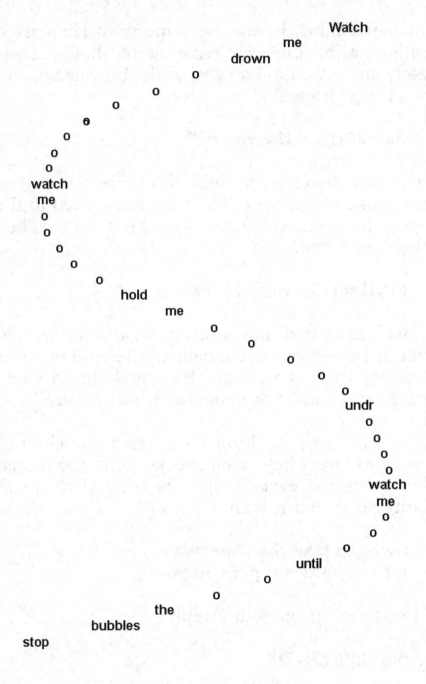

Watch
me
drown

o

o

o

o

o

o

o

watch
me

o

o

o

o

o

hold
me

o

o

o

o

undr

o

o

o

o

watch
me

o

o

o

until

o

o

the
bubbles
stop

Jimmy could barely breathe. He pushed his dress up around his waist, ran to the tall narrow mirror against the wall, trying to pull down his pantyhose as he went. But he fell to his knees first, yanked them down his thighs, scratching his thighs as he did it. He pulled the belt from his dress, wrapped it tight around his neck.

He had never gotten so hard, so quickly . . . all because of words and the beautiful images they conjured. He stared at the words as they glowed in the mirror's reflection. He was glowing too, his eyes fixed on the dwindling o's. The smartness of this boy. He was only fifteen, but he was like . . . he was . . . he was . . . he was his soulmate.

BoyUndr15, I love you.
I love you to death.
To death.
Not back again.

77

Ren sat in the office of Dr Leonard Lone, watching how the icy gray sky over Denver was draining the life from the painting that hung behind his desk.

Aren't there guidelines for psychiatrist office art? Couldn't the wrong image push someone over the edge? Especially when forced to view it while trying to avoid eye contact?

'Why did you move your desk?' said Ren.

'I wanted to have the window to my right, to have the light come in that way,' said Lone.

But I loved staring out the window behind you. I don't like your painting. You're waiting for me to answer your question — I know.

'It did feel good, yes,' said Ren.

'Because you're used to Gary berating you at the end of an investigation . . . '

'Going nuts,' said Ren. She smiled. 'Berating sounds very . . . civilized.'

'Gary is civilized . . . '

'No, you're right — he is,' said Ren. 'I was kidding.'

'Well, good job on all this,' said Lone. 'You didn't go off on your own, you followed the rules.'

Griiiim.

Lone sat back, opened his arms in a generous gesture. 'This was a case you didn't take any risks on.'

'Correct,' said Ren. *Correct.*

414

Ren sat down that evening with her laptop and a glass of wine.

Still not getting Alice Veir helping John. All her talk of why she studied the law, how she wanted to make a difference. Is that it? Do we all just aspire to be one thing, the best person who ever lived, when really, as we move through life, we realize that all we can be is the best flawed human being under the circumstances. Alice Veir was so convincing in her belief in justice. Why would she throw it all away? Was there something in particular about Anthony Boyd Lorden? Was there a personal connection? Did she know him? Weren't they around the same age?

Ren's heart started to pound.

Her thoughts shifted to Alice Veir's words about Anthony: 'I've had my life. What has he had?'

I've had my life?

She's forty-five years old. Isn't she still having her life?

She thought about Alice Veir. She thought about Patti Ellis.

How could John Veir have gotten access to Patti Ellis' medication? Oh my God. It wasn't have gotten Patti Ellis' fentanyl: it was Alice Veir's. Alice Veir is sick. She must be terminal.

Ren pictured Anthony Boyd Lorden in the interrogation video: young, handsome, clean-cut. Then she pictured the police sketch in Emma Ridley's file.

That's why it was familiar: *the photo of John Veir in the living room. At thirty years old, he looked a lot like Lorden at seventeen. And it was a pitch-dark night. Flawed eyewitness testimony.*

'You'd want a pretty tight relationship with a sibling — or anyone, for that matter — to be able to call them up and say 'I killed my child, what do I do next?'

But it would be a whole hell of a lot easier if they owed you.

★ ★ ★

Kevin Dunne's death was an accident.

And it was Alice Veir who hit him that night. Maybe she was drinking and she couldn't throw her whole future away, everything she had worked for. She called her brother for help. And he came. And they let an innocent man go to jail.

Then Alice's conscience kicks in when she knows she's going to die. She wants to carry out an act of repentance.

But John calls her when he discovers what Caleb has done. He tells her his plan, reminds her of how he helped her out of a predicament when she was in law school — how his actions meant that she got a second chance too.

She tells him that was a very different situation. She tells him that was an accident. But he reminds her that yes, it was an accident that she knocked down and killed a boy called Kevin Dunne, but it was no accident to drive drunk or recklessly or whatever she did. It was no accident

416

when she called her big brother to help her move the body, and to lie for her. It was no accident that she allowed a man to go to jail for twenty-one years until she found out she was sick, and wanted to do something good to redeem herself, wanted to set him free, so she could set herself free.

She thinks that he is making a fair point.

Ren called Emma Ridley and gave her the new information.

★ ★ ★

That night, Ren sat on her bed, holding her cell in her palm as if it was a fortune teller fish that would curl up at the edges and reveal her future. She started scrolling through her contacts.

She stopped at Joe Lucchesi.

Be brave.

She called his number.

He picked up on the second ring. 'Hey!'

He sounds cheery. I wonder wh —

'It's great to hear your voice,' said Joe. 'Really great.'

Ren felt her heart jump. *Oh, no. No.* 'Hey. It's good to hear yours. How are you doing?'

'Good, good,' said Joe. 'Are you home?'

Home . . . 'Yes.'

'How did it all go?'

Ren filled him in on the case.

'Good for you guys,' said Joe.

'Sorry I haven't been in touch in a while.' *I am falling for you, Joe Lucchesi. And it's fucking unbearable.*

417

'It's OK — you've been busy.'

'Thanks,' said Ren. 'Anyway — I better go. I've got some things to do . . . '

Silence.

Ugh.

'Well, I better let you get back to it,' said Joe.

'Thanks,' said Ren. 'Look after yourself. And . . . thanks for Denver. I had a great time.'

But I realize now: it isn't what I thought it was. You're not falling for him. You're staggering out of some hellhole looking for purchase. Someone familiar. It felt intense because we were drunk and because we were broken. I was confusing intensity with the need to attach to something.

'Me too,' said Joe. 'I was thinking maybe — '

His voice was distant. She was already ending the call.

78

Jimmy Lyle walked the aisles of the department store. He stopped at swimwear. His heart pounded. He ran his fingers along the line of swim trunks on their little hangers. They weren't organized by size, and it flooded him with anger.

He was looking for tags with the letter S. That was the size that interested him. He chose a plain yellow pair. He chose them because BoyUndr15 said that was his favorite color. And he chose them because of the days and nights he spent jerking off to the drowning boys and girls of *Surf Rescue*. And the lead actress in her yellow swimsuit. He loved her.

But he knew she didn't care about him. She didn't reply to any of his letters. The last one, the one he tried to hand-deliver, was taken from him before he even got a chance to get near her trailer. It didn't matter how he explained it to the security guard, it didn't matter how much he sobbed. He still remembered the cruelty of that man: 'Dude, if she hasn't replied to the first one hundred and twenty-seven letters, why do you think she's going to reply to this one? What's so special about one twenty-eight?'

'Because there's a gift in there with it,' Jimmy had said. 'It's a package, can't you see?' And he knew that if she just watched the video that she would get it, that she would know. She would see how much she meant to him, she would see how

419

everything he did was done while the show was reflected in his mirror. When she watched, she would be watching him watching her watching him.

His dick was hard by the time he reached the register. He smiled at the woman behind the counter, kept his eyes on hers.

'You going on vacation?' said the sales assistant.

Jimmy nodded. 'Yes.' His heart swelled. 'And it's my birthday today.'

'If you show me some ID, I can give you our ten per cent birthday discount.'

It was Jimmy's birthday. Just not the birthday that was on his fake ID.

He handed her cash. 'Don't worry — next time.'

She laughed. 'You'll only have to wait a whole year.'

He laughed, but he didn't like anything about her.

'So you're going on vacation?' she said.

With my boy. BoyUndr15.

* * *

Four hours later, Jimmy Lyle was standing by the pool, lost in the warm, shimmering water. Indoor, heated pool: BoyUndr15 had rich parents who didn't give a shit about him. They would come home from their European vacation to find him. Jimmy expected that this was BoyUndr15's plan. Jimmy knew what it was like to hate your parents, to want to punish them. He just wished he was as brave.

Across from him was a wall of glass that looked out on to snow-covered mountains. It was beautiful. But not as beautiful as what was about to unfold.

Jimmy's hand was on his buckle. His swim trunks were under his jeans. He knew what was inside them was always bigger than people expected.

He had spent a lot of money at the store — the yellow shorts, the beach ball, the towels, the oil, the condoms. He unbuttoned his shirt, unbuckled his pants, slid them down. He had his father's skinny limbs. He hated them. But that didn't matter now. He was here, feet from this swimming pool, moments from his wildest dreams, hard and ready. He unpacked his camera, set up the tripod.

He thought of his father. He felt a spike of anger in his chest.

Nothing will spoil this. Nothing will spoil this.

★   ★   ★

He had run through what would happen when they met: he would greet the boy with a smile, he would make him feel relaxed. His heart was bursting.

His phone vibrated with a text.

BoyUndr15: Opn gray door! Cmng thru the shower room . . . :-)

There was a knock, and Jimmy walked over to the door, his heart pounding, his legs weak. He

421

opened it. In the half-darkness, he could make out two figures standing there. One pushed past him, stood to his left. The other stood in front of him:

'Jimmy Lyle? I'm BoyUndr15.'

It was a woman.

Jimmy Lyle stared. 'But — '

She was holding up a badge. 'Or Special Agent Ren Bryce . . . ' She smiled. 'Happy Fuuucking Birthday, Jimmy.'

79

Gary was pacing up and down his Safe Streets office. Ren was standing, motionless, eyes on the floor.

'Jesus Christ, Ren,' said Gary. 'What the fuck were you thinking?'

I was thinking if nobody knows what I'm doing, nobody can get hurt. I am the only person who could get hurt, and that's fine with me. I can accept putting myself at risk.

'I was thinking: there is a psychopath out there,' said Ren. *I'm not good with psychopaths being out there. Look what happens. Look what happens: people fucking die. People you love fucking die. They die.*

'I was thinking,' said Ren, 'that I couldn't let that be, and that if I was the only one who knew, then it wouldn't be screwed up. The first thing got screwed up because too many people knew.'

'This is vigilante shit,' said Gary.

'But I had Ruddock!' said Ren. 'I brought Ruddock.'

'At the eleventh hour!' said Gary. 'You manipulated him — '

'Oh, come on,' said Ren, 'Ruddock's a big boy. I went through all the evidence. It was — ' *Don't say watertight.* ' . . . watertight'.

'Are you fucking laughing, Ren?' said Gary.

'No! That was — '

423

'What the?' said Gary. 'I can't believe — though I should! — that despite everything, you're still doing your own thing. Ren Solo. What is it going to take? What the fuck is it going to — '

'Stop!' said Ren. 'Stop!' *Don't. Don't. Don't. Do not say a word.*

'I'm sorry, Ren, but you're going to have to listen to this. You really are. Everett is dead. Robbie is dead. Ben — '

'Stop!' She was screaming. 'Stop!'

Gary grabbed her by the arms, squeezed them tight. 'Ren, look at me. Look at me.'

'No!' She shook her head. Gary shook her until she locked eyes with him.

I can't. I can't. She was sobbing. 'Don't say it — don't. Don't.'

'Don't say what?' said Gary.

I want to die. I want to die. 'Don't say that if I hadn't gone off on my own that they would still be alive. I can't bear it. Don't.'

'What the — ' He stared at her. Tears poured down her face.

Don't. Don't. Don't.

Gary released his grip, pulled her into his arms. Her body was wracked with sobs. He held her tight.

'That was the exact opposite of what I was going to say,' said Gary. 'Jesus, Ren — the exact opposite.'

I'm in Gary Dettling's arms. Jesus.

She pulled back. She could feel strands of her hair hot and damp against her cheeks. She checked his shirt for mascara.

424

My hands are on his chest.

She felt his hands on her face. She looked up at him.

'I was trying to say to you: it's not your fault,' said Gary. 'None of it was your fault. It would have happened another day if it hadn't happened that day. It would have happened another way. He could have taken more of us with him. This wasn't about you or something you did or didn't do. This was about Joe Lucchesi, it was about me. I shouldn't be here, Ren. I shouldn't be alive. I think about it all the time: I shouldn't be here, but I am. And I am, thanks to you. And Joe Lucchesi is here, because of you. But if you listen only to one thing, listen to this: it was not your fault. And do not spend the rest of your life trying to fix it. Do not die trying to fix this. Do not die on me, Ren.'

'OK!' said Ren. 'OK! OK! OK! I won't. I won't.' She slumped down in the chair and cried, and cried and cried.

Can't blink back a flood.

⋆ ⋆ ⋆

That evening, Ren sat on the sofa with a bottle of red wine, her phone in her hand.

Phones are a disaster. It's too fucking easy.

It's too hard.

She scrolled down, stopped at Joe Lucchesi.

He's met someone else.

In twenty-four hours . . .

She lowered her thumb on to his number.

Don't.

What's the worst that can happen?
I'm the wrong person to put that question to.
The phone started to ring.
He picked up. 'Hey . . . ' There was a smile in his voice.
'Hey.' She took a breath. 'So I'm sorry about the last call. I was . . . tired.' *Jesus!* 'I . . . had a lot going on. I'm sorry. My head is a little all over the place.'
Why can't I just be honest?
'Really?' he said.
Nice teasing. He knows. He knows me already. Black Mark Number 1. 'How are you so sane, though? Seriously.'
'I am seriously not sane.'
'You're doing a lot better than me.' *You don't know that.*
'For someone who likes evidence to back things up . . . ' said Joe.
'No, I don't,' said Ren. 'Shit. That's where I'm going wrong.' *In all aspects of my life.* 'I'm not sure I am always driven by evidence.' *I come up with shit and decide it's the reality. Which part of bipolar . . .* 'I think this might be a changing day in my life'.
'Don't be so quick to presume you know what's going on with me,' said Joe. 'I'm under no illusions — I know I come with . . . history.'
Like, of the Roman Empire.
'And with more baggage than most,' said Joe.
Like those trucks beside aircraft.
'But,' he said, 'you can ask me anything and I'll give you an honest answer.'
Unlike me.

426

'Don't be fooled by this tough exterior.' He laughed.

'Well, I can't ask for fairer than that,' said Ren. 'While we're getting it all out there, I'm an emotional cripple. You can ask me anything, but I probably won't be honest. Not in a bad way, but I think there's some override switch that, if anything is too roaring red of an emotional hotspot, these little builders come in with fire bricks.'

Joe laughed. 'Well, that was pretty honest.'

'Pretty . . . exactly.' She paused. 'OK — here's a question: what's been going on in your world? I didn't even ask last time, sorry.' *I was too busy panicking.*

'Work and Grace,' said Joe. 'Which means assholes mixed in with ballet classes, the zoo, *Frozen*, playgrounds, frozen playgrounds . . . '

'I'm sure you meet assholes in playgrounds too,' said Ren.

And moms who want to fuck you. If they only knew how amazing you are, you'd never make it out of the playground alive.

'How is Grace?' said Ren.

'Well, she's twirling around here with her hand out for the phone, so I'll let her tell you herself.'

She could hear the scuffle of Joe handing the phone over.

'Hi, Ren! It's Grace! Will you please come to my birthday party?'

Ren and Joe laughed.

'Daddy said you come to New York some-times!'

'Well, yes,' said Ren. 'I go visit my family.'

427

'Daddy said come at the exact same time as my birthday! I'm having a clown!'

Clown? Fuck, no. 'Well, thank you so much, Grace. I would love to come. I'll definitely see what I can do.'

'She said yes!' said Grace.

Ren laughed again. Joe came back on the phone, laughing too.

'You haven't given her the John Wayne Gacy talk, then . . . '

'I'm holding out for her tenth birthday,' said Joe. He lowered his voice. 'I did not know she was going to ask you that.'

'I don't think you're a master puppeteer somehow,' said Ren. 'So, what date is her birthday?'

'June sixth. She's an organizer, this one.'

'That's hilarious. Well, she's definitely given me enough notice . . . '

But are we all just assuming that I'm going to be around in three months' time? Jesus. I don't know how I feel about that.

Why don't I ever fucking know?

You do know. This is so boring.

'But I hope I get to see you before June . . . ' said Joe.

Ren smiled. 'Yes, I'd like that.' *Way too much. I hate this. My stomach. My heart. My limits . . .*

'I'm . . . glad you called,' said Joe.

Where did that come from?

'I thought you'd run away,' he said.

From that kind of sex?

Nice try.

'No,' said Ren.

428

'I'm thinking you did . . . for a little while,' said Joe.

Damn you! 'I ran maybe as far as . . . ' *The place where all the tears were. The place I didn't want to reach. The place I couldn't bear to be. To come back to the scariest place I've ever been in my life.*

Fuck. What am I doing?

'Are you still there?' said Joe.

Ren paused. 'I'm still here.'

You, me . . . and our fucked-up hearts.

Acknowledgements

Thank you to my agent, Marianne Gunn O'Connor, and to Vicki Satlow, and Pat Lynch.

Thank you to my skilled and patient editor, Sarah Hodgson.

Thank you to Charlie Redmayne for being brilliant.

Thank you to Kate Elton and all the hardworking team at HarperCollins.

Thank you to HarperCollins Creative Director, Claire Ward, for the perfect cover.

Thank you to the HarperCollins Ireland team: Tony Purdue, Mary Byrne, and Ann-Marie Dolan.

To Anne O'Brien, thank you for your exceptional copy-editing skills, and Alex-Barclay channeling.

To gifted playwright, screenwriter, and comedy genius, Kefi Chadwick, thank you for all the Anam Cara good times. And a specific thank you, in this case, for coming up with my title.

Thank you to all the experts who gave so generously of their time. Any mistakes are mine.

To SA Phil Niedringhaus, thank you once again for answering my FBI and CARD team questions. Apologies for some of Ren's poorer choices . . .

Thank you to Aquatic Death Investigator, Andrea Zaferes, for her fascinating insight into homicidal drowning, and for the resulting plot inspiration.

Thank you to Chantelle Newman for further

research material on drowning deaths, and great conversations.

Thank you, Anne Driscoll and David Langwallner of the Irish Innocence Project at Griffith College for your enlightenment on the heartbreaking reality of wrongful conviction.

To Michael Dobersen, MD, Forensic Pathologist, thank you for your invaluable notes on the autopsy scenes.

Thank you, Professor Marie Cassidy, for your help on skeletal remains.

Thank you, Lee S. Webster, for your friendship, and for your generosity in making connections.

Thank you to Danielle Corazza for your guidance in military matters.

Thank you to Edward Kroll for answering my questions on Oregon law.

Thank you, Sue Booth-Forbes, the heart and soul of Anam Cara — the best writers' and artists' retreat in the world.

Thanks also to you and your sister Diane for granting me the privilege of opening my book with your father's stunning poem.

To my beautiful sister, Lanes. You are, among other things, kind, caring, generous, and cheerleading. If I had a banana sandwich for every time you were there for me . . .

To all my family: you are amazing and supportive and funny and beloved.

Thank you, Dick Tobin, for your excellent feedback and kind words.

To Noleen, thank you for your hard work and thoughtfulness.

Endless love to my gorgeous friends and their epic undertaking. You know who you are. But stiiiill: Aideen, Bernice, Brian, David, Derek, Elena, Emmy, Eoin, Ger, Gerry, Julie, Majella, Mary, Sue, and Vanessa. Medals all round.